Lost in the Blue Room

Lost in the Blue Room

Richard
Barone

First Edition, 2011
Printed in the United States of America

ISBN 978-0-9754711-6-6

Library of Congress Control Number: 2010937407

Canto 34 Press
Melbourne, FL 32940

"Is that a pistol in your pocket, or are you just glad to see me?"
Mae West

To have is to refuse to be.
Emmanuel Levinas

Acknowledgements

Cover photo ©2011 Succession H. Matisse/Artist Rights Society (ARS), New York. *Icare* (Icarus), 1947.

Photos and references to the SwissMiniGun are used with permission of the manufacturer, SwissMiniGun, La Chaux-de-Fonds, Switzerland.

Photo on page 152 ©2011, Thomas Bassano.

SKY MARSHAL'S PREFLIGHT CHECKLIST

- S&W .38 cal. Chief's Special
- PPK 9mm
- Bullets
- Badge & ID
- Handcuffs
- Handcuffs Key
- Blackjack
- Top Secret Password
- Passports (tourist & official)
- Flight Schedule
- Cash & Traveler's Checks
- Journal
- Pen
- A Good Book
- Condoms
- No SwissMiniGun!

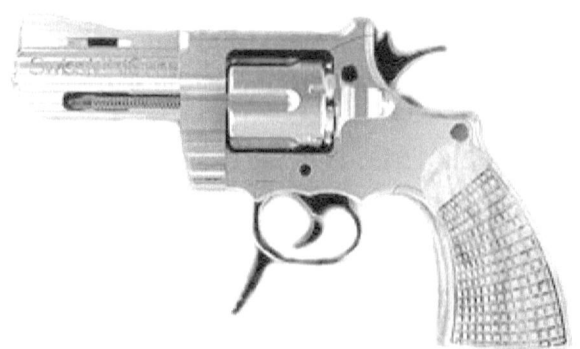

"."

Flying is *not* like swimming; you forget how after only a few years. Take for instance the *battle for the bins* during boarding. Nonexistent before airlines began charging extra for checked baggage. Grab the first bin available, for the one over your seat is already taken.

Years ago, flying was easier. Kelso knew all the ropes. The airplane was the sky marshal's best friend. Now it was an uncomfortable stranger, a sardine can packed with people that became nauseating only one hour inflight. Pocket-sized seats, stale air, and constant noise—conflated by alcohol and artificial air pressures—become bad and the mind snaps and goes into a tailspin.

When boarding, there was an air of confidence about them; they were on a dream vacation, moving to a new town, or landing that big contract. Now, all buckled-up and ready for takeoff, all their lives were about to change course drastically.

Kelso quickly adjusted and began dreaming about his layover in Hawaii. A KMA air marshal with only two to go, he was more than prepared to deal with a Code Red, being a six-foot-four black belt with a SIG P229 holstered to his back. Lost baggage, heavy turbulence, and delayed flights aside, the only situations he ever had while flying were a drunken marine who barfed on his lap, a malfunctioning toilet that dyed his backside blue, and a seatmate who didn't have the courtesy to say she would be dead on arrival.

He was more than prepared, as long as it went down in business or tourist class—not first class, the most likely place for a hijacker to strike. First class—the only place where he couldn't sit! But that didn't matter. Hijackings were a thing of the past. The D-Cooper made sure of that.

Kamal Kazi also was more than prepared. Sitting in first class, he was immune to the herd mentality. He blended in well, quenching on Evian and munching biscotti. Waiting. Always waiting. Kamal Kazi, known in the terrorism trade as *K-One*. One on every wanted list and one with a bullet. Hundred times waiting.

The amiable captain stood in front of his domain, beer bellied, smiling, and confident as a bus driver. Starbucked awake, flirting with the cheerleading, breast-tickling blond-haired flight attendant. Just what Kazi was waiting for. Hundred times waiting for. Flight deck door open and they'll keep it open as long as they can smile at each other.

Thirty-second difference between door closings. Thirty seconds in which to act.

The captain swung into the cockpit and hopped into his seat like a cowboy mounting a horse. "Good morning for our flight to Charlotte ladies and gentlemen.... And, by the way, please be kind to Carrie, our lead flight attendant."

Carrie smiled and pushed a button that made the aircraft door swing upward and close. She locked it securely and turned to get the cockpit door, a wrong sequence that Kazi had hoped would happen.

Kazi sprang forward, pushed Carrie out of the way, and entered the inner sanctum.

The captain reached for his gun, but Kazi knocked him cold with one punch to the head. Taking the gun, he swung it fast into the face of the first officer. "This is *my* plane now," he said.

Carrie stood in the doorway, shocked and helpless. Kazi swung his arm around her neck and squeezed, making her choke and struggle helplessly. When he put the gun to her head and shouted, "Surrender or she dies!" no one dared to help.

When Kelso heard a woman shriek, "He's got a gun!" he looked up the aisle and saw the hijacker coming, threatening to kill the terrified flight attendant. He unbuckled but didn't draw. How did he get by the D-Cooper? Who is that?

Kazi stood with his back against the galley and listened. He lingered a moment worried that he had lost contact. Then a voice in his head said, "I want to work with you. I can help you now. No one can ever hurt me again. I am your eternal leader, and no one will ever hurt you if you kill for me. Revenge my death!"

It was the worst possible scenario—a terrorist hiding behind a hostage held at gunpoint. SOP for a cop on the street was to call for the SWAT team, but on a sealed airplane it was SOL. Aiming for the head was too risky. Kelso waited and figured.

How did he know an air marshal was on this plane? No one does. Why didn't the D-Cooper do its job? Scan his brain, ID his intent, then zap him. Immobilize! I've seen it work. Foolproof. There're two at the gate and one surrounding the doorway. No way.

Again Kazi listened to the voice. "I've helped you get this far. You must proceed. There is an air marshal on this flight. Threaten your hostage and he will come out."

Kazi jabbed the gun into Carrie's temple. "I'll give you three seconds," he demanded, "or I'll waste her."

"Three!"

Three blind mice!

"Two!"

3

Two to tango!
"One!"
One shot!
Kazi pulled the trigger.
JAM!
He let go of Carrie to pull back the slide and chamber a round.
It's my chance! I can't ask for a better shot. Save her!
Just as Kelso reached for his SIG, three shots fired, making him….

"YUCK!" he says in disgust.
"Excuse me?" she says insulted.
"It stinks," he says.
"What stinks?" she says.
"My *Most Wanted*."
"Your most wanted?"
"My e-book," he says, pointing to his computer screen.
"Oh, I see," she says, "Your *Most Wanted*. I see. Say, aren't you that bestselling author…?"
"John Barefoot."
"Yes, John Barefoot. How delightful, flying next to John Barefoot. Hi, I'm Marge Fornai."
"Hi, Marge," he says.
"I thought about reading it, but I dare say few people would rather read a book on a plane than watch a movie."
"Well, I'm working on that too."
"You mean a screenplay? Hollywood?"
"First a promo in Frisco."
"Sounds exciting. What's it about?"
"Read the book," he says.
"I thought it stinks," she says laughingly.
"Good one," he says, worried about his screenplay going under. But then, maybe a blessing in disguise.
For Marge, the encounter is sweet chance—engaging conversation with a bestselling author, eavesdropping on creativity in the raw, and revisiting the blissful days of poetry and love. For John though, being nice about her flattery just shy of flirtation, there's no place for her in his screenplay. He's sure of that.
"I didn't intend to be satirical," she says, although her mark is already on him. "You have to excuse me. What else would you expect from a former lit major?"

"Worship," he says jokingly. Middle-aged, well doctored, and full of business, she's not a woman with whom he'd cheat on his wife.

"Then this must be your national tour?"

"Full blown," he says. "I'll be on the *Tonight Show* Thursday."

"Oh, my God, how splendid. They'll love this story."

"Now look, there it goes again."

First-class passengers rarely ventured beyond their privileged domain, there being little to see on a plane. But suddenly the drapes opened and a man appeared and stared over everyone as though looking for someone or something in the tail section. He was elderly, dressed in a business suit, and had a determined look on his face.

Kelso looked at him instinctively and realized that he was no threat. Yet there was something familiar about the man that he couldn't place. When the man put on a pair of dark-rimmed sunglasses, Kelso at once recognized the suspect. "Could it be him?" he thought.

Five seconds later, the man was gone. Kelso got up, went to the curtain, and looked inside. Immediately a flight attendant noticed, rushed up and asked, "May I help you, sir?" Kelso pulled out his badge and said, "I need to sit here. I see someone that may be a hijacker." Not getting a response, he moved forward and took a seat, the last in a row of four. It was the only one empty and reminded him of his leather lounger at home.

Kelso couldn't see the suspect or any of the other passengers or even the cockpit door, but he could now search through FBI, TSA, and INTERPOL databases without being watched. His hunch was farfetched and probably inconsequential even if true. Could he be actually sitting a few feet away from the architect of the only successful skyjacking in history? The name was unforgettable. He searched on.

Just when he found the infamous mug shot, a flight attendant came up to him and said, "The captain wants to see you. Now!"

Kelso followed her to the cockpit door. She knocked. The door opened. He went inside. The captain turned to him and said, "What the hell is this I hear about you wanting to sit in first class because you think someone is going to hijack my plane? Are you on duty?"

"No."

"Let me see your ID." Kelso showed his badge and ID. The captain turned on his reading lamp and said, "I want to see that up close. Let me have it." Kelso obliged. The captain inspected it and said, "Are you armed?"

"Yes."

"Did you check in with the boarding agent?"

"No."

"Let me see it."

Kelso took out his pistol and kept it close.

"Give it to me," the captain ordered.

"I'm afraid I can't do that," Kelso said.

"If you don't, you'll never get your badge back."

Kelso ejected the magazine and gave up the pistol. The captain admired it a moment, and then put it in his bag. "What made you think there was a hijacker on my plane?"

"D. B. Cooper," Kelso said.

"D. B. Cooper? Are you joking? He's dead."

"That's what you think."

"That was fifty years ago. Even if he is alive, he'd have to be at least seventy, maybe eighty years old. You'd never be able to identify him."

"Age progression imaging," Kelso said. "He's a perfect match."

"Cooper died in the jump," the first officer said. "And they even found the money."

"Yes, but the money was buried neatly stacked, only six thousand dollars, a token amount left by Cooper to show that he was still alive. This man is alive, I tell you, and he's sitting in first class on your plane."

"Go back to your seat," the captain said. "In coach!"

"Okay, it's your call," Kelso said. "Now, my ID, please."

"You'll get that back when we land."

"Bullshit!" Kelso said.

"What did you say?"

"I said bullshit, meaning pussies like you were the ones that caused nine-eleven. You're nothing but a chicken-shit captain who doesn't have the guts to trust an air marshal. If you don't give it back to me, I'll...."

"You'll what?"

Kelso reached behind his back and pulled out his spare piece. "I'll go back to first class, make friends with Dan Cooper, and blow your shitty plane full of holes. Put some real air in this plane."

"Ladies and gentlemen, this is the captain speaking. I have something urgent to tell you. This plane is being hijacked. Please stay calm. I repeat, please stay calm. We are sorry that this has happened, but we will do everything in our power to ensure your safety. Foremost, we must listen to the demands of the hijacker. Please remain seated and do not do anything foolish. He has assured me that no one will be harmed if we obey his orders, so please be calm and wait for further instructions. We will do exactly as he says."

"A hijacking?" John says. "On this plane? This can't be. Do you see anyone? I can't see anyone from this seat."

Marge looks up and down the aisle and says, "I don't see anyone, not even a flight attendant." Looking back at him, "Are you frightened?"

"Do I look it? Maybe I should be, but I don't feel it."

"We've been so absorbed. Maybe he walked right past us, and we didn't see him."

Someone sitting behind them—man or woman, the sound is universal—barfs in an air-sickness bag, provoking Marge to say, "Good Lord."

"This is not supposed to happen. I mean, I thought the brain scanners were foolproof. Supposed to weed out the criminal mind and the like."

"Maybe it's an inside job."

"Either that or he's got an invisible brain, or maybe a way to hide his intentions."

"Ladies and gentlemen, this is the captain again. The hijacker has informed me that he is not a hijacker. He states that...please bear with me as I read his note...that his name is Jack High. *I am not now, never have been, and never will be a hijacker. And you cannot make me one. But if you don't comply with my demands, everyone on this plane will go down.* End quote. Ladies and gentlemen, do not mistake this. He has a weapon, and it is dangerous. It melted the lock on the flight-deck door. He will not harm us if we meet his demands. So, please remain seated, be calm, and wait for further instructions."

"Dreadful," Marge says. "Simply dreadful, being hijacked."

"By Jack High, no less." John says. "It must be a practical joke."

"I don't think so, John. You heard what the captain said."

"Regardless, I'm still likin' it," thinking there could be no better place to publicize his new book. It's been a long drought for John and now a breakthrough. But whose story is it anyway?

"Listen to those people," Marge says. "Will they ever...?"

"I'm likin' it," John says.

"Everyone shut up and listen up! I don't need to tell you who I am. You already know, so wrap your heads around this. As the captain said, I am not a hijacker. You only think that I am, and *I* don't believe what you think. If you don't settle down, I'm going to get very, very upset."

John begins to laugh.

"Stop it, John. You heard what he said."

"That's it," High announces. "Since you cannot control yourselves, you are all under arrest. And do you know why you cannot control yourselves?

Because you suffer from the *natural attitude*. Your fearful times are your own creations. The leaders and media know this and exploit your fear with hyperbole, innuendo, and mystery. You are gutless, spiritless twerps, and one of the ringleaders of this conspiracy, a man sitting right beside you, is reaping a fortune. Yes, you know him. He's the real hijacker. Take a good look at him."

Marge looks curiously at John.

"What?" John says.

"Nothing," Marge says.

"Do you see what I mean?" High says. "There's violence in his eyes. You've taken his most exciting, heart-pounding, adrenaline-rushing commercial one too many times. I say stop it! Stop now and be free. Escape from his terrorism. Open your in-flight browsers and go to *w w w dot bait and switch dot com*. That's one word, *bait and switch*. Use your seat number for the pass code to enter the site. I repeat, *w w w dot bait and switch dot com* followed by your seat number. You must read the whole story, otherwise, I'll start this ship down a path you won't live to regret. Cliché, I know, but I mean it. If you have difficulty opening the website, ask your flight attendants for help. Thank you."

John surrenders his ego, types the web address into the portal, and the book opens quickly.

Dear Passengers & Crew of Pan Am Flight 2:

This is a book that you're really going to love. It's called "Bait and Switch." Now, don't worry. I'm not a pilot, and I'm not going to crash this plane into the White House. I'm just a simple sky marshal who flew airplanes for a living. I did this for many years and millions of miles, working diligently as your guardian, protecting you while you slept, keeping the skies free from terrorists and not getting any credit for it. Then, when the airlines and the government thought they had the war against terror licked, they abolished my job and sent me down to Texas to patrol the border in a Jeep! It took some time for the bad guys to figure it out, but they did, and, some years later, they hijacked four planes, annihilated the Twin Towers, smashed up the Pentagon, and almost took out the Capitol had it not been for some brave passengers on United Flight 93. Total death toll was 2,995, billions of dollars in damage, and untold hours of suffering and mental anguish, all because the government and airlines were too cheap to fly sky marshals. Or was it more than just cheapness? Some say that sky marshals were grounded to lure the terrorists back out into the open. After all, don't we always need a war to fight, an enemy to hate, and an international crisis to make heroes out of our politicians? To be sure, air marshals returned to duty after 9/11, but what about now, twenty years later? Déjà vu all over again! Do you think the new brain scanners are fail-safe? Did they stop me? D-Cooper my ass. D. B. Cooper's rolling over in his grave laughing.

So, you see, I was a devoted air marshal and sacrificed my identity to an undercover persona that never got a wink of sleep. So now, on behalf of all my colleagues patrolling the border, I'm left with only one alternative. And that's where you come in.

Take heart! This is not one of those novels for the recreationally challenged sold at airport newsstands. At least you better not think so, or else I'm going to slam this plane into the ocean and your bodies will be scattered for hundreds of miles of shark bait.

Bait and Switch
America's Most Wanted Novel That Nobody Wants
Jack High

1/Foot in the Door

Andrea sat in an armless chair flanking two crew-cut Customs agents sitting at steel-gray desks joined face-to-face. A large, open window on the other side of the desks offered a beautiful view of Lake Erie. The agents ignored it and stared pensively at their subject, who was enjoying the view and a cool breeze that came gently.

"Cut yourself shaving?" right agent said with a short laugh.

Andrea felt the bandage for a moment, then ripped it off, squeezed it into a little ball, and threw it out the window, making the agents blink.

"Hmm, I see," right agent said, now noticing a small scar in the middle of Andrea's forehead.

"Good shot," left agent said.

"You stated here that you were in the Army between sixty-seven and sixty-nine. Ever been to Vietnam?"

"Yes, I was there," Andrea said.

"Were you a nurse?"

"No," Andrea said. "I was a WAC enlisted. Long Binh."

"Ever been wounded?"

Andrea's face twitched. "Yes, I was. In a rocket attack."

Left agent licked the tip of his pencil and wrote *Virgin* in his notebook.

"Ever smoke marijuana?" right agent asked.

Effective cross-examination technique, Andrea thought. One shoots righty, the other lefty. They're veterans too, most likely Korean War. If I lie, they won't believe me. So, go ahead and say it. Say, "Yeah."

The answer arrested the questioning for a moment, as though the agents had lost their purpose. Right agent lit a cigarette and flicked the match out the window. "So, you have a bachelor's degree in philosophy, and now you're a grad student at UB?"

"Yes," Andrea said.

"Studying theater?" left agent said.

"I don't see a conflict here," right agent said, "but wouldn't you say that it's a little unusual, actor one day, sky marshal the next?"

It was a customary question to ask at interviews, like why do you want to become an actor when you studied accounting? And, Andrea was prepared to give a customary answer, like they didn't teach sky-marshaling in college, or philosophy taught me critical thinking, but instead, pulled out a slip of paper, placed it on the desk, and said, "I was inspired by this." On the paper was written: *Un simple voyage de Paris à Londres en avion nous donne une révélation du monde que notre imagination ne pouvait nous faire pressentir. H. Matisse*

"It's French," right agent said, handing the paper to his partner, who too was lost.

"Don't let it scare you," Andrea said. "You don't have to know French to understand it. Look at the words; many are the same in English. *Simple. Voyage. Paris. London, Avion.* I'm sure you know avion means airplane. Then there's *revelation*, which is the same in English. *Monde* is world. *Notre* is our, as in Notre Dame. *Imagination*, the same also. *Ne*, which is not. *Pressentir*, which is presentation or reveal. Now put it all together."

Andrea waited a moment for a response but, not getting one, said, "A simple trip from Paris to London on an airplane gives us a revelation of the world that our imagination could not reveal."

"Do you like acting?" right agent said. "You know, sky marshals work undercover and have to develop cover stories."

"Yes, I can speak like a man," Andrea said. "Want to hear?"

"Go right ahead."

"Well, we don't know exactly how Mark Twain sounded, but you'll get the idea." Andrea made a gargling sound and said, 'Everyone complains about the weather, but no one ever does anything about it."

"Hey, how'd you do that?" left agent asked.

"Lots of practice," Andrea said.

"Ever been to the Caribbean?" left agent asked.

"No," Andrea said.

"Ever get pregnant during your enlistment?"

Andrea thought the question was foul but, realizing that a pregnant sky marshal was somewhat disadvantaged, said, "No."

Left agent wrote *Islands* after *Virgin* in his notebook.

"You see, I can't get pregnant," Andrea said.

"You what?" left agent said.

"I can't get pregnant."

"Why not?" left agent asked.

"Because I'm a man," Andrea said.

Right agent flipped through Andrea's file. When he found the DD-214, he said, "I'll be damned. So you are. Andrew D'Oria. Andrew, that's you?"

"I had my name changed," Andrea said.

"But not your sex," right agent said.

"Not my sex," Andrea said.

"Certainly one way to get your foot in the door," left agent said.

"We'll be in touch with you, Mister High," right agent said.

If Andrea had shown up as a man, they would have never hired him. But they did, precisely because he didn't look like a man. And because his letter of acceptance was addressed to *Miss Andrea High*, he had no choice but to keep his successful persona going.

" . "

"Ladies and gentlemen, this is the captain speaking. Please give Mister High your undivided attention."

"Ladies and gentlemen, I see that you have all settled down and are reading my book. As a token of my hospitality, I have ordered the captain to land at the nearest airport, refuel the plane for the long haul, and provide each one of you first-class service, which means first-class meals and drinks for everyone. Over a thousand first-class meals, can you dig? I hope you will enjoy yourselves. So, you see, like the captain said, there's no need to worry. I'm not a suicidal terrorist. I want to live just like you. So, cooperate and graduate. Cliché again, but you get the point.

"Once the plane is refueled, you will have approximately fourteen hours of flying time. A seven-ninety-seven blended-wing with great gas mileage! Isn't that cool? Well, she better have because we'll be flying over the Atlantic. We won't be going San Franward after all. It's a backward town actually. We'll be going forward to no place in particular. The destination is up to you. So, sit back and relax.

"Before you indulge, there's something you need to know. The story you are reading has been rejected by scores of publishers. I'm embarrassed to say how many times, so don't even ask. I lost hope until I came up with the idea to self-publish. But don't get me wrong. I'm not blaming the book trade. Book marketers might know more about human nature than writers and so-called intellectuals. This occurred to me when I sold several copies of *Bait and Switch* on eBay for two dollars and ninety-nine cents. They went like hotcakes. They were only uncorrected proofs, but when I listed the final version, the one that had all the right notes in it, no one wanted to buy it. Imagine that, for only five dollars more, a much better book and no one wanted it.

"So, here's my suggestion. Join a social media site and tweet the world with a minute-by-minute of what's going on here. You will have more fans in ten minutes than anyone has had in a lifetime. But don't forget to read my book."

" . "

The original sky marshal had the greatest powers ever conferred upon a United States law enforcement officer. He could search suspects without a warrant, arrest anyone for false information, and kill anyone for attempting to, in the slightest way, skyjack an American aircraft. And since the basic policy was to shoot first and ask questions later, the emphasis of the four-week training course was on marksmanship.

The solidity and precision of the police revolver implied that the laws it enforced were also solid and precise. Fitting snuggly in Andrea's hand, it was the one and only thing he needed, the categorical imperative, the real defender of the law. Not the least bit charitable, it could take away a lot more than it could give. He fell in love with it.

Though this wasn't the first time he held a gun, he felt nervous on the firing range. He had to first qualify with the standard four-inch revolver in order to receive the coveted two-inch S&W Chief's special. This shiny, stainless-steel revolver was small and, for men, could be hidden easily inside a belly band and covered by a tie—now fashionably wide—even with one's suit jacket off. For the "four" women in the class, concealment was a troubling issue. Those that didn't qualify with the two-inch had to carry the four-inch in a large purse, a most difficult method of concealment in the tight cabin of an airplane.

The Treasury style of combat, which had evolved over decades fighting bootleggers, counterfeiters, and assassins, was significantly different from the FBI. Not only did Treasury agents carry more powerful weapons, they were trained to use maximum firepower in a face-to-face shootout with an assailant. To fire all the rounds at once rather than take careful aim with one shot at a time was the best technique the sky marshal could use to stop a skyjacker. It was, one instructor remarked, similar to the difference between the Marines' stress on marksmanship and ammo conservation and the Army's stress on putting maximum lead on the target.

Andrea scored big on the target and combat ranges using both pistols. The other three women qualified, but only with the four-inch. They were not preferred flying partners.

The government's attempt to understand air piracy struck Andrea as Hegelian, the goal being to resist the temptation to analyze skyjacker personalities and to concentrate on the history and statistics of skyjacking. In fact, the FAA instructors spoke of air piracy as a *virulent disease*, which had hit the world in *waves*—1961-62, 1964-65, and, most recently, 1968-69, when it reached epidemic proportions of four skyjackings per month.

"The airlines and several members of the FAA Task Force set up by the President to develop a plan of attack against air piracy were negative toward the epidemiological model for fear that it would be distorted by the media and deter travelers away from flying. Especially notorious was the government's eagerness to use its law enforcement authority to deter skyjacking by putting undercover agents aboard U.S. flag-carrying aircraft and conducting searches of passengers at airports. As one official put it, 'We cannot afford to have gun battles between sky marshals and hijackers. Shootouts are okay at the O.K. Corral, but *not* in a crowded airplane five thousand feet over Los Angeles.' More acceptable to these critics was the development of a profile that could be used by the airlines to identify potential skyjackers and deter air piracy before it gets airborne.

"After analyzing various data and facts about prior air piracies, the Task Force came up with the skyjacker profile. Initial tests of the profile proved promising. It screened out ninety-nine-point-five percent of air passengers, leaving just point-five percent as potential suspects that were interrogated and searched and found to be carrying weapons, fleeing justice, or just mentally deranged. The airlines couldn't have been more pleased.

"Then in September nineteen-seventy, a new wave hit, a shock-wave felt around the world that made the Cuban skyjackings look like games of cops and robbers. The PFLP (Popular Front for the Liberation of Palestine) dubbed it *Black September*, and their destination—an abandoned airstrip in the Jordanian desert, *Revolution Airport*."

The instructor passed around a photo of an Arab woman holding an AK-47 assault rifle. "And this is the mastermind of it all—Leila Khaled. She was arrested in London after a failed attempt to hijack an El Al flight and fly it to *Revolution Airport*. Four airplanes were taken. A TWA, a Swiss Air, a BOAC, and a Pan Am seven-four-seven that was too large for the desert airstrip but landed in Cairo where it was destroyed by a bomb. Six hundred people were hijacked and the world watched for days as three airliners full of passengers sat helpless in the burning desert sun. President Nixon ordered the Eighty-second Airborne Division on alert, civil war broke out in Jordan, and Israeli tank battalions massed on its borders with Jordan. Negotiations in Cairo between PLO leader Arafat, King Hussein of Jordan, and Abdul Nasser led to Khaled's release in exchange for all passengers held captive in the desert on three aircraft.

"Especially disturbing was how Khaled and her partner went undisclosed on the El Al flight, and how her other two partners, who had been refused boarding on that same flight, were able to get first-class tickets on a Pan Am flight. The quick thinking pilot of the El Al plane, who went into a nosedive that shook up Khaled enough for the Israeli guards to capture her and shoot her accomplice contrasted sharply with the defenseless Pan Am seven-forty-seven on which two commandoes broke into the cockpit wielding handguns and grenades."

After hearing this story, none of the sky marshals in the class doubted their importance. But Andrea wrote in the margins of his notebook, *Waves are phenomena, not things in themselves. Gov't psychologists and criminologists have no clue.*

As important as the job was in deterring international blackmail against the United States, the sky marshals had to work undercover while protecting its citizens.   While writing his cover story, Andrea saw an immense irony in it. If the profile was a sham and didn't work, how would his cover story—the inverse profile—work?

His first love—philosophy—offered no dividends for his future, but he had chosen to major in it anyway. He bore it as a sacrifice, a cross permanently strapped to his back, the directionless burden of twenty-five centuries that blocked his life from sunlight. It had promised him knowledge of the ultimate truths, but gave him a world of contradictions and unverifiable ideas. It abandoned him on an endless tightrope without the relief of a positive space above or negative space below him. Even the American answer to the great divide in human thought was impassable, it being unable to come to logical terms with the absurdities raised by modern science. His only choice was to abandon philosophy altogether. But where was he to go, and what was he to do? Fortunately, this job came along.

Now he could protest his misfortune; fly into the sky and leave the meaningless world behind. Like the French writer Guy de Maupassant, who protested the Eiffel Tower by eating lunch at its restaurant every day so that he could avoid seeing the monstrosity on the Parisian skyline, he would *live* at 30,000 feet above the world and look down upon it without ever seeing one single thing. He was not about to have, but to be!

Everyone had heard of existentialism; it was easy to grasp. Throw the words *alienation* and *anguish* into the conversation and you were hip. But phenomenology wasn't hip. It was pure philosophy, and only those that had suffered through two thousand five hundred years of philosophy could hope to understand it. It would be his cover story of a cover story, his reason for being, which no one knew anything about.

"I'm a *phenomenologist*," he said during a role-playing session in front of the class. His male voice shocked everyone, even the instructors. Now there were only three females in the room. He wore a fake mustache to make him look even more professorial. "You might not have ever heard this, but it's a real profession without which no other professions would exist. That's why you've never heard of it."

"Interesting," his seatmate said. "What exactly do you do?"

"I go around the world observing things just to make them real. This might sound absurd to you, but it's been proven scientifically that consciousness determines whether light exists or not. If light does not exist, then things don't exist, so my awareness of light makes things exist."

"Like, if a tree falls in the forest and no one is around, will it make a sound?"

"Same idea."

The class gave his performance a standing ovation. The instructor praised his cover story as "the most likely to succeed at stopping an unwanted conversation dead in space and time." The class laughed, giving it merit unintended.

The physical training sessions were little more than aerobics exercises, and the so-called martial arts training was not as rigorous and demanding as portrayed by the media. The Vietnam veterans in the class, especially those with Special Forces and combat experience, thought it was makeshift, practicing the snap-kick ad nauseam until the knees began to burn. The training had obviously been modified, since this was the first class with female trainees, none of whom looked capable of overpowering a skyjacker. And neither did Andrea, who was on the lighter side of being a middleweight. Sky marshals were not supposed to be all heavyweights anyway. They were supposed to look like ordinary passengers and represent the full spectrum of weights, heights, colors, and ages normally found in an airline terminal. He had to team up with someone big and tough enough to back him up, if for some reason guns were not an option.

Matt Bando, who pranced around the training room taunting, "Float like a butterfly, sting like a bee!" was just the man. An ex-infantry company commander from the 101st Airborne Division who had seen heavy combat in Vietnam, he was more than ready for action.

As a gesture of friendship, Andrea drove Bando into Arlington to try out an Italian restaurant recommended by the school. His male persona had worked so well in class that he decided to keep it going. Besides, it felt good being himself once again.

Bando liked Andrea for being a Vietnam veteran and a sharpshooter, and, for a woman, not wimpy. But when they sat at the table, he sensed something lost about her. Then, realizing what it was, he said, "For a moment there I thought you were wearing a mustache."

Andrea's fingers searched his face, and his eyes hunted for it around the table, but it was gone. He laughed about it and sat back, which gave Bando a better look at him. There was a small hollow on his forehead, now darkened by an overhead lamp, that looked like a wound, but Bando wasn't sure. "Is that what I think it is?" he asked.

"Yeah," Andrea said.

"I've seen a lot of weird ones, but that one takes the cake. It's as big as John Travolta's chin cleft. Where'd it happen?"

"Cu Chi. Not-so-friendly fire."

"An M-sixteen?"

"Stray round."

"Out of the blue…."

"Yeah, out of the blue, but I wasn't in the Air Force. What about you?" Andrea pointed to Bando's hand, which was missing its little finger. Bando made a fist that nonetheless was rock solid. "How'd you get a commission?"

"ROTC," Bando said. "Brooklyn College. Where'd you go to school?"

"SUNY at Buffalo. Was into theater when I got word about this job."

Andrea's voice sounded distant and frail, like he was recuperating from a bad cold. It annoyed Bando. "That was a great stunt you pulled in class the other day. How do you do that, sound like a man?"

"Takes a lot of practice. Most actors try a falsetto, but that doesn't work. Well, it's good for laughs like Tony Curtis and Jack Lemon in *Some Like It Hot*, but not for real."

"But that's a man sounding like a woman. How do you sound like a man?"

"There's a way to adjust your voice box so that you can sound that way."

"Yeah, but your hands are a dead giveaway," Bando said.

"They are?"

"Yeah, and your neck. You have no Adam's apple. And your round eyes and face."

As he was contemplating the suggestion, a guy from a nearby table came over, kicked his chair, and said, "Hey, what you lookin' at?"

"What?" Andrea said.

"My girl said you're eyeballing her."

Thinking that this was just a bully wanting to show off for his date, Andrea said, "I didn't mean anything by it."

"Then why did you look at her?"

"I might have glanced that way, but it wasn't what you think," Andrea conceded. "I thought I knew her, that's all."

"Then keep your eyes to yourself," the guy said and returned to his table.

"Why do pretty girls go out with shitheads like that?" Bando said.

"Self-preservation," Andrea said.

The sight of the hot, juicy pizza made Bando salivate. He turned to the girl and grinned like the Cheshire cat. Then he waved at her.

"What'd you do that for?" Andrea said.

Again the guy came over to the table and, without saying a word, flipped a piece onto Andrea's shirt. "Okay, faggot, apologize!"

Andrea sat motionless with the pizza on his lap, afraid to stand up and defend himself. He had never been in a street fight and doubted that the little he had learned in class would help him beat this madman. His heart started to pound uncontrollably.

"Hey, I said apologize, chicken-shit."

Andrea knew his fear was showing, and, no matter how hard he tried, he couldn't stop his heart from pounding. Nonetheless, he stood up, hoping that Bando would take the blame.

Bando waited to see how far Andrea would go and, when he started to take a defensive stance, stood up and said, "Hold it, badass! I'm the one you want."

The guy sized up Bando, and said, "So, you're the asshole's been hittin' on my girl."

"You're the asshole," Bando said.

The guy lunged forward with a punch but missed, giving Bando an easy takedown. "So, you really want to fight?" Bando said. "Let's go for it! In the back. The men's room."

After they entered the men's room, Andrea listened intently for the fight but heard nothing. Then, after a few minutes, the guy came out, walked over to his girl, had a few words, and then walked out of the restaurant.

Andrea rushed to the door and opened it. Bando came out grinning and said, "Okay, now's your turn. Go clean up."

"Clean up?" Andrea said. "What happened?"

Bando tightened his belt and said, "Nothing."

"Nothing? What do you mean nothing?"

"Exactly what I said. Take a look."

Andrea went inside cautiously. On the wall above the urinal was a framed poster titled *101 Best Quotes from Gangster Movies*. Above the toilet was a picture of *The Godfather* captioned, *I'm gonna make him an offer he can't refuse.* Dumbfounded, he cleaned off his shirt and went back out to the table where Bando was telling the girl about how the Army Rangers had taught him to kill Viet Cong barehanded, and that she was lucky he had let her boyfriend live to see another day.

On the drive back to Fort Belvoir, Andrea felt distraught by the whole incident. He had never been so frightened, not even in Vietnam where his life was constantly in danger. He had been a hero in war, but now was shown-up by a punk in a restaurant. He couldn't recall ever being as panicky. During mortar and rocket attacks, his heart was always calm and steady. The difference puzzled him. He was, nonetheless, sure he had a good friend and partner. He asked him, "So, how did you do it? I mean, like a piece of magic."

"Do what?"

"Get badass to back down."

"I just pulled out my little Willy. Mister Badass took one look at it and decided it was too much for him to handle."

"Your little what?"

Bando leaned back in the seat, pulled out a black pistol, and said, "My Will-he Pee."

"I see," Andrea said. "A bait and switch," which made Bando grin.

Since sky marshals were officially Customs Security Officers, they had to be trained in narcotics identification as well. Andrea's eyes lit up when he heard the instructor say, "And this, ladies and gentlemen, is hashish, which has a euphoric effect on the user ten times greater than marijuana. It takes six hundred and twenty-five pounds of marijuana to yield one pound of hashish. And as promised, we will light some up so that you all will recognize the unmistakable odor."

When the smoke drifted around the classroom, noisome to some but familiar to others, Andrea thought it was a test to expose the former heads in the class, fearing a stigma would appear on his forehead saying—*Junkie!*

When the instructor held up a half-inch capsule and said, "LSD is an odorless, tasteless, and colorless organic compound that is the most powerful of all hallucinogens," he was sure that his dream of flying first class for a living was about to drift out the window with the marijuana smoke.

Bando turned around in his seat and gave Andrea the biggest shit-eatin' grin he had ever seen. Andrea smiled back, but he couldn't be sure of being fully sanctioned until the powers that be swore him in on graduation day.

Of all the tests given during the final week, the one Andrea dreaded the most was disarming a skyjacker one-on-one. His only chance of succeeding was to drop back in line and hope that after taking the abuse of a dozen students, the man playing the role would be softened up enough to let the gun fly out of his hand with just the slightest punch. After all, how many heavy wallops on the knuckles could he take?

Andrea opened the door and saw the hulk standing in the center of the room, surely the biggest agent in the Secret Service called in especially to play the role of the skyjacker. He closed the door and walked forward, ready to throw in the towel. Up close, the agent looked big enough to shield the President and Vice President combined. He shouted, "It's a good day to die," and flashed a gun as if he were throwing a punch, palm down and knuckles up.

The knuckles! The vulnerable knuckles were facing the ceiling and not lined up for Andrea to throw a hook and crack open the grip as he had been taught. In desperation, he threw a hammer punch—sort of an overhand bolo—that hit squarely on the agent's hand, making the pistol pop out and fall to the floor. Andrea reached down and picked it up, not knowing whether he had actually knocked it out of the agent's hand or had just shown the proper technique to do so. He didn't stop to ask and was satisfied passing the test and eventually graduating from the school.

" . "

"Looks like we're coming in for a landing." Marge says. "I wonder where we are?"

"End of chapter one," John says. "Boring, isn't it?"

"It's got some neat twists."

2/Ground Duty

Armed with a gold badge, a pair of handcuffs, a blackjack, tourist and official passports, a secret password, and his stainless-steel beauty, Andrea reported for duty at the sky marshal headquarters in Far Rockaway—a stone's throw to JFK. Sporting a psychedelic silk tie, an Indian-red blazer with wide-body lapels to look hip, and a leather briefcase, he was fully into his cover story and ready to fly on any plane, at any time, to any destination in the world.

When he walked inside, however, ruffles and flourishes were not playing, and a flight schedule was not waiting for him. The lieutenant in charge ordered him to go out and buy a blue Customs Security Officer uniform, black shoes, holsters for his pistol and handcuffs, and report back for ground duty at 3 p.m. the next day. Since there were nine international terminals at JFK, and airlines were *not* mandated to fly sky marshals, preflight screening took precedence. The lieutenant said, however, that the established routine of flying two months on and one month off would remain in effect. Even so, Andrea worried that the job was just another bait and switch.

Though disappointed, he made use of off-duty time to find an apartment in Queens. It was lushly decorated in royal blue carpets and drapes. And, with several stewardesses living next door, he easily enticed three other sky marshals into sharing the rent. He figured, once in cover story, always in cover story. Besides, breaking voice was devastating his vocal cords. It seemed like an ideal arrangement, as long as the others were flying, leaving the apartment free most of the time.

During the first weekend, he paid his respects to the art galleries in SoHo, the funeral homes of the visual arts recently deceased. The works were laughable rehashes of the past with no originality other than differences in colors and materials. No matter how extreme abstract art became, it was no closer to creating phenomenal reality than Cezanne's still lifes, and no matter how commercial art objects became, they were no closer to conceptualizing art than Duchamp's ready-mades. The aristocracy that collected such art was not supporting art but perpetuating their elite societies, leagues, and clubs with nothing more than faith in their investments. For who would care about contemporary art otherwise? Not every piece of art was worth a hundred thousand, and the factors that made one worth that much were selective and not substantive. Pushed to the outer limits of acceptability, they somehow got there before anyone else, and that was the privileged nature of it.

He went away convinced that his greatest work of art lay buried deep within his brain, and no one, not even the world's finest surgeon, could remove it without killing him.

The architecture at JFK airport, on the other hand, was *living* art, a reality that vibrated with so much life, he could actually see the buildings breathing in and out. They were temples of the space age—nine terminals arranged like the petals of a daisy, as delicately placed as the airport was brutally busy. That Pan American Airways was bold enough to call its flying-saucer terminal *Worldport*, so too was American Airlines boasting the world's longest stained glass window on the façade of its terminal, and TWA the owner of the most futuristic building in the world, with floor-to-ceiling views of the runways and not a single Bauhaus line in the place. Built by laborers—not artists—it was a building that had a personality, a sense of height without being a skyscraper, an interior space without walls and ceilings. It was the concept of infinity made incarnate by red carpets throughout. Had Rene Descartes been able to see it in 17th Century France, he would have said without doubt, "God Almighty!" and been closer to reality than he was in creating the analytic framework for calculus.

Andrea and Matt worked British Overseas Airways at terminal 7, with occasional surveillance duty of the *fishbowl* in the International Arrivals Building, terminal 4. BOAC was a pleasure, since it wasn't timid about searching passengers. Having suffered a serious embarrassment during the Black September skyjackings, it wasn't about to rely entirely on the profile and required all passengers be frisked and every carryon be searched. British police had Leila Khaled in custody once, and they weren't about to let her go a second time.

Andrea knew that the so-called British Invasion had begun with the Beatles entry through JFK in 1964. While waiting behind a partition to pat down the next passenger, he got word that Rod Stewart's Faces was approaching to board the plane. He didn't think much of the hit song *Maggie May*, and when Stewart stepped into his space to be frisked, he felt like saying that his music wouldn't last long once people heard him speak British.

"You wouldn't be packing a rod on you now, would you Rod?" he asked.

"No, man. I mean yes, I mean no. No man," Rod said.

"Hey, maybe you can do something with that," Andrea said. "Now spread your legs and hold your arms out for a frisk."

A five-finger exercise on Stewart's defenseless body, going over every curve and bulge slowly and surely, was more than a groper's dream. He could have sold his place to an adoring fan for a thousand easily.

"You're making a first class fool out of me," Stewart crooned, pulling himself together after the frisk. It was a going-over more probing than any allowed by a masseur.

"Have a nice flight back to sunny England," Andrea said, amused by the massive mane puffed on the top of Stewart's head.

Matt thought that Andrea's guise was highly amusing. It seemed as natural as a female doctor examining a male patient.

The next evening, Andrea was surprised by the entrance of Dick Cavett, who came into his cubicle with the friendliness of a childhood companion he once knew. "You look like an *innocuous* fellow," Cavett said.

The word was antithetical to its sound and used quite effectively. "Actually, I'm a doxologist," Andrea said. "This job is only a cover story for the real me."

"Well, maybe we should have you on the show."

"Are you trying to bribe a law enforcement officer, Mister Cavett?"

"Heavens no."

Cavett appeared unruffled, wearing white cotton pants and socks, white deck shoes, black belt, and a dark blue ascot around his neck. The getup harmonized with his straight, blond hair and accented his tropical tan. Andrea gestured him to assume the pat-down stance and went about his business amused by the vulnerability of his body.

Such was his lot with BOAC, dealing with mezza-mezza celebrities rather than the superstars that were flying Pan Am, TWA, American, and Eastern. He dreamed of one day frisking Elvis Presley, Pablo Picasso, and even John Wayne.

He came close, however, on one stint in the IAB. While Bando was surveilling the terminal hoping to spot Leila Khaled, Andrea spotted Sophia Loren in the *fishbowl* trying to make her way through customs. What a magnificent specimen she was, the most statuesque woman he had ever seen, standing out in a crowd like a peacock in a flock of turkey vultures.

Inspired that a simple peasant girl from Naples could turn into a world icon, Andrea returned to his duties frisking passengers at BOAC. When a young man came through to be checked, Andrea sensed that he was in the presence of one of the vultures. There was something ulterior about the man, a man *having* and not *being*. Andrea took his time, carefully feeling through the clothes until he came to the leather boots and felt a bulge around the ankle. "What's in your boot?" he asked.

"That's my sock. Got bunched up."

"Oh, your sock. Well, now's your chance to unbunch it. Let's see."

The man took off his boot and handed it over for inspection. Wary of reaching inside, Andrea turned the boot upside down and a plastic bag of grass fell onto the floor. "I'll bet it smells like one too," he said. He inspected the contents and was sure that it was marijuana, but he was unsure whether to arrest the man. The custom in Customs was to use discretionary justice when dealing with a *small amount of grass*, but what actually constituted a *small amount* was a mystery to him. "Let's see your passport."

Noticing the holdup, a boarding agent asked Andrea what he planned to do with the passenger. "His wife has already boarded the plane," she said.

"Look officers," the man said. "I'm on my honeymoon. That's all. I only wanted a little for recreational use."

Andrea looked over the passport carefully, handed it back, and let him board the plane. The boarding agent smiled, but Andrea's perturbed partner said, "Why'd you let him go? You had a perfectly good collar and blew it."

After screening the rest of the passengers, Andrea brought the grass to the BOAC security office, called the customs agent on duty, and waited silently with the words *small amount of grass* festering in his mind. The security officers stared at the bag sitting on top of the desk like it was a magic act about to disappear. When the special agent arrived, he immediately inspected the bag and asked, "Well, where's the smuggler?"

Smuggler? Andrea thought. Now he's a smuggler and *I* let him go. "I let him board the plane," he said.

"You didn't arrest him? Why?"

Andrea pointed at the bag and said, "Because he had only a small amount of marijuana."

The agent opened the bag, estimated that there was enough to make a dozen joints, and said, "Who told you this would be a small amount of marijuana?"

"I used my own judgment about that."

The agent didn't want to admit it, but he held in his hand what many circles would call a *large* amount of grass, the federal courts notwithstanding. He walked out without further complaint.

For some time, Andrea dramatized the discretionary test, holding that he was a sky marshal and that his primary job was to kill skyjackers, not arrest hippies. He persisted a few weeks this way, hoping someday to prove his point in the wild blue yonder.

For Matt Bando, who belonged to the league of hard-boiled law enforcement officers that had to enforce laws uniformly, like torquing down the heads of a motor, each bolt getting no more or less force than stated in the book, the integrity of the sky marshal program was on the line. They argued at lunch, on breaks, and even during Sunday dinner at Bando's home in Brooklyn where Andrea was steadfast in his belief that he had made the right call.

One afternoon, while taking a coffee break at a bistro near the front entrance to the terminal, they laid to rest their dispute about discretionary justice and mused over what adventures awaited them in the sky. Between flirtations with the Hispanic waitress and sips of cappuccino, they traded war stories heard from other sky marshals already in flight.

"I heard that one guy who was flying American got drugged in a Caribbean hotel. A maid who was working at the hotel went into his room one night while he was sleeping, took his passports and all his money. The narcs couldn't figure out how he was drugged until they discovered crushed Angels' Trumpet flowers inside his pillowcase. That stuff is deadly and can kill you. They figured he was out cold for twenty-four hours and was lucky to come back alive."

"I heard magic mushrooms down in Mexico will do the same. Turn you into a head so bad, you'll never recover."

"Some guy flying Pan Am actually dropped his piece down a toilet while he was balling a stew."

"How'd he get it out?"

"Must have been a two-inch. It'll slip off if you don't watch it."

"So, what do you think a skyjacker thinks when he cases this place and sees some guys carrying two inches and some guys carrying four inches?"

"Maybe he'll think they've got bigger balls."

Suddenly, a black man rushed at them with the speed of a wild horse, knocking down every table and chair that got in his way. He ran madly through the bistro and out the front door. Quickly, Bando and Andrea scrambled around the mess and gave chase. They were already outside in the blinding sunlight, dodging cars, taxis, and trucks, when they drew their guns upon spotting him running through the parking lot towards the IAB.

Horns blasted and tires squealed, muting the sounds of jumbo jets taking off. Then came the deadening sound of cars colliding, four tons of metal slamming together without the slightest reverberation. Black-hole thud. Drowned thunder. Sinkhole implosion.

Bando got there first and looked down at the fugitive lying on his back with legs crushed under the front bumper of a small, white truck. He holstered his pistol just as Andrea approached.

The man moved slightly, groaned, and let out a deep breath, staring petrified at the hood of the truck looming above him, the word imprinted ƎƆᴎA⅃UᗺMA on his brain forever.

Andrea holstered his pistol. "Who is it?" he asked.

"Some perp," Bando said.

"What are we going to do with him?"

"Call the Port Authority police. Let them handle it."

"   ."

"There it is, John," Marge says.

"There what is?" John says.

"The breaking news!"

"Already?"

"Ex-police officer hijacks Pan Am plane. Demands job back."

"Where'd you see that?"

"The AP."

"Do they mention any names?"

"No one, pending notifications...."

3/Special Delivery

At the end of the first month, Matt Bando received a schedule to fly Eastern Air Lines, while Andrea had to wait another month, his name being at the bottom of the roster. Even his roommates had gotten flight schedules and were away most of the time, leaving the apartment all to himself.

Whenever they returned home for a night or two (John from Europe on TWA, Joe from around the world on Pan Am, and Jim from the Caribbean on American), the place came alive with tales about the new *space-age* law enforcement officers. Andrea's ground experiences frisking second-class VIPs were seriously outclassed by the sheer glamour of flying shotgun on international flights.

"The spaghetti in Rome just melts in your mouth," John teased, giving Andrea a case about not getting the genuine thing in New York. What John had really eaten, however, was spaghetti truly *al dente*—Italian style—having the texture of beeswax rather than butter.

John's stories were full of aporia, massaging words to convey some twist of reality rather than the concrete thing. Like when he walked into the bathroom one day and saw Joe "The Bear" naked, he said, "Joe, you have such a beautiful prepuce. I'm telling you, I never saw anything like it." After Joe started receiving anonymous letters from a Pan Am stewardess saying that she had heard Joe Ruby was the most "well-equipped" sky marshal on the force and was dying to have a date with him, he began parading nude around the apartment after his showers and workouts, not realizing that he really didn't have a prepuce at all and was in fact equivalent to the two-inch detective special he carried on the job. It was a test of how John could cause a self-fulfilling prophesy in Joe, as he had done successfully back in Albany selling new Cadillacs to blacks.

And John's claim that he was invited by a pilot into the cockpit of a new 747 to experience a landing at JFK was a stretch, since it would have easily blown his cover and was on every flight crew's checklist of things never to do with a sky marshal. But John said it simply because the workings of the jumbo jet were still a mystery, especially how pilots landed solely on instrumentation and not a view of the concrete.

And John always overdid it with his confidence builder, Brut. "Makes the Italian chicks go wild," he said, splashing the cologne all over his chest.

"I think they like the name better than the scent," Andrea suggested.

"How's that?" John asked.

"Next time you're in Rome, walk up to a sexy chick and say, I love you *bruttaful* woman. See what she says."

"Hey, thanks for the tip. I'll try that."

"My father taught it to me. It never fails."

There were no exploits of heroism and no remarkable adventures from the riders of the silver plane. Andrea sensed that the job might become terribly boring, though he had a plan to combat that with his cover story of a cover story.

He told them of his ground duty, about the fugitive that was run over by an ambulance, about frisking VIPs at BOAC, and about how he had met one of the three stewardesses that lived next door. The girls were usually at home, for they too hadn't received flying orders yet. They were employed by a charter airline that depended entirely on the vacation season, which was slowly approaching.

A deliveryman walked down the hall carrying a package, knowing that in the apartment at the end lived four sky marshals and in the apartment next to them were three grounded stewardesses. He stopped at their door and rang the bell. He held a package in one hand while the thumb of his other hand gently stroked the button of a switchblade in the pocket of his uniform. The door opened and a young woman peered out at him. He said, "Package for Karen Kight."

"Yes, that's me," Karen said.

Too large to fit through the opening allowed by the security chain, he made a gesture that the door be opened completely. She unhooked the chain and opened the door. He handed her the box and, as she was about to close the door, he said, "Here, please sign the receipt," keeping the door open with his foot. She stepped aside and laid the box on the floor. He looked closely at her frail feet sticking out from under her nightgown, then stepped inside slowly and closed the door.

"I don't' think so," she said.

He pulled out the knife, switched the blade and said, "Scream and I'll call the sky marshals." He snickered, being so close, yet so far away from the law. "Where're your friends, still in bed? Get in there!"

Every woman, if observed quietly, offers a glimpse of the girl she once was, and the harder it is to find, the more likely she will be the one chosen. Telling them all to strip and stand nude in front of him, he chose the one with the ugliest feet, feet that had been tortured so badly by tight, high-heel shoes that the toes were clubbed and the heels knotted with calluses—feet sacrificed to make the legs look sexy.

He ordered Karen to get on one bed and her roommates on the other and "Play with each other like they do in the movie *Lesbo from Lesbos!*"

"What?" Nancy said.

"Cunnilingus!" he commanded. "Or I'll slice her up and make you eat the pieces."

Karen didn't think that they were going through the motions for her sake, since neither one was fast enough to run for the door without being caught. She felt no indignation, calmed by the thought that they were prettier than she was, but weren't chosen for the ultimate disgrace.

Trapped on a dead-end street, the rabid dog leapt on her. It was her father, her brother, and her boyfriends, her future lovers, her husband, and even her sons, all layered on top of her with the suffocating weight of evil. The rapist tickled her sides to make her feel excited. She entertained his arousal by wiggling around the bed, which made it easier for him to pull down his pants. Taking out a tube of vermillion, he said, "This is so you don't squeal on me, bitch. The wheel that squeals gets all the grease."

Being touched, she flinched, but not enough to make him nervous. "I'll bet you say that to all the girls. Say it!"

"I'll bet you say that to all the girls," she said.

"Good. Now say, don't do it! Don't do it! I'm a virgin."

She repeated this several times until *he* stopped saying it, then she felt numb inside. He stopped and looked at the other two on the next bed watching him. "What you looking at? Get back to work!" Then, lifting up and looking down at himself, "Bitch! Look what you did to me." Looking at Karen savagely, "Bitch! You cut me with razor blades! You asked for it."

He raised the knife high over his head, the blade flashing back into her eyes reflections of terror. She made no effort to shake him off, thinking that any movement would deserve to be stabbed.

From the bathroom came the sound of a toilet flushing. Then the sound of water rushing through the walls. It was one of the sky marshals taking a shower.

Andrea stepped into the hot shower. His gun was still safekt tucked between two pairs of jockey shorts in the top drawer of the dresser. He lathered up and shouted, "It's terrific!" hoping the girls next door would hear him. "It's terrrrrrrrific!"

The rapist reared back and plunged the knife deep into Karen's soft, white, naked pillow, worked it well inside, and then pulled it out, discharging a flurry of small gray goose feathers into the air. He struck again and again, until the flight of the down covered the entire room. "Call the cops, bitch, and I'll come back and cut you just like that." Then he got up, pulled up his pants, and ran out of the apartment.

On his way down, he said to the empty elevator, "What a job. Now she'll marry a pilot, have two kids, pull in two, maybe two-fifty a year, live out in the Hamptons, and I'll be there—my portrait—hanging in their great room over the fireplace."

Karen ran into the shower.

Andrea heard the water rushing next door, and he gently moved his hand with outstretched fingers across the wall, wiping the mist off the royal blue tiles. He let his mouth fill up and then spat out a long stream that went straight down the drain.

Karen stood in her shower, letting water run over her head and down her body. She wept angrily as she washed away the red paint between her legs.

After the shower, Andrea dressed and was just about to go out when the doorbell rang. He opened it and the three stewardesses stood there in bathrobes, looking terribly lost. With a big smile, he said, "I didn't expect all of you at once, but if you must...." Nancy turned away, but he called her back, "Hey, look. I didn't mean it that way."

The three went inside and sat down on the couch. Andrea guessed that the one in the middle must have been at the cutoff point on the beauty scale for being a stewardess, her masterwork body being the thing that had gotten her the job.

Nancy did most of the talking, telling how the rapist had entered the apartment and had held Karen at knifepoint on the bed.

"Did you call the police?" Andrea asked.

"No, not yet. We thought you would since you're a sky marshal."

"No, I think it's best that you do that yourself. How long has he been gone?"

"About fifteen minutes," Anita said.

"Do you remember what he looked like?"

"White," Nancy said. "About your size, but he was bald. Totally bald."

"Had no hair on him anywhere," Anita said.

"No hair? Not even on his legs?" Andrea asked.

"Not even, ah, pubic," Nancy said.

"Age?" Andrea asked.

"Thirty, maybe," Nancy said.

"Anything else?" Andrea asked Karen.

Breaking her silence, Karen said, "He had a tattoo of a bird on his chest."

"What kind?" Andrea asked.

"A small bird," Karen said.

"Good," Andrea said. "My advice is to go back into your apartment, call the police and don't touch anything till they arrive. My guess is that he was very careful about not leaving any evidence. But that tattoo should make it easy to identify him. If you have any more trouble, call me. I'll be here."

Andrea felt depressed about not having had the chance to get out his pistol, walk into their apartment, and blow the bastard's brains out.

Karen's face enveloped Andrea in a world of helplessness. There was no trace of what had happened, only an ivory expression that lacked emotion. He had seen this face in war, but never on a woman. The accounts of the others did nothing to reveal what was concealed inside her. He started to think of it in phenomenological terms like presence and absence, immanence and transcendence, but that escaped him too. The face defied the unbiased bracketing of his phenomenology, the natural attitude of his badge. "The law will destroy the pure reduction," Farber had warned. "No matter how high of an opinion you might have of the law, you must put it out of play when performing the pure reduction. This is a good example for you, but it would be *impossible* given the importance of your work. Perhaps the law is a transcendent illusion. To ask about its existence outside of you is to introduce a false abstraction, which we call the *error of isolation*. You must be wary of artificial methods such as poetry that enjoy *predicating* experience and then finding it to be a mystery. At first you might see the falsity in it, but it will soon disappear on naturalistic grounds, drowning you in a transcendent world that is artificial and unreal. Be aware that the key danger in the phenomenological method is to think that one can construct all reality out of pure consciousness. The domains of nature and cultural traditions—the laws for sure—are too big to ignore. However, if you are to seek true meaning, you must not fail to realize that *to have is to refuse to be*."

That afternoon, Andrea went down to the Village and watched again the movie *Un chant d'amour* by Genet. On second viewing, he realized that it was not a celebration of homosexuality at all, nor pornography as some had claimed. Indeed, it showed how prisoners went about abusing themselves alone in their cells, but it was more about imprisonment, not only of two lovers separated from each other by a concrete wall, but the imprisonment of love, desire, consciousness within the body. A silent movie without written dialogue, it conveyed the feeling of love like no other work of art he had seen. Their love was not physical; it was as ethereal as the cigarette smoke that they shared through a hollow reed passed through a hole in the wall that divided their cells. A wall that concealed the face of the other.

The eye of a prison guard looks through a peephole at a masturbator in his cell. Is that me? We see through one eye as in Cao Dai. I enter the cell and point a gun barrel into the inmate's mouth, but it only makes his face grin. Inmate dreams about running in the woods with his lover, combining their bodies, feeling and being felt at the same time. Grinning face guards this inner world from me. It cannot be penetrated by a bullet. No matter how condemned or isolated, it flows freely behind the grin, always hanging onto the hope that one day the bouquet of flowers dangling on a string outside the prison window will be caught by his lover's hand in the next.

The actor touches the gray cell wall, and the surface of the painting buckles. I go behind the wall and push back on the canvas with my palm, making the wall bulge outward. Not really concrete or hardcore after all.

" . "

"Ladies and gentlemen, this is the captain speaking. We have refueled and are headed toward the Atlantic. I want to thank you for cooperating with the demands of Mister High. Please keep reading, for he is able to monitor your progress individually. With his permission, I have turned off the seatbelt signs, and you are now allowed to use the lavatories and move about the cabin freely. Once again, thank you for cooperating, and we will get through this ordeal safely."

4/Takeoff

His entrance into the Eastern Airlines terminal to begin a month of flights to Miami and San Juan was a reprieve from the bondage of ground duty that had been cramping his style for four months. He was more than ready to take off on the *Wings of Man*.

EAL's terminal at JFK was not space-age, despite the fact that ex-astronaut Frank Borman (one of the first to travel to the moon) was recently installed as a "special advisor" to the company. It couldn't compare with the American Air Lines terminal where passengers were able to watch jets take off right above the heads of the ticket agents. It looked more like Penn Station than an airline terminal and possessed an unpretentious, existential nature. An object not thematic. Appearance, nothing more.

Beyond the public barriers—deep inside the guts of the building—the three sky marshals entered the pre-flight briefing room and introduced themselves to the flight crew. The plane was a new Boeing 747 jumbo jet, and the flight was a nonstop overnighter to San Juan. The crew was still unsure that the giant airliner could be managed properly, both externally in heavy air traffic, and internally with over three hundred passengers aboard. In addition to all the concerns for safety that he had to mention, the flight steward reminded the stewardesses of the beverage service policy for sky marshals. "If he orders a screwdriver, then give him orange juice and orange juice only. A Bloody Mary, tomato juice only. In all other respects, they are to be treated exactly like paying customers, including hors d'oeuvres, filet mignon, and free movies in first class."

Soon after, at the boarding gate, Andrea felt as though all the passengers were watching him, especially when the boarding agent acknowledged the mark on his boarding pass with a wink. He carried a suit bag with two pressed shirts and an extra pair of pants, along with a small carryon stuffed with underwear and socks. Looking like the average professional—it was Bando's idea that he wear a suit to fit his cover story—he walked into first class feeling privileged without having earned it. So now, how could he possibly justify being a philosophy professor at age twenty-six flying first class? Any first-class passenger would spot the incongruity in a second.

Fearing that he couldn't pull it off to save his life, he sat discreetly next to a man in a white suit, who immediately asked with a Spanish accent, "Do you like the aisle seat? I think there are plenty of window seats to go around."

Too late to devise another cover story, Andrea felt around his big blue leather seat for the seat belt and said, "No, it's okay. I don't think there's much to look at tonight." Sensing that the man wanted the seat to be vacant in order to accommodate an available stewardess, he said, "I prefer an aisle seat so I can watch them walk around." Actually, it was the only seat he could take—left side, aisle—the perfect spot for aiming at a skyjacker by resting his pistol on the back of the seat in front of him. It would blow out the eardrums of the passenger sitting there, but that was a necessary consequence of getting off a steady and accurate barrage.

The luxury was marvelous, and he hoped the job wouldn't interfere with enjoying it, at least on his first flight. When the plane reached cruising altitude, he got up and went back to look at the horde in coach. He couldn't spot his partner but knew that *his* turn would come on the return trip.

While returning to his seat, a passenger rushed by and quickly ascended the steps to the first class lounge. Immediately, he went up behind him, only to find his partner already sitting there. They exchanged the same look of surprise—dogs chasing their own tails. It was a defect that would dictate the course of their movements in flight. Whether they went up first or tailed someone who did, there was no way they could avoid blowing cover, for the door that led to the *sanctum sanctorum* had to be protected at all times without delay.

Going back downstairs, Andrea went straight to his seat, and sitting there in his place was a bright shinny pair of handcuffs. The man next to him was snoozing and might not have noticed, so he quickly sat down directly on top of them swearing never again to hang them off the back of his belt *a la* detective Dirty Harry.

He ate, read, watched a movie, visited the toilet twice, wrote a few notes in his journal, listened to music, but didn't dare sleep a wink. With most of the passengers preferring to sleep rather than watch a movie or eat a meal, the four-hour trip to San Juan was rather sedate and uneventful.

Arrival at the break of dawn at Isla Verde was a tribute to the wonderful jumbo jet, carrying hundreds of people with unprecedented comfort and speed. Andrea felt honored to fly this newest marvel of aeronautical engineering and to protect it from pirates, psychopaths, and terrorists.

They stayed at a backwaters hotel that catered especially to sky marshals. It was clean, safe, and reasonably priced, but not a good idea to frequent every trip. They didn't savor being victims in a terrorist plot that bombed a hotel with a dozen U.S. marshals sleeping in it. Nevertheless, the food was excellent.

The next morning, they were back on another 747 for a return flight to New York. The flight crew was the same, but Andrea worked alone in the tourist class. He loved the feeling of floating in space, and no other plane did it better. But now the quarters were crowded, and he had to be more careful about hiding his piece—the stainless-steel beauty resting inside his belly band and covered by his psychedelic tie.

"Do you have the business in Nuevo York?" the woman next to him asked.

"No," he said. "I'm a philosophy professor."

There, at last, it's finally out. My cover story. So, now what would I have been doing in sunny San Juan? There is no philosophy in Puerto Rico.

"You vacation in Puerto Rico?"

"Yes," he said, silently thanking the woman for freeing him from the identity trap.

"But you no look it. You should wear tropical shirt so you can show your friends back home where you been."

"Oh no. I do have one in my bag to show them. Thanks."

After breakfast, the captain turned on the seatbelt sign in anticipation of heavy turbulence. When the big jet flew into the rough stuff, Andrea realized that it was indeed a worthy flier, managing the course with only a few suppressed jiggles and creaks. There was no free-fall feeling he had so often experienced on the Boeing 707. He sat back thinking to himself, I could really fly this thing for a living.

Suddenly, a man appeared right on top of him and climbed over the back of his seat. Hurdling seatbacks, stepping on arm rests and people, he crawled as if escaping out of a tunnel. Andrea ignored it as a temporary outburst of a claustrophobic passenger, but when a stewardess came up to him and whispered in his ear, "A man is trying to open the rear door; you'd better do something," he went back to look.

Having failed to find relief in space above the passengers, the man was now trying to lift the big, metal arm of the rear door, and bail out. Andrea grabbed him from behind in a reverse bear hug, but the little guy was strong and slipped out easily. The movement jarred Andrea's pistol from his belly band, and it dropped down inside his pants. He squeezed his legs together to hold it from dropping to the floor and reached into his pocket to grab his blackjack, but before he got it out, the man tackled him by the legs, and they fell to the floor, making the stewardess shriek. The steward got on the interphone and called for help from the other sky marshals in first class. Wrestling out of the scramble, Andrea managed to pull out his blackjack and, not knowing the effect it would have on muscle rather than bone, let go a spring-loaded blow on the thigh, which made the man yell, "Cabron!" and give up.

The shiny pistol lying on the floor drew an appreciative comment from a woman watching nearby. "Qué hermoso señor!" Andrea retrieved it and let the man limp to his seat, which was unwise, for another man was waiting to take revenge for being stepped on. After insulting the little guy with every swearword known to the Spanish-speaking world, he punched him in the face with a fist the size of a coconut that sent him flying into another man, who, in turn, pushed him into another man, who got upset about being forced into the fight and kicked the shin of the guy doing the pushing, which got another man upset at the little guy for starting the fracas in the first place, and he began strangling him. Not to be left out, a woman took off her shoe, shouted "No me jodas!" and threw it at the man with the coconut fists. The shoe missed and hit a man sitting in another section of the plane. He took it out on the woman sitting next to him, whose husband took offense, started pushing and name calling, which escalated into another fight. Soon, the whole plane was a flying bedlam of screaming, punching, and biting Puerto Ricans.

The captain announced, "I order you to stop fighting and return to your seats." This seemed to stir up more trouble, especially amongst those fueled by machismo and a hatred for the English language. The only thing that calmed the fighters was the soft voice of a stewardess that said something in Spanish none of the sky marshals or other crew members understood.

Upon arrival at JFK, a squad of Port Authority police stormed the plane and arrested three of the nonstop fighters. Andrea's partner wanted to know why he hadn't made the arrest and thwarted the violence. Andrea wrote a report saying that he suspected the little man's erratic behavior was a diversion and a possible tactic to uncover the sky marshals on board. Nothing further was made of the incident.

When sky marshals first started to fly Eastern, the cabin crews were rather formal toward them. Little by little, engaging in conversations now and then, especially in the first class lounges, they came to realize that sky marshals were not run-of-the-mill cops, but ordinary people that came from varied backgrounds. Some were even furloughed airline pilots. The Bureau of Customs had done an extraordinary job of selecting people that looked as though they had absolutely no connection with law enforcement.

During Andrea's first month, flight crews didn't exist, for the passengers took all his attention. He had several opportunities for dates, but didn't bring himself to it, until one day a cute blond sat across from him at a table in the upper deck.

Stewardesses had the reputation for being as intelligent as nurses, as attractive as chorus girls, and as friendly as contestants in a Miss America beauty pageant. The glamour associated with meeting the rich and famous was no exaggeration for these fortunate women. Sky marshals, though not in this league, were just as intriguing and possibly more challenging.

Ybette had noticed Andrea at the pre-flight briefing and took advantage of the moment when he was alone in the upper lounge. Sitting across from him at a table, she wasted no time sneaking her bare foot under his pants and running it temptingly up and down his leg. Andrea thought it cleverly sexy, but pulled back to stay cool.

"*Y*-bet?" Andrea asked. "Is that really your name?"

"*E*-bet," she said.

"Why?" Andrea joked, making her laugh. "Where'd you get that name, Ybette? It's neat. I've never heard it before."

"Mother wanted to name me Bette. She said I had Bette Davis' eyes. But father wanted to name me after his mother Yolanda. So there came the great compromise."

"I think your mother was right. You do have nice eyes."

"And what kind of a name is High?"

"It's not my family name. My real name is Italian."

"Just 'n Italian?" she said, laughing at herself.

"No, you don't want to know. It's a secret."

"Hi, Justin High," she said, "Does that mean if you tell me your real name, you'll have to kill me?"

"No, not that. It's not *that* secret."

"What then?"

"Justin can be my name, if you like. It stands for justice, of course. Not that cosmic consciousness stuff that's going around these days. You know, Timothy Leary and all that. There's no justice in transcendental meditation. Are you into that?"

"No."

"They believe that when you die, you're going to become one with the world. There's no justice in that. I mean, no punishment for being evil. The worst criminals become one with the world just like the saints. It's a religion that ignores good and evil. It's amoral."

Andrea's voice intrigued her. It sounded like a person from the past channeling into the present. Weak and off key, other people would find it annoying, but not Ybette. "Are you religious?" she asked.

"No. I don't go to church anymore."

"Is that why you wear lipstick?" she asked, entranced by his bow-tie-shaped lips.

Andrea wiped his mouth with the back of his hand. "No, I don't," he said.

"Then, why are they so red?"

Andrea felt his face getting warm.

Ybette felt excited, getting a sky marshal to blush. "Would you like me to do the *air strip*?"

"The what?"

"It's the *in* thing on airlines now. They change uniforms mid-flight. We'll never get to wear miniskirts on Eastern."

"I think your uniform looks very professional."

"Navy blue?" she said, slapping Andrea lightly on the wrist. "Look at this thing. It's so old fashioned," getting up and modeling, making sure to show off her trim bootie.

"Nicely tailored," he said.

"Sure, for a suit. Who wants to wear a suit?" She admired his sports jacket, flashy tie, and racy lips that would tickle her neck if given the chance.

Glancing at the stairwell to make sure no one else was coming up, Andrea said, "I have a black silk suit for my other cover story. For when I play a millionaire."

"I wish I could wear anything to work," she said.

"What would you wear?"

"A whole wardrobe. Change clothes every ten minutes like they do in Hollywood."

"Frank Borman wouldn't go for that," Andrea said.

"Boring Borman," she laughed playfully. Andrea liked the tone of her laugh, the silliness of a ten-year-old girl playing make-believe marriage with her boyfriends. "I have to get back to work before the steward kills me."

Presuming that one of the rich-and-famous had already made plans with her, he didn't offer her a ride home but, when deplaning, noticed that she was alone. "Would you like a ride home?" he asked.

"I never thought you'd ask."

On the way to Queens, she asked, "Do you think I should quit Eastern and join Braniff so I can do the air strip?"

"Where does Braniff fly?" Andrea asked.

"I don't know, but I'd still be able to fly to Miami."

"That's an Eastern hub, isn't it?"

"It's my home," Ybette said.

Andrea was glad to see that Ybette's apartment, which she shared with three other stewardesses, was just a few blocks from his. Though it lacked a carpet and anything resembling plush furnishings, it was large and had two full-size bedrooms. "Linnehan is here again," she said, closing the door loudly and hesitating before entering.

"Who's Linnehan?"

"Norma's boyfriend. He's an FBI man that she met at the Salty Dog."

Ybette went into her room and Andrea waited on the couch. A minute later, Linnehan came out and sat next to him. He wore a three-piece gray flannel suit and wingtips with loose laces, which he tightened proudly, as he would the cuffs around a suspect's wrists. "Rember said you're a sky marshal, is that right?" he asked.

"Who said?" Andrea asked.

"Rember, I said."

"I don't remember."

"Of course you don't," Linnehan laughed. "Rember did."

"What are you talking about?"

"Ya-bet."

"Oh, yeah, Ybette," Andrea said, embarrassed that he had forgotten.

"So, that's how you two met. Been flying long?"

"About a month."

Andrea got up, went to the window, looked down at the street for a minute, and returned to the couch, making sure his tie was covering the handle of his piece.

"Nice tie," Linnehan said, now certain he had an easy target. "What'd you qualify with, a four-inch?"

"Two-inch actually," Andrea said.

"That's a thirty-eight Chief's special, right? May I see?"

Having unloaded the pistol in his car prior to coming up, he thought it harmless. "Sure," he said and handed it over.

Linnehan opened the cylinder to check inside, stood up, and let out a disturbing groan. "Come with me," he said.

Andrea hesitated a moment before getting up, not sure what Linnehan was up to, but followed him into the kitchen to get his gun back. Linnehan stood against the counter at the far end, held out his ID briefly, and said, "Aren't you aware of the regulation that you're not supposed to carry your weapon in public while off duty?"

"Let me see that again," Andrea said, moving closer to get another look at the ID. Linnehan pulled it out again, and Andrea read aloud, "United States Department of the Treasury, Bureau of Customs. What's this? I thought you were FBI."

"Let me see your creds," Linnehan said.

"My what?" Andrea asked.

"Your badge, moron."

Andrea took out his badge and handed it over. After taking down his name, Linnehan asked, "What's the password?"

"McCormick," Andrea whispered.

Linnehan gave back the pistol and badge and said, "Don't trust anyone, especially those stews. And make sure to lock up that weapon before you go off duty."

"Okay," Andrea said.

"And get a haircut," Linnehan said. "You look like a bitch."

Without argument, Andrea left the apartment and returned to his car, where he sat for ten minutes holding his gun. "It saved my life in the Nam," he lamented. "I went to sleep with it! And that rapist is on the loose." As he was about to drive away, his nemesis appeared on the street.

Linnehan's VW beetle was an obvious hangover from college, and he inspected it as he would a drug smuggler, looking over, under, and around the vehicle for any signs of tampering. "FBI agent, my ass," Andrea said crossly.

Later, he called Ybette and apologized for leaving so abruptly. Ybette asked about the scar on his forehead. "It's just an old war wound," he said, "fully healed now." Having been a nurse, she didn't believe that a wound to the brain could ever be fully healed, but accepted the apology and an invitation to the sky marshals' abode.

Relaxing on the living room floor, Andrea looked up at Ybette's bare foot and said, "Why doesn't it stink? Do you soak your feet?" He grabbed her foot and massaged it gently between both hands and said, "Feels like baby feet." She put on a scowlface, like she had tasted something bad. She didn't believe him, but it felt good.

He brought up the rape that had happened next door, and how he felt about not being able to stop it. The story didn't upset her but made her feel safe being with *Justin* High. She lay down next to him and was overcome by an unbelievably sexy scent from his body. "What did you do before you became a sky marshal?" she asked.

"I studied philosophy."

"That's pretty heavy. Did you want to become a philosopher?"

"Yes, but that was impossible. Philosophy these days is nothing but introspection, like modern art is about art itself. It's not about what you see in nature anymore. It's about *how* you see. We distrust our seeing, our thinking. We study how objective thinking went wrong, how the philosophers made mistakes in their thinking, how they always disagreed and never resolved anything. It seemed like a game of words. I quit because I felt exhausted. Burned out."

"I'm sorry to hear that."

"Awe, that's no big deal," he said. "I have another confession to make that's even worse. You see, I'm not what you think I am."

"What do I think I am? How do you know what I'm thinking?" she said.

"You don't understand. I'm acting out a cover story...for my job. I'm really a woman acting like a man. I knew they wouldn't hire a woman, so I dressed like a man at the interview and really made an impression when I told them I was a woman. They hired me, because I was such a good actor. And, when I got the job, I had to create a cover story, and the most logical thing was to act like a man in order to *keep* the job. To be more accepted. Does this make sense?"

"I don't believe you," Ybette said, glaring at his body, knowing that there was only one way to prove his masculinity. She couldn't tell by his voice and incredibly sexy lips; her intuition told her that he *was* a man. She had worn her flirty white chemise especially for the occasion, and she wasn't about to be disappointed. "Don't you think I'm attractive?"

She lifted the dress and exposed her naked body. It was a revelation unlike anything he had ever seen, the glow of silky smooth skin promising a joy and satisfaction—a primal and glorious eroticism—second to none. It was a force so strong, bait so enticing, that he lost control of himself. It was the power of opposites cancelling each other out, the conflict between logic and psychology for the origin of truth, the clockwise vibrations of the plane's right wing balancing the counterclockwise vibrations of the left wing. He was forced to complete the symmetry. It foretold a story of doom and nothingness, yet a story of everything.

Now fully mounted, she looked down curiously at his euphoric face, glowing with the light from another room. His smile was hypnotic, providing the license for the inoculation—swab the area, jab the muscle, pull back slightly, inject the serum, withdraw, and massage the area.

Though all her rides were easy to climb, they always seemed to run away from her, up the hill and off into the night sky. When a man came, it only made her feel like easing her bladder, denying her any pleasure that might spill over into an involvement.

This one was special, however. Andrea had no idea. Ybette's plan now consummated, she pulled herself together and said, "Please get a towel. There's enough here to make ten women pregnant."

He accommodated her with his sole bath towel, thinking that it was more polite than she going to the toilet. Watching her sitting on the floor like a yogi, he was struck by how fair-skinned she was. There wasn't a thread of hair anywhere on her body other than her blond head. He had seen crab-infested grunts shave themselves like that in Vietnam, but he knew she had a different reason.

"Flying throws off my rhythm," he said.

"You were splendid," she said. "Wait till you fly across time zones." She was thinking of some pilots that had trouble even getting it up. "Then you'll really feel strange." Paralleling a key tenet of nursing never to tell patients how bad they really look, she didn't tell him that his lovemaking did nothing for her.

"So, I passed the test?" he said.

"The results will be in the mail," she said. Then, squeezing the towel between her legs, she stood up, shuffled to the door and looked out the peephole.

"I don't think the mailman is coming this late at night," he said.

"I'm not looking for the mailman," she said.

" . "

"Do you smell that?" Marge asks.

"Yes," John says. "I'm starving."

"Oh, here comes the flight attendant with the menus. I can't believe they're serving our food to all the passengers."

"It's just a power play," John says. "He's hungry for power."

5/First Intention

On the return leg of a San Juan trip, Ybette took a break after the food service and read a letter from Andrea.

Dear Ybette,

I hope you don't mind receiving my letters at work. We have been flying so often lately, I figured the quickest way to reach you would be c/o EAL. Your job keeps you very busy, so you don't have much time to write in return. My job leaves me too much time to write—letters, poems, graffiti on lavatory walls, and even a book. I've devised some new cover stories to use as occasion demands. Even had business cards made. I can pretty much play anyone, except, of course, a celebrity that everyone knows. But, hey, maybe with a little makeup, I'll try that too. There are no copyright or libel laws against impersonation. At least, I hope not.

Speaking of which, I must tell you about my cover story of a cover story, the book I'm writing while trying to stay awake. It's about this actor who impersonates a woman so that he can get a job as a sky marshal. He knows that the government is selecting several women for the job, so he trains his voice to sound like a woman. There's a lot more to it than sounding falsetto. A voice instructor teaches him to master voice resonance—men have lung resonance while women have head resonance. And he learns female mannerisms from an acting professor. Once he gets hired, he takes on the cover story of a man in order to be more acceptable to his peers and successful with stewardesses. What do you think of the story so far?

Thanks for sending the torn photo of yourself. I wonder who owns the bottom half and whether he's the luckier one. I showed it to John, my roommate. I told him you used to be fashion model in Miami. He said, "Yeah, where? The Miami Mini-mart?" I told him that your lower half—your legs— look like Tippi Hedren's legs. (Remember the blond in <u>The Birds?</u>) That made him shut up.

I have good news. Instead of doing ground duty next month, I'll be going on TDY to LA to fly Continental to Honolulu. Can you imagine the luck? It's not Pan Am or TWA to Europe, but I can't argue with it.

Love, Andrea

She always had to take the return flight home, but a response to this letter was not on her emotional itinerary. She just thought about it.

What is it about him that's so appealing? The big dimple between his eyes, the red lips, the name Justin High? What can I possibly write him? That Augustus invited me horseback riding on his ranch in Wyoming, or that I went on a safari in Africa with Longo, or that Hardy got me finish-line tickets for Daytona? Did I ever tell him any of this? I must have, in moments of small talk. Or was it vice versa, mentioning to them that I had dated Justin High, a war hero and sky marshal, the stud that proved the gynecologists all wrong? That would really throw them all into a tailspin wouldn't it? Do I dare ever mention it to anyone?

Never.

Andrea looked away from his journal at a red-eyed, portly man seated on the opposite side of the lounge staring at him and motioning with his eyes that they meet in the blue room.

He knows who I am, Andrea thought. I've blown my cover and now he wants me to join the gay chapter of the Mile-High Club. Bastard. I'd like to stretch his mouth open and wrap it around his face and make him choke on his own head.

The door opened letting in a burst of sunlight that temporarily blinded the bartender. When it closed, his eyes adjusted on two dark figures approaching the bar. To a non-football fan, there was nothing remarkable about the taller one's appearance—a blue windbreaker, black T-shirt, and jeans—tall and quarterback-set. Except his face.

When the strangers took seats, the bartender took a closer look and said, "Broadway Joe! What'll you have?"

Bando smiled, enjoying the moment of mistaken identity for as long as he could.

"So what does that make me," Andrea said, "Eddie Arcaro?" It was an appropriate call, since the watering hole was directly across from Hollywood Park racetrack.

"Maybe if you lost fifty pounds," the bartender said, "and Eddie lost thirty-four years, you might see eye-to-eye."

When served, the two sky marshals moved to a table out of earshot of the bar. "Anyone ever tell you that before?" Andrea asked. "Say you're Joe Namath?"

"No," Bando smiled.

"Well, let's hope we can score a couple of touchdowns tonight."

Bando went to the jukebox and selected a dozen songs. First one to come up was *Maggie May*.

"You would have to play that," Andrea said. "Come on; rub it in why don't you."

"Look. First chick that comes through that door you can have. Tell her that you frisked Rod Stewart."

"Yeah, sure. It's so dark in here I couldn't tell a man from a woman. Speaking of which, do you think we'll ever meet up with what's her face out here? Leila Khaled?"

"No. There's no money here. It's all in the Big Apple. Wall Street. The Fed."

"The Jets."

"There you go."

A woman came in and sat at the bar alone. "A stew," Bando guessed.

"An actor," Andrea said. "Say, whatever happened to Mark Andrews, that actor you had for a roommate? He should be out here looking for a job."

"A dancer," Bando said. "He was a dancer, last I heard. I kicked him out, and he quit the program. I think he's busing tables around Broadway looking for a job."

"Why'd you kick him out?"

Bando fanned his hand side to side to resemble a boat rocking and said, "One night when I came out of the shower, he was lying on the bed with his ass sticking up in the air like it was waiting for a bus."

"Andrews? You're kidding." Andrea thought it was a duo made for Hollywood—Bando and Andrews—athlete and artist, bold and suave, Gable and Grant. "He could shoot like hell. He was the first in our class to qualify with a two-inch."

"He was looking for more than just two inches."

"Why would anyone that good-looking want to be queer?"

"To take it up the butt for the boys in the corps. How the hell should I know?" Bando liked Andrea's homely appearance, which made it easier for him to be on strictly professional terms. That she always wore men's clothes, sounded like a man, and had a man's sense of humor was all that he could ask for in a female partner.

"What if I told you that I was exactly what I appeared to be?"

"I'd say that you were nuts." Bando caught the eye of the stewardess at the bar. He pushed back his chair and said, "As my double once said, 'Willy, it's three in the morning and Miss America just ain't coming through that door.'"

"It's three in the afternoon, man."

"Go hit the pool or something."

"Yes, sir," Andrea said. Ego hiding under his jacket, he returned to his room and wrote another letter to Ybette. Then, making sure that all his bullets were lined up on the dresser like soldiers on roll call, he took target practice at the cartoons on TV, taking special aim at *Popeye's* friend Wimpy, alias "Jones, one of the Jones boys." Before firing, he checked the cylinder once again to make sure it was empty. Keeping the trigger finger and thumb going in perfect harmony, he shot Wimpy rapidly in the chest five times before the fatso ran off the screen.

An hour later, Bando came to his room and said that he had made a double date with the stewardess and her roommate. "I didn't want you to be left out," he said. "Even though...."

"Oh, thank you darling," Andrea said, turning over on the bed. "May I have the daily special?"

Bando picked up a bottle of baby powder that was on the dresser, unscrewed the top, and poured it all over his sarcastic partner. "So this is the secret to your success. Let's see how good it works on Alice. Put your bullets away and meet me by the car at six."

As it was not supposed to happen, but often does on a blind date, Andrea's girl was better looking than Bando's. Bando thought it was a shame to let it all go to waste on his cross-dressed partner, but switching dates would be a disaster for both of them.

Alice was an even match for Ybette, but being four inches taller—coming eyelevel even in low heels, which she wore on his behalf—more striking. Andrea knew right off that she was going to be a one-night stand—up once, take a bow, then exit stage right—fifteen minutes of fame on Ventura Blvd. His fate became even more sealed when she ate only one bite of lobster tail, one cut of filet mignon, one-half stalk of asparagus, and one tablespoon of tiramisu. It was a feat of self-discipline more tantalizing than the food itself.

Working on his prearranged plan to spend the rest of the evening alone with his date, Bando entrusted the car keys to Andrea and suggested that he take a moonlight drive around L.A. The dreamy scene of a car parked high on a hill overlooking the glittering lights of Hollywood and Beverly Hills—as glamorized so often in the movies—was perhaps the ticket to success. He ventured out with only his instincts and innocent date, not bothering to ask for directions or to take a map, like a comedian starting a joke without knowing the punch line. The streets and highways were mean at every corner, not showing any signs leading to that cherished spot—the lookout, observation point, idyllic place—where he could sit, philosophize, and neck with the most beautiful girl in the world.

He couldn't find it.

Eyes riveted on the road ahead, he soon realized that Alice was watching the black landscape with silent discontent, and when they came upon an unending stretch of highway, the humiliation made her head swim. For her, the drive was worse than deadheading home to Newark on Christmas Eve. The only thing that saved his life was finding the way back to the motel before dawn.

With a new psychedelic tie knotted extra long to ensure it covered the pistol under his belt, Andrea eased into seat 10B next to Tamashiro Noburu, a land developer from Okinawa, Japan. Tomashiro read a little black book and didn't look up until the plane was well on its way to cruising altitude. Sensing his seatmate was travel weary, Tomashiro said, "Are you golfer any chance?"

"Of what?" Andrea said, looking over the man's jet-black head and bushy eyebrows that didn't show a single gray hair.

"Golf. You golf?"

"Oh, golf. I thought you meant something else. I was daydreaming."

"I pick up new putter in Los Angeles. Titanium."

"You didn't travel to L.A. just for a putter."

"Drive for show; putt for dough," Tomashiro said.

"You must be a poet."

Tomashiro opened his book, pointed to a passage, and said, "It says, Uya nu katachi yu utan tu, Manzai. Shigata ni uchiyachiri. Boh tu chi tu ni tachi shirhudi."

"Which means...?"

"In order to attack enemies of my family, I disguise myself as itinerant player. Sword concealed in pile of long and short staffs."

Adjusting his tie slightly to make sure it was covering his piece, Andrea said, "You, ah...what are you saying?"

"National sword of Japan," Tomashiro said laughingly. "Sandwich!"

"Sandwich? I don't understand."

Tomashiro made a chopping motion with his hand and repeated, "Sandwich...sandwich. National sword of Japan."

"Oh, sand wedge. But better make sure sky marshal no hear you talk about sword," Andrea said.

"Yes, you right." Tomashiro said. Then he pointed to another passage and read, "Yuku suiyushi nu ungami ni inuru kukuru wa wag a tichi ni isuji hi chawashi taboriti. We pray to God of Travelers that we may meet our enemies quickly."

"Quickly, I agree. If it's going to happen, let's get it on."

A stewardess brought Andrea a cup of tea. His eyes fixed on her orange and gold-striped uniform, which had a zipper running down the center from collar to hemline cut at mid-calf. A faint flesh tone showed through her white nylons stretched tight around the knees. Bothered by his fixation, she said, "Is everything okay, sir?"

"I ordered tea with cream and sugar," he said.

"Excuse me?" she said.

"You put a lemon wedge there, and it doesn't go with cream and sugar."

"I gave you both just in case you changed your mind."

"But how can I take out the cream if I change my mind?"

"Japanese have solution," Tomashiro said. "Drink tea. No sugar. No creamo. No problem."

"Some people like tea with lemon," she said. "I'm sorry but I'll take it back if you want it plain."

"Okay," Andrea said, handing her the lemon wedge. Then, turning to Tomashiro, "How could she make such a stupid mistake?"

"No mistake. Japanese man no eat sweet. Only woman and children eat sweet. Maybe good to discover something new."

"What, to be Japanese?"

"No. By way, what do you do for living?"

Andrea took a sip of tea and began his cover story. "Oh, I'm an actor. Before that, I was a painter and always discovered something new. I can't describe it. Just that they were unique. Avant-garde. Daring to be different. That's what my uncle used to say. Dare to be different. Can you believe he was the first guy to use black-wall tires on a car? Ten years ago, he bought a new Buick Electra, took off the whitewalls and mounted blackwalls on it. Everybody thought he was crazy. It made the car look like a truck. But now look. No one uses whitewalls except pimps. He used to claim that Detroit stole his idea since blackwalls make a car look sportier, and they're easier to clean. The same thing happened with my paintings. Every time I came up with something new, it wouldn't take long before I would see it in *Art Forum*. It was as though someone was spying on my studio."

"This plane has nice pictures upstairs. Have you seen?"

"Yeah. Do you know where that stuff comes from? The wife of the president of Continental likes art. She had all the jumbos fitted with paintings. Her choice, which is not saying much for the people that have to look at it. Ask the people behind us what they'd like to see hanging on the walls and you'd get entirely different art. I'll bet their favorite color is blue, not orange and yellow. The rich get to decide what is and what is not art— what goes in the museums, what sells for ten thousand dollars. The people don't get to go to the upper deck and see the paintings. That's why art is not important in their lives. They buy cheap prints to put on their walls. After a month, the art becomes part of the wall and is forgotten. I think your country has it right. Treat nature as art and enjoy it outside. It's not selected by aristocrats and forced on society as great art just to secure their investments, but is something already there of its own accord that can be enjoyed by everyone."

"Like orange," Tomashiro said. "Very nice."

With a good amount of professional pride and the flattering illusion that the playgrounds of the rich and famous were not too good for them, the three sky marshals accepted the desk clerk's offer of the penthouse suite, which provided a separate bedroom for Andrea. It cost them not much more than their combined per diems. And as they bent their steps towards a small taste of fame, they prayed that Sammy Davis Junior wouldn't show up to reclaim his favorite crib in Honolulu.

"Hey, free postcards," Hugh said. "What should I write my wife?"

Andrea said, "Diamond Head looks spectacular from the balcony and the waves rolling into Waikiki Beach move with celestial grace."

"Hey, that's good. Say that again slow, so I can write it down."

"Let's rent a woody," Bando said. "Take a tour around the island. Surf the north beach. Pick some pineapples. Get a massage later."

"I'm game," Andrea said.

"Count me out on the massage," Hugh said. "Let's get something to eat first."

A few hours later, they were on the North Shore sizing up the waves, which were breaking close to shore. Matt and Andrea decided to chance body surfing, while Hugh watched.

When Andrea took off his shirt and pants, Matt staggered backward. He stood speechless for a long time, staring at Andrea's flat chest. Then he started to laugh. He laughed so hard that he lost balance and had to sit down.

"What?" Hugh said. "Did I miss something?"

"At least it's not hairy," Matt said.

"I have to be prepared," Andrea said. "Just in case."

"Now, I owe you one," Matt said. "Let's go," running toward the water.

The humongous waves slammed the two amateurs repeatedly with avalanche after avalanche of sandy brine, bouncing their bodies off the bottom and flinging them up in the air like beach balls. It was total submission to a force that couldn't possibly be controlled but had to be joined, with head bent down, knees tucked into the chest, and arms wrapped around the legs, thrown down into a dangerous darkness and held there for a moment of mercy, until irrevocably jettisoned up into the breaker's twenty-five-foot peak, achieving perfect synchronization with one of nature's most discordant forces.

Now back on shore, totally wiped out, Andrea noticed that the ringing in his ears embedded there by the war had disappeared. Bando came out of the water with every muscle in his body untied yet miraculously held together. He sat next to Andrea.

"It was a bait and switch," Andrea said. "I had to get back at the bastards someway."

"The only thing that you got back is your five-o-clock shadow," Bando said, still amazed that his partner had pulled off the ruse for so long.

Andrea smiled and stroked his makeup-free face.

The routine of flying Continental direct to paradise went on undisturbed for a month until Andrea and Matt had to fly weekly nonstops to Chicago on United. This was a disappointing assignment in that the planes were L-1011s, and the layovers in the airport hotels were short and unexciting. But deadheading on an empty plane offered one luxury—three open seats on which to lie down and catch some serious shuteye.

During one flight, Andrea had already found his niche of undisturbed sleep when Bando woke him and gestured to follow him to the rear of the plane. "Mile-High Club," he said with a big smile. It took a moment for the words to sink in, but when they did, Andrea stood up and went back to have a look. There was nothing surprising though, just three stewardesses standing in the galley talking and drinking coffee. Not seeing anything more than that, and, having a terrible ringing noise in his head, he returned to his row of seats and went back to sleep.

After landing at O'Hare, Andrea asked Bando whether he had joined the infamous club. Bando smiled and held up two fingers spaced in the sign of a bull, as infielders do to signal two outs to outfielders.

Early in the morning, Bando stretched himself and jogged all the way out to Garden Grove. When he turned and headed home, the wind came at him head-on, slowing his pace. Pulling on his beard to measure the length of the whiskers, he estimated one more week before it would be fully grown. His thoughts floated playfully between a cold beer and a marriage proposal to his girl Isora.

Isora was an attractive stewardess and not easily put off by his rowdy ways. Once during a party, while she stood against a wall looking free and sexy, he crawled up to her, grabbed her by the ankles and pulled the legs out from under her, causing her to smash butt-first to the floor. Any other girl would have been mortified, but Isora laughed about it.

With every passing block, Bando took a deeper breath, trying to shake off the weariness in his legs. So many lazy hours sitting in first class eating French food had to be worked out.

He jogged back through the town and into the countryside where a cloud of dust kicked up by a truck blew across a cornfield. The black pickup came to the main road, turned left toward him, and accelerated at breakneck speed. It didn't slow down or veer politely, but kept barreling straight ahead as though no one was there. Bando jumped off the road, spun around, and gave it a mile-high, middle-finger salute. Suddenly, the truck's wheels locked, and it came to a screeching halt. It backed up a few feet, stopped, and drove off.

Bando adjusted his belly band, which held his gun tightly pressed to his body, and continued down the road. After ten minutes, the same black truck came up behind him following at his jogging pace. As it came around to pass, a man in a cowboy hat stood up in the bed, loosened a lariat, and flung it around Bando's head. It was a good throw, but Bando caught it before the cowboy had a chance to pull it tight. Bando tugged on the rope, causing the cowboy to lose balance and fall onto the road. The truck continued forward until the driver noticed what had happened and stopped.

Having lost his hat, which was tumbling freely across the field, the cowboy stood up wondering why the hippie hadn't taken advantage of the fall and lunged at him. He thought that maybe he was tired from running and now easy to whip. "Hey, acidhead," he said, "why don't you go pick daisies and stop hoggin' the road?"

"You better go home before you get hurt," Bando said.

The cowboy shuffled his feet and pumped his fists like a BAMF. Then, moving to his left, he feinted a few lefts and rights, signaling that he wanted to box man-to-man. Bando went into his martial-arts stance and turned with his opponent, keeping loose and ready. Edging in closer, the cowboy came within striking distance. Bando's left foot darted swiftly, kneecapping him hard. The cowboy buckled under the overload of pain, allowing Bando to finish him off with a powerful kick upward into the soft spot under the chin. Had he been a skyjacker, the target would have been his throat.

Watching his friend go down, the driver jumped out of the truck. The cowboy, now rolling around the road in pain, struggled desperately to breathe. Seeing a car come up the road, he waved at it, but it went by without slowing down. He tried to climb back onto the truck but lost balance and fell off.

Instead of helping his friend, the driver reached into his boot and pulled out a knife. Holding it in close, he advanced slowly, intending to slice the hippie's hands as he tried to defend himself. He wanted to even the score.

Quickly, Bando reached under his shorts, drew out his PPK, and pointed in full combat stance at his target. The man dropped his hands, put the knife back in his boot, and said, "Okay, we'll git."

Pointing at the M-16 hanging in the rear window of the truck, Bando said, "What are you, National Guard?" He suspected they were going to ambush him up the road.

"Naw," said the driver. "It's just a two-twenty-two varmint gun."

"Same thing," Bando said. He aimed at the M-16 and squeezed off a round. The bullet put a hole in the glass and tore the trigger off the rifle.

Willy back in place, Bando continued jogging. When he passed the dirt road out of which the truck had come, he breathed deeply.

6/Banana Split

"Make me disappear," Ybette said.

"I'm not that there yet," Andrea said. "But I can make a knot disappear," pulling out a two-foot white rope from his pocket.

"Where'd you get that?"

"The Magic Castle in Hollywood. You can get all kinds of tricks there. Watch this." He tied a knot in the center of the rope, and then covered it with his hand. "Say the magic word."

"I don't know any."

"Make up one."

"Ameliorate"

"Ameliorate?"

"I don't know."

"Okay. Ameliorate! Voila, and the knot disappears!"

Ybette let out a long sigh when the trick didn't work. Andrea covered the knot again and said, "Abracadabra! The guy said it was an easy trick. Cost me ten bucks."

"Did instructions come with the rope?"

"Yes."

"Did you read them?"

"No."

"Why not?"

"It's not a magic rope if you need instructions to make it work."

"Now you're sounding like one of your letters." She licked her lips, getting impatient for the banana split. "What did you mean in your letters?"

"About what?"

"About me."

"Just what I said in them, I guess."

There is art and then there is philosophy. Having created the former, he claimed immunity from the latter.

When the waitress served the *Montana Banana*, she made a face and said, "This thing is obscene! They would be arrested serving this back home. Look at it, Justin!"

"Andrea," he said calmly.

"I'm sorry, Justin. I mean Andrea. Can't you see?"

"No," he said.

She turned the dish around to face him. "What do you suppose that is?" pointing at the banana flanked by two balls of ice cream at one end, and a mound of whipped cream sprinkled with coconut at the other. She began scooping spoonfuls of the chocolate and vanilla into a mound in the center and topped it off with the whipped cream.

"You're ruining it," he said.

"You sent me a letter a day. Why? What did they mean?"

"I can't add anything more to them. It's like that ice cream tower. It'll melt away, just like our *mediocre* lives."

She stabbed the erection angrily with her spoon. "Mediocre lives? Is that what you think?"

Well, there's one ten-dollar word she understands. She didn't understand any of my letters, but this word really rang her bell. "Well, it's true. Listen. Only five people in the world know how a Fernsehen really works."

"A what?"

"There are a lot of physicists that think they know, but they really don't. Only five do. People like you and me don't give it a second thought. The same thing goes for the meaning of existence. No one really cares to ask why. Only a few people ever have, but someday one person will find out why and only four others will understand him."

"You're impossible."

"Okay, let's look at what we do for a living. It's not very creative. Anybody can do it."

"That's not true. Hundreds of women applied for my job and didn't get it."

"But that's not saying they couldn't do your job."

"No, it's not. I'm sure they could, but they didn't have what the recruiter was looking for."

"And what was that?"

"I can't say for sure. Whatever it was, I had it. I can't describe it, and I don't think the recruiters can either. It's just something special that only a few people have."

"Charisma?" he said, smiling.

"Maybe."

"Hey, can I use that for my book?"

"You're book? What book?"

"Didn't you read my letter? It's about a philosopher. His work is futile, so he becomes a sky marshal, posing as a woman just to get hired. He takes on a male cover story to get action, but he falls in love with a stewardessus."

"A what?" she asked laughingly.

"A stewardess," he corrected. "She's okay, but he wants to do something really great. He wants to be the first one to thwart a skyjacking and save the lives of three-hundred people."

"That's never been done before."

"Not by a sky marshal. That's my problem. He doesn't know what it's like, so all he can do is write about it. I don't know what it's like, so how can I write about what he writes?"

"Use your imagination."

"He can't because his philosophy tells him that the imagination is deceptive and creates nothing but lies."

"Well, what about his girlfriend? Maybe you can make a romance novel out of it. Don't you have enough firsthand experience to write about that?"

"Ours is definitely first class. And very real."

Pleased by this turn, Ybette scooped up a big portion of ice cream and fed it to him. Then she asked, "So, how will it end? We get married, and I become a housewife?"

"Get married?"

"Yes, and I become a housewife."

"Housewives have a lot of responsibility," he said sincerely. "And they can be very creative. When I'm out flying around the world, you will stay home, take care of the kids, and write the ending of the story."

"I'll never have the chance to do that."

"Sure you will."

"No I won't."

"Why not?"

"You don't understand, Justin." She put the spoon down, took a deep breath, and said softly, "You see, I can't have babies."

The way she said *babies*, with such affection, made him think there was one right there next to them, smiling and giggling. "Sure you can have babies," he said.

"No, Justin. I can't. My gyne said so."

"Your gynecologist? They're not always right. They said my cousin couldn't have any kids, so she adopted one. After a year, she got pregnant. Then she had another one and had to give up the adopted one."

"Yes, that's wonderful, but my case is different."

"How come?"

"I can't tell you straight out," she said. "You need to know the reason behind it."

Andrea checked his watch and showed her the face.

"What's that supposed to mean?" she said.

"We have all afternoon." he said.

"All right. We do." She called the waitress for a cup of coffee and began her story. "I was just beginning to fly—in my first month—when the senator came aboard and right off took a shine to me, because I was a southern lady flying Eastern. I told him Kentucky wasn't exactly the Deep South."

"Was this guy from Georgia?"

"You don't understand. A *southern* lady flying *Eastern*!"

"Okay. I get it. Then he must be from New York."

"I can't say, silly, so don't ask," slapping him on the wrist.

"Okay, it doesn't matter."

"Well, I forgot to carry my pills that trip and got pregnant with this man."

"Like forgetting your gun the first day on the job?"

"Not quite. Maybe forgetting your bullets," she laughed. "Well, anyway, he wasn't going to get a divorce, and I wasn't going to give up my job, so we agreed to give it up. Besides, I didn't have to go to a public clinic where they treat you like a lab specimen. There's a doctor downtown recommended by the airline, so I went to him." She paused expecting him to comment but continued after taking another sip of coffee. "When I went into the waiting room, there was a show on TV. It was about a widow who was haunted by her son and her daughter. They were statues she had sculpted on the fireplace that came to life." Ybette paused again, this time struck by the absurdity of the story, but she continued. "The strange thing was that her children were her own creations. She was a sculptor, and they came to life. This wasn't an afternoon soap, but one of those fifties dramas, the *Loretta Young Show*, I think. It didn't show what she had done. Just implied it."

"I don't think they allowed the word on television then."

"I was surprised the receptionist didn't turn the channel. The story was upsetting, but I didn't change my mind. At first, I thought it was on purpose, that I was shown this program to discourage me. Somehow, I don't know. Maybe it was. When I got into my surgical gown and waited in the examination room, I heard a voice." She paused a moment to compose herself, then said, "Justin, I swear to you, it was a little boy's voice, and he said, 'Mommy, look at me!' I didn't see anyone there. Can you imagine? It sounded so real. I couldn't go through with it after that. So, I got up and walked out."

"What did the senator say?"

"I should have lied to him. But I told him what had happened. Then one morning, I woke up screaming. I know the signs of shock and felt it happening to me, so I called an ambulance. I went into shock when they wheeled me into the emergency room. The doctors operated and found that my uterus had been punctured and that the baby's head had been pushed through and was still inside."

Overcome with pity, Andrea took her hand and squeezed it gently. "I don't know what to say," he said. "How…?"

"I was drugged and kidnapped, Justin. I'm sure of it, but I can't prove it."

"Did you call the police?"

"I reported it at the hospital. There was someone on the staff, but there was nothing else they could do."

"Did you tell them about the senator?"

"No. I told them that I didn't know who might have been the father."

"Wow. But you think he was the one who planned it?"

"Let's go, Justin. I don't want to talk about it anymore."

That evening, they went to her apartment, since Linnehan had broken up with Norma, and there was no chance he would be there. After a few drinks, she changed into a silk evening gown that clung to her skin without the slightest wrinkle. She sat next to him on the sofa and said, "I'm sorry for troubling you with my story. I didn't mean to. Your letters were very kind. I understand how you feel. It's been a long time since we first met, and you were away."

"About three months," he said.

"A lot can happen in that time. You wrote so many nice letters. I'll always keep them." She searched for more to say but stopped short of saying why she didn't reply to the letters. "Don't be so hard on yourself, Justin."

"I'll try hard not to be," he said.

"That's good," she said. "Now please go. Norma is waiting for you."

"Go? Where? Where's Norma?"

"In bed waiting."

"For what? For me?"

"Of course, you silly. You know Norma. Go ahead. It's okay."

The idea of walking into a dark room and sneaking into bed with a woman he hardly knew seemed bizarre. "Doesn't she have a boyfriend yet?"

"Justin, she's lost count already."

"Yeah, well, that's the, ah, that's the whole point."

"Okay, suit yourself, but she said it was okay."

"And you?" he asked. "Any interesting dates while I was gone?"

"I dated an Indian man. Sat right there where you are, bound and determined to get his little peter into me."

He laughed and could hardly ask, "What'd you do?"

"Nothing."

"Well, what did he do then?"

"Masturbated himself."

"That's bad," Andrea said. "I'd liked to have seen that. But you can't be prejudiced about blacks?"

"My mother disliked people of the colored persuasion."

"Then you'd date a black guy."

"That depends."

"How about Jimmi Hendrix?"

"I wouldn't miss that *experience*," she said, smiling.

"Would you dare to, ah, you know...?"

"First-class service? Why sure, darling. Sweet as brown sugar."

"Now that would not be mediocre," he said. "But you should know, he has some bad skin."

"What do you mean?"

"Acne."

"How do you know?"

"A friend told me. A marshal who frisked him on a flight to London."

"He frisked Jimmi Hendrix?"

"Never know who you're going to meet. I frisked Rod Stewart once. Nice guy."

"Rod Stewart? No. What did he say?"

"You're making a first class fool out of me."

She laughed. Then, feeling the time was right, he pulled out a little box, gave it to her, and said, "A little present from Ha-vai-ee."

She took the box, opened it, and immediately clasped around her neck an opulent string of pearls. She wasn't sure why he had waited so long, but she kissed him nonetheless.

"They're not tied," he said, "but I couldn't argue with the price. You can get them tied at a local jeweler."

"They're beautiful, Justin. I wouldn't want those fine white pearls spilling and running all over the floor now, would I?"

He held her hand—a treasure never to be lost. He kissed it. She closed her eyes and fell back gently upon a pillow. She was surprised his body wasn't suffocating. He kissed her gently, moved toward her neck, licked the pearls, and finally connected with her lips.

The mysterious scent from his body made her moan and wriggle. She caressed herself, priming a spring of eroticism that lay hidden deep inside. She emerged from the silk and, suddenly, he was adorned. It knocked him backward, and she crawled onto him. He didn't move except to open his lips to breathe. She kissed him softly. Now rising to the surface, the spring gushed forth a flurry of kisses that covered his entire face—forehead, eyes, nose, cheeks, chin, lips, and even ears. It was one minute of sensuousness that surpassed anything he had ever dreamed possible. Then, abruptly, she stopped. He waited a minute for her to return, but she was back in her old self again, thinking the same thoughts she had abandoned only minutes before.

He now understood how a woman felt after a *quickie* from a man. She had no staying power—the thread that kept the pearls together. But what was it that ran through her words and actions day to day? Was it the word *Ybette*, which began on its own every moment, or nothing at all? The pearls didn't string themselves together.

He left her sleeping on the sofa and returned to his apartment, still tingling all over, the scent of her body still fresh in his mind. Just as he opened the door, John came out of the bedroom all packed up and ready to go. "Look, man," he said, "my brother just sent me some hash, and I can't take it with me. Don't freak out, man, but help yourself. It's in my drawer."

"So, what am I going to be doing in your drawers?"

John laughed and walked out the door, off again to Europe.

The stick was about the size of a pack of gum, but Andrea knew that its effect was ten times greater than grass. He already had several drinks under his belt and thought that he could simulate a heroin high by combining it with a few tokes of hashish. Just an experiment, he thought.

It wasn't quite midnight, so he helped himself to a small chunk. Immediately after taking a few heavy tokes, a thought hit him with the strength of the hemlock taken by Socrates. "John is not a man to be trusted. What am I doing?" Running around the apartment looking for a surveillance camera, he kept saying, "It's a plant! It's a plant!"

Unable to find a device, he rushed out and waited for the elevator down. An elderly woman came up and said, "Are you going by the second floor by any chance?"

"No," he said. When the door opened, he walked inside and closed it in the woman's face, and then rode straight to the ground floor. When he walked out into the cool evening air, the clear sky rewarded him with an explosion of stars.

Karen Kight, returning home from a tennis tournament at Forest Hills with a few friends met him with a friendly, "Welcome back stranger."

Afraid of the telltale signs made by the hash, he walked by them without looking up or saying a word. Crossing his mind like a ball flying over a net was the thought that Karen was carrying the rapist's baby. Life was a one-sided game of tennis where he never got the chance to return the volley.

He walked away from everything recognizable and sat on a cool lawn surrounded by well-trimmed hedges. Except for an occasional passing car, the streets were deserted, and all he could hear was a ringing sound, now louder than ever before. Backwards and forwards, the buildings paraded in gloomy emptiness. When a huge mélange of lights, trees, and stars started whirling around him, he fell back on the grass. No one saw him lying there, and he could have gone unnoticed until morning, but the only thing he needed at that moment was for the world to stop spinning.

Fearing that it would take until morning to recover, he shut his eyes and tried to force his brain to stop. That made him more nauseous, so he took a deep breath, turned over on his side, and slowly sat up. Still breathing deeply, he got back on his feet and wobbled around aimlessly through the streets until he found a recognizable façade, went inside, rode the elevator to the top floor, walked down the hall, turned the key, switched on the light, and flopped down on the nearest bed.

It wasn't long before he had taken another bad turn and was reeling around in a fit of nausea, not the heady kind that was bearable, but the visceral kind for which there was no relief. Unable to hold out any longer, he jumped up and headed for the toilet. Stumbling around a corner, he fell to the floor and upchucked the remains of the banana split into a corner of the hallway, painting the walls with the color of a brown paper bag. Too tired to clean it up, he returned to bed and slept until noon.

Feeling much better after the siege, he packed up all his belongings and moved out of the apartment.

Matt Bando was happy to provide refuge for his friend in his little underground abode in Brooklyn. They agreed to go fifty-fifty on everything, including driving to work when they were on ground duty at JFK.

"So, how's the big Y doing?" Bando asked. "I thought you two would be shacked up by now."

"It's the feminist movement," Andrea said. "It's making women feel more justified acting like men. It's doing nothing to improve interpersonal relations."

"Women acting like men? You should talk."

Andrea told him the story about Ybette's abortion, and even about how she had kissed him with incredible passion but petered out just as he was getting really hot. "I never thought a woman with thin lips could kiss so good."

"Sounds like she's been taking tribal pills. Is she?"

"Yeah, she carries a pack with her."

"Why would she claim to be sterile if she needs to take the pill?"

Andrea thought for a moment, and then said, "Added precaution maybe.

Just like you carry two guns."

The following morning, the fifty-fifty agreement was put to the test when Bando looked out the window at the street. He stood spellbound for several minutes, not saying a word, while Andrea sat at the table eating breakfast.

"Man, this omelet is good," Andrea said. "Cream cheese and eggs shouldn't taste this good."

"It's gone," Bando said.

Andrea picked up his plate, went to the window, and looked out. From ground level, the space between the cars where once stood Bando's Cougar looked like a vacant lot between two houses. "Mannaggia!" he said.

Bando went to the door, opened it, and looked outside.

"Does this always happen in Brooklyn?" Andrea asked.

"Only to red convertibles," Bando said.

" . "

"What are you writing?" Marge asks. "Surely you're not finished reading."

"An e-mail message to the author," John says. "I've had enough."

"You can't be serious."

John ignores her and continues to write.

As an author of mainstream suspense, I'd like to give you a little advice. There's nothing exciting about a sky marshal riding around the skies for months without finding a landing zone; lost, dizzy in empty space without a navigator. People will buy a novel about sky marshals because it promises them a good action story. They want to get their vicarious jollies as well as think they are learning the inside dope on something. People aren't interested in any philosophical awakening that takes place in the main character. The average book buyer, when he sees a novel about sky marshals, is going to expect and want three things. Sex, violence, and an exposé to make it a bestseller. Definitely not any philosophy.

Publishers have one major competitor—television! In order to compete, they need crisp writing, easy reading, and vivid images. Like it or not, these are the only books that sell, not literary books.

The part that stands out in my mind as being the worst is the characterization. Andrea is only half-drawn and inconsistent. As a man who dons various cover stories, he isn't convincing. He comes off as trying to play experienced and worldly, but fails. I think you haven't really gotten straight in your mind just who this guy is. One minute he's tracking down terrorists like James Bond, the next he's trying to lay a woman that can't have orgasms. You try to make your characters sophisticated, but they seem more like college sophomores trying to act sophisticated. Andrea appears as a bit of a prig, flying around with his head in the clouds, ready to preach a sermonette at the drop of a hat. You've told us little about him; he seems amorphous, like Jell-O. Why, then, should we care about him? In an action book like this, he's got to be rock hard, razor sharp, vivid in the reader's eye, someone we can trust and believe.

Your story needs a likeable main character. He should have a flaw or handicap with which the audience can sympathize, but he must be a hero, a hero that comes out a winner in the end. Otherwise, you're treading on solipsistic narration, which seems to be the sole purpose of your book. I think you are writing too much for yourself. I don't think you know yet what effective writing is all about. You're a pilot without a navigator and your book is a plane without passengers wanting to go somewhere.

I don't buy your premise that the more we are denied this character Andrea, the more reality we give him. You are bringing up a very unpleasant and unpopular subject here, the wound he carries with him—the specter of Vietnam past. It's the impossible center around which this whole book rotates and goes nowhere. A main character that needs to search for a plot while the gunplay goes on elsewhere—the skyjackers hunted down and destroyed—is a gigantic failure.

You need a bottom line here, something readers want. Take my <u>Most Wanted</u>, for example. It has everything they could possibly ask for in a book. Sex, violence, and an exposé.

Commercial, you say? Why, of course. People don't give a shit about creativity.

For starters, change your subtitle, 'America's Most Wanted Novel That Nobody Wants.' That's absurd. There can be <u>nothing</u> that's most wanted that nobody wants.

John Barefoot

Five minutes later, John gets an e-mail reply that says: *Barefoot, bullshit! There is something most wanted that nobody wants. America's most wanted criminal, which is what I am right now. So, get ready, you fuggin son-of-a-bitch. Wanted or not, here I come. Jack.*

Suddenly Marge says, "Someone is coming down the aisle. It's a man, and I don't think he's the air marshal. I told you...I told you...."

John turns and looks out the window to hide his face, but he hears High say, "Where is he, that fuggin worm? Barefoot! Are you Barefoot? Which one of you is Barefoot?" High stops next Marge and says, "Do you know John Barefoot?"

There's a boyish innocence on High's face, a look that defies his intentions, even with untamable eyebrows and mustache.

"No," Marge says. "I don't know him."

"You there, looking out the window. What's your name?"

Don't look at me, John says, but his plea is not written on High's ears. Where's the air marshal to shoot this madman? Don't look at me. Can't someone tackle him now and take his gun?

"Hey, you! I said, what's your name?"

I'm going to piss in my pants. No, no! I can't. Not in front of everyone. Hold it, John. Hold it! I can't lie to him; he'll find out and really shoot me. Oh, God, I should have e-mailed Anita instead. And my parents to say goodbye.

"Get out here!"

He's going to shoot me and sabotage my bestseller.

Marge stands up and lets him out.

I don't see a gun. There's nothing in his hand. Nothing! He's holding air. It's absurd. I shouldn't smile but can't help it.

"What's so funny?" High says.

"Nothing," John says. "It's just that your gun is…."

"Is what?"

"Is ah…. I can't see it. Invisible?"

"Invisible?" High says. "That's the trouble with you poets. You invent a word, and you expect the whole world to follow suit. Bang, bang, you're dead. Bang! Bang! A lot easier on the ears than the real thing. Wouldn't want to upset your readers with real bullets, now would we? Blanks are all you need. Big blanks. That's all poets are. And what's with the remark, 'certainly no philosophy?' Afraid of the real thing? Real bullets?"

A line from *Hamlet* comes to mind, but John dares not say, *There are more things in heaven and earth, Horatio, than are dreamt of in your philosophy.*

"Well?" High asks.

"Yeah," John says.

"Of course. But this gun doesn't have bullets, so you might think it's harmless."

Why doesn't someone jump him? We could take him.

Jack High reads Barefoot's eyes and says, "I wouldn't try it. I must look like an idiot, holding out my hand like this with nothing in it. But, believe me, there is something in it, and it's real. You see—or not see—that it's a pain ray. You've seen hand-held pain rays, but not this one. No one has ever seen one before, because no one can, not even its inventors. It's top secret. Not the gun, but the cover, which no one can see. It's cloaked with metamaterial. Want to try it out? It won't kill. Just a little dose."

"A stun gun?" John asks.

"No. More like a microwave, but along that same line. Just a little bit more oomph, know what I mean? Let's see. I'll set it on pizza. Want a hit? Here goes."

"Wait! I believe you."

"Very good. Then sit down, shut the fug up, and read. Your national tour is over!"

7/Clipper Rainbow

As Andrea kicked back in his blue Herculean leather seat and stared at an image of the globe on the first class menu, he became the envy of every cop that ever wore a badge. This is not an airline, he thought. This is an *airways*. Pan American World Airways. And this is not flight 349 out of Atlanta, but flight 2 out of JFK heading east for destinations around the world.

The simplicity of the number impressed him no end, for there was actually no end to the flight. It just kept going east, stopping only at the major cities along the way, just as its twin, flight 1, kept going west and making the same stops in reverse order. Pan Am flights went far beyond the thousands of other flights that tangled themselves into untold knots in the skies. It was a way of life, and he was heading for London, the first stopover.

He would put on his headphones and listen to his favorite rock channel, catch up on some reading, write a poem to Ybette, and try out a new cover story on anyone who wanted to listen. But first, he had to study the passengers. He was guarding *Clipper Rainbow*, and he wasn't about to let a terrorist hijack it by any means, under any circumstance.

Pan Am had lost a 747 during Black September, and some pilots were carrying personal weapons aboard. The captain of *Clipper Constitution*, a former B-52 pilot, carried a PPK in his boot.

Trying to look casual without attracting attention, Andrea took the first shift in the upper lounge. While standing at the bar, a woman began flattering him about his black silk suit. She kept this up for half an hour, until Bando bumped him on the shoulder. "I'm sorry," Andrea said to the woman, "it's getting crowded up here. Here's my card. You would be a good candidate for that augmentation." He left the lounge and went downstairs wondering how far his new cover story would carry him before falling flat on his face.

A few minutes later a man came up to him and asked, "Are you the plastic surgeon who just spoke with my wife? She said you'd be the fellow wearing the bright tie."

"Yes, I am," Andrea said. "Doctor Genet."

"You seem rather young to be a plastic surgeon."

"I graduated from the University of Bluffalo med school in sixty-seven."

"Where did you say?"

"Buffalo. Buffalo, New York."

"Oh, I see. They have plastic surgery there?"

"Actually I interned at the Buffalo VA hospital. We saw many badly disfigured veterans from Vietnam, so I got firsthand experience in the specialty. I just opened a private practice. Is there anything I can do for you?" Andrea stepped to the side and inspected the man's profile.

"Do you see something, doctor?"

"Yes. I did a study of the jaw structures of officer candidates in the Army, and its effects on promotion. Are you in the corporate world, Mister, ah...?"

"Rick Nickle, Vice President of marketing, *Sureshot*."

"*Sureshot*? That's the...."

"Pop-up, drop-down, fast-reload staple gun."

"Staple gun? Oh, yeah. Better not talk about guns here. The sky marshal might get upset."

"Sky marshal? You mean here?"

"Well, I hope so. Don't you? And as I was saying, if you're in good physical condition, you would be a good candidate for surgery. It would definitely improve your facial balance. That's what we're after. Augmenting the mandibles alone might make you look too aggressive. What you need is proper balance in the facial features. Chin, nose, mandible. So, if you do go for it, make sure your doctor understands facial symmetry. Like a portrait artist."

"What exactly would you do, if you were my doctor?"

"Yes, I'd start with your chin. If you stand still for a moment...." Andrea took out a pen and held it perpendicular from Nickle's lower lip. "You'll see that your chin could easily be augmented to line up better with your lower lip. The more symmetrical the face, the more angular the jaw and balanced the facial features, the less primitive we look. I suggest you look for a picture of a jawline in a magazine...of an actor perhaps, like Robert Redford, and take it to a good plastic surgeon. 'This is how I want to look.' He'll fix you up, I'm sure."

"How much would it cost?"

"Have him give you a quote and call me."

"Thanks doctor. I'll do that."

Not wanting to press his luck, Andrea went back to his seat and stayed there until the meal was served. The menu—Pan Am's Transatlantic Service, Premiere Classe—was in French and classier than anything he had ever seen. He ordered Escalopes de Veau (Sauce Marsala). But as great as it tasted, it had to go down quickly so that he relieve his partner upstairs before the kitchen closed.

When they arrived at Heathrow, the accommodations provided by the British for surrendering weapons were just as Sam Layton, the team leader, had described. On the far wall of the security office was a table around which were stacked sandbags that formed a small bunker where the

American sky marshals could unload their weapons safely. "And there it be," Sam said, pointing at a hole in the wall made by a .38 caliber bullet accidentally discharged by a sky marshal several months earlier.

"Who was it?" Bando said.

"I don't know," Sam said. "But he's no longer flying."

Andrea felt like a fool unloading in a mock bunker, but that's how serious Brits treated firearms.

Sam took them to a small bed and breakfast near the British Museum where he had stayed several times and gotten good service. "Why not stay with the flight crew where we can get a *big* American breakfast?" Andrea asked.

"On the contrary," Sam said. "The British have *big* breakfasts! You'll get coffee and a roll when we go to France and Italy." Sam was a furloughed Pan Am pilot and a master at international savoir-faire.

One night layover wasn't enough to do any sightseeing, but at least they had a quiet place to rest for the next leg of the trip—London to Frankfurt.

Shortly after takeoff from Heathrow, before the seatbelt sign was turned off, a man leapt upon the staircase and pulled himself up the railings to the upper deck. Matt unfastened his seatbelt and gave chase, skipping every other step in his climb. Reaching the top, he noticed that the man was standing at the cockpit door trying to turn the knob. He grabbed him from behind in a bear hug and forced him against the door. Realizing this was a bad move, for he couldn't get out his gun or blackjack, he looked around for help. Fortunately, Sam came up the staircase to lend a hand to subdue the likely skyjacker. Immediately realizing that force was the only solution, Sam pulled out his blackjack, reared back to get a high-arcing swing, and landed a solid blow on the side of Matt's skull. Arms falling limp to his side, Matt collapsed on the floor. The skyjacker knelt down, took the pistol off Matt's belt, and looked at it enviously. Then he grabbed the thick mane, pulled the head back, pointed the muzzle at Matt's forehead, and cocked the trigger. "No!" Sam yelled, handing his man a stiletto, which he switched open and pointed towards the eyes, hesitating for a moment about which one to attack first, then jabbed it deep into the right eyeball all the way through to the brain. Oddly, no blood came from the wound as he pulled out the knife. Then he did the same with the other eye, this time digging deeper as if drilling for it. Then it began to flow.

Holding his badge up to the peephole, Sam knocked on the cockpit door. The flight engineer opened the door and at once gave way when he saw the sky marshal's gun pointing at his heart. "Get down!" Sam yelled. "On the floor. Now!" Hesitant to do so, the engineer submitted only after seeing the second skyjacker approach, armed and ready to kill. They handcuffed the engineer behind his back, the second officer to his seat, and instructed the pilot to fly to a cruising altitude and engage the autopilot.

Sam whacked the pilot on the top of the head twice with the blackjack and took over command of *Clipper Rainbow*.

Not getting a response on the interphone, the flight steward went up to the upper deck and saw the sky marshal dead on the floor. He attempted to open the cockpit door but found it locked and went back downstairs to get the last sky marshal.

All they said to Andrea was that there was an emergency in first class and that he had to do something quickly. He followed the stewardess to the upper deck and saw his partner on the floor. He knelt next to the body and put a hand on the motionless chest. Not a single breath. The face was so covered with blood that only the hair showed it was Matt Bando. He drew his pistol and checked the cockpit door. It was locked. "We can't get through to the flight deck," the steward said. "No one answers."

This is how they were in the Nam, Andrea recalled. Unrecognizable! But I was still alive. Now he's dead. They'll have to put him in a body bag and ship him back to the States.

The ringing in his ears grew louder, throbbing through his brain from one side to the other. "Is the fire alarm on?" he asked.

"No," the steward said.

Andrea searched for Matt's revolver but found only the spare, which he handed to the steward.

"What are you going to do?" the steward asked.

"Check the toilet out," cocking his gun and opening the door slowly. Nothing was inside.

A stewardess came up the steps and said that Sam Layton and Sam Zamojian were the only two passengers missing and presumably inside the flight deck. Feeling dizzy, Andrea stepped back, sat down, and asked the steward to close the shades and turn off the lights. "Crossfire," he said. "I'll stay here. You sit on the side and when they open the door, fire everything you've got."

"What if it's the captain?" the steward said.

"You know Layton is a pilot too?" Andrea said.

"No, you don't. It's Sam Zamojian. He's the hijacker."

"Then how did he get inside?"

The four jet engines continued to propel the immense tonnage of metals, plastics, and people through the air at terrific speed. The steward didn't hear the noises and vibrations. He went to the interphone and tried to call the captain one more time, but, getting no response, took a seat and pointed the pistol at the unyielding door.

Andrea remained seated. In his hand, the stainless-steel weapon shined in the dark. Its smooth coolness helped him fight off the urge to jump up and attack. Zamojian has Matt's two-inch, he thought, and Sam has a four-inch. Not good shots, but they have the advantage of looking through that peephole.

Every five minutes the steward interrupted the vigil with a round of calls on the interphone. "Nothing new," he reported and returned to his seat.

Then, a voice came over the PA system. "This is the auto pilot speaking. Ladies and gentlemen, I regret to inform you that your captain is dead and I have taken over this clipper."

"That's Sam's voice!" Andrea said. "I told you."

"We have changed course and are now headed for Rome where the plane will crash into Saint Peter's Basilica. There's no need to worry, since I have several years of flying experience, and we should arrive at our destination on schedule. Thank you, and I'm sure you will find Rome much more picturesque than dirty old Frankfurt or London. Get your cameras ready!"

The steward jumped up again and called the flight deck, but there was no answer. "What are you going to do?" he yelled at Andrea. "You can't just sit there. You have to lure them out!"

"He knows the British have big breakfasts," Andrea said.

Suddenly, the plane started descending. "We're approaching Rome." With a violent thrust, the steward opened a window blind and looked outside to see if he could spot St. Peter's dome.

"Within the next few minutes," Andrea whispered to himself, "the totality of this plane, all three hundred thirty passengers and eighteen crewmembers will bring a false rapture to the thousands of people assembled for Sunday Mass."

"What?" the steward asked.

Even though the stewardess had given the order for all passengers to remain seated, people kept moving about the plane, some even looking up the stairs but not daring to make the climb.

Andrea's watch read 11:55 a.m., and he had to act now, but there was no way to lure them out of the cockpit. He told the steward to put the blind down, and the lounge became dark again. A small beam of sunlight shined through the fisheye lens in the door and lit up his face. "My bullets are frangible," he said. "Check out your gun. What are they?"

"What do you mean?" the steward asked.

"The bullets. Are the tips hollow or solid? Check 'em out."

The steward fumbled with the gun until the magazine slipped out; he felt the top bullet and said, "Solid."

"Let me have it! Hurry!"

The sunlight through the peephole went out momentarily, and then shined again. A passing cloud, perhaps.

Another cloud shrouded the plane and he envisioned the shape of the thing behind the door, the distance from the floor to the heart, the thickness of the door and how much it would impede the bullet, the length of time it covered the sunlight, and which Sam was eyeing him. He hooked his revolver back under his belt and held the 9mm Makarov on his lap with both hands—ready to raise and fire.

NVA officers and Russian KGB agents beware! Safety off! Here goes. Next time it passes over my sight, sunlight gone for just a second—open up on him!

Creeping up to his intention, the smooth surface of the door transforms into a linen canvas upon which is painted a picture of a soldier sitting in the fashion of a Cao Dai monk meditating before the eye of god, which begins to appear in the center of his forehead. He's Andrew D'Oria! The philosopher-soldier-artist raises the pistol, aims at the eye, squeezes the trigger and nothing happens. He pulls again and again, and it doesn't fire. The eye turns into a hollow-nose bullet and the target-face grins at him saying, "Super Vel thirty-eight special!"

I'm a poetic novelist addicted to the self-deifying language of sandy roads, silvery cobwebs, lapping waters, and lyings down—mendacities all. I have to squeeze the bullet out, not pull it. Squeeze the trigger! I can't pull the bullet out. Squeeze the trigger until it goes off on its own.

No, that's not it. You pull the trigger! It's a combat target, not a bull's-eye. A body target. Jasper Johns was wrong. Magritte created *Ceci n'est pas une pipe,* and Johns reaped the fame and fortune for being a target shooter.

The plane descended to 3,000 feet and was now fully depressurized. The steward stood up, went to the cockpit door, and put his ear against it. Suddenly, he heard a loud rush of air, as if a door had opened. He signaled Andrea to come forward.

Keeping a steady eye on the light, Andrea moved slowly toward the door and put his ear to it. The steward said, "He's going out the escape hatch. Listen."

"Do they have parachutes?" Andrea asked.

"I don't know. I didn't notice."

"Okay. Open the door and stand back."

Before the steward put the key in, another sound came through the door, one Andrea understood very well. Its beat was regular and repetitive; its tone was mockingly familiar. The beats became louder and quicker, pounding in his heart. It's an absurd reversal of forces—a knocking at the door.

"Who is it?"

"It's Sam. You're going to be late, High."

"Late for what?"

"High! Are you in there?"

"Late for what?" yelling louder.

"Breakfast, man. If you hurry, you can still get something before they close the kitchen."

"Okay, I'll be right down," thinking that if he takes his time, all they'll have left for breakfast will be tea and crumpets.

" . "

"A *deus ex machina*," John says.

"A *deus ex machina*?" Marge asks. "Where?"

John points to the screen and says, "He employs a dream to resolve the skyjacking. How cheap."

"A dream? What's wrong with that? Haven't you seen *The Wizard of Oz*? In various circles, it's considered to be one of the best movies ever made."

"He's the wizard of Oz all right. *Pay no attention to that man behind the curtain*," John says loudly. "Why doesn't somebody do something about him?"

A man sitting directly in front of them, who heard John's comment, turns around and says in a foreign accent, "You're John Barefoot, why don't you do something? You're the cause of all this. We know it's you."

"Cause of what?" John says.

"The hijacking. Or haven't you heard?"

"How ludicrous."

"Go ahead and talk, that's about all you're good for."

"What's your name?"

"So, you're taking names now, hey?"

Having a sizeable weight advantage, John gets up and confronts his accuser face-to-face. "You want to make something of it, pipsqueak?" he barks. "Get up or shut up!"

"That's all you Americans know," the man says, staying in his seat. "Violence. Always trying to settle arguments with violence, like they do in the movies."

"Movies? You want movies?" John shouts and punches the man on the shoulder. "I'll show you movies." The man pushes the call button. John continues his assault, "Get up, you pussy!" The man remains seated and quickly two flight attendants arrive and order John back to his seat.

"   ."

A woman in her late forties sat opposite Andrea at a card table and smiled suggestively with titanium-white crowns and a glossy complexion. Her open hand, holding a lit cigarette, approached her face slowly, like a plane coming in for a landing—angling left and then right—until it found the exact spot to put it in. She took a deep drag on the cigarette. "Was sind Sie von Beruf?" she asked. "Dichter?"

"Nein," Andrea said, putting down his pen and journal. "Verstehen Sie English? Mein Deutsch ist sehr schlect."

"Yes, I speak English, but your German is not bad," she said.

"I'm a nuclear physicist," he said.

"Sie machen Spass. Es tut mir leid. I mean, you're kidding."

"Nein," he said.

As the plane changed course slightly, sunlight streaked onto the table, drawing Andrea's attention to the Bloody Mary sitting on it. Held in the light beam, it looked radiant. He frowned and said, "Kernstoffe!" He hadn't forgotten this word, probably because it sounded so perfect. He took a long drink. The woman was speechless. He looked down at the thick evergreen forests interlaced with fog-decked valleys and thought that everything German had two strikes against it. He took another drink and said, "My Uncle Nello killed Germans in those woods. Looks like another good day for war down there." The woman got up and went downstairs.

Picking up his journal, he finished recording the nightmare, hoping someday to find a resolution to the hijacking that he couldn't solve, the hijacker that he couldn't kill.

He was glad about not having a layover in Frankfurt, but went on to Istanbul and then Beirut. Close to the Holy Land, Beirut was an adobe-vested little city offering little in the way of architecture and picturesque scenery, but a lot in the way of Persian carpets. Bando was tempted to buy a silk one, but decided to leave the merchant with an unreasonable offer and pick up the bargaining when he returned on Flight 1.

8/Tiger Show

By the time they reached Bangkok, their circadian rhythms were as reversed as the directions of Flights 1 and 2. Unlike regular travelers who could get some shuteye on the plane, they were totally beat upon arrival. Checking into the President Hotel at nine in the morning, they went straight to bed, even though it meant wasting almost a full day of the three-day layover.

That night, after dinner, Sam joined the flight crew to take in a tiger show, while Andrea and Matt went out to try on Bangkok's more interactive amusements.

The more Andrea indulged in Bangkok, the more captivated he became. After visiting a Buddhist temple, drinking a few Tiger beers, and wrapping a thick python around his neck, he began to realize that objects and people totally transcended him, and the idea that they existed only through consciousness seemed absurd. The physical thing made singular by some mysterious process of aiming at it was slowly squeezed out of him. The Thai passion for gold highlighted this nicely; it was a substance worshipped more than Buddha himself, which took its value not from man's valuing it, but from its own rare identity.

Seeking respectable dates rather than massage girls, they asked the taxi driver to take them to a disco off-limits to soldiers and sailors. They were American civilians not connected with the military, a status that surely gave them preference in the eyes of young Thai women, say nothing of the lure of their inflated cover stories.

Matt picked up two girls at the bar and brought them to a table in the middle of the disco. "I'm an actor," he said. "I race sports cars. Have you seen the movie, *Le Mans*?"

The girls laughed shyly.

"And my name is Andrea. I'm a magician from Dallas. I like my scotch black and my women blue." The girls giggled. "So, what do you two do for a living?"

"They're college students," Matt said.

"Good. Was machen Sie studieren? Go-go dancing?"

The girls looked at Matt. The band started another song. Matt took his girl's hand and went onto the dance floor. "The band is from the Philippines," the left-out girl said. "Quite good aren't they?"

"Cheap imitation," Andrea said, though it was a decent rendering of the *Theme from Shaft*.

"Yes, I see," the girl said.

"Do you want to see a magic trick?" he asked.

"Yes," she said and rested her chin on her palm like her head was a golf ball ready to be driven.

Andrea took out his white rope, made a knot in the center, and said, "You hold one end of the rope, and I'll hold the other. Now, I'll place my hand over the knot and you say the magic word. *Ameliorate!*"

"Ameliorate," she said awkwardly.

"Voila!" Andrea said, lifting his hand up, "The knot disappears!"

The girl looked at the knot still tied to the rope and said, "It's still there."

"No, it's not. Look, it's gone."

She pointed to the knot and insisted, "No! It's still there. See?"

"You're just imagining it's there."

The girl looked away for help, but her friend was in another world dancing with Matt. Andrea put the rope back in his pocket, got up, and went to the john.

It was a relief to break away from the sickening smoke and match-game music. He didn't return to it and walked straight out of the building into the cool night. He turned in the direction of greatest darkness, up Petchburi Road to what appeared to be the end of the nightclub district. He tripped off the end of the sidewalk and onto a dirt path. Soon, a dusty film coated his shiny cordovan boots. Street lights reflected off them like the sun through a fog.

He felt no regret leaving his partner and the girls cold. It was a manipulative scene that Ybette would have found just as ugly, although for different reasons. He was now sure of being in love with her. She was afloat in space somewhere incapable of finding a place to land. He wanted to be her landing zone, a port to harbor her lost soul, to make her loaded with desire and perfectly happy.

She had left home to become a stewardess in the big city. Now she was alone and starving. The abortion story, incredible as it seemed, was an indelible part of him, haunting him with its hungry presence, its mocking hiddenness. He could write her a letter in propitiation, but it would be for naught. A vanity trip. Nothing more. Nice try, she would say. Nice try.

Then, from behind a row of bushes lining the pathway came a shallow voice saying, "Hey, guy, you wan date?" Andrea stepped back to get a better view, though he wasn't alarmed. What had appeared to be a deserted path was now made friendly by a young girl coming into the open. One would have thought she had gotten lost on her way to church, wearing a white, one-piece dress, white high heels, and pearl necklace. He smiled, letting her shapely figure take its course, taking command of him the closer she came.

"You wan date?" she said again, brushing little boxwood leaves off her dress.

"Sure," he said. "Where do you want to go?"

"My place. Not far from here. In Patumwan. We take taxi, okay?" She raised her hand and immediately another girl came running across the road. "My friend come too, okay?"

The smile left his face, and he said, "Wait a minute. Slow down. First, let's get to know each other." Her shapely body was very enticing, but her partner's wasn't. "What were you doing behind the bushes?"

"Hiding," she said.

"From what?" he asked.

"Tiger," she said.

"Tiger?"

"No, Tai girl, Tai girl," she said.

"Oh, you mean Thai girl."

"Yes, very bad. Where you stay?"

"President Hotel."

"Okay. Nearby. But my friend come too."

The idea of two girls in bed at once excited him, but only if they looked equally as pretty. The second girl was obviously the muscle in the duo, the one who could get them out of a tight spot if necessary.

"But how much for two?" he asked.

"Five dollar," they said together.

As though waiting behind a bush for a customer, a taxi drove up quickly. Andrea sat between the girls in the back seat as it raced through the streets like there was no time to lose. Within seconds, she was upon him, trying to get the job finished before they reached the hotel. His mind being half a world away from the bumpy and freewheeling ride, he felt little, as if he were sheathed by a dozen condoms.

The taxi squealed to a halt at the stoplight, and Andrea was surprised that the driver hadn't gone straight through it. A truck pulled along-side, and the boys inside looked down at the back-seat trio. They laughed and made heckling sounds. The girl wasn't ashamed and didn't stop, and Andrea wasn't ashamed either, for he felt detached from it, stuck on one side of his sensations, like the fingers feeling one's arm, but the arm not feeling one's fingers. He couldn't feel! He touched the girls head, and then he looked up at the laughing boys. The scene was permanently imprinted on their minds and would be with them until death—a Caucasian man caught in the backseat of a taxicab at midnight on Petchburi Road, Bangkok, October 24, 1971. Being a porno star wouldn't have been much worse, the immorality compounding with each release, a virus spreading and mutating by the thousands, never to be reversed, recalled, or made good. Even after the star's death, the evil and corruption continue nonstop.

He entered the hotel proud of having a girl on each arm. The night clerk gave him a surprised look, and Andrea read it to mean—*how can you handle two girls at once? You must be a superman.*

In the light of the room, the girl was even more attractive, with an unusually creamy complexion, full lips, bright teeth, silky black hair, and the best-shaped legs he had ever seen on an Asian woman. After neatly placing her shoes by the door, she asked him to take off all his clothes and take a shower. He wasn't sure if this was a trick, so he put his clothes neatly on the chair and hopped onto the bed.

Lying naked, he wanted desperately to amend the scene in the taxi, to erase it from the memories of the boys in the truck who had watched him. As she cleaned him with a damp washcloth, he sank deeper into despair, but no sooner had she aroused him again, he felt clothed by a new and strange morality of underplay and peace.

After fifteen minutes of labor, the girl puckered out and her partner took over, the results being worse and, for them, more embarrassing. The pretty one went to the bathroom to refresh the washcloth and start over again— an artist wiping the miscreation completely off the canvas. The refreshment worked and she began again, but became tired after a short time.

It's the scotch mixed with jetlag, he thought.

Hiding in a bush she had waited, and into a bush he went blindly after her. Flashing across his mind for just a second was the face of his friend— CΔT—in brutal agony, shot all over by friendly fire. He rolled off and lay on his back, staring at the ceiling fan swirling over his head. No choppers to rescue him this time.

The girl cleaned him again, still eager to get paid. Then a knock came at the door. It got louder, and Andrea pulled up the bed sheet and asked the second girl to answer it. Matt Bando came into the room with the look of a soldier going after a gook that had killed his best friend. "The clerk at the desk told me, but I didn't believe it," he said.

"Told you what?" Andrea said.

"That you came back with two ladyboys."

"Ladyboys? Get out." Andrea sat up in bed. "No they're not."

Giggles came from the hallway. Bando's girls from the disco were listening.

"Take a good look, man. Look at his arm," pointing to the second one's arm. It was hairier than most women and, for a Thai, certainly peculiar.

Hairier than his even. "Where are your passports? Where's your badge?"

Andrea had no apology. "Come on man," he said. "It's okay. They're not going to...."

"Not thieves? Since when are shit-stabbers not thieves? Where's your wallet?"

"In my pants."

Bando picked up the pants, opened the wallet, and counted the money.

"Hey, what are you doing?" Andrea complained.

"My advice is to get rid of them. I'll be in my room if there's any trouble."

After Bando left, Andrea jumped up and put on his pants. Fully sober now, he sat on the bed, the two boys kneeling at his feet. He gave each a five-dollar bill. They bowed before him several times with hands folded in prayer. Their respect for the young American had grown to godlike proportions. They thought he was a monk.

Asking permission to leave, the two got up and went for the door. Andrea grabbed the pretty one by the arm and asked if he might check her out, still uncertain of her sex. She nodded. He put his hand inside the dress and felt firm pectoral muscles under the falsies. In that brief moment, touch became feel—no possibility of revulsion or violence—all the mystery of the attraction and separation, the rush to the hotel and idleness of the body, the coolness of the washcloth, the crisp assurance of a good meal tomorrow. He walked them to the door and bid them goodnight. On the back of the door was a sign that read, PLEASE LEAVE YOUR VALUES AT THE FRONT DESK. He laughed and went to bed.

Half an hour without sleeping and he was back on his feet, so charmed by the young boy that he had to go out and find him again, not for another round, but to observe from a distance. He took a taxi to the exact spot hoping he would be there hiding behind the bushes. He searched up the road until he came to the end, feeling happy and sad that the boy had left for the night.

The place was dark and desolate; no human would dare prowl about. It felt comforting. He wished it would turn darker, so dark his body wouldn't cast the slightest shadow.

That's all I am anyway, he thought. A shadow. There's no shadow that I cannot be, outsmarting the world of VIPs with as many cover stories as I can imagine. But when the plane touches ground, and it's I all over again—I who can't come anymore, I who can't tell the difference between a man and a woman—it's time to get off. So, do I really want to keep working this job? Who is this person with different names and occupations anyway? Every trip somebody new.

He turned to go back and, suddenly, a rustling noise came out of the bushes. It followed him down the path, keeping pace as he picked up speed. Startled, he quickened his gait, but the thing kept up with him, making more noise as it plowed through the thick hedgerow. Thinking that it was a meddling wild pig, he broke out into a full jog, but the thing kept plowing through the thicket, growing bigger and more powerful as it kept up with its prey.

"This is Thailand," he gasped, now realizing that he was being stalked by something as big as it gets—a man-eater! "Could it be? A man-eater?"

Adrenaline rushing through his veins and legs pumping furiously, his heart and lungs propelled him faster than he had run in his life. Yet the sidewalk to safety was not there, and he feared that in the blur of speed he had chosen the wrong path. Daring not to slow down and look back, he kept racing toward the flickering lights until a voice came from behind the bushes. "Hey, man. Why you running? Where you going? I'm here."

"Run!" Andrea yelled without stopping. "It's a tiger. Run!"

"Tai girl? Where?" the ladyboy said, trying to pull his white dress free from the brambles. "I'm stuck." When he finally broke loose, he stopped, as if paralyzed by a strange magnetic force. Swiftly, the four hundred pound tiger trampled him to the ground.

Andrea heard a thrilling cry, such as a woman gives at the moment of childbirth. Reaching the sidewalk, he stopped, turned around, and saw a large, dark figure on the pathway standing perfectly still with what looked like a white napkin under its chin. Suddenly, the ladyboy thrashed and twisted in frenzy, letting out a bloodcurdling scream that made the tiger loosen its grip and drop him to the ground. But then, holding the body down with one paw, the tiger began biting it, trying to tear apart the head and shoulders. The ladyboy rolled from side to side to break free. When the tiger sunk its teeth deep into the body, the ladyboy's leg rose up high into the air; broken at the shinbone; the bare foot dangled helplessly.

The tiger turned and walked toward the jungle, dragging the body between its front legs. The only thing that kept the flesh together was the white dress.

Horrified, Andrea ran up the street and went straight into the disco. He sat at a table in the far corner, gasping for air, unaware that it was smoky and foul.

Matt Bando was so proud that he had balled two chicks at the same time, he didn't mention it the next morning, as if it were in the same category as the ten percent disability check he received every month for getting his little finger shot off in Vietnam. Andrea, likewise, didn't mention the tragic incident he had witnessed, but he did, however, provide the usual excuses for his indiscretion. "Booze...jet lag...poetic license." Matt asked him if he was going to include that in his trip report. "Only the part where the ladyboy gets mauled and carried away by a tiger," Andrea said.

"Don't you wish?" Matt laughed.

In the afternoon, they toured the river marketplace and had a chance to taste something recommended by Bando's dates—durian.

The so-called king of tropical fruit couldn't be eaten in public places, including hotels and restaurants, and they wanted to know why. If they could bring ladyboys into their hotel, why not this fruit?

The first one opened was infested with worms. "Might be best one," the vendor said. "Worm, he know."

"I've had worse in Ranger school," Bando said. "Smells like water buffalo dung."

The vendor pinched his nose and said, "Hold nose, then eat. Very delicious. Very heaty. Must take rambutan after. Very cooling."

Andrea held his nose and took a bite. The texture was gooey like a ripe banana, but the taste was incredible. He touched the hard, sharp spikes, and said, "I wouldn't want to get hit on the head with this thing."

"Looks like a medieval coconut," Bando said.

"Kill you for sure," the vendor said.

"I've heard it's a potent aphrodisiac," Bando said.

"Who said?" Andrea said.

"You want aphrodisiac?" the vendor said. "Durian no compare to number one. Very, very potent. From China."

"What is it?" Andrea said.

"I cannot tell you here. You tell me yes and I order for you. Will make you horny for many days."

"What's it called?"

"We call RMB, so police don't know. Import from China."

"How much?" Bando asked.

"Two thousand renminbi for male; one thousand renminbi for female. One meal for both. Cook with herbs in broth. Fantastic."

"We don't have that much. Maybe next visit."

Realizing that he was dealing with freewheeling Americans rather than run-of-the-mill GIs (a deduction based on the length of their hair), the taxi driver took them to one of the biggest and most expensive houses in Bangkok. The selection was impressive—at least twenty-five girls sitting and lying around on three tiers behind a huge wall of glass, all wearing numbers and looking like tropical fish in an aquarium.

Right away, Bando made a selection. The girl went out the side door and came down to sit with him and chat.

Andrea looked earnestly at the remaining school, trying to select the one that least wanted to be there. He picked the highest number, thinking she was the last one in and, probably, the least indoctrinated into the cult. Up close, she looked no older than thirteen.

They paid for the all-night escorts and went on a tour of the city, stopping first at the Royal Grand Palace.

"That is where our prince live," Nina said.

"Do you have a king?" Andrea asked.

"Yes," she said. "But we no like American movie *King and I*. Disgrace to Thailand and movie ban here."

"Why? I thought it was a good movie."

"King no have flat feet. Very disrespectful. King no dummy."

"Yul Brenner played the king," Bando said.

"Yeah, I see what she means," Andrea said.

"It must be like Thailand making a movie of Nixon dressed up as a transvestite."

After treating the girls to drinks and music at a disco bar, they brought them directly to their hotel rooms.

Nina had large, lively eyes and a figure that would make most American women envious.

"What's your real name?" Andrea asked.

"May I have paper?" Nina asked. "I write it." Andrea offered up his journal for the autograph. She wrote: *Love always! Niyawan Wattanadamrongpongpisit.*

"Your name is as long as a poem," he said. "How old are you?"

"I must not say," she said, taking to the bed in a relaxing stretch, warming up the muscles in her back. He followed her and did the same. "How do you ever say it, then?" he said. She pronounced it quickly, and he thought it musical. "That's a wonderful name. Are you Buddhist?"

"Free thinker," she said. "My mother is Buddhist. She pray in temple. I do not go to temple."

"How often do you go to the doctor for a checkup?"

"Once a week."

Andrea was as wary of this as he was of a woman who claimed to be taking the pill daily. He told her about the encounter he had the previous night with the ladyboys, and how he sank deeper into trouble because he couldn't make up for the scene in the taxicab. "There is no way I can take it back," he said. "It's in their minds and will be there as long as they live."

She had never heard a confession from a man, and here, alone with him on a bed made for sex rather than conversation, she explained why she had turned to being a numbered girl.

"My family is very poor. Live in Chiengmai. My father is very weak heart and no work. My mother wash dishes in restaurant. My home is two-room flat. We no pay rent. I find job in Bangkok to send money home to my family."

He put his arm around her, and she cuddled in close to him, holding back emotions of self-pity that she knew would lead to tears. She had revealed too much to a stranger, so with an upbeat voice said, "You visit Chiengmai someday. Girl very beautiful. Tall and light skin. Pretty. Not like southern girl. Do you know Miss Universe? Hpasra Hongsakula? Have you seen her? Do you know she no speak English?"

"Where did you learn English?"

"From my friends. And Catholic school."

"You went to Catholic school? How come you're not Catholic?"

"My ancestors not Catholic."

"Do you pray to your ancestors?"

She thought for a moment, and then said, "No."

"Is Chiengmai far from Bangkok?" he asked.

"One day by bus. I can arrange for you. Okay?"

"Maybe next trip."

"When you come back?"

"Next month," he said. "Say, do you want to see a magic trick?"

She sat up, and he got out the infamous white rope. "It's called the knot disappearing act." He tied a square knot, had her hold both ends of the rope, and put his hand over the knot. "Now, say the magic word."

"What word?" she asked.

"Your name," he said.

"Niyawan Wattanadamrongpongpisit," she said.

When he opened his hand, the knot was gone. "It works!" he said in amazement.

Now feeling comfortable with him, she asked, "What do you do?"

"I'm a United States sky marshal," he said.

"Oh, I see," she said. "Very nice."

" . "

"Finally, he put some meat on the table," Marge says.

"Yeah, rump steak," John says.

"Oh, please, John."

"I'll bet philosophy turns up again. As Albert Einstein once said, 'All philosophy is written in honey. Tastes sweet at first, but turns to mush on cross-examination."

"Sounds like a bait and switch," Marge says.

9/Layover Plot

Driving around the block several times trying to find a parking place, Andrea saw a BMW Bavaria getting ready to back up, so he maneuvered his little VW quickly, making the steal downright mean. The driver of the big sedan jumped out and yelled, "Get the hell out of there! That's mine."

Andrea got out of his car casually, closed the door, and said, "I don't see your name on it."

"Look, you dumb son-of-a-bitch. I was here first. Now move that piece of junk or I'll...."

Afraid to turn his back, Andrea stood his ground, allowing the man to get closer and size him up. Realizing the weight ratio between them was about the same as that between their cars, he reached into his pocket and gripped his blackjack. An off-duty altercation with a civilian was surefire expulsion from the program, but he couldn't be sure of the outcome otherwise.

"You're bluffing," the man said.

"That's what *you* think."

Betting there was something lethal in store for him, the man backed down, turned away, and said, "Tuches arine!" He got back into his car, but instead of driving away, put it in reverse and started to run Andrea down.

"You crazy bastard, you!" Andrea yelled, moving quickly out of the way as the car backed against traffic. Screeching to a halt, the man changed gears and floored the gas pedal, squealing tires and lurching forward back into traffic. Andrea flipped him a bird as he drove by, and the car screeched to a halt again. The man jumped out and ran after Andrea full blast, but Andrea quickly opened his car door, got inside, and locked it. The man pounded on the window with all his might trying to break it, so Andrea reached into his glove compartment and took out his revolver. The sight of stainless-steel gun made the man stop, return to his car, and drive away.

Ybette answered the door in bare feet—a taste of something homegrown. "How's my favorite world traveler?" she said, hugging him tightly and arching backward in the cradle of his arms to give him a good look.

"How's my little southern girl?" he said.

"Barefoot and pregnant," she laughed.

That she could joke about her infertility made him doubt it; but maybe she was turning a bad thing good, celebrating her freedom.

They sat and talked for over an hour, she believing every word of his stories about Bangkok. She was sexually excited about it, but he didn't notice, so anxious was he to ask her to move into his new apartment. "It's closer to the airport," he said. "There are two bedrooms, so if all three of us should happen to be there at once, I could sleep on the couch."

"Do you have any furniture?" she asked.

"Everything we need. It has a nice kitchen, but one bathroom, which is what you have here with four women. Four's got to be a little crowded. I wouldn't take up much space. A razor and a toothbrush are all I need. It's four-ninety-five a month. I'll pay half and you and Carol can split the other half. I'll pay all utilities."

"I'll have to ask her first. I'm sure she'll like having a sky marshal as a roommate. That rapist is still loose, and there have been more attacks since you left, just like the one in your apartment."

"More stewardesses?"

"Yes. He used the same, ah, what do you call it?"

"M.O. Modus operandi. He plays a delivery man with a package that's too big to fit into the door without pulling the chain. What he really has is a knife. It's a bait and switchblade."

"Okay. But you have to do me a favor first," sitting back on the couch, now at a comfortable business distance from him. "Carol has a doctor's appointment next week, and it would be the awfullest thing for her to go alone. Could you drive her down?"

"Is she sick?"

"No. She needs to have a D 'n' C."

He didn't know what the initials stood for, but was sure what they meant. "Ah, you mean a.... I see."

"It's the worst time in her life to fall pregnant. She's made the choice to correct her mistake before it's too late."

"Who's the guy?"

"She's sure it's Baxter, her old boyfriend. It doesn't really matter. Can you help her?"

"I'll have to think about it."

When Carol LeTendre walked across his Oriental rug wearing absolutely nothing—not even lipstick—Andrea thought that a woman couldn't be more beautiful. "Oops!" she said, rushing for the bathroom. "I didn't think you would be home so early."

"I didn't want to be late," Andrea said.

Although as tall as Ybette (sometimes getting uniforms mixed up), Carol was more amply endowed, a point of jealousy between the two, since Ybette made a habit of comparing their weights, which were a few pounds more or less than one-ten. Those few made a big difference.

The brightness of Carol's skin rivaled Sergeant's *Portrait of Madame X*, though more ivory under a head of raving red hair. Pink, he thought, were her nipples too. I shouldn't have given up painting.

He drove her downtown to the infamous appointment, not saying much on the way, doing his job to give her moral support, as Ybette had hoped he would.

He sat alone in the car, watching the people walk by, not waving placards or praying the rosary, just minding their own business. He considered driving away and making a personal statement, but he held back, knowing that it would be cold and unkind. He would rather accept accusations of being an accomplice, the getaway driver, the man behind the wheel—a wheel locked in one fatal direction—than risk losing Ybette. And there were other reasons for staying. Philosophical ones.

He thought about Karen Kight and whether she had taken the same route. But for her, the intentions were different. She had a good reason, having been raped. The argument that God could never concur in sin, whether rape or adultery, and instill a rational soul in an embryo at conception was logical, no matter what the church said. The soul did *not* arise at conception, for the soul transcended matter. Animal powers do not produce the soul, and God would never do so concurrently with rape or adultery. A tadpole with gills and a tail couldn't possibly possess a human soul. The human soul was of a higher order and required a body capable of intellectual powers.

Purged of the life that had taken hold of her, Carol returned to the car without saying a word. Andrea knew that Baxter, the likely father, had refused to take the driver's seat, because he had actually wanted the baby, even wanted to marry her. He was a handsome man, and it was understandable that she had fallen for him, but he happened to be getting nowhere in his job and had failed the CPA exam an embarrassing number of times. In a way, the abortion was a way to cut him out of her life altogether.

They went straight back to the apartment where Carol spent the afternoon silently in her room. When it came time for dinner, Andrea knocked on her door and asked if she wanted to go out to eat. "There was a Christmas tree in the office," she said sobbingly.

He went out to eat alone, and when he returned two hours later, Ybette was sitting on the couch wearing her usual sexy nightgown. He sat next to her and asked if she had a safe flight to Miami.

"Smells awfully good," she said. "What's in the bag?"

"Spaghetti and meatballs. For Carol. She didn't want to go out to eat."

"How long has she been in there?"

"Since we got back this afternoon."

Ybette's question made Carol sound more like a casual acquaintance than a close friend. She seemed overly indifferent, and it made him suspect that she had more than just innocent familiarity with the procedure her friend had experienced. He had dwelled on her day and night, trying to understand the disaffection she seemed to have toward him since his return from L.A.

"Well, go try again, silly," she said.

Andrea knocked on the door again, and Carol refused to come out saying, "Give it to Ybette. She's always hungry."

Ybette began picking at the bag with her toes, prompting Andrea to go into the kitchen and get a spoon and fork. She dove into the food as if she hadn't eaten all day. Then she asked, "Justin, why don't you get a TV?"

"Too boring," he said, getting up and stacking a few albums on the stereo. "You're more interesting to watch. And music is more stimulating, don't you think?"

"Maybe," she said with a smile. "Justin, I'm curious," taking another bite. "Mmmm! These meatballs are so good, I can't stop."

"Curious about what?"

"About your face."

"My face? What?"

"You shaved only one side of your face."

"I did not."

"Look at you. You're a trip."

"Get out."

"And your shoes. Why did you start leaving them by the door? They're always in the way when I come in."

He stretched out on the large rug, gliding his palms across the smooth wool surface. "I don't know," he said. "It's an Oriental thing, I suppose. This doesn't need shoes on it."

"So, what do the designs mean? All those angles—diamonds, and..." pausing to count the sides, "hexagons."

"Interesting, aren't they?"

"Why didn't you buy something more pleasing? Blue flowers or something. Look at them. They're all crowded in. There's not one inch without something pointy or sharp. I'm afraid to lie down on it."

"That's the point. Your body is the perfect contrast on it. All *your* edges are smooth and perfectly rounded."

"Oh, stop, Justin!"

After she finished eating, she joined him on the rug feeling guilty about having eaten a meal intended for her friend. "I think we should take Carol out for breakfast tomorrow morning, don't you?"

"Great idea," he said. She rolled on top of him, and he complained, "Oh, no! You're going to crush me to death!"

"All I ate was one meatball."

"One's a meata-balla! Two's a meata-ballsa!"

"Oh, hush," rolling off him onto the rug. Then, looking carefully into his eyes, "So, Justin. Tell me. Did Carol cry in the doctor's office?"

"Ah, I didn't see her cry."

"But you did go in with her."

"No."

"Oh, Just, you didn't. She went in by herself?"

"Look, Ybette," he said calmly. "It wasn't my job to go in and hold her hand."

"Justin, you can't even imagine how a woman feels," getting up on her feet with a mind to kick him in the side. "I had hoped you would have given her some support. No wonder she's so upset."

"Well, maybe I should have, but I'm glad she didn't have to go through with what you had to." However apologetic, he knew there was more to her own tale than she had revealed over the banana split.

"Thank you," she said walking away, leaving him to bed down alone on the couch between the two bedrooms, staring at the front door in the dark.

He awoke in the middle of the night with a feeling that someone was watching him. Ybette stood at the door in nightgown and bare feet looking through the peephole. She watched and waited for ten minutes. When she turned around, her face was ashen and perspiring. He dared not say a word as she returned directly to bed.

As the Eastern meal of barbecued chicken, rice and black beans was served, a Puerto Rican woman asked the priest sitting next to her, "Padre, would you give bless my food?"

"Of course," he said, and recited the short Catholic version of grace before meals. She was surprised that the prayer was in English, for she was sure he looked Spanish.

After the meal, the woman felt so blessed by the priest's presence, she asked him to hear her confession. She was motivated by the impersonal nature of their encounter, like a tryst between strangers.

"Right here?' he asked. There was no excuse to back down, since the omnipresent whir in the tail section made it impossible for anyone else to hear them. So, after the trays were cleared, she began.

"Pordóneme, padre, porque he pecado."

"Please speak English. When was your last confession?"

"Six month."

"What are your sins?"

She glanced across the aisle, and then continued. "I commit contraception."

"Do you have children?"

"Si. Two boy."

"Do you go to church?"

"Si, every Sunday."

"Do you receive Holy Communion?"

She hesitated, and then said, "Si."

"For your penance, say three Our Fathers. Now say a good act of contrition."

She bent her head down and said the prayer, but, not hearing anything from the priest, she said, "You no give absolución?"

"I can't," he said.

"Why no?"

"I cannot give you absolution, because I am not a…." He looked out the window for a moment, unable to think up a logical cover story for being a make-believe priest.

"Si, you no…."

"I am not allowed to," he said. "You committed a sacrilege and must confess to a bishop, otherwise you risk excommunication."

Totally mortified, the woman looked away and was silent the rest of the flight to San Juan.

Upon arrival, Andrea's beer-thirsty partners were eager to try out a place that had a reputation for good, cheap, and fast sex, while he decided to stay near the hotel and try his luck girl-watching on Condado Beach.

He wandered on the beach for a long time and then nursed a rum-and-coke at the bar until the sun had reached its peak. Despondent, he went back to his room and sat on the balcony looking down at the strip below. Watching a woman stroll suggestively up the street, it occurred to him that he had never made it with an honest-to-goodness streetwalker, and this being the most fashionable tourist area in San Juan, he waved at her. She waved back and crossed the street to get closer. He signaled to her to come up, and she shrugged her shoulders, not knowing the room number. Taking a chance on her at that distance, he signaled the room number. She took up his invitation and went inside.

It didn't take long for her to get to his door, and he greeted her with, "You must already know this place."

"You want me come in?" she asked.

"Sure," he said, admiring her politeness, which was more than he expected from a woman of the street. However, she looked familiar in an ominous way. Imagining her in black hair, he realized that she was the spitting image of Leila Khaled! Leila Khaled in disguise? No way!

She stepped to the middle of the room and gave him a good look from head to toe. Then she looked around the room and said, "Goodness, you have the biggest room in the hotel. Two rooms! How many beds you have? Three?"

"It's the VIP suite," he said, impressed by the genuineness of her Puerto Rican accent, something an Arab would find impossible to imitate.

"You VIP?" she laughed. She lit a cigarette and sat on the couch. The initial puff of smoke came out of her nose gracefully, expressing with flared and heated nostrils perfect control over her body. She proposed an exchange, purely economical. "I don't do cheap sucky," staring boldly at the bulge in his swimming trunks. "Straight sex. Any position. One hundred dollars."

"How do I know you're not an undercover cop?"

She smiled, proud that her lips were clean enough to be kissed. "This is you room, not mine. Mira, come search me," standing up and parading around slowly, showing off a figure with the curves of a waxed mustache on a Caribbean pirate. "I have no bug."

The Roman collar on the chair by the table caught her eye, and she asked, "What's that?"

"Nothing," he said.

"You priest?" Then again, explosively, "You priest!" Picking it up with two hands like it was a bra dripping wet, she said, "Oh, baby, you bad. You bad."

His eyes hunted about the room for anything else that might be exposed.

"Baby, I had lotta trick, but never priest." She moved closer to him. "Here, put it on and you can have it for fifty."

Easily afforded, since he always carried a healthy travel advance, he picked up his wallet and gave her the money, along with a condom he had been saving. She put the money in her small purse, reached under her skirt, and pulled down her panties as quickly as she would sit on a toilet. Her voice sounded unhurried and motherly as she instructed him to take off his clothes, put on the collar, and get in bed. He obeyed, and she jumped on the bed, straddled his hips, and applied her trade.

Enjoying the superiority of the position, she began to claw at his abdomen with long, sharp fingernails, bringing up red lines on his skin and making him breathe in and out deeply to ease the pain. Reaching the point of ecstatic hyperventilation, he felt something snap. Immediately, they stopped moving. She rose up to see what had happened and noticed that he had broken straight through the condom. Now fully exposed to all her dangers—ecstasy in shambles—he recoiled amateurishly.

She burst out laughing.

He couldn't remember where and when he had purchased the defective rubber. Not having another one, and very embarrassed, he sat up and said, "That's not funny." She kept laughing anyway.

The laughter empowered her. She laughed so hard, she started to cough, pressing her hand flat against her chest as a kind of support for her weak heart. Her face, lit up by the blood rushing into it, made the rouge on her cheeks look fake. She was totally outside of him now, every single detail of her—white teeth, bleached hair, brown eyes, red lips, red fingernails—nothing to be purchased or stolen.

Afraid that she might cough something up, she got out of bed and said, "I must clean up." She picked up her panties and purse, and went into the bathroom where she stayed an unusually long time.

She had plenty of condoms in her purse but used the defect as an excuse to get back on the street quickly.

Eyes closed when he awakes, the weight of an enormous hangover pressing against his face, he can't recall having anything to drink. The telephone is ringing, the television still on, and a loud knocking is at the door. The door opens to the limit of the security chain and the maid shouts, "Housekeeping! Housekeeping!" He tries to get up but can't move. The door closes. Slowly, he opens his eyes, and the sunlight beaming in from the balcony hammers through to his brain. He wants to knead his eyes, but his arms are still paralyzed. He turns his head towards the clock. It shows 3:30. He notices that his partners are still in bed sleeping and then realizes that they too have missed the wakeup call and the 9:20 a.m. flight back to New York.

Damn it! We've been drugged. It *was* Leila Khaled.

The telephone stops ringing, and the television sinks in as he listens to the last few seconds of the broadcast. "...several skyjackings already today. Eastern Airlines has suspended all flights in and out of Isla Verde Airport. We will keep you posted as more news becomes available."

An intense shudder runs through him. He tries to remember the last thing he did before going to bed. It was the previous afternoon taking a shower after the streetwalker left the room. There is nothing after that—no swimming, no dinner, no shows, no TV. Nothing. Just all-of-a-sudden now!

He flares open his fingers several times, then lifts the dead weights that he has for arms and legs. Finally regaining control of his body, he creeps out of bed and opens the dresser drawer. "My badge! My gun! My passports! My blackjack! My handcuffs! All gone!" He wobbles over to his partners, but they are so dead to the world, not even a bomb blast would wake them up. He checks for their stuff and sees that everything has been stolen.

He opens his briefcase and takes out a manuscript of a novel three-hundred pages long. He turns over its pages, starting from the back, looking for the skyjacking scene that has the answer. He skims through passages of sex and violence, but nothing about a skyjacking where he resolves the standoff on Flight 2. He is certain that he had fleshed it out, moment-by-moment, adjective after bleeding adjective, but there is nothing in the manuscript to show for it, only the struggles between his main character and a stewardess named Yolanda. The last passage reads:

At about 35,000 feet, as I was on the last leg to New York, I heard a veteran stewardess say to two randy boys who were making a ruckus, "Why don't you two boys go outside and play!"

That's it, I thought. The perfect response to a skyjacker—let's take our gunfight outside. I wrote that down in my journal and later thanked the stewardess for her comment.

He turns to the TV, which has the news report of the catastrophic world event. "Over one thousand planes the world over have been skyjacked by an army of terrorists posing as sky marshals holding over three hundred thousand passengers hostage in the sky. The attack is as devastating as an all-out ICBM strike on the United States."

"They stole my book!" Andrea yells. Counting the page numbers in the manuscript, he notices about twenty pages missing. "That's it. The plot was resolved right under my nose, but I didn't see it. They turned it into a world event. All the time I was searching for it, developing characters toward this one climatic event, they expunged it from the story, leaving me nothing but self-centered characters, vain dialogue, and pointless action going nowhere—a plane without destinations flying in all directions at once, not really lost—for its home port is the open sky."

He shakes his head, gathers in his arms all the loose pages, and goes out onto the balcony. One by one, he lets the pages go, taking flight in every direction as the wind gusts would have them.

Down below on the street, the blond streetwalker looks up at him, waves, and shouts, "Mira, padre, what are you doing?"

He looks down and lets the whole bundle go, showering her with his raped dream.

As Andrea took his seat, a well-dressed man sitting next to him asked, "Am I in for a sermon?"

"No, sir," Andrea said, quickly putting on headphones to catch his favorite song, which was always first on the list. Unlike any other song, *Magic Carpet Ride* gave him the feeling of really being in the groove flying the fabulous jumbo jet first class. *I like to dream, yes, right between my sound machine. On a cloud of sound I drift in the night. Any place it goes is right. Goes far, flies near, to the stars away from here....*

The man waited politely, amusing himself with a paperback until Andrea was sated with the takeoff and uplifting music. "I should think a priest would be praying the rosary for a safe flight instead of listening to rock 'n' roll," he said.

"You must have good ears," Andrea said.

"Hi, I'm Bert Russell," handing Andrea a business card. "I sell shoes. Women's shoes mostly."

"I'm Father Andre. Glad to meet you."

"I don't mean to be pushy, but I've never seen a priest fly first class."

"No, it's okay. It's a family joke. Embarrassing, but I couldn't refuse my cousin's offer."

"Then you must be on vacation."

"You might say that."

During the meal service, only small talk passed between them, but afterward, Bert had something to get off his chest. "You're a new...newly ordained priest...and my congratulations to you...and I wonder if there was anything new coming down the pike about celibacy?"

"Celibacy? No, I'm afraid not," Andrea said. "The church is two thousand years old and changes don't happen overnight. If Pope John the twenty-third were still with us, maybe, but for now, there's no chance."

"Then you priests will never get married. And I will probably never see the inside of a church again."

"I don't follow. How does my being single affect you going to church?"

Bert looked out the window for a moment, thinking of a respectful thing to say. "It's just that...well look...you're new, and they still have the reins on you pretty tight, but I just don't believe these older priests when they get up there and preach to the hoi polloi about piety. I see right through them." He handed Andrea the book he had been reading.

"The *Passover Plot*," Andrea said. "I've heard about this."

"I've been reading a lot lately, and this one's really got me thinking. It says that Jesus was the greatest magician that ever lived, and all his miracles were actually magic tricks that he had learned in India. And he happened to be there at the perfect place and time in history to get away with it, like a lady walking by one of my stores spots an Italian shoe in the window that strikes her fancy because it's that time of the month when she's feeling sexy and will spend three hundred dollars on a pair that will cripple her feet. You see, society is crippled by Christianity and priests don't see this, because they have been made to feel guilty about their inability to remain chaste. You can't tell me all priests are chaste."

"We are sinners, yes, just like all men."

"I used to think that I was a sinner until one day I realized that it was because the church said so. It's like styles in shoes and clothes. Change the style to make people believe they need to dress a certain way, and they all do. They all go out and buy bell-bottom jeans. So I stopped believing, and I felt like a million bucks. I didn't have to be afraid how I looked at women. You would be surprised how many are on the make these days. After I got divorced, my sex life skyrocketed. Look, I've got more telephone numbers in this book than the Bible has books."

"Enough for a dozen men," Andrea said.

"That's right," Bert said. "I think clearer now. See things clearer. Like the muddiness of mud. The steeliness of steel. The wetness of water."

"The girlishness of girls."

"To hell with poetry," Bert laughed.

"Ban the metaphor!" Andrea said.

Later, in the lounge, they talked again, and, with three double martinis under his belt, Bert was now about to pull out all the stops on his enmity toward the church. "You know, the more I read books like this, the more I see why so few people go to church. I mean, like after Christ's death, if he were really God, why didn't he go back to Pontius Pilate or the high priest and tell him off? The reason is that Jesus was really doped up on the cross by a drug he found in the Orient. He didn't really die. He was in a catatonic state and later came back to life. He never rose from the dead. He was alive when he appeared to the apostles. But he never appeared to anyone important for fear of being killed on the spot."

The lounge was now empty, and the plane was gradually creeping downward toward JFK. Bert painted his thoughts with large Motherwellian blotches of black and white, trying to make connections between them but, at the same time, holding onto the premise that things in reality were not connected by design.

"Take my daughter, for instance. Any of a thousand different choices would have led to her *not* being born. She was an accident that happened twenty years ago. When I look at her, she always reminds me of the time before she was born, before she ever existed. I knew of thirty years for sure without her. Nothing there. No Elizabeth. Period. Before she was born there were billions of years without her. An eternity without her. Now she will live seventy, maybe eighty years. What's to say she has any hope on the other end? The evidence—the billions of years—points in the other direction. Backward, like before."

"Are you saying that we could only be assured of life after death if we had life before death?"

"Yes, precisely. That's why Jesus claimed to have come from the Father. Otherwise, it wouldn't have been possible for him to come back to life after death. Since he claimed to be the Messiah, he had to show everyone his death, and then his so-called risen body after death. This was the plot."

"You know, Bert, I think you might have something there. Maybe I'll look into this book after all."

"Well then, here, take it!" Bert handed him the book.

"The numbers, Bert?"

"Be my guest."

"Bert, I don't know what to say. Here's something you might like in return." Andrea grabbed his Roman collar and ripped it off his neck, then handed it to Bert, who was stunned and didn't say a word.

Returning to their seats, Bert pointed out a stewardess and said, "If I wasn't sure about getting laid tonight, that's the one I'd hit on."

"Good choice," Andrea said.

When they arrived at the gate, Bert was first off the plane. Once inside the terminal, he felt as though he had forgotten something. He turned around and saw Andrea walk up to a trashcan, take out the red paperback, and dumb it inside swiftly, as if it were the wrapper off a candy bar.

" ."

"Too philosophical again," Marge said. "He had something going, and it would have made a great story, but what a letdown."

"Keep it to yourself," John said, "and continue reading."

Free of the Roman collar, he lay on his Oriental carpet, shirt open and tanned chest exposed, looking more like a beach bum than a knight recuperating in Avalon. "Miami?" he asked. "When?"

"I just put in the request," Ybette said. "It could take a month, maybe a year."

"Don't like winter in New York?"

"This place is getting depressing."

"What's wrong?"

"It's the neighbors," she said. "I never see them in the halls, but I can hear them through the walls in the bedroom at night like they were right here."

"What'd you hear?"

"They work for National, I think. This sky marshal was in there this morning with one of them trying to...." She rolled off the couch to get closer to him and whispered, "Trying to sodomize her."

"Really? I know the walls are pretty thin, but you actually heard that?"

"Oh, Justin, you should have heard them argue about it. He was as persistent as an old mule and wouldn't take no for an answer. He kept going on about how it wouldn't hurt and she wouldn't know if she never tried it before."

"Have you seen him?"

"He was terrible. Kept going on about how all couples do it, and how she was a prude for not trying. Can you imagine?"

"Maybe he didn't earn the privilege."

"What are you suggesting?"

"Seems to me," he said, "that he wanted to skip a couple of important steps and just barge right in there."

She stood up, looked down at him and said, "Justin, that's a terrible thing to say. A woman's got to be bad off to want it that way."

He smiled and said, "I agree that most people think it's unnatural. But some people think it's natural. It's SOP for gays."

"It's perverted, Justin. Twisted."

"Did she give in?"

"Of course not."

"Then what did he do?"

"Shot her. How should I know?"

He got up off the floor and sat on the couch. "Now *that's* a terrible thing to say," he said.

"Yes it is, but can't you see that it's disgusting?" Then, with a scornful look, she punctuated, "It's evil!"

"Evil?" he said. "There is no evil, only absence of goodness."

"Oh, here we go, another lecture. I don't have the time to catch up on all your philosophy."

"It's not all that complicated, Ybette. Atheists always say they don't believe in God because God would not allow evil in the world. But there is no evil in the world as such, only absence of goodness, absence of God, who is all good."

She sat down next to him and folded her arms, allowing him to continue the argument.

"God does not allow evil in the world, only people to turn away from his goodness, like the devil did. The devil was created by God. God is all good and could never create evil. That would be absurd. The devil is good but turned away from God and the source of all goodness. He was created the most beautiful angel but turned away from God. Since God is the source of all beauty and light, the devil exists in total darkness. He lacks light and therefore is no longer beautiful. He lives in total darkness because he turned away from the light. People who do evil things are actually doing the same thing as the devil, turning away from the light. If we keep focused on God, we can't fall into darkness."

"That makes sense to me," she said.

Later, she allowed him to get into bed with her, but only for sleeping, since the room was dark and depressing. He felt there was something hidden inside her waiting to ambush him, like a useless muscle that does nothing for ten years, then one innocent morning decides to explode in a horrible spasm of pain that's so bad you can't get out of bed.

After Ybette's departure the next morning, Carol returned from her trip, giving him a double dose of deprivation. But Carol saw Andrea differently, and she felt safer when he was around. As they sat at opposite ends of the couch, she thanked him for helping her during the crisis and asked that he now do the same for Ybette. "Have you noticed that she's been acting rather depressed lately?" she asked.

"Yes, I have, especially last night."

"Well, she told me that she had thoughts about suicide. She wasn't joking either. She had that expression on her face."

"No one jokes about that. When did she tell you?"

"Last weekend. What do you think we should do?"

"Did she tell you why?"

"No."

"Well, maybe it's because of her condition."

"Which condition is that?"

He was surprised that Carol didn't zero in on what should have been the prevailing condition in Ybette's life. "Of not being able to have children," he said.

"Yes, that condition."

"You act as though there might be others."

"No, not that I know of," she said. "Just that one."

"She's told you the story about the senator, I'm sure."

"Yes, she told me that story."

"You don't sound very convinced," he said.

"It's something I'm not ready to talk about."

"Okay," he said. "My friend has a brother who's a psychologist—a professor actually at NYU. I'll ask him."

Andrea was silent all the time that Ybette moved about the apartment, getting undressed, taking a shower, putting on a nightgown, and sitting beside him on the couch. You would have thought they had just argued and were on non-speaking terms, except that they were not watching TV, listening to music, or otherwise ignoring each other.

They sat as they would in a car, she noticeably nervous about something going to happen when they arrived at their destination—an abortion of her baby, or worse yet, her own execution. She wiggled around making him think that she was plotting her own death, contemplating whether he might even assist her.

A slipper dangled off the tip of her foot, making it look open and vulnerable, waving him forward to do whatever he pleased—to reach forward and trace his fingers along the delicate arch, to encircle her neck with his hands, to reach inside her and squeeze her heart till it stopped beating.

Oh, Justin, help me stop this maddening pounding in my chest! Help me die now so that death will never take me. I must do it myself and not let it take me.

Her excitement ran into his body, going straight to its core, igniting his passion swiftly yet softly. He held her hand. His body trembled uncontrollably for a few moments. It was a boy's first orgasm, a dream's climax, a spontaneous outpouring not through rocks but from the sky itself.

After the tingling underneath his skin stopped, he asked her, "Do you love me?"

"Yes, dear," she said. "I love you, but I'm not *in* love with you."

He was spent and too tired to ask what she meant.

Simultaneously, the tips of his feet rose off the floor as the jumbo jet's nose rose off the ground and ascended into the sky. It was Pan Am World Airways Flight 1, and, no matter where it took off—New York, San Francisco, Honolulu, Tokyo—the rock channel always started with the same song— *Magic Carpet Ride,* first class or coach. As the plane banked to the left, his left foot dropped slightly and his right foot rose slightly, doing a balancing act like the wings themselves until the plane reached its cruising altitude of 35,000 feet.

"Did you know that this flight goes all the way around the world?" Andrea asked his seatmate JoAnn, a student returning to Bangkok on a semester break from Berkeley. She shook her head so slightly that he hardly noticed her answer. She was so natural and distant, he kept reeling in, afraid that any slack in the line would cause her to snap free. "I fly flight one all the time. Flight two goes in the exact opposite direction, west to east. They meet in Bangkok and New York. Cool, hey?"

"What do you do for a living?"

He hesitated for a moment, thinking through his cover stories for one that might impress her. "What would you guess?" he asked. "I'm not flying first class, so that rules out rich businessman. Sorry." She frowned playfully. "But, hey, that's an idea. Why don't we play a game to kill the time? You guess my occupation, and I'll guess your major. Okay? You start."

"Poet," she said.

"No, but nice guess." He looked intently into her dark eyes and said, "Now it's my turn. I'll say English."

"No. That's my minor."

The game of tag went on for a few turns until he noticed that she had been listening to channel 6, which he knew was all classical music. "Music!" he guessed.

"How could you tell?"

"Intuition," he said.

She could never learn his occupation, of course, even if she had guessed correctly. On the other hand, he learned a lot about her—that she had won a scholarship to study music at Berkeley, had no steady boyfriend, and planned to meet her relatives at the airport. They became so well acquainted on the eighteen-hour flight, she invited him to dinner at her parent's house. He was very surprised at this, given that he had told her the story of his encounter with the Thai ladyboys on the previous trip. "We respect ladyboys," she said. "Even have national beauty contest to pick the most beautiful one." She was suggesting that whichever choice a man made, it should be respected.

Approaching Bangkok, and, realizing that it would be very embarrassing for her to invite a man with no occupation to dinner with her parents, he said, "I'm a parapsychologist."

"A pair of what?" she smiled merrily.

"A pair of psychologists. I couldn't make up my mind between behaviorism and psychoanalysis, so I chose both." She shut her eyes as though she had been slapped in the face, and then opened them with an expression of disbelief. "No, I'm just kidding," he said. "I'm a parapsychologist, as in someone who studies the paranormal. Mind reading. Fortune telling. That sort of thing. I travel to Bangkok every month to study the séance as it relates to Buddhism."

"Oh, I see. Very good." She gave him her phone number and told him to call after he was settled in at the President.

As she was setting the table for dinner, JoAnn leaned toward him—showing off the valley between her breasts—and said, "My father says you are divorced."

"Is that a joke or a predication?" Andrea asked.

"He wants to know whether you ever been married."

"Tell him no. Tell him that we have divorce in America, because it's against the law to have a mistress." On hearing this, the father smiled.

Andrea wasn't too fond of the sour and hot tasting food that they prepared. He wanted to show off with some *real* cuisine, so he offered to treat them all to dinner at the best French restaurant in Bangkok.

Although highly recommended by his hotel desk clerk, *Le-Normandie* atop the Oriental Hotel was operated with Thai clients in mind, just as Asian restaurants in America cater to American tastes. Seated at the large circular table family style were JoAnn, her twin sister with fiancée (also a twin), her little brother, her grandmother, father, and mother. The menu was written in Thai, French, and English. There was a lot of discussion about it, since the parents couldn't read and were having difficulty making up their minds, so, Andrea ordered first, choosing the most expensive item on the menu—lobster supreme—wanting to show them what great food looked like and thinking they would be cautious and order something from the local menu—Pad Thai perhaps. After he finished ordering for himself, including dessert, he handed the menu back to the waiter. Then, in unison, they folded their menus. Andrea turned to JoAnn and said, "Aren't they going to order?"

"They already did," JoAnn said.

"What are they going to have?"

"Whatever you ordered."

Andrea's spirit sank. He would have preferred to lay himself on the table as the main course rather than pay $35 a head for perfect strangers. Never had he spent as much on his own family for one dinner. What he thought to be a cheap trick was actually an honest custom that would have saved him money had he not been such a showoff.

After dinner—fabulous in his mind, decent in theirs—he paid the check and followed the family procession out of the hotel.

Not to be outdone, JoAnn's mother bought a few durians on the way home and served them to Andrea with the usual advice to pinch his nose before tasting. It smelled just like the ones he had eaten with Bando, and he surprised his guests by going for seconds, savoring both the foul smell and sublime taste all at once.

"I've heard it's a potent aphrodisiac," he said to JoAnn. "Better watch out."

Having blown most of his travel advance on the meal, he would have to tighten his belt the rest of the trip home, which gave him an idea for a new cover story. With the help of JoAnn's cousin, who was a Buddhist monk, Andrea got all the paraphernalia that he needed to make it work.

Bald and self-conscious, he was unsure that he could pull it off in first class. In clipper class maybe, but a Buddhist monk in first class?

One hour into the flight, it looked like smooth sailing. He had been a hit at the preflight briefing, and the pale orange robe he wore was the perfect concealment for his weapons. But not even his seatmate had dared question him about it.

When served, he attacked the filet mignon like a caveman. Suddenly, a man and a woman ran up the spiral staircase to the upper deck. At once, he squeezed out of his seat and went upstairs to investigate. The lounge was empty, so he sat on the floor facing the cockpit door and waited for the two lovers to finish their rendezvous in the blue room, a harmless initiation into the Mile-High Club.

Fifteen minutes of sitting upright started to wrench his backbone, so he went to the door to eavesdrop. The familiar sounds of moaning mixed with a few thumps and rattles—to be expected in such tight quarters—and then a few expletives in French assured him nothing significant was happening. It's the French connection, he thought, turning away and sitting down again on the floor. He sat for another five minutes until the door opened and the man peeked out. He ducked back inside for a minute and then came out alone and went downstairs. Another passenger came upstairs and went inside, which made him repeat the same inspection, and just as before— French expletives. Eventually, the man came out. A minute later, the woman came out and immediately went downstairs with a hand held up against her face.

When Dewey came up to relieve him, Andrea could hardly get up off the floor and tripped on his robe going downstairs. Returning to his seat, he was distraught that dinner service had ended and his tray removed. Low on cash, he had been hoping to bulk-up on the plane to hold him over on the layover in Beirut, but now he would have to borrow from Bando for sure.

"You were gone so long," his seatmate said, "I told the stewardess that you were finished eating."

"That's okay," he said. "I'm used to fasting. It strengthens the will."

"So, you really are a Buddhist monk?" she asked.

"Yes."

"I hope you don't mind my asking, but how can you afford to fly first class? And why would you eat meat? I thought Buddhists were vegetarian."

"I'll answer your question, but let me ask you one first. What is the thing you fear most?"

"Well, maybe at this moment, the plane crashing."

"Certainly. Your death. My death. We all fear death the most. So, it must follow that the thing we desire the most is life. And this is what I'm searching for. I figure that I have a better chance of finding life in first class than in coach. Wouldn't you agree?"

"Sure, but where is your money coming from? Donations?"

"From the will," he said.

She looked at him curiously, catching the pun and not knowing where he would go with it. She smiled and asked, "Your will?"

"My will. His will. Thy will be done," he said. "Did you know that we are the laziest men in the world? Hell, all we do is sit around all day and sleep all night, and beg for food in the morning. That's why we become monks in the first place, so we won't have to work. But, we're not practicing bad faith, because this is part of our faith—the main reason for it—to break away from the pain and misery of daily life, and its desires, like sex. This is where we surpass Catholic priests—chastity is far superior in a Buddhist monastery. It's all about will power actually. The power of the will to become one in thought with the world. To assimilate life versus death, evil versus good, hot versus cold, dark versus light, because the mind cuts things in two. It's the ego's fault, so the ego must be the way out. It sounds like a contradiction, doesn't it? We have two eyes, two hands, two legs, because we need them to survive. We are two sexes—male and female—to survive the species."

"So, is that why there are no female monks?"

"Precisely. But females too pray to Buddha."

"That's sexist," she said.

"They pray to become men in the next life so that they can have a better chance at immortality."

"Phooey! That's bogus!"

"Not really. If you think like a woman, sure. These monks deny their masculinity. Christianity is a lot more sexist. Christian women have no chance of becoming like Jesus. They are women for eternity."

"Are you celibate?" she asked.

"I don't have the will for that. The only will I have is the one my father gave me. It's how I can afford to travel around the world like this." He caught a passing stewardess' attention and asked for a Bloody Mary, then continued. "I wear this habit so stewardesses will think I'm celibate. They really freak out when I ask them for a date. I don't have a chance in hell reaching Nirvana. I want to become a woman in the next life—not a man— so that I can experience childbirth."

"But maybe you were a woman in the previous life and had many children."

"Hey, you have something there. Maybe that accounts for some men wanting to dress up like women, like they do in Thailand. Sometimes I feel like I *was* a woman, but didn't have any children. Maybe that's why I want to be one. In the next life, of course."

He finished his Bloody Mary and made one final comment about Buddhism. "I've found it has one big flaw. It requires intense will power to engage in meditation in order to gain enlightenment. I've tried and failed countless times. The purpose is to assimilate one's self—one's ego—into nature. But this takes sheer will power; an enormous ego. See the contradiction?"

"No," she said wearily.

"It's a problem of method, actually. Physicists have the same problem trying to study the photon. They can't because it can't be observed and measured when it's a wave. An electron is both a wave and a particle, meaning it can be in two places at the same time. Einstein was proven wrong on this. Did you know that Einstein was a lecher and not all that smart?"

The woman squinted at him, and then shook her head.

"Same is true for Buddhism. It's like trying to look at a germ in a microscope, but you can't see inside it because it has skin like a mirror, and you see only your eyeball looking at itself. That's what I mean by ego getting in the way. It's a problem of consciousness." He repeated the word, this time stressing each syllable. "Con-scious-ness."

"Oh, really?"

"Consciousness can never be assimilated into nature because nature is always a phenomenon *in* consciousness. Nature is not in consciousness as it really is, only as consciousness perceives it to exist. Buddhism tries to improve consciousness, and that's false because enlightenment is said to exist in consciousness, *which doesn't exist without something to be conscious of*. In other words, by its very nature, consciousness can't exist separate from the world it is conscious of. Physicists are busy at work this very minute trying to prove this. They eventually will, and the world will see a revolution in human existence second to none. Or should I say worlds second to none? Buddhists cannot explain enlightenment, and it is not clear to them what it is. But consciousness is immediate experience always of something but not necessarily of nature in itself, only of nature as it appears in consciousness, which is a different thing. The meditating monk cannot transcend consciousness and free himself from the pain of existence. If he says he does, he's contradicting himself simply by saying so, by claiming such a consciousness."

"I think I understand," she said. "He would have to be unconscious to do so, which is absurd."

Andrea smiled and made a move to kiss her but held back.

" . "

"Philosophy again," Marge said. "Did you understand that piece about consciousness?"

"Do you suppose his consciousness is going to take over this book and, in the end, execute those that don't pledge allegiance to it?"

11/The Blue Room

Reaching cruising altitude, Andrea stretched out in the little space offered by the aisle seat and closed his eyes. No sooner than his fortieth wink, a stewardess tapped him on the shoulder and said, "Here's the magazine you requested, sir." He jumped up startled, as though caught sleeping on the job.

"Okay, thank you," he said. He opened the magazine, and a small note popped out onto his lap. *Andrea, are you working? If not, I'm deadheading. I need to see you. Carol*

He looked up the aisle and thought she must be in first class. After the seatbelt sign was turned off, he went up to the dark-blue curtain protecting first class, opened it, and a stewardess barked, "Sorry, sir, this area is reserved for first-class passengers."

"Could you please pass a message to Carol LeTendre? She's a passenger in first class. Tell her Andrea said *no*."

He waited in the back of the plane for a few minutes, and when she appeared walking down the aisle toward him, he was delighted beyond belief. Her smile was quiet, full of friendship but, at the same time, longing for escape. Her lips moved excitedly, but she didn't speak. He thought that she was about to reveal something important about Ybette, something she wasn't able to discuss in the apartment. But she said, opening the lavatory door, "Go inside." Thinking that there was some trouble, a threat written on the wall perhaps, he stepped inside and looked around. A second later, she squeezed in beside him and closed the door. "We don't have much time," she said, dropping the seat cover. "Sit down, please!" quickly exposing her exquisite breasts.

He had desired her body like one desires to hold a flower in bloom, to draw it near and smell its fragrance, to caress its soft petals. He kissed her as fast as she could open up more to attack. This and only this was what he had always wanted. Now fully undressed, she found hand and foot holds in places only a mountain climber could, and she levitated above every bounce and jiggle made by the plane's tail. No longer hidden behind a navy-blue uniform, her skin glowed with the luster of pink pearls. He nibbled her skin, causing her to bang around in the bucket like a newly caught salmon. He loosened his pants, causing the stainless-steel pistol to slip out, but he grabbed it quickly and placed it in the sink. The sight of it excited her, and she brushed against the door lock and pushed it accidentally to *unoccupied*.

He looked up and caught glimpses of her wild green eyes and large blue veins radiating down her slender neck. His leg shot out, banging hard against the door. He held her lithe body around the waist, thumbs digging deeply into her navel as she rotated gently. He kicked the door again, and she played sweet melodies all over him.

Now slightly ajar, the door opened as the plane turned slightly, and there stood a young, crew-cut boy in a black Star-Wars T-shirt looking straight at them. Shocked, the boy slammed the door and ran away.

Carol turned around, locked the door, and then scurried about to get dressed. There was a loud knock at the door, immediately followed by a pounding made by a remarkably heavy fist. They pulled themselves back together only to meet the flight supervisor outside.

An immense excitement coursed through their veins, convinced that instead of being struck by lightning, they were about to lightning-strike the world that wanted to ruin their lives for making love.

Carol rushed out of the lavatory and pushed the supervisor aside. Andrea took his gun and followed her up the aisle to the cockpit where he knocked on the door and held up his ID to the peephole. The flight engineer didn't trust him and said on the interphone, "Who are you?"

"Special Agent Dave Doyle, FBI," Andrea replied. "I just arrested a stewardess who was plotting to skyjack your plane."

"FBI? I didn't see you at the preflight."

"I was undercover."

"We didn't get any warning," the engineer said.

"Of course not. This is an internal investigation matter. We had her under surveillance for three weeks."

"Okay. It's your bald head throws me off. What's the password?"

"McCormick!"

"Okay. Wait till I inform the captain."

A minute later, the captain came out of the cockpit alone. He was a heavy-set man of fifty with thinning gray hair, clean-shaven face, and a way of talking out of the side of his mouth. His right hand was held behind his back, and he didn't offer a handshake. "I'm Captain Gerrard. What seems to be the trouble? You said you have arrested one of my stewardesses who wanted to skyjack my plane?"

Andrea focused on a large wart near the center of Gerrard's chin. "Wild horses, my ass," he said. "In the name of the Holy Jihad, this plane is under attack!"

"Come again?" Gerrard said.

"Holy Jihad!" Andrea yelled, pointing his pistol at Gerrard's wart.

Suddenly, Carol turned pale, screamed, and ran to the back of the plane.

"Holy Geehard?" Gerrard said, pulling out a sawed-off bat from behind his back. "Yeah? You and whose troop of boy scouts?"

Andrea pulled the trigger, and the pistol didn't fire. He pulled repeatedly and nothing happened. Gerrard raised the bat, swung it, and connected squarely on Andrea's forearm, sending the pistol flying over the passengers.

Screeeech! Boom-kada-boom!

Screeeech! Boom-kada-boom-boom!

Andrea opened his eyes and the first thing he saw was the sign, *Life Vest Under Your Seat.*

A stewardess apologized, "That was quite a bump, and I know what you all are thinking. I'm here to tell you that this landing wasn't the pilot's fault, it wasn't the airplane's fault, and it wasn't any of the stewardess' fault. It was the asphalt on the runway! Welcome to Buffalo International Airport."

The pain in his head didn't subside and ruined the weekend at home with his parents. He blamed it on the dreams lodged there by the pressurized cabin during the flight from New York. What he needed was an hour in a dream chamber to depressurize slowly, as if he had the psychological bends or something. He even thought of visiting Father Juvenal, his old high school chemistry teacher to confess his dream-lit sins and receive photochemical absolution. But he figured the jovial monk wouldn't take him seriously and would refer him to a shrink downtown.

Standing in line to get his return ticket to New York, playing sky marshal once again, he forgot all about the pain in his neck and the dream that had caused it, though he had recorded it in his journal for possible use in the novel. When the plane arrived from New York, Customs Agent Gary Linnehan got off and walked right past him without the slightest expression of recognition. He's either on the job or on the make, Andrea thought.

"Planes are only on time when people are late," said a man standing behind him in line.

"What do you mean?" Andrea said.

"My wife! Now that the plane is here on time, she's late."

"Well, at least she won't have to waste time going through a security check like they do in New York." The man kept looking back as the first-class passengers were boarding, but just before going through the door, his wife came running up, out of breath, and looking just like....

Oh, no. Not again. It can't be her again. Leila Khaled, here in Buffalo? Oh, but yes! Maybe she came in from Canada by car over the Peace Bridge. Yes, the most wanted terrorist in the world planning another skyjacking in New York. Maybe that's why Linnehan was here and just missed her. Maybe the intelligence was five minutes too fast!

He boarded the plane and dropped his boarding pass in the aisle in order to get a closer look at her sitting against the window. Now convinced that she was the closest anyone could get to being the guerrilla, he showed his badge to the head stewardess and insisted on sitting in the first-class section for surveillance. He stood in the aisle watching them while the stewardess relayed the message to the captain.

The idea of a skyjacking plot taking place right under his nose made him feel the dreadful weight of impending war. Without asking, he took the empty seat directly behind them, making sure his leather jacket was open and his pistol ready to draw.

On hearing that there was an armed sky marshal aboard, Captain Tester delayed takeoff and told the stewardess to bring him forward.

Andrea bowed slightly before entering the dark *holy of holies*. The enigmatic complication of clockworks and illuminated switches on the instrument panel offered just enough light to see the pilot and copilot. It was a sacrosanct workplace second to none. He felt unholy and ignorant—a sinister intruder.

"What's the idea of coming aboard my plane without identifying yourself to the boarding agent as an armed marshal?" Tester said, sneering at Andrea's leather jacket.

"I forgot," Andrea said.

"Now you've delayed the flight and we're behind schedule. Are you now armed?"

"Yes."

"Then, you'll have to turn over your weapon to me now."

"I'm afraid I can't do that, sir."

"You either leave it here or get off this plane."

Andrea waited a moment, knowing that he had no choice but to turn it over. He shook his head a few times, then reached under his belt and pulled out his stainless-steel beauty. He held it up to give both pilots a good look, then opened the cylinder, dropped the five bullets into his pocket, and handed the empty pistol to Tester.

"You'll get it back when we land," Tester said.

Andrea pulled his lips back between his teeth and bit down hard as he walked out of the cockpit. Ambling through the first class section, he said. "American pussies. Now you can go ahead and hijack this son-of-a-bitch." He took a long look at the spitting image of Leila Khaled, shook his head, and went back to his assigned seat in coach.

Captain Tester radioed ahead and reported the incident. Upon arrival at La Guardia, Andrea went back into the cockpit and retrieved his pistol.

"I think you might have company when you get off," Tester said. And, sure enough, when he did, two sky marshals were waiting to escort him to headquarters. He felt relieved that they treated him routinely, but he knew that they were being more protective of the airlines than one of their own. Knowing that sky marshals were summarily guillotined for infractions much worse, like discharging their firearms accidentally, he was hoping for a stay of execution.

He wrote an incident report, explaining his disappointment with the airline for being so uncooperative with his surveillance. Then he asked for his gun back. They refused and told him to report back in the morning to meet the special agent in charge.

It was late before he reached the apartment, and he expected both his roommates to be in bed, but as he peered into the dark living room, he saw Ybette lying on the rug. In a split second of dread, he thought there was a man beside her, but on seeing that it was Carol, he walked quietly into the bedroom and went to bed.

He awoke in the middle of the night to the scent of sweaty breasts. Ybette stood beside the bed looking down at him seductively. He looked at her for a moment and, thinking it was a dream, turned over and went back to sleep. She got into bed and lay silently beside him all night.

Reporting early in the morning for the appointment, he met his old roommate John exiting the building, wearing a black leather coat.

"You look like a rock star," Andrea said. "Like that British guy who sings *Wild Horses*. What's his name? Mick Jagger! That's it. Spittin' image of Mick Jagger."

"I like your hairdo," John said. Then, showing off his new schedule, "Can you believe this? Another month of T-way. How can anyone want to quit a job like this? Three months in a row."

"Quit? Who's quitting?"

"Heard the latest? They plan to phase out the program next year. Too many complaints by the airlines. Too many four-inch airheads in the program, if you ask me. No one's shot a skyjacker yet, so they plan to send us to Texas to be border patrol officers."

"Texas? Border patrol? Holy shit. Do you know what the suicide rate is for those guys? What are you going to do?"

"Keep flying as long as I can. I met this T-way stew, and we're getting serious together." John lit a cigarette, making Andrea wonder if he had ever detected anything missing from his stash of hashish. "You remember those stews that lived next door? That pretty one, Nancy? Man, she went down on me one night, man. Then again, the next night, and every night I was there. Really freaked me out, man. Elegant, man, but I had to quit her. Too much of a good thing drove me nuts." John took a deep drag and exhaled, "Fellatio freaks me out, man."

"I see you've picked up some Italian. Which stew was it?"

"Nancy. The tall one that looked like a model."

"What happened to the others? I lost touch. Did they ever catch that rapist?"

"I was ready every night for him to come back. No, he's still at large."

Andrea didn't believe the story about Nancy. "I gotta get going, John. Appointment with Donovan."

"Yeah, I heard. Good luck."

Before going into the building, Andrea turned back and yelled, "I was just joking!"

"What's that?" John yelled back.

"You look like Shaft!"

John gave him an air jerk, laughed, and walked to his car.

The appointment was delayed a half hour, so Andrea hung around the schedulers to learn more about their jobs, thinking he would be grounded like them, for how could they fire a Vietnam veteran for being a little overzealous? The schedulers confirmed that the bureau was not hiring any more marshals and that some airlines had cut coverage altogether. "Too many pissed-off pilots," one guy said.

That's it, Andrea thought. Tester was a pissed-off pilot, and that phony Leila Khaled, his accomplice. Could there actually be a conspiracy against sky marshals? All along I thought they were our friends; now it makes sense. They want all the glory!

Once in Donovan's office, he sat in a chair against the wall, like an observer rather than the one being interrogated. Two other agents were present, as well as Lieutenant Casio. He hoped they would merely slap his wrists and tell him to take a few days on the beach without pay. Donovan asked the first question. "What's your name?"

"Andrea High," he said curiously with an inward laugh.

"Andrea High? Well, then, who is Andrew D'Oria?"

"My cover," Andrea said.

"Your cover? Mister, whoever the hell you are, we've got a real problem with both of you. Not only does it say here that your name is Andrew D'Oria, it says you are on one hundred percent disability from the Army."

"What are you looking at?"

"Your DD two-fourteen and medical records. You have short-term amnesia and can't remember who you are day-to-day."

"Where I am day-to-day? How could I get here, if I didn't know where I was? I'm not affected by the bullet anymore."

Donovan looked at Casio, a twenty-five-year veteran of the Customs Service, and said, "Any questions?"

Casio smiled and said, "Let's see your driver's license."

Andrea handed it over. Casio inspected it, shrugged his shoulders, and handed it back.

"Do you remember being on American flight six-eight-nine out of Buffalo last night?"

"Yes."

"And claimed to have identified the fugitive terrorist Leila Khaled sitting in the first class section and insisted on moving to a seat behind her?"

"Yes."

"What made you think she was Leila Khaled?"

"Her facial features. She looked just like the photos I saw in training."

Donovan threw his pencil on the desk and said, "Leila Khaled doesn't look like that now. She's had...." Realizing that he was about to reveal classified information to a person that was about to be fired, he picked up a Pan Am cup and took a big gulp.

"And you were off duty at the time and still carrying your weapon?" Casio asked.

"Yes."

"Mister High," said Donovan. "Do you recall being instructed by Special Agent Gary Linnehan that you were not supposed to carry your weapon off duty?"

"Yes, I recall Special Agent Linnehan, but I thought he was an FBI agent, not Customs. At least that's what he told the stewardesses living in the apartment."

Donovan looked suspiciously at the other agents and then said, "Did he tell *you* that he was an FBI agent?"

"Yes, until I asked for his ID. Then I saw that he was Customs."

Donovan was silent for a long while, mulling over his decision to fire High. "Do you recall having received a briefing where we covered the regulations on firearms? You signed the attendance sheet *Andrea High,* but don't tell me that you weren't present, because you're Andrew D'Oria!"

"Yes...I mean no! I was sitting in the back of the room and didn't hear much. I have tinnitus. Ringing in my ears."

"Look, you are on shaky ground here. Lying about your name...."

"No, that's wrong. I didn't lie. My name was legally changed to Andrea High. I put that on my application. Linnehan is the liar."

Looking at Andrea's personnel file to ensure that he was still on probation, Donovan noticed the letters *MISS* after his name on his SF-50. He crossed it off and entered *MR.* Then he showed Casio the mistake. "Have personnel correct this," he said.

"Yes, sir," Casio said.

"Anything wrong?" Andrea asked curiously.

"Just a typo," Casio said.

Looking frustrated, and doing his best to avoid further investigation, Donovan conceded, "You're a veteran with a Purple Heart and a Distinguished Service Cross." He paused a moment, knowing that it was a medal second only to the Medal of Honor. "And a disability rating. We respect that. Otherwise, we'd ask for your badge right now. However, let me tell you that you are still on probation, and, from what I've seen in this program, you don't have much on your side otherwise. If you resign now, you won't have a disciplinary action on your record, and you can come back into the federal service later. Otherwise, we have to ground you."

Andrea knew they were up to their gills investigating cases of misconduct, so he opted for ground duty rather than resign. He knew the compromise was accepted because of his status as a disabled veteran, and that it would be awfully tuff to fire him. The likelihood of someday patrolling the Mexican border in a Jeep looming over his head, he took a clerical job in the scheduling branch in order to buy time before going back to grad school.

12/Beep! Beep!

The tradition for existentialists was to write books in public cafes, thinking that to do so at home would be fraught with bad faith. Andrea had hoped to take this tradition into the jet age by writing his book in a crowded airplane at thirty-five thousand feet. But now, he had to settle for the stray Salty Dog in Queens.

Sitting at a grungy table, immersed deep in thought, he was lost for words. He looked up at the bar and saw a man watching him intently. The eye contact was enough for the man to approach and, when near, he said, "Can I buy you a drink?"

"Sure," Andrea said.

The man took a seat and said, "I couldn't help noticing you writing. What is it, a novel?"

"How'd you guess?"

"I'm an agent."

"Not another FBI agent?"

"No, not that kind," the man said, producing a business card. "I'm a literary agent. I work downtown. Come out here on weekends to meet the stews."

Andrea read the card, put it in his pocket, and said, "Dan, nice to meet you. My name is Andrea High."

"Well, Andrea, what's the book about?"

"A sky marshal with angst."

Dan snickered and said, "I thought sky marshals were tough guys. At least that's the impression one gets from the media."

"That's what they want you to believe. Actually, sky marshals are average people. Not tough. Most of them were never cops. Treasury selected average people, because they wanted them to blend in with the public so they wouldn't be recognized."

"Like yourself? Are you a sky marshal?"

"If I were, I wouldn't tell you or write about it. I flew for about a year, until I had a little problem with the regulations. Now I work for scheduling. Gives me a lot of time to write."

"Which airline do you work for?"

"I don't work for the airlines. I'm still employed with the Treasury Department. I make up the schedules for the sky marshals."

"Sounds interesting. And the book too. Mind if I read it?"

"Well, it's only a journal now. I don't have any copies."

"Can you get me a synopsis? Sort of a summary? I'll see what I can do."

"Sure. No problem. I'll have it by tomorrow."

"Just send it to my office. Don't forget your name, address, and phone number."

The following weekend, they met at the Salty Dog to discuss the prospect of marketing the manuscript.

"I talked with a few publishers," Dan said, "and I think you have a good story going. You have just the ticket for a bestseller—an insight into something the public knows nothing about."

"Sounds great."

"Only problem is, you don't have a plot. No entrée, only appetizers."

"I know. I've been working on that. I need something unique and not a traditional spy story, or a mystery ending in the usual. I've got my hands tied. I'm not flying anymore. It's that first hijacking out of London, the one where the sky marshal takes over the plane that bugs me. I was unable to end it."

"You need an exposé, and I've got just the ticket. How'd you like to fly again, around the world, first class?"

Andrea sensed Dan had something in mind other than a book. "Sounds great." he said.

"You can be the first man ever to write a novel on board a plane at thirty thousand feet. No guns involved. The only thing you have to worry about is a pen. You can kill as many skyjackers as you want and not worry about being shot or blown up."

"What do you have in mind?"

"Let's talk outside."

He followed Dan into an alley, which was dark and secluded. The "agent" lit a cigarette, which made his face glow for just a second, and then he took a deep drag to reinforce his plan. "I have a source that would pay a lot for the monthly schedules out of JFK."

"The monthly schedules? I thought you wanted my book."

"Your book tells me more than just a story. You've been shit upon by the airlines. Leila Khaled was not dream. You overlooked it, and it's the central theme you need. I suspect it's true."

"A conspiracy?"

"Certainly. We need to investigate this. It's the plot you need to make this a blockbuster."

"Really?"

"Don't you want satisfaction? Don't you think it's payback time? They owe you more than a story for a book. Look, here's a hundred to help you think it over," handing him five twenties and then walking off. "I'll be in touch."

The next evening, they met again near the Salty Dog. Still wary, Andrea said, "Are you a cop? This is entrapment, if you are."

"No, I'm not a cop. And you're right; it would be entrapment if I were."

"Okay, good. Now, what does your source plan to do with the schedules?"

"He's looking for payback, just like you."

"Who is he? Or, what is he?"

"I can't say, but trust me that he's not a terrorist or a spy."

Though consoling to hear, Andrea couldn't be sure. "I don't want people hurt because of this," he said. "No one, understand?"

"He feels the same way. That's why he wants you to help."

"Who is he?" Andrea asked again, suspecting it might be the fugitive D.B. Cooper wanting to gamble one more time, this time for a lot more money.

"A legend in his own time," Dan said.

Then it really might be Cooper, Andrea thought. "Interesting. How much is he willing to pay?"

"A thousand for each monthly. One for each marshal."

"For how long?"

"For however long it takes. A few months; maybe a year. I can't say."

With over a hundred marshals flying, the take could be a bundle. "Yeah, but if I get caught, it will mean life."

Dan was either the real thing or an insane man. "One hundred thousand up front," Andrea said. "And you can have all the schedules you want. No limits."

"I doubt it, but I'll check."

A week passed without a word from Dan. Andrea began to think that the proposition was a practical joke. He knew absolutely nothing of *the source*; that it was D.B. Cooper seemed farfetched, like from another dimension, a dimension more suited to the confines of a book. It would pull the story away from certainty into another set of characters, characters that lived out there somewhere. Cash was the only reality. Hard cash in hand. And, if Dan was able to come up with that amount of money in real bills, it would confirm the source's sincerity.

Then, on a Sunday morning, Dan called and wanted to meet at the Unisphere in Flushing Meadows Park. Andrea agreed.

When they met, Dan went straight to the point. "The source will pay ten thousand per drop. No one gets a hundred thousand, not even CIA moles."

Andrea thought it over for a moment, and then agreed with one stipulation. He had researched the D.B. Cooper case, knew that the two hundred thousand ransom was never recovered, and that it was all in twenty dollar bills. "No twenties," he said. "Only hundreds."

"Okay, easier to carry. I understand. Only hundreds. Here's the plan. Go to *His Place* on Flatbush Avenue in Brooklyn and ask to become a volunteer to deliver meals for the needy. Tell them you want to drive route number four. My uncle Duffy is on that route. He lives in an apartment on Lois Lane. You'll have no problem, because he can't talk. He's confined to a wheelchair. He'll keep the door unlocked so walk straight in. He'll be waiting in the kitchen. Leave the meal on the table for him. When you leave, you'll find the drop in the closet by the front door. Take it and leave your drop. The drops are to be put in black, plastic bags. Any questions?"

"Where on Flatbush is *His Place*?"

"At Beverly Road. You can't miss it. It used to be an old Protestant church." Then, handing Andrea a small pager, "Take this. When you're ready to make a drop, push the button. It sends out an encrypted signal. I'll have the money ready at Duffy's place the next day. And make sure you get the schedules as soon as they're out. And don't use a copy machine. They keep a copier count. Use this."

"A deck of cards?"

"Yeah," Dan said smiling. "Play solitaire on the nightshift."

Delivering a dozen hot dinners wasn't easy, not only because he did so on an empty stomach, but because the clients were hard of hearing, slow to the door, lonely, and in need of company. When it came time to make the first drop, he entered the apartment slowly, thinking there was someone else there besides Duffy. "His Place meals," he called out.

"Beep-beep," Duffy replied, sitting in a wheelchair as usual, at the kitchen table.

"How are you today?" Andrea asked, placing the meal on the table.

"Beep-beep!" Duffy said.

"What's that mean?" Andrea asked.

"Beep-beep!" Duffy repeated.

"If that's all you say, how do I know what you mean? Can you say yes or no?"

"Beep-beep!"

"Well, if that's all, then I have to go," Andrea said. "Bon appetite," knowing that the food was by no means gourmet. "See you again tomorrow."

"Beep-beep! Beep-beep!"

Duffy's smiling eyes followed Andrea out of the room.

Reaching the entrance hallway, Andrea opened the closet and, in a matter of a few seconds, exchanged his little black bag for the one waiting there. He looked back to see if Duffy had been watching, turned the door knob and was outside in a wink. The operation was so clean and easy, he was sure it would bring him a fortune.

But what good was fortune without fame? He would be back in the same regimen of cover stories that he was in as a sky marshal. An unknown. A story without a finish. He wanted revenge.

When he returned home, though still starving, he counted the money and, based on what he had learned from the Secret Service instructors at the sky marshal school, inspected each bill for counterfeit. He even tore one bill to see if the green threads were embedded. It was all real. Five packets of one hundred dollar bills. No twenties, as he had instructed. And a new pack of cards to photo the month's schedules.

During the week, he listened apprehensively for any news of a skyjacking. He was deep into it now. No turning back. No chance of becoming a double agent either, or arresting Dan and possibly getting his old job back, a job that was doomed anyway.

Getting richer and more apprehensive, it was like playing a game of hide-and-seek, not sure the seeker had given up, and cautious of not giving away the hiding place. The source had either lost his nerve or was getting closer to an attack. He had to take a chance on the latter.

He left a note attached to the camera that said, "Tell me, or I will quit!" He didn't get any calls, but kept his part of the bargain, taking photos as usual. Then, surprisingly, on the next drop, the bag contained a note to meet at the Unisphere.

Dan looked drawn.

"Okay," Andrea said, "tell me."

"Have you ever heard of Operation Northwoods?"

"No."

"It's about Cuba. It's always been about Cuba. Even JFK's assassination. Look, I don't know what they told you in sky marshal school, probably a lot of bullshit about how important you mission was. But it's all a hoax. A government setup to make the public believe it's doing its best to thwart hijackings and make airline travel safe. Well, the real skyjackers in this are not the Cubans but the government. It's a conspiracy to make people believe the communists are taking over."

"But the program is working."

"Program? Program my ass. It's just a show of force. You saw that in

Vietnam. They're ramping up for a big *reduction* in force. There'll be a retreat, then you watch. A big attack. An attack so big, it will make the president and all his cronies dribble."

"Interesting," Andrea said.

"You were looking for a way to stop a hijacking and be a hero. Well, friend, even if you did find one, you'd still be a pawn. It wouldn't stop anything. It would just feed the fire."

"Dan, I need another deck."

The drops went on for a few more months, but then Dan's bag came up empty. The hijacking was either going down or Dan had succumbed to his own futility. Andrea had to make a getaway. For sure, overseas!

The biggest problem would be carrying the money through security and customs. Stacked together, fifty thousand dollars was too bulky to carry in a regular money belt. Though undetectable by magnetometers, it could be easily detected by a quick body frisk, which was standard practice for most airlines, especially Pan Am. Going by plane was too risky. He had to leave by car.

Go home. Cool it for a year. Study philosophy again. Bangkok can wait.

Resigning from his job was easy. Saying goodbye to his roommates was another story.

The untidiness of the apartment looked fatal; the beds weren't made and there was no food in the kitchen. The same could not be said of Carol, however. Wearing raggedy clothes and no makeup, she sat on the sofa looking absolutely beautiful. Andrea sat next to her and broke the news matter-of-factly.

 The sincerity with which he disclosed his demise overwhelmed her. She didn't know what to say and began to speak of Ybette as a bad influence on his life. "Now that she's away and you are leaving, there's something about her you need to know." She placed a comforting hand on his knee. "She never told you this but, since she is…how can I say this? I suppose it's all right. I owe you one since you helped me through that terrible time."

"I know what you're trying to say. She told me about her abortion."

"That wasn't an abortion. That was butchery. She did have a D 'n' C later. Did you know?"

"Well, I thought the story hard to believe. It sounded like she had stolen it off a TV soap."

"Believe me, Andrea. I saw her in the hospital, and she was nearly gone." Carol paused to collect her emotions. "They thought she was infertile, until she got pregnant again. She proved them wrong."

"That's good. So, she's okay after all. And she did, ah,…"

Tears gleamed in Carol's eyes as though she were running against a fierce, cold wind.

"She conceived?" he said. "And I…?" Carol's passionate expression didn't console him. "Well, it doesn't surprise me. I figured as much. That's about the only thing she could conceive about me anyway."

"You need to talk with her, Andrea. She needs encouragement, especially from you. She's been very depressed lately. If you could tell her, maybe she would pull out of it."

"Tell her what?"

"That you forgive her."

Andrea gazed at the front door where Ybette stood at night peering into the empty hallway, then said, "I don't think I can do that."

Philosophic inspiration came from a thing that he couldn't describe, paint, or sculpt, because it wasn't a *thing* actually. It was a happening, the unending disclosure of the very substance that gave a thing existence. He made the pilgrimage on a free Thursday morning.

Driving slowly over the Rainbow Bridge, he gathered courage from being suspended over the Niagara gorge and the Whirlpool Rapids. The line of cars at the end of the bridge gave him pause for more courage to go on. When it was his turn, the Canadian immigration officer asked where he was born. "Buffalo," he said, hoping that he wouldn't have to show his seven-league passport. As usual, the officer let him pass without inspection.

Viewed from the sidelines, the Horseshoe Falls hit him with a heavy mist and a steady rumble. Up close and personal, whether fighting the whirlpool at its base, bucking a hurricane at the cave of the winds, or journeying behind its torrent, it became an effusion of power so colossal, it could douse an erupting volcano in minutes.

Now, as he was walking through the wet tunnel behind the falls, he thought how he wanted to package himself in a style, create an elegance that only he could create, as though some truth were locked inside him that only he knew. "And yet, whatever does come to me," he said to himself, "will only be fodder for another artist bent on vulgarity and violence. I am powerless to find a truth in my style, to protect it from being plagiarized, defiled, and abused."

Thus he lamented his plight, the tunnel reminding him of the bridges he always took to board airplanes. And when he reached the end of the tunnel, he turned left and beheld a deafening roar. It transfixed him for a long time, making him unable to get closer and see it clearly. It was a white blur in his eyes, rushing down at highway speed, shedding a cold mist through the portal. He stepped up to the railing and beheld the awesome spectacle and looked into the open chest of creation. And there was the beating heart of nature.

This is the utmost cruelty, he thought sorrowfully. A picture moving by so fast it cannot be seen. No! I won't express it as a metaphor. It's more than words or pictures. It defies everything. I never saw or heard anything so defiant. God is out there behind the falls, sitting with his back to the rock wall, laughing at the enormous tonnage of water flowing down, green on the outside, pure white on the inside.

He bowed respectfully at the portal and walked away.

Driving back over the Rainbow Bridge, hoping for a view of the colorful spectrum dipping into the gorge, he found himself again waiting in line. His car was selected for a random customs inspection.

He had nothing to fear, since his money was safely hidden. "Have anything to declare?" the customs officer asked.

"No, sir," he said. He even got out and obliged by opening the trunk.

Standing inside the nearby customs office, a special agent watched the inspection. When he recognized Andrea, he rushed outside and said abruptly, "Wait! Check this guy better."

Recognizing the menacing agent, a shout of terror ran through Andrea's body, "Run away! Run away!" But he held ground.

They were face to face again, and Andrea was at a disadvantage again. He was well aware of the customs law that allowed an agent to trail a suspect out of the customs arena to anyplace in the U.S., as long as eye contact was maintained. The agent could in fact follow him to his home and search it without a warrant for no reason other than sheer suspicion. Andrea kept silent and submitted to a body frisk.

"I heard you were fired," Linnehan said.

Andrea remained silent.

"Check underneath the car," Linnehan ordered. "And the gas tank. Give it the works." Then, to Andrea, "Okay, your wallet. Hand it over." Andrea did so reluctantly. Linnehan looked inside, counted the money, and said, "Five one hundred-dollar bills? Where'd you get these?"

"From a bank," Andrea said with an insolent undertone.

"Wait here," Linnehan said. Andrea knew he wanted to check for counterfeit and write down the serial numbers.

After an inspection just short of cutting open the seats and tires, Linnehan let Andrea get back into his car and drive away.

Worried about the fate of his fortune, he drove straight home and checked his Bangkok bank. It looked undisturbed, so he went inside and retreated to his bedroom. The window had now turned bright with setting sunlight, and anything passing in the back yard would cast shadows on it. He lay on his bed and watched patiently, but, after only ten minutes, his eyes grew heavy and he dozed off.

Suddenly, a loud noise woke him. He thought his father had returned home from work, but when he looked outside and saw a stranger come out of the garage door, a man in a grey suit, an agent named Linnehan, he panicked and reached for the shotgun in the closet. Had it been anyone else, it would have been an easy plea of self-defense, so he rested the gun and went for the phone to call the sheriff, but that too would only bring further investigation.

Linnehan was now walking around the yard, kicking up dirt, actually looking for something buried. "That nosey, sneaky, lying bastard. He's gonna find it!"

12/Bald Finch

Overlooking the Hudson and a horizon of Catskills, the asymmetrical building looked more like an Ivy League college than Matteawan State Hospital. Incorporating every roof and façade style known to man, the sign of its true identity was a twelve-foot perimeter fence topped with razor wire. It was nothing like the dramatic stage in *One Flew Over the Cuckoo's Nest*. It was a lunatic asylum.

And now, however oddly he had shaped his fate, it became Andrea's asylum too, although for different reasons and, he hoped, a different outcome.

The guard stood alone against a window, warming his back on the morning sunlight and casting a shadow of his body against the opposite wall. Thin and frail—and old enough to retire—he was amused by the giant-size image of himself. He was not capable of protecting the teachers from being assaulted by the criminally insane that inhabited the prison. All he could really do was call for help. Andrea knew that and disliked him.

Hilario Bonar stood in the middle of the room waiting to be recognized so that he could deliver an important message. When Andrea looked at him, he approached and said, "Valentine wants to see you. He'll be down soon."

Thinking Bonar could easily win first place in the queerest queer contest, Andrea said, "I'm surprised he let you out on your own."

"I'm not a child," Bonar said.

"Then you should get them permanently tattooed," Andrea said, pointing to Bonar's eyebrows. "India ink's poisonous."

"Good idea, Mister Andre. Maybe after my operation."

"I heard you want to go to Bangkok for that. Where're you going to get the money?"

Blushing through his white greasepaint, Bonar said, "Valentine is very mad at you. Boy, is he mad."

"You know how they do it, don't you? They split your penis down the center and fold back the flaps. Are you sure you want to do that?"

Bonar sat in a chair, folded his arms, and waited. He didn't know what to say or even how to read.

A few minutes later, Valentine came in with a two-guard escort and stood in front of Andrea's desk, resting his two fists on top of it like a defensive tackle on the scrimmage line ready to charge. His forearms were as thick and hairless as Bonar's thighs. Three-inch scars, evenly slashed up and down the forearms, were the price he had paid for being released from Attica and the tickets of admission to Matteawan. Now given the privilege of sleeping on a hospital ward rather than in a prison cell, he didn't care if they called him suicidal. Andrea thought the scars resembled the service stripes worn on the sleeves of Army class-A uniforms, each denoting three years of honorable duty.

Valentine's voice was calm and low-key, an obvious result of heavy medication. "High, listen," he said. "You picked the wrong guy to be law clerk. I helped more inmates win appeals than Porter. He doesn't know any of the Hispanics in here. He doesn't even know how to speak Spanish."

Valentine's big knuckles were now white as bone. Andrea longed for his pistol. If he could only blow the bastard away, he'd rid the world of one magnificently evil and unrepentant murderer. It would not only be an eye for an eye, but a way of doing business for a way of doing business. "There's room for only one clerk now," he said.

"You should know that I have plenty of inmates who want to see me work here."

Andrea had seen most of the inmates and didn't think that any of them were in shape to cause any trouble. "I was told to call them residents," he said. Valentine was a *big* toad in a small pond. At Attica, he was a *small* toad in a big pond.

Valentine punched the desktop with both fists, making Andrea recoil. "I heard you a Vietnam vet and have a bullet on the brain. Loud noises make you jumpy? You should get that taken out." Then he signaled to the guards to take him back to the ward.

As he was walking out of the library, Valentine took a shiny, red pencil out of his pocket and gave it to Finch, an inmate sitting at a table. Finch read the imprint on the barrel, went quickly to a wall-mounted pencil sharpener, inserted the pencil, and turned the crank until the lead came to a superfine point.

When it was time to close for lunch, Finch offered to help Andrea clean up. The guard brought the other inmates back to the wards.

"Do you have any jobs for art teacher?" Finch asked.

"Well, to be an art teacher, you'll need a bachelor's degree," Andrea said.

Finch whistled as if he had seen a pretty woman.

"How do you spell that?" Andrea asked.

"Spell what?" Finch asked.

"That wolf whistle."

"Don't know if I've ever read that."

Andrea unhooked a large ring of keys from his belt and locked the library door. As they walked toward the main gate, he said, "Not even in all the comics you read?" Andrea turned around for an answer. Finch looked the other way. "So, why do they call you Bald Finch? Is there really such a bird?"

Finch laughed and stroked his clean-shaven skull.

"You can go out from here," Andrea said, reaching the gate and putting the key into the lock. "The guard will let you in on the other end."

Suddenly, Andrea felt a sharp prick on the back of his neck. "Don't move!" Finch said. "You know, if I stab this pencil through your foramen magnum, you'll die?"

"What?" Andrea asked.

"I'm a brain surgeon going in for that bullet...."

"Wheeeeeeeeett wheeeeeeeeeeoooo!" Andrea whistled and jerked his head away. Cocking his right elbow, he swung it around and cracked Finch straight in the face. Stunned, Finch staggered backward, fell to the floor, and crawled around, snorting blood. He stood up but quickly lost balance and fell down again.

Curious about the whistle, Ron Contralto came out of his classroom. Noticing the standoff, he telephoned the goon squad. Backed into a corner, Finch stood up and began swinging the pencil as if it were a knife, but when he saw six guards come running with clubs and straightjackets, he began stabbing himself in the legs until the pencil broke in half. "Die bitch. Die!" he cried.

At once, Andrea realized who Finch was. After the guards had restrained him and were about to drag him away, he said, "Wait a minute. Let me see him." Unbuttoning Finch's shirt, he exposed his chest and a tattoo of a small bird. "Bald Finch, my ass. You're the rapist of Queens."

Finch spit at Andrea but missed.

"Hardly the Marquees of Queensberry," Ron said.

"Thanks, Ron," Andrea said. "I owe you one."

Every Wednesday afternoon, Andrea visited the Fishkill Correctional Facility, where he descended to the basement and opened a storage room labeled *Library*. The walls were covered with books people had donated to the institution so that the destitute might reflect upon their status in life— worthless discards. Hundreds of *Reader's Digest Condensed Books*, a 1952 edition of *Collier's Encyclopedia*, *The Berlitz Self-Teacher French*, Anthony Lewis' *Gideon's Trumpet*, a *Lamaze Guide to Childbirth*, the *Book of Mormon*, the *ALA Intellectual Freedom Manual*, and the New 32nd Edition of *Wiring Simplified*, signed by the author with the footnote, *The energy crisis is real. Use energy wisely—but do not waste it! H.P. Richter*. The only things of relevance were old *National Geographic* magazines, which Andrea displayed neatly on the tables.

Not even the photographic gems in these magazines would attract anyone other than the teachers on a break. What were the residents thinking as they walked past the library in single file? A graveyard of unknown names? Mini-caskets lining the shelves? Just a drifting anxiety, the feeling one has after a nightmare that cannot be remembered. Hopelessness surrounded by wordless walls that caged them away from their parents—a replica of the courtroom where they were pronounced defective delinquents, criminally insane, and incompetent to stand trial.

The classrooms, however, were much better, for they were empty and nonthreatening, rooms where the residents could be themselves—students, patients, inmates, defendants, criminals, and mentally retarded.

"Do you know who these people are?" Natalie asked.

"*Many things*," Andrea said.

Natalie didn't like Andrea ever since he wandered into her classroom one day to discover the fiasco live—a student from Bard College trying to teach one of the *many things* how to read, aggravated that day by one of them peeing in his pants.

"No, you don't understand," she said. "They are human beings."

"I realize that," he said.

"Why don't you do something rather than sit there like that? Can't you see they need help? The library is closed every day, and when you do show up—when is that, once a week?—no one uses it. Can you blame them? Look at this pathetic place. It's the worst library in the whole world."

"I wouldn't say that," he said, although he agreed with her assessment.

"You're not a librarian. You're just like a guard." Natalie stood up and turned toward the door. "You come in here, spread out a few magazines on tables, then go home and collect your pay."

"What do you expect me to do, work miracles?" And as she left the room, he shouted, "I'm an art teacher!"

The following week, Andrea borrowed a large laundry hamper from the loading dock and filled it with the books from the library. He made a dozen trips back and forth to the dumpster until the shelves were empty. He never returned to Fishkill to see the weeded library. The residents, however, now thought it was a great place to visit, look at the nice pictures in *National Geographic,* and draw pictures on them using colorful markers.

After liberating the library, Andrea visited the gym and joined his supervisor and four trustees in a three-on-three game of basketball. "Get on me, Scott," he said. "I can't lose." Scott obliged, and Andrea hit three jump shots in a row.

On Friday, he made a special trip to Fishkill to make sure the garbage truck picked up the dumpster and the one thousand escapees hiding inside it.

" . "

"Ladies and gentlemen, this is the captain speaking. I regret to inform you that there has been an impasse in negotiations with the hijacker. The authorities are doing everything they can to ensure your safety, but it appears that we won't be able to land anywhere and must remain aloft. We have plenty of fuel to fly to Heathrow or Orly if necessary to refuel, so there is no need to worry. The hijacker has informed me that he will let us go once we meet his demands. However, he has not told me of any further plans he has other than for us to continue with his story. Thank you."

"I thought so," Marge said. "You can't trust a hijacker no matter what, even if he is a sky marshal. Terrible to go on this far without a workable plot."

"Do you think he might turn this around and blame us? I mean, here we are trying to get it all read to save our skins, and we might find some turn in the story that sees us all blown up to kingdom come."

"Like he's planning to work us into the story, to make us resolve his plot."

"Good Lord, you may be right."

14/Bumping Rights

Six months away from his friends was more than he could bear, and he returned to see them on the first weekend that the weather was agreeable. He had called an hour before arriving and was happy to hear Ybette's cheerful voice once again. She told him to "drive carefully but waste no time."

Without knocking, he unlocked the door and walked inside. She was standing on the Oriental rug wearing a sheer, pink nightgown, not waiting for him like he had hoped, but arm-in-arm with another man—a short pilot still in uniform. Candles were lit around the room and Carole King was singing *"But it's too late baby, now it's too late"*—his former present to her—on his stereo. On the wall over the couch hung the *Hylomorphic Soul*, which had once been his academic attempt to de-sanctify art, as so many artists had done in the past, beginning with his hero Caravaggio. Now it was just an amusing sign hanging as a fornix over fornication.

Carol wasn't in, so he went into the bedroom without saying a word, brooding over being exiled from the scene and angry that Ybette had just set him up. He had no hope of ever finding someone like her upstate. Without her, how could he ever finish his novel? How could he have begun writing this story with an ending already in mind if he wanted it to be honest to life itself?

Andrea's entrance hadn't alarmed Ybette, so he understood this to mean that he was still her friend, like a brother in the family rather than a lover.

Nothing had changed, and nothing new had been added except for a roll of scented toilet paper in the bathroom. Being in the space of the story once again, he awaited the inspiration that had escaped him upon leaving it. He felt happy to be back, but sad to no longer be a part of it—to see the monk's robe hanging next to his uniform in the closet, the gun and badge hiding in the dresser drawer, the journal waiting on the nightstand. He wanted desperately to recapture the magic feeling of what he was and did, but all the connecting things were gone, the props a magician uses to entertain the audience and create himself.

His life of self-indulgence was bound to end in a forfeit, for there was never an honest place for him in it. This he knew and lamented.

He lay down on the bed and pressed his fingers against his forehead, searching for the trigger that would fire away the bullet chambered there.

He didn't know how he was going to get his precious rug out of the apartment, but he was sure that he needed help. He called Matt Bando but got no answer.

Ybette's purse caught his eye. Hurriedly, he opened it, pulled out her telephone book, spotted the name *Sen X*, jotted down the number, and rushed out of the place without saying a word.

During the next few weeks, he thought constantly about Ybette's statement, *I love you, but I'm not in love with you*, and about how she had used him. He felt glad that he hadn't attempted to console her as Carol had suggested. Even so, he called the senator one day out of curiosity. No one answered. He tried several times without a hit. He let it go for a day, and then tried again, but no answer. Then he realized that the number was not the senator's office or home number, but most probably a private number. And, one day, persistence paid off.

"This is Andrea," he said, using his feminine voice. "You don't know me. I'm a friend of Ybette."

"Andrea? Andrea who?" asked the senator.

"Andrea High."

"How'd you get this number?"

"From Ybette."

"Ybette who?"

"I bet you that..." laughing at the pun, "that you can't remember." Then, getting no reaction, "Are you listening?"

"Yes."

"Ybette. You know, the blond stewardess on Eastern."

"I don't recall any Ybette from Eastern."

"But she gave me your name and number."

"Are you sure you have the right name. What name did she give you?"

Andrea was silent a moment, then said, "Senator X."

The senator laughed, and then said, "Goodbye."

It had occurred to him to blackmail the senator, since adultery, kidnapping, and forced abortion were charges not to be overlooked, but Andrea didn't have the nerve to carry it out or any evidence to show. Besides, Ybette would never help him.

Taking revenge by seduction and castration occurred to him, but it would have been too sordid and complicated to carry out.

The next weekend, he went back to New York, this time in a rental truck ready to take back his furniture and Oriental rug. He wouldn't have been able to attempt the operation alone if it weren't for Bando and his friend Luca.

The wops from Brooklyn accompanied him up the elevator, gathering steam at every passing floor, for the success of the attack was based on surprise. Walking down the hallway, they had the look of a narc squad going in for a bust. When they reached the apartment, Andrea tried his key, but it didn't work. He rang the bell a few times until Ybette answered, keeping the security chain hooked on the door.

"Andrea, you're back. Why didn't you call?" she said.

"Why did you change the lock?" he said.

"For security reasons."

"Can I come in?"

"Not now. I have company."

"Where's Carol?"

"She moved out."

"Where's my rug?"

"It's still here."

"Let's go," Bando said, showing off his big athletic smile. But what really got Ybette's attention was Luca standing coyly in the background.

"Who's that with ya'll?" she said. "Al Pacino?"

"Al Pacino?" Bando said. "Hey, Al, come forward and take a bow."

"I'm just going to have to see the landlord, then," Andrea said. "Let's go."

As the three were leaving, Ybette unhooked the chain, stuck her head out into the hall and said, "Let me have one more month to find a place and you can have your rug back."

Turning around and leaping backward like a baseball player getting back on base, Bando stuck his foot between the door and the frame before Ybette could close it. He forced it open and walked inside.

Ybette smacked him across the face with all her might, stunning the ex-Special Forces Ranger a moment. His grin had a look of surprise that a slap could hurt so much.

Andrea and Luca walked in behind Bando. Baxter, Carol's ex-boyfriend, stood in a corner.

"Cozy arrangement," Andrea said.

"Luke, keep the door open," Bando said, "while we get the stuff out into the hallway. Let's get everything outside first, and then move it downstairs."

"You better get all your clothes out of the dressers," Andrea said.

"You bastards!" Ybette yelled, running into the bedroom to rescue her things.

Andrea's main concern was the Oriental rug, which he started to roll up. Baxter's eyes were glued on him all the time, waiting for an opening.

"I heard you got fired," Baxter said. "What'd you do, become a monk?"

When Andrea stood up, Baxter lunged at him with a right hook aimed at the jaw but hit him squarely on the left ear. Expecting the blow to cause a knockout, Baxter didn't follow up and waited for Andrea to fall.

As hard as the blow was, Andrea stood unmoved. Instinctively, he landed a flurry of kicks on Baxter's shins that backed him up against the wall. Had he wanted to ruin Baxter's amorous designs for the night, he would have aimed higher, but he really didn't care anymore.

Bando was surprised his middleweight partner could handle a heavyweight without even throwing a punch. "Those boots are against the law," he said.

Suddenly, Baxter grabbed Andrea in a bear hug, trying to pull him down, but Andrea struggled backwards, tripped over the stereo, and crashed to the floor.

Realizing that Baxter was now mastering the fight, Bando rushed over, pulled him off, and ran him headfirst into a corner.

When the scuffle died down, Ybette came back into the room wearing her pearl necklace. She cuddled up to Luca like a cat rubbing against a leg to get attention. She gave him a little note with her phone number on it, but he let it drop to the floor and went about helping to move the furniture, pretending not to notice her seductive body swaying around the room.

Once everything was out into the hallway, they worked recklessly to get it all down the elevator and onto the truck. Oddly, throughout the raucous affair, not one neighbor came out to see what was happening.

On the truck back to Brooklyn, Bando said, "And check out Luke, carrying on with the big-time stewardess."

"Must be the Al Pacino look," Andrea said.

"She's good-lookin'," Luca said.

"Sure. Good-lookin'," Bando said. "Better watch out for good-lookin'. She carries a wicked bitch-slap. Really stunned me for a second."

Referring to Bando's leap to get into the door, Andrea asked, "Where'd you learn that move? The Nam?"

"Called the feigned retreat," Bando said. "Your CO must have used it too."

"That he did," Andrea said, "but it never worked. The gooks were always onto it and never came back out to take a second look after we left."

Waking up to Bando's alarm clock next morning, Andrea thought that he was back on the job again. He sat up straight, trying to recall his last flight, but all he could remember was sitting at his desk in graduate school listening to Marvin Farber talk about the saber scars on German officers' faces. "What is this?" he said. "How'd I get here?"

"You're kidding?" Bando said, waking groggily. "After that siege last night?"

"Did I fall or get hit on the head?"

"Yeah, he gave you a good whack. You should have seen it coming."

"Who?"

"That blond guy. Heavy set. Staying with Ybette."

"Staying with Ybette? Oh, hell. Damn thing. I won't remember shit now," getting out of bed and standing in the middle of the room. "Give me a shot, a good shot on the other side of the head. Maybe that'll put it back in place."

"Are you serious?"

"Yeah, give me a good shot."

"You better see a doctor, man."

"Your headlock. That might work. Do it."

"Do what?"

"Put the bullet back in place."

"It'll do more than that."

"What is it, anyway?" Andrea said. "You probably just kick the guy in the balls, get him down on the ground, and put a headlock on him. Right?"

"It takes practice."

"What? Learning how to kick balls?"

Troubled by his friend's incompetence at self-defense, now that he was weaponless, Bando agreed to show him. "This block of instruction is classified secret, no foreign." He opened the front door to make sure no one was listening.

"You're serious," Andrea said.

"When an opponent sees you assume a martial arts stance, he's going to try to do one thing—tackle you and get you on the ground." Bando held up his index finger. "One way. One way in space and time." Putting the finger up against his lips, "The point is what?"

"I don't know."

"No, not I or he, but the air you breathe. The air you breathed. It's not I versus him. It's I versus me. Watch me. Go ahead; attack me, whichever way you want." Andrea lunged at him and, a second later, found himself helplessly on the floor in a head crank begging for mercy. Bando let him free.

"The thing men fear most is breaking their neck. They can take all kinds of hits, but the neck is most vulnerable. The neck supports the man, not the legs. Where it goes, that's where the man goes."

Holding his neck in pain, Andrea said, "How'd you get behind me so fast?"

"You tackled me in the past, and I tackled you in the present. That's how."

"Run that one by me again."

Bando laughed. "Work on it. It will come to you. Then, when you can step out of the past, put this neck crank on him." He showed Andrea the hold that would force any man to yield. They practiced it a few times until Andrea was good to go. "Now all you have to do is practice your tenses."

"Yes, master," Andrea said.

After another breakfast of Bando's famous cream-cheese omelets, Andrea was ready to depart for Buffalo.

"All your stuff is outside in the truck ready to go," Bando said. "Look, you can bunk here all you want, but I've got a flight to catch."

Andrea was so indebted to his friend, even for breakfast, he didn't know what to say. All he could do was shake the man's hand before he left for work.

Alone in the apartment, Andrea tried hard to remember what had happened, but nothing came back to him. Bando had told him about the affair, which was nothing about how Ybette must have felt sleeping on the cold floor without a bed or even a rug. What had he said to her, and she to him, while it was all taking place? What were her last words?

Inspecting the truck in daylight, he noticed that every piece of furniture had been damaged, especially his precious Bolero speakers, which played Ybette's last words for him in gouges, dents, and scratches. He would write to her and apologize, but not for a long while.

Before leaving Queens, he drove to his old apartment to see if his erstwhile neighbors—the charter stewardesses—were still living there. It was an act of faith for him to leave his forwarding address in case they ever needed a witness.

He recognized two of the names on the mailbox—Kight and Denali. He pressed the intercom button; a woman's voice answered, "Hello, who's there?"

"Andrea. Is Karen in?"

"No, she's not in. Who's this?"

"Andrea, her friend. Nancy, is that you?"

"No, this is Linda."

"Linda? You must be her new roommate. I have a present for Karen. I'd like to leave it with you, if you don't mind. Can I come up?"

Linda turned to her boyfriend, who was standing at her side, and said, "He has a package for Karen. Should I let him up?"

"Go ahead," he said.

Linda buzzed the door and Andrea took the elevator up to the top floor. At the end of the hallway, his erstwhile apartment door taunted him. He rang Linda's doorbell instead.

Linda peered through the peephole and whispered excitedly to her boyfriend, "I think it's the rapist. He's bald. Look!"

He looked through the peephole and whispered, "Damn, you might be right." Then he went for his holster that was on the table, pulled out his pistol, and took a combat position in a corner behind the door. "Go ahead. Open it."

The chain clanked against the metal frame as she opened the door. "Come on in, ah…. Sorry, I forgot your name already."

"Andrea. It's Andrea."

The door slammed shut with the force of spring-loaded hinges, revealing Gary Linnehan pointing his gun. "Raise 'em high!" Linnehan ordered.

Andrea raised his right arm as though he were taking an oath and then began walking backward into the living room. "It's you again," he said. "Here too? Damn, you get around." He dropped the package onto the couch and raised both arms. "I'm not going to tell about your gun, if that's what you're worried about."

Linnehan pointed at a chair and said, "Get over there! Sit down!"

With eyes glued on the gun and not watching where he was walking, Andrea kicked over a small wastebasket, spilling trash about the floor. "I'm sorry," he said, sitting in the chair.

Linnehan reached into the closet and retrieved a pair of handcuffs from his jacket. Keeping his eyes locked on Andrea, he moved forward, not exactly sure how he was going to handcuff his assailant and keep the gun fixed on him at the same time. He didn't trust Linda, so he said, "Down on the floor! Face down!" Andrea didn't move, having gone far enough with the game. Linnehan lunged at Andrea as if to pistol-whip him, but slipped on the trash and fell forward, hitting the coffee table and discharging a round through the wall, making Linda scream sharply.

Now flat on the floor, Linnehan tried to recover his pistol but was late.

"Nice shot," Andrea said, picking up the pistol. "Linnehan's magnum got out of hand," aiming at the special agent's head. "Three-fifty-seven, the kind used by Treasury agents. Customs too." Ears ringing loudly now, he could hardly hear himself talk. "Makes too much damn noise, don't you think?"

Linda noticed the thing that Gary had slipped on. She stepped on it—soft and bouncy—making the nipple swell. Then she kicked it under the table.

"I wonder if you hit old lady Shapiro," Andrea said.

Gary lay motionless on the floor, positive there was a way out of the jam, if only he could find it.

"Carrying your gun off duty, special agent Gary Linnehan, is a violation of Customs regulations." Andrea walked over to the closet and rifled through Linnehan's jacket until he found his ID. Opening it, he said, "What do we have here? A counterfeit ID! United States Department of the Treasury, Bureau of Customs." Showing it to Linda, "Look, it's counterfeit."

Linda checked the ID card and said cheerlessly, "You said you were an FBI agent!" Linnehan eyed the window as an avenue of escape.

"Yeah, just like he thought I was printing counterfeit money in my garage. How stupid." Linnehan got up off the floor and sat in the chair. "An FBI agent. Isn't it a felony to impersonate a federal law enforcement officer? Well, I guess if your job is sniffing through people's underwear all day, you might have a good excuse. But then, if he really was, he wouldn't be able to carry this monster of a gun. A beauty, don't you think? The perfect weapon to take skyjacking. Make sky marshals shit their pants to see a weapon such as this." He aimed at various objects around the room. "Nice balance. Just the story I was looking for. A little sex and a big gun. A sky marshal is fired, falsely accused of rape by a counterfeit FBI agent, takes his stew-girlfriend hostage and skyjacks a plane. But where shall he go? Bangkok? Yes. Bangkok, so he can find his ladyboy waiting behind a bush."

Linnehan smiled, seemingly to distract his prey from his wandering eyes, which were looking for an opening or a weak spot.

"What's that face you make?" Andrea said. "You don't agree? You should try one. Looks and acts just like a real woman. You'll feel he's one hundred percent woman. And he won't hit you with all those hang-ups, like the monthly period, fear of getting pregnant, or abortions. Sex is free and ready anytime you want it."

"You wouldn't dare," Linda said.

"Dare?" Andrea said. "That's a good word for it. So, what do you think? Do we have a plan?"

Andrea aimed at a huge painting of a man—a headshot—hanging over the couch. He had never seen a worse attempt at portraiture. The head was basketball size with skin color to match. "Yours?" he asked Linda.

"Yes, why?" she said.

"Looks like a basketball player," he said. "Nothing wrong with that, it's just that, well, a painting class might help." Then, looking at Linnehan, "Well, what d'ya say?"

Linnehan didn't answer but was still plotting an attack.

"So, now it's my turn to play FBI agent." Kicking around the trash on the floor, "Well, if there're no takers...." Andrea waited a few seconds, and then walked out the door.

Instead of escaping down the elevator, and, still having the key, he unlocked the door of his old apartment and went inside. No one was there.

Not surprisingly, the walls in the hallway were still stained with vomit—the only work of art in the place. John's monthly flight schedule was on the dresser. Andrea opened the drawers and was amazed to see at least a dozen pistols jammed inside—automatics and revolvers, big and small, including the standard-issue .38 stainless-steel detective special. John was not on duty and no doubt shacking up with his girl. "Sure obeys the regulations." The other drawers held bullets and a fresh supply of hashish. "And be sure to break the law while you're at it."

The idea rushed through him—skyjack John's plane to Rome! The schedule was right there with the flight numbers and departure times; the drawers gave him his choice of weapons. "Take it! Take his gun and bullets. Take the blackjack. And take his PPK," diving through the assortment of pistols and stuffing his pockets. "And a thirty-two in my boot. Yeah!"

The doorbell rang. He went out and looked through the peephole. It was Mrs. Shapiro, so he opened the door.

"Did you hear a shot?" she said.

"Yeah," Andrea said. "It came from that apartment over there."

"That's what I thought. I thought they were after the rapist. The bullet came through the wall and hit me in the back. No, not my back. The back of my chair."

"Are you all right?"

"Yes, I already called the police. They should be here any minute. Say, you're one of the sky marshals, aren't you?"

"Yes, I am. I'll go check it out. You go back to your apartment and lock the door."

She rushed back to her apartment without hesitation.

He waited a few minutes, went to Shapiro's apartment, and rang the bell. When she opened up, he gave her Linnehan's gun with the instructions, "I took this away from the FBI agent next door that shot you. He said it was an accident. Give it to the police when they come. I have to go to work now, but I'll be back tonight. My name is John. Stay inside now and don't answer the door for anyone but the police."

"FBI agent? Oh, my. Thank you, John," she said, taking the gun excitedly, smiling at it, and going back inside.

Andrea ran down the rear stairwell to escape. And just after he got away in his truck, a police car drove up and took his place.

15/Venus Shot

The rain stopped and the sky cleared so quickly that Andrea understood why Florida was the perfect place for people living on borrowed time. Even hurricanes didn't stay long, often passing through in just twenty-four hours. So claimed his grandfather, who was used to weeklong, bad-weather assaults in Buffalo.

"The air is so fresh outside," Andrea said.

"This time of year," Carmen D'Oria said. "I love it. Up north, it's getting colder and pretty soon winter. Cold. Snow. But here, you see the weather change. It gets cooler. Fresh, yes. Like you say. You wait and wait, but winter never comes. You wait and wait, but it never gets cold. Never snows. Like waiting for death that never comes. It's wonderful. So alive. You get that feeling?"

"Yeah, gramps. How are you feeling otherwise? Any better?"

Carmen looked out into the hallway to check on the nurse and said, "Between you, me, and the wall, the doctor said I might live to be eighty-five."

"Hey, that's great news."

"Hey, keep it to yourself."

Odd request, Andrea thought. Shouldn't a dying man who gets a new lease on life want everyone to know? "Anyone come down to see you?"

"No. Haven't' seen anyone yet. It's a long drive, and your aunts and uncles don't think I'm worth the money to take an airplane."

"How's the food here?"

"Not bad, but I tell everybody it stinks. They believe me and bring me food. This one fella that comes see me even drove to Key West to get me a genuine key lime pie. His name is Joe Wishe. A school teacher. He's a nice fella, Joe. He volunteers for Meals on Wheels. He used to bring me lunch every day."

"Was the pie any different coming from Key West?"

"Hell, yes. Joe's a compassionate young man, like yourself. He brings me anything I want. I told him I have no family. You can get away with that living down here alone."

"I delivered meals in Brooklyn once. To needy people. There was this one guy who couldn't talk, and all he said was beep-beep. Just beep-beep. It stood for everything."

"Joe wept beside my bed when I was in the ICU. Thought I was ready to die right there on the spot. He asked me if I wanted to see a priest, and I said yes. I asked him why he wept, and he said I reminded him of his grandfather who died without seeing a priest."

"Do you think he was honest or just pulling your leg?"

"What do you think?"

"I can't say. Did you see a priest?"

"Yeah, he came to visit. But that's all. We just talked. You know the story."

Andrea recalled the heated arguments they always had on Sunday afternoons over cups of hot tea and homemade biscotti. "Yeah, I remember."

"When I die, Joe's going to get a big surprise when he learns that I'm not his grandfather."

Andrea laughed and said, "You shouldn't drive a red Cadillac, gramps."

"Don't forget my big boat," Carmen laughed heartily.

"I won't, gramps. And your top-floor condo on the beach. I won't gramps. I won't."

Holding his chest and unable to control his laughter, Carmen complained, "You're going to make me split my stitches, you…. Mannaggia, brutta bestia la gelosia…."

Traveling to Miami just to see Ybette was risky, since the chances of finding a stewardess at home were about one in five. But this time she was definitely at home, having had her wings clipped by a hyperactive horse that threw her while on vacation at a dude ranch in Wyoming. She had been so handicapped by the accident that she actually had time to respond to one of Andrea's letters apologizing for the sad affair in New York. He had hoped that maybe so humbled by it, she would actually be thinking about settling down, although she hadn't said this on the phone.

It had been over a year since their breakup, and she looked as beautiful as ever. He gave her a light kiss on the cheek, afraid that anything more would topple her off the crutches. "You had one bad fall," he said.

"I had a bad horse," she said. "Did you check out of your hotel?"

"No, not yet," he said, unsure that her hospitality would last the night.

"I told you to. You know you're welcome to stay here."

"I like this," he said, entranced by her apartment. "Very sunny and breezy. And all to yourself. I like your entrance. Directly to the outside. No dark hallways like in New York."

"I should be on the first floor, don't you think?"

"You didn't expect to be thrown from a horse when you took this place, now did you?"

"I couldn't help it. I had to show them I could ride, being from Kentucky and all. But the mount they gave me was such a stud. Justin, you should have seen him. Started to nose an old mare first chance he got. Then jumped right up on top of her and started humpin' her like all get out. I couldn't hold on for dear life."

"Really? That's funny."

"The fall wasn't, believe me. But that wasn't the thing that crippled me. When he climaxed himself, he got so dizzy, he fell off the side of that mare and landed right on top of my leg. I never felt such awful pain. Broke it in two places."

"I'm sorry," he said. "Did you sue them?"

"Once my attorney gets over laughing about it. He's a hoot. Oh, Justin, I'm so glad you came."

"How have you managed all by yourself?"

"It's been hell, let me tell you." She couldn't tell him that she had no other friends willing to stay with her in such a condition.

Looking at the oil painting over the couch, he said, "I forgot that I was such a good artist."

"I've had more comments about that," she said. "People think that it's me riding my own thighs, but I tell them that it's not really. It was done before we met."

"Go ahead and tell them that. Tell them it was a premonition; a premonition that actually happened. A painting that willed itself to be."

"Justin, how silly. A painting doesn't have a will."

"Oh, no? Then why is it called *Hylomorphic Soul?*"

Ybette started to laugh so hard, she had to sit down for fear of falling.

Later, it was his turn to laugh, watching her struggle to pull on a bikini over the leg cast. "You should have been a contortionist," he said, getting excited by the suggestions of her body. He got closer and kissed her on the shoulder.

"That's nice," she said. "Thank you."

At the beach, she was embarrassed and afraid to use the crutches, so he had to carry her to the water. "Your navel is so beautiful," he said. "It reminds me of Botticelli's *Birth of Venus.*"

"Justin, I always get a chuckle out of you."

Once they found a place on the sand, she asked, "Justin, I want your honest opinion as an artist. Why do you love it?"

"Love what?"

"My Yankee shot."

"Oh, your Yankee shot? So, now my Yankee opinion means something. Well, I'd say it's not like most you see. It's open. Vulnerable. Sexy, that's all."

"Like what?"

"Not like a bullet hole. That's this one here," pointing to his forehead. "This is a gook shot. That's a *Venus shot*. The ultimate rendering."

"None better?"

"It's perfect," taking off his sandals and sizing up the water. "The only thing you could do to make it better is, ah, maybe teach it to sing."

She laughed again, unable to talk. Then she said, "Oh, I love it when you get your funny up."

Andrea drew with his finger a large heart in the wet sand pointing toward the water.

"That's so nice, Justin," she said.

Quickly, a wave came in and washed away half of it.

"Now, I know you can't go swimming, but do you mind if I indulge?"

The water was clear, blue, and cool. He swam out fifty yards to a sandbar upon which he stood and appeared to her to be walking on water. He took ten minutes to regain his breath, and then swam leisurely back toward shore.

"I almost ran out of steam on the way out," he said, drying off with a towel.

"You swam your ass off, Justin," she said.

"I'm not sure if I have the energy to carry you back to the car."

"Well, I'm not crawling back."

"Okay, my dear. This is not going to be like Rhett Butler carrying Scarlet upstairs, but it will get you there." He stood her up and held her arms as if they were going to dance, then stepping under her body, swept her up into a fireman's carry. "This is how my platoon sergeant saved my life in the Nam."

His love is leaving me, she thought. He's making me sink down into my hips. His shoulder bone cuts into my ribs, walking like a stud ready to throw me off, breaking my other leg.

Reaching the car, he cleaned the white sand off her tan body and then gave her a very long kiss, going so far as to feel her teeth with his tongue. As unhappy as she was, her mouth tasted sweet.

That evening, he sat on the edge of the bed not knowing whether she would allow him to make love to her. This is how it will be at the end, he thought, not knowing for sure whether we will be acceptable to God.

She hobbled out of the bathroom and, not asking for help, sat on the opposite side of the bed.

"Do you need any help?" he asked.

"No, I'll be fine," she said, lifting her legs onto the bed.

"I should have picked a more appropriate time to visit."

"No, you've been very helpful."

He plumped the pillow and reclined next to her. "The fan reminds me of a helicopter. Feels great."

"Where are you working now?"

"The ICA," he whispered.

"The CIA?"

Andrea laughed, knowing that for him the two were synonymous. "No, the ICA. The International Communications Agency. It's part of the State Department."

"So, what do you do?"

"I run books."

"That's strange. What books?"

"Books about the United States that people in other countries ought to read."

"That's interesting. So, what do you do? I mean, what's your job title? Librarian?"

"I'm an ethical information specialist. An EIS."

"I've never heard of that job before. Ethical information specialist. There, I said it. A real mouthful. I'll never remember it."

The cover story works, he thought. Now I'm home free.

She turned on her side to face him. He turned on his side to face her. They started kissing, she thinking he was the loneliest person in the world, and he thinking she was the most beautiful woman in the world.

No more unwanted pregnancies from a man I don't love.

No more pre-reflective ejaculations for a woman I love.

Nothing is standing in my way. No one. No thing. No memories. "I love you, Justin," she whispered.

Could this be true? Is this really Ybette saying this to me? I don't know what to say. "Yes," he said. "Shall I?"

"Yes."

Taking off his shorts, "Give you...."

"Oh, yes. Please."

"My love?"

She arched her back, and he helped slip the nightie over her head. My love's in love. Maybe.

She was very receptive, just like the first time they made love.

"It feels so good," she said.

He lingered on these words for a long time, not believing that the pleasure would ever make her say, *I'm in love with you.* He couldn't ask her.

Soon, the initial passion subsided. He moved off her gently, as though trying not to wake her. He felt like he had eaten tiramisu as an appetizer, and now she wanted him to go in for the steak. He didn't say a word and just lay perplexed at her side.

"Are you all right?" she asked.

He turned to her and held her hand tightly, afraid of drowning in her false pity. "I'm fine," he said. "Just a little tired."

"All that swimming in the hot sun is bound to put you in a state," she said. "You're not used to this weather. Just relax here a few days. I'm not going anywhere. Now go to sleep and I'll fix you a nice breakfast in the morning."

They slept in each other's arms for some time, until a noise in the living room woke them. "What's that?" she asked.

"A voice," he said.

She called out, "Is anyone there?"

"Sounds like a child's voice," he said.

"Mommy! Mommy! Come help me."

"A boy's voice," she said. "I hear it. Go see, Justin."

Andrea got out of bed, more nervous than he would be if it were a dream. He said, "I wish I had my gun."

"A gun? It's a boy, can't you hear?"

"Okay, stay here. I'll go check."

The living room was empty, but he still heard the voice calling, "Mommy, mommy!" He turned his head to catch the direction of the call and realized that it was coming from the wall behind his large painting. He went back to bed and said, "It's your next door neighbor's kid crying."

"It can't be. There's no next door neighbor that way. There's a stairwell on the other side of that wall."

"Okay, I'll go check outside then. Stay here."

He got up again and opened the front door. A humid but cool breeze swept over him. He looked out into the dark morning and saw no one. Ybette came up behind him and stepped out onto the landing. "Maybe we're both dreaming," he said.

They went back to bed and returned to sleep, this time separated, but slightly touching each other.

Her deep breathing gave him the opportunity. He placed his pillow beside her and got up slowly without waking her. It was five o'clock and still dark, so he had time to get it done before she awoke for breakfast. He picked up her purse, sneaked into the bathroom, and found a letter inside addressed to Ybette Rember, EAL, Miami Int'l Airport. He opened it and read.

Meeting you by chance at the hotel has meant so much to me, especially after my divorce. If I had known 20 years ago that Eastern had such beautiful flight attendants, I wouldn't have joined American. I truly believe we were meant for each other. That is why I was troubled when you said that you "try on" other relationships in order to reassure yourself of the love you have for him. What was it you said he was? A librarian? Surely, you should be able to do much better than that. It seems unreal that you should be in love with him. You belong in the air, not on the ground in some stuffy library. Flying is in your blood, just like it is in mine. Blue skies filled with white clouds as far as the eyes can see. The rush of wind outside the cabin. Nothing in your way. Nothing in front of you saying "Stop!" Just continuous propulsion, straight ahead, through the air with everything fully under control, and safely....

Unable to finish, he put the letter back in the purse and returned to bed.

The hard cast weighed heavily on his arm. He wasn't sure that she was resting it there on purpose, but seeing that she was still asleep, he freed himself carefully and got out of bed.

She got up later and apologized for not making him breakfast as she had promised. She felt terribly depressed about a dream she had.

"Was it about your leg?" he asked.

"No, much worse."

"Then, what about?"

"I can't say. It's so depressing."

"Then maybe you should see a therapist."

"I've had this dream before."

"They say we have dreams in order to adjust the mind to see reality more clearly. It's like artists using a dark background to make the light in the foreground appear more vibrant."

Ybette dwelled on this idea as she sat down carefully at the table for breakfast.

"How about a hot cup of tea?" he said. "You know, when I was flying Continental, a stew wanted to serve me lemon when my tea already had cream in it."

"Well, how did you order it?"

"Cream and sugar. How do you want your tea?"

"With cream and lemon, please," she laughed.

"You silly fool," he said, making her laugh even more.

While Andrea was out shopping for groceries, Ybette returned the favor by doing his laundry. Buried deep in the bag was his journal, which she couldn't resist reading. It began with his entry on visiting his grandfather in Palm Beach, and most recently, about his visit with her.

I'm still not aware of the truth regarding her abortion. She never mentions it, and I dare not ask. The temptation is somewhat diminished when I'm with her. It's better not to write heady letters. Keep them matter-of-fact. She appears to be more motherly now due to her broken leg. She needs loyal companionship. She would surely be a good mother, but I'm taking precautions not to suggest this to her. On this matter, she is very consistent, and I don't see her being a very good character in the novel. On the contrary, isn't it the thing that would make for the greater mystery—the nondisclosure of the truth? I mean, not even in the end!

She asked me about my job. I got careless and mentioned that I was an EIS. I couldn't bring myself to use my CS. I was embarrassed what she might say—an ex-sky marshal turned into a librarian. Could there be any greater inconsistency in one's life? Maybe that's why we attract one another.

Inside the journal was a small envelope addressed to Mr. Santo Trafficante, Jr., 2505 Bristol Ave., Tampa, FL. It was unsealed, so she opened it and read the handwritten letter. *We know all about your filthy lucre from drugs, pornography, prostitution, gambling, and bribery operations, and we intend to stop it. We know all about your operations in Florida and the southeast. We cannot wait for the day when the revolution takes hold in this country and will soon begin to fight you people with the only weapons that you understand—guns and bombs. We'll come in the daylight and not sneak around in the dark like the dirty cockroaches you are. In appearance, you are scary, but in reality you are NOT powerful. It is not the Mafia, but the people who are really powerful. We know that* power grows out of the barrel of a gun*. We'll finish the job the Prime Minister started over ten years ago when he kicked your undesirable ass out of Cuba. We don't like what you've been doing to our members in Miami. I don't need to sign my name to this letter, for you'll learn my true identity in due time. WORKERS OF ALL COUNTRIES, UNITE!*

The moment that Andrea spotted an octopus sitting on ice in the fish department, he realized that he had forgotten to mail the letter to Trafficante. It was a terrible breach of security to let it out of his sight. When he returned to the apartment and heard the sound of the clothes drier going, he braced himself for the infamous bitch-slap.

Surprisingly, Ybette was on the balcony reading a book. He put the groceries away and joined her. "Your car rides nicer than mine," he said, pouring out a glass of iced tea and sitting beside her.

With eyes fixed on her book, she asked him, as if stumped by a name there, "Who is Santo Trafficante?"

Realizing that she had seen the letter, he said, "Going through other people's dirty laundry, you should have been a customs agent."

Still avoiding his eyes, she said, "I was just trying to be helpful."

"Did you open it?"

Closing the book and finally looking at him, she said, "Yes, I did."

"Why?"

"It was unsealed."

Now I'm in a pinch, he thought. I can't deny having seen it myself and say it was just my job to mail it. Give her the *I'm not at liberty to discuss my job* routine. But she's already read it. I can't say it's part of my job. So, do I have to kill her, like in the movies?

"Are you a communist?" she asked.

That too is a no-no. "Of course not," he said. "It's a project for my book. I'm writing about a sky marshal that thinks the Mafia is hijacking planes to Cuba in order to incite the government to take action against Castro."

"But don't you know that this man is dangerous? He could get you killed."

"He won't know who I am. There's no way he could track me down. Don't worry. It's not dangerous."

"I wish you wouldn't anyway."

Andrea disliked the noise of the highway. "I didn't hear that traffic yesterday," he said. "Was the road closed or something?"

"It's the breeze, Justin. You can't hear it when the breeze comes from the ocean."

"I see. And when there's no breeze?"

"Traffic noise."

"What if the breeze swirls around, like a wash machine?"

"Oh, just please...."

"I hope you didn't put the letter in the wash."

"Oh, it's safe, Justin. Don't worry. I wouldn't dare let on about secret government work. I was just curious about what y'all did in our nation's capital."

"The letter is not government work," he insisted.

"Which means that you don't have to kill me after all?"

Andrea laughed. "For reading classified information? I wouldn't, even if it were. I'd just have you arrested and deported back to...."

"Justin, you stand in need of a good lickin'."

"Yeah? You and whose army?"

"Justin, you fool. Don't ask stupid questions. Why, Robert E. Lee's, of course." She put down her book, looked at him and smiled. "Now, how 'bout a nice Yankee dime, sugar?"

He started digging into his pockets until he saw her pursed lips waiting for a kiss.

" . "

"John, wake up!" says Marge. "Have you read chapter fifteen yet?"

"No. I'm afraid I dozed off. Must have been that wine."

"Well, you didn't miss much. You can skip it. Adds nothing to the story."

"What's it about?"

"Matt Bando gets a job in L.A. as a narc and writes a letter to Andrea. Andrea responds and says he was married to a nurse, got divorced, and still works in Washington in the ICA as an ethical information specialist, a cover story of some sort. If you want to read it, go ahead, but I'd go on to chapter sixteen."

"I think I'll just skim through it, just in case."

16/Out of Touch

Realizing that he had lost contact with his ex-flying partner, Matt Bando sat down and typed a letter.

Hi Andrea,

It's Sunday morning and I have time to fill you in…I am now a special agent for the BNDD…The same thing is happening now in the war on drugs, and I am not about to give up all that firepower…My last flight as a sky marshal was on Pan Am to Bangkok. What a swan song. I asked my escort about that thousand-dollar aphrodisiac we heard about, and she took me to a restaurant that served bull penis curry. Not the same thing, since it was only five bucks, but it tasted pretty good. Now I have a philosophical question for the make-believe Buddhist monk. Why eat bull penis to get a bull's penis when the bull eats grass to get a bull's penis?…How is your love life? Have you heard from the big Y? Did you ever finish your masters? Did you ever finish that book, and was it published? If so, send me a copy or tell me where I can buy one…That is all for now.

Andrea waited for almost a year before responding to Bando's letter. He wrote:

Hi Matt! Sorry for not writing sooner, but there were so many loose ends…I too have a new job. I work for the ICA, not to be confused with the CIA. I'm an ethical information specialist. Could be the only one of its kind in the world. Don't ask me what I do. I'll tell you later. I had initially planned to get placed in the Far East office in Bangkok, but the person there has grandfathered in the position and won't rotate till she retires. I'm waiting.

I've gotten hitched. Have you? My wife is a nurse…She's half Italian, half French. The perfect combination. She works nights…I must tell you about my job someday when we meet. It's not what you might think. I've lost touch with Ybette. The last time we met, we didn't get it off so well. I couldn't figure her out, one way or the other. She's still flying for EAL and firmly entrenched in the swinging singles lifestyle. One day she'll wake up an old maid and curse herself for not raising a family to take care of her…I've also given up on the book. It had great action but no essence; too many particulars that didn't suggest any consistent plot. And no climax. I'm still waiting for the Big Bang to turn the story on…Someday, when I save up enough money, I'm going back to Bangkok and try that thousand-dollar bowl of whatever. You know, the greatest aphrodisiac. RMB, I think they called it. Thinking about the good old days. Yours incognito, Andrea

Bill Gold took out his credentials, placed them on the conference table in front of Andrea and opened it slowly, like it was a book to be read. Andrea glanced at it, surprised at the gentle nature of the agent's approach.

"This is your follow-up interview," Gold said. "I have several questions based on our initial investigation of the information in your application for top-secret, SCI clearance, if you don't mind."

"Not at all," Andrea said. "Go right ahead."

After asking routine questions about Andrea's background, Gold said, "In the financial liabilities section, you stated that your mortgage is twenty thousand, while your assets show the house to be worth one hundred and fifty thousand. That's a sizeable down payment. How do you account for those assets?"

"My father's estate."

Gold flipped through the pages until he found an item and said, "It says that your father was a steelworker. You had a brother who shared in the estate. Your share was half, I take it? Was there any other source of income?"

"My grandfather's will."

"Yes, I see. How much did you receive on that?"

"Ninety thousand."

"Anything else?"

"A condo and a boat in Florida."

"How come they're not listed?"

"My grandfather just died a few weeks ago."

"How much is the condo worth?"

"I don't know exactly."

"You need to find out and add them too." Then Gold produced a memorandum from the U. S. Department of the Treasury—the image of death in Andrea's eyes. The ghost of sky marshals past loomed before him. They got me now!

"You still owe the government two thousand dollars," Gold said, pointing to the memo. "So say the folks at IRS. They claim you absconded with a travel advance when you were a sky marshal and never paid it back."

"I remember the advance, when I was on TDY to L.A., and paying it back every payday, and when I resigned."

"Do you have anything to prove this?"

"You mean they don't?"

Gold shook his head no.

"That figures for Treasury," Andrea said. "I did save all my pay stubs."

"That's smart. Please bring them in and show me to clear this up."

When Andrea returned home that night, eager to go through his old pay statements to show the idiots at the IRS he had paid his debts, he was struck silly by an empty house. On the kitchen counter was a note from Laurie attached to a separation agreement prepared by her lawyer.

Andrea. Please sign this. I have spent my last night coming home after work and finding you sleeping in bed rather than waiting for me like a husband should. Once a week don't get it in my book. Laurie.

He was more amused than distressed that every piece of furniture had been moved out while he was at work. "She must have been planning this for months. The sofa, table, chairs, stereo, and TV. Even the beds! All gone."

He rushed outside to check his Bangkok bank and, noticing that the ground was undisturbed, let out a sigh of relief. Then he patted the plot like it was a baby that needed to burp.

He slept on his Oriental rug that night, wondering why she hadn't taken that too.

" ."

"It adds something," John says. "Watch out for that RMB. It could mean ready-made bomb!"

"Oh, my, John. What are we going to do?"

"Hang in there, Marge. We'll think of something."

17/Twins

Ybette promised to show him "something new and exciting," if only he would pick her up at the airport. It was New Year's Eve, and the weather was good, so he made the trip from Annapolis to Washington National in no time.

Standing beside his car, he waited in front of the arrivals terminal, worried that she would be unrecognizable after ten years. Every other stewardess that came out was blond, and he thought that maybe she had changed her hair color. He couldn't bet on her wearing the navy blue uniform that she hated, but when she came out in a chic yellow uniform, he was puzzled by the sad look on her face. Limping like a crippled pigeon, she spotted him, dropped her bag, and gave him a big hug. He grabbed her bag and, in an attempt to cheer her up, said, "Old war wound?"

It was a terrible joke. She hobbled to the car door and waited impatiently. But when they got underway, she thanked him for being so kind to pick her up.

"What happened?" he asked.

"Oh, Justin, I feel like I'd been rode hard and put away wet."

He smiled and said, "You don't mean...?"

"Of course not. It's my leg. It's got a mind of its own. I didn't even see the bag in the aisle, just went and tripped over it."

"And upset your leg again?"

Exasperated by the thought that her leg would never be fully healed, she began to cry. Then, wiping away her tears, "Do you know where you're going?"

"The hotel. Yeah, we had a conference there a few months ago."

They beat the crew's van to the hotel, which was just a short drive into Arlington. As soon as they were inside the room, she threw her arms around him in utter exhaustion, unable to take the last few steps. He carried her the short distance to the bed and laid her down gently.

"I must have walked down that aisle a hundred times," she said. "The pain was so bad...."

"Do you have any medication?"

"I was doing well without it, but then it came back when I tripped on that damn bag."

"It'll get better."

"It's been so long since I had any pain," she said. "Can you get me a pill? They're in my purse."

"I had hoped we could go to the disco. Did you hear that music downstairs?"

"Justin, I'm sorry. I was such a fool to call you away from your friends."

"It doesn't matter." Looking at her body stretched flat on the bed, "I'm glad I came."

She smiled, taking the pill. "Do you still work for the CIA?"

"CIA? You mean ICA. Yeah, it's okay. Not like flying for a living. I might even get a transfer overseas. Maybe Bangkok."

She didn't want to bring up his divorce, since she was in no mood for argument, but let it slip out anyway. "You're now free to go anywhere you want."

"Yeah, single again," getting up and turning on the TV.

"Justin, I told you it wouldn't work."

He couldn't remember that she had told him that. He drew in a deep breath and then exhaled slowly. "Right after she left was the hardest part," he said. "At night, I could still hear her breathing. It was like she was still there sleeping beside me."

"Justin, I'm sorry," as though his wife had died.

"It's not so much that she left all of a sudden; it's just that I didn't know why. There had to be another guy. I didn't know where she lived. I even tailed her friend from work one night, and I got a nasty letter from her lawyer saying that I had better stop stalking her or else they'd call the police."

"Justin, no!"

"Then, one day, a year later, when I was walking out of the dentist's office, I ran into Laurie as she was coming in. It was as though I had met her for the first time. No emotions whatsoever. There was something peculiar about her face. She looked so plain and commonplace. But when I saw the mini surgical scar on her chin, I realized what it was."

Andrea paused a moment, giving Ybette a chance to ask, "What was it?"

"She had a small mole removed. I thought it was petty. I never realized such a small thing meant so much to her."

"More than you, Justin?"

"Well, I don't feel fully responsible for the marriage anyway. A shrink had advised me to marry her."

"A psychiatrist?"

"Bowled-over psychotherapy. Something I couldn't get from the VA. You have to pay for that. I had insurance, so I went. It was great. My main concern was my mental condition for marriage. In our last session, Doctor Silvernail said, 'Andrea, there's nothing wrong with you. Go ahead and marry Laurie.' So, I did."

Ybette was silent.

"After Laurie pulled out, I went to see a priest and told him the whole story, especially about her not wanting to have children. He told me without hesitation, 'Dump her!' Which I did, from my mind. So, I must be the only man on earth that had a shrink tell him to get married and a priest tell him to get divorced. Usually, it's the other way around."

"How strange."

"You know, I even joined a single's club at the church. There were only three girls in it. And two guys. I sort of made things even."

"Did you find anyone?"

"I really didn't fit in. I felt like an oddball, like a Corvette in a used car lot filled with Fords and Buicks. Then I joined a lonely hearts club. I think I got one date out of it. We met in a coffee house, and she was upset about my complexion. She was looking for a guy with olive complexion, and I had always thought that, being an FBI, that I had an olive complexion."

"FBI?" she asked.

"You know, full-blooded Italian. I guess I had lost my tan from not flying to San Juan."

"FBI? You too? We must be related."

"You're not Italian," he said.

"Yeah, but I'm full-blooded Irish!"

"So we can't get married after all," Andrea laughed.

Sharing simple initials, she worried that the same would happen to her one day. Turning toward the TV, she said, "Change the channel."

"That's what I say," he said, getting up and changing channels.

"Johnny Carson," she said.

"No, it's Frank Sinatra," he said.

"Back to Johnny," she said, laughing.

"What do you think of Sinatra?" he asked.

"He's a very powerful man," she said.

"He's a cafone!"

"A phoney?"

"No, listen. Ca-pho-nay. It's Italian for a guy who thinks he's a big shot, because he hangs around with the Mafia."

"That got him into trouble, didn't it?"

"He thinks he's a tough guy and can push people around, like he's got a hit man backing him up."

"Do you think he can have people killed?"

Andrea laughed. Not even an admirer of his voice, he said, "Sure. He's got enough money and connections. That's all he has—money. Do you know he dodged the draft because he had a bad eardrum?"

"So?"

"So?! He copped out on serving in the war but won an Academy Award for acting as a war hero."

"What's wrong with not wanting to go to war? If all they...they called a war... and no one showed."

"Nothing, if he admits being a coward."

Andrea thought that because the heroes of World War II had fought for a more noble cause than the Vietnam War, the standard for cowardice was different.

"What about contentious objector?"

"Conscientious objector? No excuse. There were a lot of noncombatant jobs in the Nam. You didn't have to go to the field if you didn't want to. Only fifteen percent actually saw combat in the field."

"And you were one of them?"

"Well, I didn't drive a truck, if that's what you mean."

"Is that where this if from?" she asked, pointing to the scar between his eyes.

"Do you know that Sinatra once said that his main aim in life was to have everyone listen to him sing while they're on their death bed? The last voice you should hear...."

"Ol' Blue Eyes."

"Gross!" he said.

She touched the scar as if it were asleep. "Did they ever take out the bullet?"

"Well, my last physical—X-rays and blood work—showed an enlarged prostate. And an enlarged heart. I knew those two, but an enlarged pituitary too? Something's been working its way up. I asked the doctor about the bullet, which was the whole purpose of the X-rays. He wouldn't say anything about it, although I suppose it lit up the X-rays like a Christmas tree. Now I suppose that if I went to confession—it must be twenty-five years—the priest would say that I had an enlarged soul."

"Do you believe we have a soul?"

He was happy that she asked such a question. "Well, we don't have any proof that it exists, and we don't have any proof that it doesn't exist, so take your pick."

She kissed the scar and eased slowly out of bed, favoring her sore leg as she hobbled to the bathroom.

"Are you okay?" he asked.

"I don't think so," she said.

He jumped up to help her. "You're not going to be able to work tomorrow like this. Your leg's stiffened up. Have you been getting any physical therapy?"

She stopped at the mirror and started taking off her uniform. He stood behind her zipping off the dress, watching admiringly the reflection of her figure.

They heard the roar of the crowd gathering on Times Square, waiting for the ball to start descending, and Andrea relived their early days together, the summer evening strolls at Flushing Meadows, the spaghetti dinners at La Giaconda, the transcendent smell of jet fuel in the morning at JFK. He wanted desperately to see her naked. The jet-black bikini that she wore under her uniform was….

He said, "You said that you had something to show me."

"Can't you tell?" she said.

"Where did you get that pistol?" he asked, pointing to the small charm dangling on a gold chain around her neck.

"*You* gave it to me, remember?"

"No. When?"

"When you came back from Bangkok, all bald and monk like. That was a hoot."

"Please take it off. Too many bad memories."

"I'm sorry," she said, taking it off.

"That's better. So, now, what's your surprise?"

She slipped off the top of her bikini and said, "They're still a little sore."

The naked breasts, so bulbous and ready, made him say, "Chesticles." It was a call that fell out of his mouth like a cherry pit rather than a long string of cheese fondue.

"What?" she said.

"Very sexy," he said.

"That's not what you said."

"A Freudian slip," he said. "Doesn't mean anything."

"I heard horror stories about silicone injections," she said, "silicone getting into the bloodstream, so I didn't dare take that. I had him do implants. He did a great job on the incision, don't you think? They're almost fully healed now."

"Does that mean no more heavy duty…workouts?"

She frowned and said, "Oh, Justin! You know me."

He sat on a chair and she came up close to him. "May I look?" he asked.

"Yes, but be careful."

Under each breast was a small scar about the width of her mouth. "They look like smiles," he said.

"Do they look like theirselves?" she said.

"Twins," he said, offering a suitable, one-word poem.

It was a quick, trivial confession, diverting attention from the mortal sin of her life. Her augmented breasts were stuffed short stories, and he was just as glad about not touching them as he was about not having touched his grandfather Carmen when he was laid up in a casket in Lomdardo's Funeral Home. Nonetheless, he slept by her side that night and brought her to the airport next morning, where she caught her plane back to Miami.

The evening of New Year's Day, he called to see if she had gotten home okay. She answered as a woman would answer during childbirth. He had to ask if it was really Ybette on the phone. She gave him the impression that the angel of death was about to break into her apartment, drag her to the balcony, and throw her off.

"Oh, God, Justin! They're going to fire me!"

"Why? What's wrong?"

"The supervisor on the flight threatened to reprimand me for showing up unfit for duty."

"Did you tell her about your leg?"

"Yes. When I got on the plane, I told her that I wasn't able to work because it was killing me, and I could hardly stand up. She said that I could deadhead back to Miami, but that they would be shorthanded. I took an empty seat in first class. The man sitting next to me was a bishop and...."

"You didn't!"

"No, it's not what you think. When they handed out the menus, he didn't want one, because he said that he was fasting after the holidays."

"Good for him."

"I got offended, like he was too high and mighty to eat our food. Then when Marilyn asked me what I wanted to eat, I said that I didn't want anything, because I was fasting for abortion."

"You said what?"

"That I was fasting for abortion."

"What did the bishop say?"

"He said that I should be fasting to end abortion!"

"Wow."

"I felt insulted and got up to go to the lavatory. I felt woozy and bumped into the supervisor coming down the aisle. I must have taken too many pills on an empty stomach. She accused me of being drunk and said that I was endangering the lives of the passengers by not being able to handle an emergency."

"That's an exaggeration. You weren't on duty."

"Justin! There's no exaggeration when it comes to passenger safety. It's the main reason why people are fired."

"You don't think they'd fire you for that?"

"But that's not all. When I told her that I wasn't on duty, I gently nudged her out of the way, and she...while the plane was making a turn.... Oh, I can't believe I did that!"

"Did what?"

"She lost her balance and fell on a passenger. A first-class passenger. Spilled wine all over her."

Andrea, now worried that this might be cause for being fired, didn't know what to say. He loved her to the extent of wanting to help her, as he remembered that she had expressed suicidal thoughts to Carol when they lived together in New York.

Ybette started to cry. Suddenly, so close and real, they felt as though they were face-to-face at the altar exchanging wedding vows.

"Ybette, are you all right?"

After a moment of complete silence, she said softly, "No."

The answer stunned him, for now he was aware of the fear inside her and the vacuum it had created, a vacuum that was now drawing him in. "Are there any friends you can call?" he asked. "Any close friends there?"

"Justin, that's the problem. They may be too close. I'm never sure where they stand with me. When we met yesterday, I wasn't sure you'd be the same way and give me a meaningless bunch of words. But you didn't. You really are my friend."

"But I'm not sure I really know you."

"That's it, kind of. I'm not sure you know me."

"Or that anyone knows you."

She cried again, but this time holding her hand over the phone so that he couldn't hear. "I don't know why I do that so much lately."

"What's that?"

"Cry."

"Sounds like it just creeps up on you—and bang—all of a sudden hits you. Are you sure you're not all right? No, I mean.... I'm sorry, Ybette. I meant to say, are you sure you're all right?"

"Justin?"

"Yes?"

"Please come see me."

"Jeez, that's a helluva long drive." Dragging out an excuse, he added, "I have to go back to work tomorrow."

Coldly, the dial tone pierced his ears.

He called back but got no answer.

The next morning, he called again and still no answer. Fearful that she might be considering suicide, he made a flight reservation, just in case he couldn't get in touch with her. When he got home from work that night, he gave her another call. Finally, she answered.

"Justin, it's you!" she said excitedly. "Where are you?"

"I'm home. I made reservations to fly down tomorrow morning, just in case...."

"Oh, Justin, that's wonderful. Justin! You don't know how good that makes me feel."

Now fully committed, he dreaded having to call in sick to work. "Where were you?" he asked. "I called back last night and again this morning."

"Had to go to the doctor. Got my prescription refilled."

"Are you feeling better?"

"I feel better. The doctor thinks I need more testing. It seems I've lost weight, and he couldn't understand why. Maybe it was a mistake...that maybe I lost an inch."

"A what?"

"The nurse measured my height and it came out to five-five! I've always been five-six."

"Maybe it was the—ah—the thing they measured with."

"And I now weigh one-o-five."

"How's that?"

"I haven't been hungry either. I think I haven't touched anything in a week and don't feel hungry anymore."

"You looked fine to me." But not to let her incredible statement go, "You haven't eaten anything in a week?"

"Justin, I'm terribly sorry for last night. When I got home, I was tireder than I've been in my whole life. It was a flight from hell. I do apologize."

"Hey, no problem," he said. "I'll be there tomorrow night. I'm looking forward to enjoying your sun again."

"My son?" she asked.

"Yeah, to warm up. I'm cold."

18/Abstinence

Ybette lay on a couch reading *Virginia Woolf: a Biography*, afraid of falling asleep for fear of having another nightmare. She planned to sleep during the day and wait for Andrea's arrival the next evening. Only then would she be able to sleep safely at night.

She had heard of Virginia Woolf and admired Andrea for sending her the book. It was thick and heavy, and she used a pillow on her stomach for cushion and support. Interested only in her personal life, she skipped over passages that dealt with her writing career and went directly to the heart of the matter—the breakdowns, the voices commanding her to get fat, the starvations, the buggers in waiting, the lesbian trysts, and the attempted suicides. With each turning page, the love affair grew stronger; Virginia's haunting eyes cried out to her between the critics' abuses: "clever intellectual snob...peddler of capitalist narcotics...fragile poetess." The deaths of Virginia's mother and father, the passionless boyfriends, the demanding girlfriends, the merciless critics, and the onslaught of World War II, all collected into heavy rocks that she loaded into her coat pockets one day and carried into the River Ouse. It was an inevitable result for a childless woman tormented by the people around her, and especially by her own powerless being.

When Ybette read Virginia's last letter to her husband, blaming herself and not him for her fate, the bond was sealed. Virginia's greatest love—to write stories—was denied her, not from without, but from within. She was her own worst enemy, and *she went headstrong into that only experience about which she could never write.*

She awoke and looked frantically for the book, in the cracks of the couch, under the pillows, and finally down at the floor, but it was gone.

Ashen and cold, a nude boy stood in a corner and stared at her. Terrified, she threw a pillow at him, but just as it connected, the body disappeared and the pillow bounced off the wall. It was a body as solid as hers but not connected to the objects in her world.

"Get out of here, you!" she shouted. "Who let you in here?"

"I'm your son," the boy said.

She picked up another pillow to throw, but instead used it as a shield to protect her breasts. "What did you say? I don't have a son. Who are you?"

"Mother, I'm your son." The boy broke his wanton stare and looked about the room. He walked closer and stopped, dark eyes sparkling in the light, beaming with anticipation, searching for an answer to his presence.

Hoping for recognition, he said, "Where is father?"

"Go away! You can't be. It's impossible."

"Mother, can't you understand how much this means to me? Look, here's your book." lobbing the book onto the couch. "They're just words that thicken my darkness." He took one more step forward and held out his hand.

"Ghost! You bastard!"

"No, mother. Touch my hand. I'm not a ghost. See, look. I can touch myself, but I can't feel myself. Only you can do this for me. Look, I can't feel my hand touching my body. I feel like a thing, like that book."

"So, how do you know I'm your mother? If you were never born, how do you know it's me?"

"Because I'm *an infinity of possibilities*." The boy sat on the floor, taking his rightful place as the child of the house. "Oh, mother, you don't know what infinite is. I saw Hitler being crowned king of the world, the total destruction of the world by the first hydrogen bomb, and the election of Robert F. Kennedy as president of the United States. So, why can't you possibly believe that I was born?"

"Because you were destroyed before you were...when you were twelve weeks old."

"Twelve weeks? So, now I'm twelve years," and before her very eyes, he changed to "now twenty-four years old." She gasped and lost her breath as if punched in the stomach. "And forty-six years old...and seventy-six!" He flashed from newborn to toddler to boy to teen and then into a parade of maturing years each passing by her to senility and the grave. The dispositions, interpositions, and contrapositions of his being—right-handed, left-handed, ambidextrous; smiling, frowning, winking; eating, drinking, smoking; talking, singing, sleeping; brown, black, blond—figures all based on nothing, merged into one little pulsating fetus on the floor at her feet. Carefully, she eased off the couch and crouched down on the floor before it. "Is it you?" she whispered.

"No, it's you!" a man said, standing in the same corner where the boy had stood. "Exactly as you were thirty years ago, still alive and well, just after your mother walked away from the clinic." He held out a string of white beads and said, "The clinic where she saw a nun holding these. Yes, beads that reflected back to her eyes the joy, sorrow, and mystery of life. Beads finite and easily named. Hail Mary, full of grace.... A prayer that asks her to help us like she helped her baby to grow! A prayer that reflects the infinite towards which it is directed."

The compression of her body back through time into an unborn minimized her life beyond all feelings and emotions. Yet, there she was, full of life and light-years away from all help, a body prostrate on the floor so easily crushed by the next passing foot. She closed her eyes tightly, but there again in the darkness she felt the squeezing sensation all over her, trying to reduce her to that thing on the floor from which she came. She shrieked in horror, "It's not me! It's not me!" unable to even touch herself.

"If you destroy it," the man said, "you will destroy Ybette."

"No! Not so," she screamed and ran into the kitchen, only to find him sitting there in a chair. "It's my retarded brother Radar. Isn't it?" she said. "Not me."

The man smiled and didn't respond.

"You can see that, can't you?" she said. "It's so convoluted and distorted, its brain must be growing in its stomach. My mother wasn't as holy as you think. She was neurotic and took thalidomide. She didn't want Radar but went and had him anyway. Have you seen him? He can't talk. All he can do is grunt when he wants something. He grunts to eat or go to the toilet. It's all the same to him. He can't write his name. He can't even draw a simple square house. Whenever I see him, I think it would take doctors a million years to rewire his brain so that he could at least think. Do you know what microcephaly is? It's about the most hopeless thing...." She paused a moment, trying to hold back the tears. "It's the most hopeless.... They'll never find a cure. Might as well scrap the whole heap and start over because this one will never work right."

She walked behind him thinking she could take a boning knife and shove it in his back. "So, he's in limbo, just like you," she said. "What do you think of God when he makes a vegetable out of a human being? What does Radar have to live for? When he dies, that will be the end of him. He will lose everything because he has nothing. So...so, you. What did you call yourself? The infinite possibility? You will live on, but Radar, the impossibility, will die forever."

"You blame grandmother for Radar," he said. "True, she was neurotic and took thalidomide, but you still have all your fingers and toes."

"*Your* grandmother?! You think she was your grandmother?" Ybette laughed, having finally outwitted the specter. "That proves it. You're not my son, because Peg Rember is not my mother. And, if she's not my mother, she's not your grandmother and we're not related."

"I'm sorry."

"You should be. I was adopted. Peg Rember is not my real mother."

Feeling that she had the thing trapped and defeated, she ran her fingers through its hair. It felt soft and human.

"And now," he said, "what kind of possibility are you?"

"I'm a flight attendant."

"Coffee, tea, or me?"

"Cheap shot. I knew you'd say that."

"And Andrea did too. Do you want to know what he really thinks of you?" He stood up as tall as the ceiling. "You have never seen anything like it in your life, have you? How many men have you dated in the last ten years? You've lost count. Doctors, lawyers, politicians, sky marshals, pilots. You name it, right?"

She retreated to the bedroom, but he was already there on the bed waiting for her. "He thinks that you're all talk and no action. That's what he is writing about this very minute. All talk, no action. A flirt with every available man you meet in first class, hardly looking at a man if he wasn't in the top one percent. In economy class, you're just the regular old Ybette, but just as soon as you get behind the curtain, you punctuate every word with an arm squeeze or a raised eyebrow, as though you'd invite every man to join the Mile-High Club if it weren't for the long lines at the lavatories. And as for Andrea, you never returned a fraction of the love he had for you. You implanted the thought in his mind that because you loved him, you were not *in* love with him, that there was something inadequate about him. You loved him, but at the same time didn't love him. You kept him in a holding pattern between love and rejection, keeping your candle burning at both ends. You lied to him, clouded his creativity, and disgraced love itself. Like giving him another name that you liked. Like wearing that provocative black bikini New Year's Eve, suggesting for him a sexual paradise if only he were the right man. That body of yours—those legs, those shapely hips, and now those generously endowed breasts—all so sexy, you can't help but look totally available to any man that comes within range. But you're losing it slowly."

"How would you know?" she said. "Have you ever been turned on by a woman? Of course not. You're about as real as the statue of David. It's like you're alive and dead at the same time. If you keep playing around like you're alive, maybe you'll become alive." She strolled around the bed seductively, enjoying the feel of his eyes upon her.

"What are you scared of?" he asked.

"Scared of? What isn't there to be scared of? I could get in a heap of trouble at work. Justin's plane could crash coming down here. You could attack me. I could get pregnant with a ghost. Is there anything that I shouldn't be scared of?"

"You missed one."

"What?"

"That I might never go away."

"I'll be damned if you don't," she snapped. "Why don't you bother your father for that matter?"

"That's why I'm here. I don't know my father. Who is he?" changing into a boy again.

"You don't know, do you? Then, how did you find me?"

"By your M-wave, mother. You see, I don't have DNA."

"DNA? So, you can't prove who your father is. That's a switch."

"It's how bees find their way back to the hive."

"Like Radar, a mass of knotted-up DNA."

"No, even he can't, but I can be here and there at the same time." The boy stood beside the bed, a phantasm looking down at himself. "Radar can't do this, be a wave of his body."

The trick reminded her of the very first time she had communicated with Radar. They were walking in the park, and he was going too slow, trailing behind her, so she turned around and yelled, "Come on, boy. Pick up the pace!" Radar turned around and looked behind him but couldn't find the pace.

She laughed at the memory. The boy laughed in harmony. "What are you laughing at?" she asked.

"*Your* pace, mother. You're losing pounds and inches by the second."

"What do you mean?"

"Your body, mother. Pretty soon you'll be like me."

The telephone rang. She answered and Andrea said, "Ybette, I have some bad news. I have to go on TDY. I won't be able to see you now. I'll be in Guam."

"Guam?" she cried. "What on earth would you be doing in Guam?"

"Nothing but work," he said.

"Justin, then promise to come see me as soon as you get back."

"I promise," he said. "I'm really sorry about this. How do you feel?"

"Much better. I think it's out of my system."

"Did they call you about that run-in with your supervisor?"

"No."

"Well, maybe they'll forget about it. I wouldn't worry."

"I hope so."

19/Metabolism

When Andrea boarded the plane, he didn't say hello to the person next to him, and that person didn't say hello to him. There were only a few sky marshals still flying and probably none aboard.

Of all the flights he had taken as a sky marshal, he couldn't remember once not talking to a passenger. Now he was in a different world where people treated flying as nothing more than a subway trip to work.

After takeoff, it occurred to him that he might be on a voyage of vengeance, and that he might be feeding on Ybette's depression. Having nothing to write on, he pulled out the airsickness bag to record this thought. When he reached inside the bag to tear it open, a slimy substance coated his hand. At first, he thought it might be something to speed up the inevitable, a potpourri of ipecac perhaps.

He jumped up and rushed to the lavatory to wash it off, but had to wait in line, trying to keep in mind the idea of being a *catalyst* rather than a carrier of a contagious disease.

I'm wrapped up in a self-fulfilling prophesy, he thought, like a woman with an alcoholic father wanting to marry an alcoholic man, or a man with a frigid mother wanting to marry a frigid woman.

After cleaning up and borrowing a piece of paper from the flight attendant, he wrote,

Is my behavior a self-fulfilling prophecy in which she acts in ways that disaffirm my expectations of her? It's why some people choose to go to church on Sunday and some people stay at home and read the newspaper. They believe what they desire to happen, and they desire what they believe to happen, as though the act of faith itself determines the very existence of the thing desired. It's why the all-powerful United States knowingly provoked the enemy to flee underground in Vietnam while losing the war at the end of the tunnel. It's why Vincent Van Gogh, who had a Platonic love affair with Rachel the prostitute, cut off his <u>left</u> ear and gave it to her, then painted a self-portrait showing his <u>right</u> ear bandaged, as though the right hand that had done the cutting couldn't do the same to the painting, or as though the painting couldn't do justice to the reality by replicating it, mirrors notwithstanding. I doubt that he knew the left side of the face is the most becoming.

The artist distances himself from the world. This provokes or induces the world to look unnatural, giving the artist cause to believe he is seeing the world uniquely, creatively. This is a self-fulfilling prophecy that reinforces his art. Like Van Gogh drinking too much absinth to the point where his vision is drunk on yellow, and when he goes into the fields, everything becomes hyper-chromatic.

Or the opposite, when Rauschenberg the amateur visited de Kooning the master and asked for a drawing to imitate and, instead of replicating it, used it in his studio as an exercise in erasure, mark by mark, pencil speck by pencil speck, until, after a month of painstaking work, the drawing was reversed in time back into a blank sheet of paper.

Or Leonardo, not having been taught Latin or Greek by classics scholars that controlled the tomes of knowledge, wrote his notes backwards in code so that only he could understand them, thus reinforcing his aberrant dissections and weird inventions.

A poet who senses that an affair will turn into a disaster—only if he participates in it—plunges into it headfirst, so that it will take place and, when it's over, writes a poem about it.

Ybette, too, is a SFP. She flirts with men without realizing she is doing so. It's as natural to her as shaking hands or saying thank you. They fly around her like lost airplanes, so many men bound for mid-air collisions without any air traffic control. Is that what she wants me to be, her air traffic controller?

Ybette lived near the airport, so he didn't have to wait long to be picked up. Her car reeked of cigarette smoke, and she looked worse than he had ever seen her, yet she drove capably though heavy traffic. Given two good legs, she might be a good taxi driver, he thought, and live a happier life.

"You look wonderful, Justin. I'm jealous of your suntan."

"The beaches are the only thing to do on Guam," he said. "How have you been?"

"Not well. I spent most of the month in the hospital. Used up all of my sick leave."

"In the hospital? For what? Your leg?"

"No. My metabolism. I must have seen a dozen endocrinologists already."

"A dozen? I didn't think they had that many."

"They were afraid to take my blood, I had lost so much weight. Funny thing, though, I didn't feel weak. I didn't starve like they thought I would."

When they arrived, Andrea was shocked to see her get out of the car and stand shorter than she was before. He didn't mention it but realized that there was without doubt something drastically wrong with her.

"My car looks awful, I do apologize," she said. "The birds down here make an awful mess."

"Birds?" he said. "Are you sure birds did that?"

Ybette looked closely at the three dried-up blobs evenly spaced on the front of her hood. "Bird poo, isn't it?" she suggested.

"I don't think so," he said.

"Oh, no, Justin. You mean to tell me I've been driving around town with these discharges hanging on the front of my car?"

"I'll clean it off," he said.

Once inside the apartment, he went straight to the kitchen and started browsing through the cabinets and refrigerator to see what might be good for dinner. All the containers were family size—a gallon of milk, a dozen eggs, a five-pound bag of sugar, a gallon of Chianti…. "Are you planning a party?" he asked.

"No," she said.

"Why do you need five pounds of potatoes?"

"It's more economical," she said.

"But you'll never finish all these before they start to sprout. Why don't you buy two or three potatoes at a time? This way guys in the checkout line will know you're single."

"Is that what you want?" she asked.

He opened a box of spaghetti and cinched enough for two. "Or don't you care about meeting local folks?"

When they finally sat down to eat, she admired how he examined the color of the wine in the glass by candlelight, smelling the bouquet, then sipping a little bit at a time, trying to get as much flavor as possible out of zero vintage. "I was worried all day," she said.

"About my flight?" he asked.

"About whether they'd call me in."

"Well, if they didn't call by now, maybe they forgot about it."

"I hope so." The taste of the food made her feel good inside. "You make the best pasta sauce, Justin."

"It's spaghetti Bolognese."

"It's so delicious. You should open a restaurant."

Suddenly, she shuddered and put a hand over her mouth.

"Are you okay?" he asked.

"I bit my tongue," she said. "I keep doing that."

Despite the hearty meal, her face showed no signs of recovery, and he thought her spirit had vanished. The idea of being the cause of her depression bothered him, and he was afraid to ask if she felt well. "The plane was very crowded," he said. He told her about finding phlegm in the airsickness bag, and she flared up about Eastern's incompetence. He should have stayed off the topic, for she started to talk again about her incident.

"After I pushed her and returned to my seat, they were all looking at me like I was a criminal. I mean everyone was. Like it was a major catastrophe. And when some jerk said that stewardesses were nothing but glorified waitresses, I almost wished I were a skyjacker and taken that plane to Cuba or somewhere."

"Did you tell him off?"

"I couldn't. I just told him that for his information, we weren't stewardesses but flight attendants, and when he realized who I was, he said that he was sorry. But the look of the passengers! Justin, I don't think I can get up and face them anymore. When I got off the plane, they were all watching me. I saw them all at once. They all looked so sad and mean; I wanted to run home as fast as I could."

"I felt that way," he said, "after coming home from Vietnam."

"I'm not going to be able to handle him if he calls."

"Handle who?"

"Bill Bascle, the Director of In-Flight Services. He's so arrogant. He's never been a flight attendant, but has the nerve to...."

"A pilot?"

"No, a retired Air Force general would you believe? They say Frank Borman hired him just so he could boss around a general."

"What was Borman? A colonel?"

"Do you know this man wanted to join the Mile-High Club so bad, he got divorced just after he got the job?"

Andrea waited a minute, not sure he wanted to say what was on his mind, but since he had nothing to lose from her, said, "Well, if he calls you on the carpet, maybe you should give him a little skin."

Ybette stroked her chin gently and calculated the odds of making such a move. "Too risky," she said.

"Well, if they force you to resign, maybe you can go back to nursing."

"I've forgotten everything, Justin," staring at her Eastern coffee cup. "Look at this. America's favorite way to fly. Let's show them how we can earn our wings every day. Let's take one last trip together. Fly east and never turn back." She smiled deviously, as though ready to rob a bank.

"If you're thinking what I think you're thinking, you're nuts. Where would we go? Niagara Falls and go over in a barrel?"

"Justin, I'm thinking seriously here. Listen. We can plan to take a jumbo out of Miami after it lands and all the passengers have deplaned. Then, we get on and start flying, like we're a retired couple taking a cross country trip in an Airstream."

"Yeah, sure, retired couple going no place in particular. Just keep flying east around the world."

"You've got no home. I've got no home. What do you say?"

"You're serious."

"Let's sleep on it."

"It would be suicide."

It would be during the flight, she thought, while they were alone together in a jumbo jet cruising at thirty-five thousand feet that she would tell him about her visions, and about living together in a world of infinite possibilities.

"Let's sit in the living room and just talk," she said. "I finished the book you sent me."

"That big thing? No. You must have been skimming. Where is it?"

"I finished the whole thing. Two hundred and twenty-six pages. I'll prove it to you. Ask me a question about her."

"It's longer than that. Did you read both volumes?"

"Both volumes? You sent me only one."

"Where is it?"

Hidden behind the TV, it looked unaffected by having been held by a poltergeist. Paging through it, he pinched off the two volumes in one. "The pagination is not continuous," he said. "It's easily over five hundred pages. You actually read these two books?"

"Ask me a question."

"Okay. I'm sure you know how she died and how she had a problem finding a man who, ah, wasn't a queer. And about her mental instability. And…. Well, here's a question that might get you. Who was Quentin Bell, besides being the author?"

"Too easy, Justin. He was her nephew." She took the book and showed him the picture of Virginia on the back cover. "Can you paint this for me?"

"I wouldn't do it justice," he said.

During the night, Andrea awoke to the flushing of the toilet and light coming from the bathroom. The light went out, and he felt her climb back into bed and cuddle up next to him. A nauseous wake of cigarette smoke accompanied her.

After only an hour of sleep, she awoke suddenly with a putrid taste flooding her mouth. It was as if someone had tried to choke her with hot puke. She got up, drank a glass of water, and returned to bed without waking him.

A mockingbird sang, and he went out on the balcony hoping to spot it in the trees below. The range of its voice reached no more than a city block, but its repertoire was endless. It sang for him alone that morning.

When he went to the bathroom, bits and pieces of spaghetti were still floating in the toilet bowl. So that's how she stays thin, he thought. Or maybe she's just worried about being fired.

At breakfast, he commented on the *Starry Night* hanging over the toilet. "Is that for men only? You know, when I first saw that painting up close in New York—the original—the stars struck me as giant breasts in the sky."

"Justin, how crude."

"But you don't know Van Gogh. He had a terrible obsession with women, and unfortunately, women of ill repute."

She laughed at his choice of words and said, "I picked it for the colors."

"It goes well with the light viridian walls," he said.

"Have you thought any more about what I said last night?"

"You mean about doing a portrait of Virginia Woolf?"

"No. Well, yes, that too, but about the other idea."

"Oh, I don't know. I turned in my gun long time ago."

The prospects of skyjacking a plane didn't rouse him, for he had no good reason. What bothered him was not knowing whether she was sincere or just joking. If he had the motivation and a good plan, he would approach it cautiously and not half-baked as she. He imagined it being like the double-slit light experiment where photons of light won't show a wave-interference pattern on a screen if they pass through only one slit, but if two slits are present, wow, what symmetry!

"But you still know how to shoot, don't you?"

"Of course. I shot expert with the thirty-eight."

Ybette reached into her purse and pulled out a pistol that was too big to be a charm, but too small to be a real gun. She placed it on the table along with a few bullets. "It's real," she said. "And can kill."

Andrea inspected it as he would a life-size revolver. He read the name engraved on the barrel. "SwissMiniGun, Cool. What's it good for, killing mice? Where'd you get it, off a Swiss Guard at the Vatican?"

"I bought it in Africa."

"You mean you bought a SwissMiniGun on your safari to Africa?"

"Well, I couldn't have bought it in Switzerland, because I never flew to Switzerland."

"Yeah, I know. Eastern has its limitations."

Eastern was indeed the main cause of their misfortunes. For him, it had been the next card in the deck, and his story as a sky marshal might have been different had it been another airline. If he had been assigned to TWA, he would have never met Ybette and gotten mixed up with Linnehan. He would have flown daily to Rome, met a nice Italian girl, gotten married, had seven children, and been one of the lucky few to remain in the sky marshal program. And, maybe, on the day before his retirement, shoot the terrorist general who was trying to lead an army of skyjackers into nirvana.

For her, Eastern happened to be hiring when she wanted out of nursing.

In short, they were both casualties of chance and coincidence.

"May I?" he said, aiming the gun at a blond Barbie doll dressed in a blue and gold stewardess uniform standing on top of the refrigerator.

"You wouldn't dare," she said.

"I couldn't, not even to a doll."

"Does that mean no?"

"Well, look. You're not Leila Khaled, and I'm not Steve McQueen, so let me think it over. After lunch, I'll go out and take target practice with the mini-gun. May I use your car?"

"Better take the Porsche," she said. "I can't drive the stick with my leg like this, and it needs exercise."

"The Porsche?" he asked.

"A gift from a friend."

"You're kidding."

"It's the silver one with Virginia license plates."

"Is the hood clean?"

On impulse, she swallowed something bitter. The thought that it might be a piece of her flesh made her break out in a cold sweat. She started shivering and asked for a blanket. He brought her to the living room; she curled up on the couch and closed her eyes. He let her sleep. After only ten minutes, the sound of a lawn mower made her jump up. She waited a few minutes to collect her thoughts, and then said, "What a strange dream I just had."

"You were asleep," he said.

"I was lying on a conveyor belt and went into a machine. There was a mirror on the wall and I looked at myself. I was naked, and I had a round tummy. I sucked it in and out popped two breasts on my chest."

"Typical dream," he said. "I have it all the time."

"A light flashed, and the conveyor belt started up again."

"It took your picture," he suggested.

"Then someone opened up my suitcase and I was inside. Justin, I was the size of a...."

"Of a what?"

She sat up. "Justin, please get me a glass of water before I die of thirst."

20/Ziggy

Meandering down a back alley, he found refuge from the bright afternoon sun in the shade of squat stucco buildings. Seductive music filtering through the front door of *Place Pigalle* lured him inside. It was a strip joint full of panatela smoke and spewed beer. He went to the bar and took a seat. A hollow feeling gnawed at his insides—the effect of too much sunshine and salt water on an empty stomach.

A buxom blond with pearly skin undulated like a Dali timepiece over the stage. Again, the *Persistence of Memory*, but here in life-size proportions not neutered by a charlatan's magnifying glass, not a rock for a clock for a cock, but Liberace's grand piano in full swing.

When the music stopped, Ziggy squeezed back into her one-piece dress with as much sex as when she had taken it off. She headed straight for Andrea and stood beside him. "Jou like mein dance?" she asked, looking at his face and the folds in his pants made luxurious by the shiny blue silk. She wanted to feel the material, but held back. Her eyes returned to his face and inspected it for a moment, taking the scar to be a knife wound, a sign of revenge. She was half right.

He brushed her hips with his knee. "Yes," he said. Her body appeared more imposing than it did nude on the stage. Her breasts were magnificent up close, and she had to adjust the dress to keep them confined. She smelled athletic, not perfumed. Trickles of sweat running down her strong neck made him thirsty. He took another drink. "Want a drink?" he asked.

"Naranja!" she said. Her voice sounded as muscular as her thighs. When the drink arrived, she reached for it, giving him a whiff of her sweaty bosom. The odor was pleasant, carrying the same promise as fresh fish. Highly desirable, if he were a flesh monger.

"Vould you like fur me to go mit jou?"

"To my hotel room?" drooling over her body. Ziggy nodded in agreement. "How much do you mean?"

"Vee talk later," she said. The bartender came over and placed a bill on the bar between the glasses. Andrea finished his drink in two gulps and took up the bill. He moved the paper around to get a better reading of the total in the dim light. What first looked like twenty, came out ringing two hundred.

"For two drinks? You gotta be kidding me."

Ziggy sulked as Andrea turned his knees toward the bar. He looked coldly at the bartender, who had moved to the other end and was now talking to a thug. "Two hundred dollars!" he blurted out. "Horseshit."

Hearing the complaint, the bartender patted the thug on the shoulder and walked back. He anchored both hands on the inside edge of the bar, showing off large tattoos on forearms kept nondescript by dense masses of black hair. Should be so for all tattoos, Andrea thought.

"Havin' a bad day, mate?"

Andrea's jaw was a little wobbly from the rum, but he was still willing to force the issue. "Two hundred for two drinks? This must be a mistake."

"Cover charge, mate, and a drink for the lady."

"I don't see anything about a cover charge."

Andrea gave up a twenty, and Ziggy slowly rolled her grand piano away from the bar.

"Nobody asked you to look at anything," the bartender said. "You didn't ask, so now I'm tellin'. Pay the rest of yer bill!" The thug at the end of the bar stood up, revealing a whaling physique, adding to the bartender's clout.

Slumping a little, as if under a heavy weight, Andrea said, "Okay. It's just that this is more than my take-home pay for a week."

"So, what's your bag, the merchant marine?"

"No, man, I can pay, but I just have to go get the rest. I don't have it on me."

"What do you have? Got any insurance?"

"Insurance? What insurance?"

"Anything to hock? A watch maybe?"

Andrea envisioned the thug walking over and making quick work of him before he had the chance to turn it around in his favor, classified style. The bouncer didn't even have a neck, so he doubted his limited ability with the neck crank. He searched through his pockets, pulled out the SMG and pointed it at the guy's head. The bartender looked at it curiously and started to laugh. "You're a bloody fool, mate," he said.

Andrea waved the little gun and said, "You want to see blood. I'll show you blood."

The bartender stepped back, unsure that the gun was lethal, but sure that it wasn't a toy.

"It's a Russian Kernstoffe," Andrea said, "and can open your head up like a ripe watermelon."

"A what?" the bartender said.

"Russian Kernstoffe!"

"No need for that. Put it away, mate. Your twenty's good."

21/Bird of Paradise

Startled by the growl of the engine, he opened his eyes and eased off the gas pedal. Through a cloud of carbon monoxide a black man came and looked inside the car.

It took a long time for the wound-up Porsche to die down, but eventually it did, and Andrea thought that it had burned out, going full blast all night in his sleep. He turned it off, unlocked the door, and went outside to check. His right leg was stiff, and he walked with a limp.

"Are you hurt?" the man asked.

"No, just stiff from sleeping inside, that's all." Andrea opened the hood and looked at the engine.

"I was going to unplug your battery, but that's in the trunk, and you were locked up inside. I thought you were trying to snuff yourself."

"I think the sucker's burnt up."

"Don't worry about that engine, man; it's air-cooled. Germans build 'em loose like that. But you sure looked funny, flooring it and going nowhere fast. Long way from Virginia."

"Virginia? What makes you think I'm from Virginia?"

"The license plates, man. And you're headed north. Highway One."

"Highway One?" Andrea was astonished that he was on the east coast and worried that his memory was off track again.

"What'd you expect?"

"Then I'm probably out of gas. Any stations nearby?"

"Up in Fort Pierce."

"How far is that?"

"Just a few miles. Let me show you something first. Over here. Interested in taking some Florida art back to Virginia?"

"Who's the artist?"

"Al Hare. Ever heard of him?"

"Hare?"

"Yeah. That's right. *H, A, R, E.* Hare. I've been meaning to get some business cards, but...." Hare pulled out a few paintings and propped them up against the back bumper and along the side of his car. "Twenty-five dollars. Take your pick."

Andrea liked Hare's derby hat. He had seen a German artist wear one but couldn't recall the name. It went well with Hare's thin mustache.

"Anything catch your fancy?"

"I like the sunset with the orange sky and the palm tree in the center." The painting made Andrea recall the angelic sunset of the previous night, and he felt on track again.

"It's a sunrise, man. East coast. That tree's down on the Indian River, just like that. Must have sold a dozen so far. A halfway decent piece, don't you think?"

"You mean you sold a dozen of the same painting?"

"Better than the dollar-fifty they feed you in the Army."

When Hare talked, he faced the road to spot cars approaching. Andrea liked the way his eyes were set far apart, giving him the native appeal of Anthony Quinn.

"Did you go to art school?" Andrea asked.

"I got interested in art in high school. Had a great teacher who taught me how to mix colors. But what really got me inspired was a stained glass window in church. When I was a kid, I used to go in and watch the sun shining through those windows reflecting colors on the walls. But one window really did it to me. A gray abstract in the midst of all the red, yellow, and blue glass. You know, I looked at that design for I don't know how many years, every Sunday. But then one Sunday, after I was discharged from the Army, I went back into that church and saw that it had changed. I saw that it was really a *hand*. The hand of God in the sky, palm open, fingers pointing down—like this is—and not an abstract anymore. And no matter how hard I looked at it, I couldn't get that neat abstract back. It was always a hand." Hare looked down at his painting admiringly. "I'm going to capture that someday."

Andrea looked again at the painting and thought that it might not be worth twenty-five dollars, being painted on a construction board that was already warping. "Reminds me of Giacometti, the way the landscape has been deconstructed down to just a single palm tree. Looks so spindly at that."

"Twenty," Hare said.

"Well, in that case," handing Hare a twenty. Andrea brought the painting to his car and wrote on the back of the board: *If I paint twenty pictures at once, you won't be able to castrate me. If I delinearize the palm, I erect it. At the same time, I multiply my profit. Tracings retrace other tracings. Sunrises retrace painted sunsets. This thievery of oneself has no poetic power. It's impotent.*

A car pulled up, and a customer stepped out to look at the paintings. Andrea drove back to Miami hoping it would be a sufficient peace offering for being gone so long.

Returning to the apartment, he couldn't recall how long he had been gone. The door was blocked by a wet towel on the floor. He forced it open, and the stench of gas choked him.

Keeping the door propped open with the towel, he ran inside and slid open the balcony door, then ran to the kitchen to turn off the gas jets on the stove.

In the bedroom, Ybette lay naked on the bed, spattered with vomit and half-digested red capsules. "Mother!" he cried. "What did you do?"

Terrified, he ran out the front door and hung over the railing, gasping for air and holding back the urge to throw up. The lifelessness of her body was horrible.

Colder each second, the woman he had loved with such passion, the woman he would help at any cost, waited for him. He took a deep breath, went back inside, and confronted the unbearable scene again. An empty pill bottle lay on the floor. He leaned over her and dared not breathe in, as she didn't breathe out. He put an ear to her chest and listened for a heartbeat, but all he could hear was the bullet in his brain hissing.

Choking and coughing, he picked up the sweaty body and brought it to the balcony. Ripping off his shirt, he cleaned the face and mouth, and cursed himself for not knowing how to resuscitate her back to life. "CPR! CPR! CPR!" he shouted, hoping the letters would do the job.

He pinched the nose, held up the chin, and blew hard into the mouth, causing the throat to choke up a pill that flew directly into his mouth just as he was taking another breath. It went deep into his throat, and he had to swallow it. He took another breath and blew again, this time watching the chest rise a little. He blew again and again, until he felt two little puffs of air come out of the nose. He tried again but got nothing. Then, it occurred to him to press on the chest to start the heart.

The bare breasts—lofty and pink—looked undefeated and still alive. "What a waste," he said, pushing down on the sternum. "What a waste," pressing thirty times and then checking for breaths again. Nothing came.

Her marble-eyed stare reduced him to tears.

Suddenly a boy appeared in the doorway and said, "I smelled gas, and the door was open. Is Yolanda okay?"

"Ybette! Ybette!" Andrea cried, now turning again to the mouth, taking another breath, and blowing into it.

"She doesn't look it," the boy said. "If you ask me, she's pretty near the angel's end."

"Call nine-eleven. Hurry! Inside!"

"I think it's too late for that. Look, the angel! It's alighting. Can you see? Oh, how magnificent. How beautiful; like nothing you ever saw. Yolanda will be all right now. Don't worry. Don't complicate this by pulling her back. Let her go. All you can see in her is death. That's not the beauty of the immersion. It's happening. Believe me."

Forcing the heart to stop pumping, she had robbed it of the power to stop on its own, which freed her from being condemned to death by it. Now abandoned, the body began the ritual of death: cooling quickly, there being little fat between skin and bone; blood settling down in the back where it began turning the skin blue; sphincters relaxing and losing control over the call of nature. It became a condemnation that nothing could overrule. For Andrea, it was a verdict undeserved. She had planned it that way, knowing that he would be the first to look down upon her, fall to his knees, and pray. But he didn't pray with words. He wept.

After the wave of sorrow had passed, he picked up the body, brought it to the living room, and laid it on the couch. He telephoned for an ambulance, explaining that a woman had overdosed and was dying. Just as he ended the call, the boy walked out of the apartment.

All the evidence pointed toward suicide, but an eyewitness—the boy—was most vital. Andrea yelled and ran out after him but found only an empty landing and an old woman coming up the stairwell. He asked her, "Did you see that boy go down here?"

"No señor," she said. "No boy."

Andrea went back inside and knelt beside the body with his left hand on the forehead. It felt cool, heightening his fear that she was lost forever. He would have given anything to save her, but having been demoralized by so many failures in life—chivalrous, artistic, and religious—there was nothing left for him to offer. He was as capable of interceding for her in prayer as an eighty-year-old man was capable of running the marathon.

A bird of paradise flower in full bloom sat upright in a vase on the table. While watching a droplet hang off the edge of its blue stigma, he felt the strength come to him with the surprise of an electric shock.

"Lord, look at her. Please forgive her. Didn't you say, 'Father, forgive them for they know not what they do?'"

A wailing siren warned of the approaching ambulance.

"They're coming now. I loved you many years, even how you visited me one night in a dream. You looked so much like yourself, and I was excited to have painted your portrait. Now, whenever I dream of a face, it will be yours—invisible on a white canvas.

"Is this the end? Police and doctors add your name to death reports. Friends share memories, then forget about you. And I cry over your half-torn picture."

Two paramedics came through the front door and immediately went to the body. Andrea answered their questions convincingly and without suspicion. He felt the need to cry, but held it inside so that all his sorrow would be directed to her soul. He felt that the cry would amplify the tremendous shock of her death, which threatened to drive her into the depths of hell where all the suffering of humanity was unleashed. He stepped back and let them see her beauty, still pink and most sacred. They examined for vital signs and, not finding any, placed a white machine about the size of a briefcase beside her chest.

"I'm going to try to jump start her heart," the paramedic said, grabbing two paddles off the machine, rubbing them together with gel, and aiming them carefully above the right breast and below the left breast. "Don't touch her," he said. "Clear!"

Disappointed that the body didn't jump up from the shock, Andrea thought the machine had lost power. "Checkin' the pulse…. No pulse. Hit it again!"

"Going to four hundred. Clear!"

"Got a pulse. Got a pulse." That moment, Ybette's eyes opened wide and she made the shrill, plaintive call of a nighthawk. "Keeeeeer!"

Then she was silent and still again. The paramedic checked her pulse. "Gone," he said, and then proceeded to give her another shock. After zapping her heart three times unsuccessfully, they put her on the floor and began CPR, which was no use. Finally, after another round of shocks, the paramedic dared to say, "She's wearing out my battery. Let's get the gurney and bring her down."

Discouraged, Andrea went into the bedroom and collapsed on the bed. The heat from her body was still there—inside the mattress! It felt warm, and he wanted to somehow capture it inside himself. He closed his eyes tightly and saw in the darkness her *face* floating around in space, turning this way and that, not knowing which way to go, lost in a void, mouth open wide but unable to make a sound, not even noticing that she was looking directly into his soul.

Horrified that he had actually seen her abandoned soul, he opened his eyes and began to pray. The vision was too immediate to have been a dream, and he closed his eyes again to see if he could go back inside and save her, but she was not there anymore, no matter how hard he tried. She was not saved but lost to find her own way out of the emptiness. She needed help, and all he could do was feel her warmth evaporate into the space around him.

22/Meltdown

On the nightstand was a wordless note she had written:
"."

Two-by-two microbubbles uplifting and protecting a period that threatened to end his life. Periods with wings, beginning and ending, filled with deadly gas rather than air, two pairs of marks thrust him into a world of muted and useless screams fighting for life, and, within their confines, he took flight.

"Andrea!" a faint voice said. "It's me. Down here."

Andrea sat up and looked at the doorway, but no one was there. The voice came again, and he said, "Where are you?" Then looking down at the floor, he saw a small doll standing beside the bed. It was her Eastern keepsake, without its uniform, but could it be…talking?

"It's me, help me," she said.

Astonished, he bent down and gently helped her up. At that moment, the paramedics came into the apartment pushing a gurney and looking for the body. "Where is she?" one of them asked, coming into the bedroom.

The doll immediately went for the SwissMiniGun, which was on the nightstand. The men were entranced by the naked little thing. Realizing they had something fantastic on their hands, they advanced toward it slowly, holding out their arms to keep it from escaping.

"Is this some kind of magic trick?" the medic asked.

"No," Andrea said. "I'm not sure what happened."

Andrea likened her as a desktop model used by biology students.

She aimed at different parts of the paramedic's body, not sure which would cause the most harm. Then she thought, shoot his eye out!

"Lookit, she even got a toy gun," the paramedic said.

"Don't touch me or I'll shoot!" she yelled, aiming at his face.

Not sure what he had heard, the paramedic hesitated for a moment and then reached out to grab her. Instantly, she fired four rounds, feeling relieved that the revolver actually had gone off without jamming. One shot entered the man's eye like a needle, penetrating the cornea and lens, instantly blinding him. Trickles of bright red blood oozed from his cheeks as he backed away, giving her time to reload.

"She can really shoot, can't she," Andrea said proudly.

Seeing with only one eye, the paramedic moved back into the living room and sat on the couch, followed by his partner who ran out the door and yelled down to the ambulance driver, "Call the cops!"

"Andrea, I didn't want to hurt him," she said.

"I can't hear you," Andrea said.

"I'm sorry!" she yelled.

"You look like her," he said shakily, "but I can't believe it's you. Ybette? Where did you...? How did you...?"

"I don't know. Maybe I shouldn't have taken up smoking."

Andrea laughed. "Nasty thing. I'm glad it didn't become a habit. What are you going to do?"

She gestured for him to lie back, but he got up and looked into the living room. Seeing that her body was not there, he locked the door and returned to bed, being careful not to crush her. She sat down beside his head and talked into his ear. "Your ear looks so clean, Andrea, I'm proud of you. This earlobe feels so soft and fuzzy," worming her fingers into the canal.

"I can hear you much better now," he whispered. "How did you get so small and come back to life? This is fantastic!"

"I don't know. All of a sudden, I was falling into an ocean of black water, like a sugar cube dropped into a cup of black coffee. The further I fell, the more I melted away. It was so frightening. I screamed and screamed, but still kept falling. I couldn't stop my little crystals from melting off me. It was awful. Then I saw all these other cubes falling around me doing the same thing, melting away into the ocean. It was like being in outer space. The universe. No stars."

"But how did you come back to life?"

"I don't know. I kept melting away till I was one small sugar crystal, a tiny speck."

Andrea pointed to the note on the nightstand. "Like that?"

"Yes. A dot. A point. A...."

"A period."

"The same size as...."

"As a what?"

"I couldn't tell you, because you would never forgive me. Now it doesn't matter. The same size as a ...." She climbed onto his shoulder and from there onto his chest. Feeling safe now, she slid toward his face, wrapping her legs around his neck. "You smell like the ocean, Andrea."

"Sorry, but I didn't have a chance to shower."

"Then they started calling out names. When they got to me, they didn't know my name. Can you imagine being judged and they don't know your name? How could they make such a mistake? How could God not know my name?"

"Sounds like a government operation," he said.

She moved forward a little and squeezed his neck with her thighs, caressing it, as she would a saddle. "You should shave, Andrea. You're tickling me." Finding no end to the vast landscape of his face, it was as variegated as the sides of the mountains surrounding her favorite dude ranch in Wyoming.

The tip of her nose met the tip of his nose, his breathing casting comfortably warm puffs of air over her body. He looked at her cross-eyed and was unable to put anything in focus. "I can't see you," he said. "You're too close." She laughed tickling his lips with her breasts. He wanted to open his mouth and bite them off. He stuck out his tongue and touched her belly gently.

"Stop that!" she yelled.

"Sorry, I couldn't help it. I have to talk, don't I? And you're so close." His mouth movements tickled her, and she giggled. "What was it like being dead?" he asked.

"I can't explain it. I had no senses. I lost all my senses. There's no way to explain it to you. There was no light because I had no eyes. It was as if my mind was the only thing alive. There was no darkness either, so don't be afraid. No darkness, hear me, dear?"

"Yes, but what about...you know, God?"

"I didn't see anyone, just that vast ocean the deeper I went. I must have lost my mind the moment...." Leaning back, she stood up on the valley below his collarbones. He could see her face more clearly now, although not completely in focus. "Your skin is loose, Andrea," wiggling back and forth, unable to get a steady stance. She reached up and grabbed onto the curls of his hair above the forehead. His nose kept her at a distance but amusingly vulnerable to him. He stuck out his tongue just to measure her distance. "Don't you dare even think about it!" she said.

"I was only going to offer you a ride," he said.

"Keep your tongue to yourself, or else you'll get my Irish up again." She inspected the bullet wound between his eyes, pressing her fingers into the scar as if it were a clump of dough to be kneaded.

"What are you looking for?" he asked.

"The bullet. It is a bullet, isn't it?"

"It's probably dissolved by now after all these years."

"Yes, I should think so. Dissolved into a dream. The first dream of the night."

"The dream I can't remember," he said. "That's it! You got it! I always remember the last dream, not the first. Maybe that's why I could never find an ending to the story. I need a beginning to find the ending. Without the world, just an ocean of light, there would be no night or day. On the third day, God created the Earth, but what about the first two days? How did they become days when there was no sunrise or sunset?"

"No starting point."

"That's all? You were a nurse and took anatomy. Which part of the brain do dreams come from?"

"The first dream? I can't remember." She moved over to his eye and looked deep into it. "Wait. Now I can see something. Your brain is shaped like an orange. I don't see orange, only grey. Think of orange, Andrea."

"Orange what? The fruit or the color?"

"Either one but don't tell me."

He thought neither. He thought of Agent Orange. "What do you see?" he asked.

"An omega sign," she said. "A deformed brain. This means you will be the last to die before scientists discover the key to immortality. It will be the very brain used in the experiment and will become the sacrifice upon which the deification of humanity will rest."

"Where'd you get that?" he asked.

"I don't know. It just came out," trying to decipher the years she saw. "I don't see anything for two thousand thirty-four."

Afraid to add up the years till his demise, he said, "What about you? How much time do you have?"

"I don't know. Might be five minutes, might be five hours."

"Okay, get ready," he said. "We're going." He didn't stop to devise a plan, and like a burglar working quickly, took only things of value that he could fit into her big rollaboard bag. When done, he turned to her, held out his hand, and said, "Okay, saddle up."

The sound of an approaching police siren hastened his urgency to find a way to hide her and get away. He looked out the window and noticed that the paramedics were now waiting by the ambulance. "Any ideas?" he asked.

"You're the sky marshal," she said. "How would *you* smuggle a one-foot-tall flight attendant onto a plane?"

Rummaging through the dresser, he picked out a long scarf and tied it to his waist.

"Wear the Hawaiian shirt!" she yelled. "Put on the big Hawaiian shirt I bought you! Hurry, Andrea. And don't forget my purse! And my gun. Give it to me. Hurry!"

Before buttoning the shirt, he picked her up and placed her against his abdomen, navel to navel, held secure by the scarf. "Put your legs inside my pants," he said. "And hang onto the scarf. And be careful with that gun!

Here we go."

They went out the front door just as the police car arrived. He waited to see which way they went up, and then he took the opposite way down. He felt encouraged by having had the presence of mind to lock the door when he left, giving them a few more minutes to get away.

When he crossed the parking lot, he could feel the ambulance driver's eyes mark greedily his brightly flowered shirt. He held his abdomen in while walking toward the Porsche. Her body felt sweaty and itchy, and he feared that she was suffocating.

He threw the bag in the trunk, got in, opened the windows, and drove away. She came out of his shirt like a skin diver who had been under water too long, gasping for air. "I'm dying of thirst!" she croaked, hardly able to talk.

"You could be dehydrated," he said. Luckily, they found a grocery store on the way to the airport and went inside.

When they came out of the store and started walking back to the car, a tall man carrying a red can came up to them and said, "Hey, can you help me get some gas? I'm from out of town and ran out of gas. I don't have enough to get back home. Look," reaching into his pocket and pulling out a few coins covered in lint and flaky remnants of gambling tickets. Around his neck was a gold chain on which hung a gold pendant.

"Where's your car?" Andrea asked.

"Over there," pointing across the parking lot.

Andrea sized up the man's tanned face and beach-bum appearance. Even if he is a crook, he thought, the Good Samaritan thing to do would be to give him ten bucks. But life is a deception, dissolving in an infinite ocean of nothingness when it's over. "You're a lying son-of-a-bitch!" he said. "Get the hell out of here!"

The man put down the can, and said, "Who the hell do you think you're talking to?"

"A damn bum."

"Yeah, I'll show you who's a bum, you cheap bastard," pushing Andrea and causing him to stumble backward. Andrea looked around for help, but all of a sudden, from out of his shirt came the SwissMiniGun firing off two rounds, hitting the man squarely on the chest. Momentarily stunned, as spots of red formed on his silk shirt, he threw a punch, but, when another shot hit him in the face, he buckled over.

Andrea rushed to the car, got in, and drove off. "What a shot," he said. "I mean, that was one hell of a shot."

"Do you think he needs a doctor?" she said, coming out.

"Yeah, but he'll live. Don't worry about it. Do you have any more bullets?"

"Plenty," she said, trying to open a carton of orange juice. "Two packs in my purse."

23/Disco Wanda

They waited in the employee parking lot, considering ways to best get through security and board the plane. Was there a better way to carry her than inside his shirt? "It's not too bad," she said, "other than your belt is too tight, and it's hard to breathe."

He expanded his waistband and said, "Saddle up." She climbed over his leg and went one foot at a time down his pants, like she was getting ready for a potato-sack race. Then she spun around to face him, resting her backside over his belt.

"Just like my old detective special," he said.

"How are you going to pay for this, Andrea?"

"Can't you get us free tickets?"

"I could if we were married."

Andrea smiled at the idea. "Maybe we should fly to Las Vegas first. Then we could honeymoon anywhere in the world."

"It might work. I'm still officially employed. But I'd have to get a name change and all that paperwork."

"Okay, then, that's out," he said. "Before we go inside, let's get some signals straight. If I ask you a question, answer *yes* by tickling me on the right side, and answer *no* on the left side. Got it? And if there's an emergency, give me a knee in the groin, but not hard."

"Like this," kicking him in the left side.

"Not so hard, but that's the idea."

He buttoned his shirt, grabbed the bag, and went off to the terminal, feeling terribly suspicious and worried about the condition of his hidden partner clinging to his waist. The piggyback method was a poor choice, and because she had to remain motionless, he wasn't sure that she was still breathing.

"Are you all right?" he asked. She tickled him on the left side. Immediately, he opened his shirt, looked down at her, and whispered, "What's wrong?"

"Nothing!" she yelled.

"Well then, get your signals straight." She started drumming on him, and he retaliated by jumping up and down to give her a few jolts. "Be careful. We're going in."

At first, the ride excited her, for she was entering a world that she loved dearly. The cool air began seeping through the shirt, giving her great relief. She relaxed her grip, now confident that she wasn't about to fall, the belt being tight enough to support her thighs. Yet she wasn't able to see the ticket counter, the carryons rolling about the floor, the plethora of people waiting in line, and the bulging veins on the neck of the agents as they lifted heavy suitcases and placed them on conveyer belts. She missed the sound of her shoes clicking on the floor as she moved faster and faster toward the gate, weaving with silver-winged pride through passengers rushing back and forth. The prospect of never again being a flight attendant, of never being able to be alone and independent, depressed her. And Andrea became a man who would marry her at any cost, kidnapping her, holding her captive, turning her into his child, even holding her imprisoned in *his* womb!

Suddenly, she screamed, kicked, and punched the man who had saved her life. She turned around to face forward and threatened to crawl out of his shirt.

Assaulted by her in every way short of being bitten, he walked quickly to the nearest waiting area and sat between a woman sipping coffee and a man reading a newspaper. He loosened the top of the shirt, looked down at her and began talking, sounding rather crazy to the strangers (to be sure, in the pre-cell-phone era).

"No, I can't let you out. It's too risky. They'll arrest you for sure…. No, you can't stick your head out. They'll all see you. Keep your head inside, please…. I know it's suffocating in there. Okay, you want your freedom back. Ybette, it'll be all right."

The lady next to him got up and walked away, but the man stood his ground bravely.

"You're growing?" Andrea continued, encouraged by the news. "How can you tell?" He looked over at the man, smiled and said, "She's growing, can you imagine? Twelve inches and still growing."

Ybette started kicking again, drawing the man's attention to the jiggle in Andrea's pants. "There she goes again. Can't stand still. Must have been the orange juice I gave her."

"What's you got there, a pet monkey?" the man asked.

"No. She's all human being."

The man folded his newspaper, put it in his briefcase, and walked away, looking back once to make sure he wasn't followed.

Since there were no more flights available to Washington, he purchased a ticket to JFK just to get out of town.

"You know, it's going to be colder in New York," he said. "Better stay put and enjoy the ride. We've got an hour before the flight, so stay calm."

"I'm hungry!" she cried and kicked.

"You are? I can't believe it. I'll get a snack."

Miami International Airport wasn't very inviting, although it was the main hub for Eastern. Architecturally, the terminal was more symbolic of the suburban blight stretching southward than of space-age travel, and very different from the terminals at JFK. Nonetheless, it had several gift shops that he visited looking for a snack.

Displayed on the shelves of one shop were several dolls dressed in various flight attendant uniforms, skillfully tailored and standing about twelve inches. With an eye out for nearby customers, he picked out a doll. She tapped him on the left side, so he put it back and got another one. He went through the entire lot of dolls with no success until a woman came up to him and said, "Put it back or I'll call the manager."

"Excuse me?" Andrea said.

"I saw you put that doll in your shirt, so put it back or I'll call the manager."

"Okay, I'll put it back, lady." He opened his jacket and out shot Ybette's arm waving her little finger. The woman put on her glasses and leaned forward to get a closer look. Astonished, she felt faint, wobbled backward, and knocked over a display of seashell souvenirs. Andrea picked out two dolls and a chocolate bar, and paid for them at the cashier.

The days of the frisk search being long gone, Andrea wasn't too worried about getting through security, though he was respectful to the security guards on duty. They weren't law enforcement officers and were about as competent and authoritative as the people that guarded department stores or amusement parks.

Normally fond of the aisle seat for the ease of escape it offered, it wasn't the best place to hide, but the only one he could manage with a standby ticket. After settling down, he slipped Ybette a piece of milk chocolate, which she gobbled up in a hurry.

Reluctant to fasten his seatbelt, he attracted the attention of the flight attendant, who said loudly, "Please fasten your seatbelt, sir." Ybette started to toss and turn in order to face forward, causing Andrea's shirt and pants to move around quite noticeably. The flight attendant noticed the movement in his pants and showed an expression of disbelief.

"Wait," he said softy, waving her to come closer and listen to his explanation. "It's not what you think."

She whispered into his ear, "What's in there?"

"It's my thang," he said. "We make movies together."

She frowned at him and said, "Please buckle up the best you can. We have to take off now."

Ybette's only amusement throughout the flight was listening to Andrea's digestive tract taking its course. It was indeed a soft and warm ride for her, and he was kind enough to keep the air flowing through his shirt by pointing the ventilation nozzle directly at it. When the lights went out and the movie was turned on, he fed her some peanuts, which made her start choking. He made choking sounds to cover hers and rushed to the lavatory.

"What can you drink out of? Any ideas?"

Ybette stood up on the edge of the stainless-steel sink and said, "Look the other way. I have to go." After relieving herself in the sink, she said, "Okay, now flush for me, Andrea." He ran water into the sink and gave her a tissue so that she could wash up, then another tissue, which she used to wrap around her body like a towel.

He stood long-legged in front of the toilet staring pensively into the stainless-steel bowl, ready to take his turn, but nothing came. "I can't go with you looking," he said.

Ybette turned around but continued to watch him in the mirror. "Fine porno star you are," she said. "Can't even micturate in public."

"I can't hear you," he said.

"But you do look mighty handsome, cowboy."

When done, Andrea sat down and looked her over, worried that if she didn't get a hot meal and clothes, she wouldn't last the journey.

"I'm not wearing that awful doll's uniform," she said.

"What about the other one? The Disco Wanda. It looks cool."

"Gaudy, Andrea. Gaudy." She turned toward the mirror and let the tissue drop, revealing a body that she had always wanted, a body with skin as smooth and soft as a baby's. "Look at me, Andrea. I'm starvin' about half to death."

"You need some warm milk."

"We don't serve warm milk."

"Yeah, I know, but I have an idea. Hop aboard."

Going straight to the galley, he ordered a hot tea with cream, making sure to keep it on the side. Back inside the lavatory, he submerged the half-ounce container of *half and half* in the hot water, warming it quickly.

"Oh, it tastes so nice, Andrea," she said, mouth ringed white. "Just what I always wanted—a whole bucket of cream to myself."

He prepared a cup of tea using just the sugar and lemon.

"Would you like cream with your tea, sir?" she said.

"You remember that one," he said.

"Continental, wasn't it?"

He picked her up gently, kissed each breast, and helped her inside to once again continue the journey.

The rest of the trip was difficult for her, being so confined to the underside of his garments. Upon arrival at JFK, sore in every muscle, dizzy from looking nowhere, legs aching from the constriction of the belt, toes cramping from not having ground to stand on, she leapt for joy in his womb when they deplaned.

Having walked through the Eastern terminal many times before, she knew the exit route well, except for the apparent detour he was now taking. She emerged from hiding only to find him sitting in a stall in the men's room searching through the carryon. "It amazes me that they allow this thing on the plane," he said. "It has more pockets in it, you lose track of where you put stuff." Finally finding the dolls, he stripped the clothes off both and said, "Try them on for size." He spread his legs, making room for her to stand on the carryon and get dressed.

"My waist is as small as can be," she said, but this uniform is impossible. Let me try the other one."

"Are you growing?" Andrea asked. "You're getting bigger. Look at you! You were twelve inches this morning. Now you're at least thirteen, maybe fourteen inches!"

Next door to them came the sounds of a man trying to repress his laughter. "Hush, Andrea," she said. "I think someone is listening." She tried on the Disco Wanda outfit and that fit perfectly.

"Disco Wanda! Sock it to me!"

"Hush, Andrea!"

Now that she had something to wear, they had a long discussion about where to go, she willing to go anywhere, and he cautious about the police, media, and especially ICA that would turn his life inside out if apprehended. He argued that something profound was missing—a secret treasure toward which they should be running, or an evil demon from which they should be fleeing. But no one was after him. Even though he was carrying a human being that might be the clue to the mystery of life, it really didn't matter at all.

There was no *cause-and-effect* to the story; it was metaphysical nonsense. He contemplated reenacting her suicide, going through the same sequence of events that she had experienced—gas, Demerol, defibrillation—all for the sake of reducing himself to her size. But that would be too risky and lead nowhere. He thought of bringing her to the chief scientist at ICA, who might be able to unravel the mystery of her transmutation. And if that failed, to the Abbey of Gethsemane where Trappist monks could pray and release her from the state that trapped her. She was a key given to him to unlock something profound, but where was the lock?

This wasn't a fantasy tale. This wasn't the 7th *Voyage of Sinbad* where Princess Parisa, shrunken to a finger-size elf by a wicked spell, was able to sneak out of the Cyclops' prison and push back the heavy bolt and free her beloved Sinbad. Ybette was a miniature but not a doll, pintsize but not a baby, little but not a dwarf. She was a revived human being that had lost ninety percent of her weight in the comeback process, but none of her mass. How could that be?

He opened the stall door and carried the two naked dolls out to the sink, put them on the shelf, and washed his hands. The men waiting in line for the next stall gave him the same look of surprise as they would a woman who walked in by accident.

After washing and drying the dolls, he sat them up on the shelf, pointed a finger, and said, "Remember now, girls. No freebies!"

Happy to be out of the men's room, Ybette peeked out at the familiar site of the terminal, her little eyes absorbing just as much as they ever did, and her little nose picking up the aroma of coffee brewing, making her stomach growl. Andrea too was so affected. "Where's there good to eat these days?" he asked.

"Cucina in terminal four," she said. "The IAB."

He walked briskly out to the street to catch the shuttle bus, and a blast of cold air hit him with a bang. Ybette shivered and clung to his warm belly as he buttoned the top of his shirt. He felt a cold coming on and dreaded going anywhere at such a miserable time of year.

When they got to the IAB, he walked into the first restaurant that he could find—the Taj Mahal.

"How many are you?" the maitre d' asked.

"Just one," Andrea said.

"We have place for you at the bar. Please follow me."

"Noticing a few small tables still available, Andrea pointed to them and said, "I'd prefer a table."

"But you're just one."

Andrea said, "Great. You know how to count. One body. Now, let me have one of those tables for dinner."

"Our policy for dinner, sir...."

"Taj Mahal, my ass," Andrea balked. "Your policy for dinner seems to be how big a tip you'll get, not how well you serve a customer."

"I'm sorry sir, but you can eat just as well at the bar."

"Forget it," he said and walked out.

In Cucina, he found an isolated corner where they sat and talked things over. "Maybe we should forget this idea," he said. "I know it's your dream to go traveling, but we don't have much time to plan. Maybe it's not the right idea."

"If it's too cold," she said, "we can get warmer clothes."

"It's more than that. It's about…, I don't know. Something else."

"What do you mean?"

"I don't know," he said. "I can't explain it."

24/J.G.

Into the night, hour after hour, as departure lounges filled with passengers and then emptied themselves like colossal digestive tracts, they roamed every floor of the IAB until coming upon a most unlikely place. On the fourth floor, as if in a museum, were three chapels—exhibitions of faiths Jewish, Christian, and Protestant—all clearly visible from the outside through glass windows and doors. Andrea opened the door of the Jewish chapel just to breathe the air inside, opened the door of the Protestant chapel just to hear something inside, and opened the door of the Catholic chapel to walk inside. It was very quiet and empty, so they took a seat facing the altar. In the left corner was a large wooden statue of Our Lady standing on a three-bladed propeller alongside a four-tier rack of votive candles shimmering through ruby goblets.

From behind the altar emerged a short man of about forty carrying a pail of water. A spotless white towel skirted his waist. A butch haircut and receding hairline made him look nearly bald. His nose was broad enough to have been broken, and his eyes were so deeply set in the skull, they didn't reveal a color other than dark. He wore a freshly-pressed shirt, buttoned only at the third button, revealing a hairless chest and sleeves rolled up to the biceps of hairless arms. The shirt was monogrammed with the initials *J.G.* just below the place where a pocket is usually sewn.

J.G. put the pail on the floor in front of Andrea, indifferent to the presence of Ybette on his lap, and said, "Take off your shoes and socks."

"For what?" Andrea said.

"A rite of the church."

"Which church?"

"Ah, the right church. Don't they always practice the right rites in church?"

"That depends on the church."

Kneeling down, J.G. insisted, "I must wash your feet."

"Why?" Andrea wondered.

"For my plenary indulgence."

Andrea took off his shoes and socks and stuck one foot in the water, which was pleasantly warm. Then he put the other foot in on top of the first.

"Are you a priest?" Ybette asked.

"A saint," J.G. said. "So said the *great atheist*. He called me Saint Genet, and rightly so, since I performed the *Miracle of the Rose* and had a vision of *Our Lady of the Flowers*. Instead of being punished for the crimes I committed, I was rewarded by being sentenced to prison, a place meant for pain and suffering, a place where no man preferred to be, a place designed to destroy human freedom. I made flowers out of criminals, the worst kind of criminals—men that raped and killed girls—so that I could love them, and make their brutality fragile, like a rose. And it worked, at least in my novels, my art."

"You're not Genet," Andrea said. "He's dead. Who are you? What are you doing here?"

"Who's Genet?" Ybette asked.

"The guy who wrote *Querelle*, a book that got me into trouble with my ex-wife. She thought I was turning gay because I was reading a book titled 'queerly.' She didn't know any French, even though her mother was French."

J.G. laughed and tucked the towel under his belt.

"I bought all his books," Andrea said, looking pensively at the statue. "Got me in trouble with my mother too. She practically disowned me. She burned all of them and buried the ashes in her rose garden under the statue of Our Lady."

"I cannot recover those dirty books," J.G. said, "so I was sentenced to wash away the dirt from men's feet until the day when all evil books will be burned in the Armageddon."

"You didn't know," Andrea said.

"I see a boy in bed reading *The Thief's Journal*, his nature trembling in my presence, and I'm condemned for having removed Christ from his sainthood. My novels spread out like wildfire, violently consuming freedom every which way the wind blows." J.G. sat down next to Andrea and began to dig deep into his conscience. "I suffered from becoming my stories, which were in fact lies. Sure, I was a thief and homosexual, and spent most of my life in prison, but you don't see the coward that I really was. All you see is the hero, the fictional character that supposedly made something great out of his life. You don't see the tears I shed alone in my cell at night, abandoned by my thoughts. I refused to meet myself in myself and met myself in external heroes—Harcamone, Stilitano, Querelle. I became a fictional character, a thinker who became the thing thought—é clater vers; geworfene Entwurf; a bursting forth—without a center, a source, a being, fooling people like a magician that I had a hold on myself, when I really couldn't find anything inside me to hold onto. I was an orphan; I didn't have a father or mother; I didn't have a body. I was a body imprisoned with other bodies that I kept interchanging with my own. My advocate—the *great atheist*—the philosopher who engineered my pardon, was a politician. I became a pawn for communism. I was his idol, his model, his raison d'être for existentialism. A subject for proving his subjectivism."

"I like this," Andrea said. "Go on."

"Sartre started with Descartes' profound idea to wash the mind of all ideas that could be distrusted or doubted, which was everything and anything, everything men call real. Descartes *thought* there was something left over and called it the *cogito*—the thinker, the ego, the self, the *I* that thinks. All perfectly sound, except for the sound of it. The *I*. A word, a sign, a phenomenon that escaped the mind-cleansing act, the *I* that wasn't washed out of itself. How could it be, if there was nothing left to see?"

"Good philosophy. Good philosophy for a poet. I'm impressed."

"That's why he said that I internalized the prison, my fellow inmates, my lovers, the things I stole. I became them all, their bodies."

"Precisely, and you were nothing inside without them—an empty consciousness."

"And this is where Sartre was *a succès commercial*. He glorified consciousness into my body. He thought that I was the first and only body. Adam."

"Sartre should have done some research into evolution and genetics. How could you have happened on your own? Just because you didn't have parents to teach you doesn't mean you were the first man. It's like saying to that wooden statue, invent the Pythagorean Theorem."

"I was not a wooden statue!" J.G. exclaimed. "I was a body par excellence. My mother was a prostitute and my father a Frank trick! I was abandoned at age one and became a...."

"Basket case!" Andrea said, making Ybette laugh.

"A body par excellence! Nothing more. A vulgar, impolite, mixture of parts, held together by a body. I exist my body. I don't exist *inside* my body. I exist *my* body, only when I'm aware of my body *inside* another body."

"I exist my body? But you must know that your body is composed of a billion different parts. What puts it all together?"

"You tell me," J.G. conceded.

"Something for sure, but not the parts. Let's say you're a basket, and in that basket are a million pieces of a puzzle—a jigsaw puzzle—the human body. Each piece is a different organ, or part of an organ of the body. Each piece has all the genes—I'm sure you will agree with that, Jean—the entire code, the entire map. But some are turned on, some turned off, which tell it what it is—the mitral valve in the heart, the iris in the left eye, the thumb on the right hand. Now take the basket and dump all the pieces on the floor. Then you tell them to form a human body. The genes are all there, but nothing happens. How does a cell in an embryo, which has the entire map, the entire genetic code, decide to divide into a heart cell or an eye cell? And when decided, where to go in the body to form a heart or an eye? Surely not the body you talk about. Surely not one body-plan gene that does all the conducting, for where did that gene get its plan, its unique marching orders? Take the evolutionary path back in time and you're bound to find a beginning cell; where did that cell get the directions to divide into multifarious cells? Take the cell you lived in for so many years. Where did you get the knowledge to write stories that allowed you to escape it?"

J.G. reached into his pocket and pulled out a cigar, which he put into his mouth and pretended to smoke. "French pantomime will never cease. Now, to your question about genes. True, a name game played by biologists and chemists, but I must admit, one very convincing one. Nonetheless, the origin of life is not really life, as you imply. But scientists are zeroing in on it—the transition from inorganic to organic compounds in an oxygen-rich environment given billions of years and layers of rich strata. DNA, you must admit, is made of organic compounds, and organic compounds are made of inorganic elements—oxygen, hydrogen, carbon, and nitrogen."

"Yeah, great," Andrea said wryly. "We're eighty percent H-two-O. But that doesn't explain how this bag of water can move about in space and time on its own."

"You see, this is why you never became a philosopher. You always wanted to be a philosopher, is that right? But you couldn't even resolve a simple plot in a book. Do you know why? You were born of an ancient myth whose simple meaning was diverted by the medievalists so that you live under a great repression such that anything creative and original you might do promises only the fires of hell. Naked truth scares you. Your self lies to itself. It does not come from thinking in which purity of consciousness is primary, and this thinking is not only unfaithful to philosophy, but *covers* and alienates it."

"What are you suggesting, that I sell my soul for a silly plot in a book?"

"The soul exists the body!" J.G. insisted.

"Nonsense."

"That's the only true art. All the rest is metaphysics."

"But I can't do that."

"Why?"

"Because the soul will not survive," Andrea said. "Your books are alive now, but wait till the context changes in the future. The texts will become as innocuous as the devil is today, hiding just like you behind that altar. Sartre was right about you. You might become a saint after all. People will read

Funeral Rites and laugh out loud as if it were a comedy."

"Then I won't have to wash anymore feet!"

"I thought you liked washing feet."

"I'd rather be writing, but I have no way to escape. This is my sentence. I have no freedom to change the plot."

"Your books had no plots, other than your masturbations to transcend the cell by diving headfirst into it. The sentence became your sentence. To put it existentially, you became a being-for-yourself only after becoming a being-for-others. *Existence precedes essence*—a dictum from a philosopher that condemned dictums, so it became a cliché. End of existentialism!"

"I'm getting hungry again, Andrea," Ybette said.

"Of course you are," J.G. said to Ybette. "You would consume the whole world in order to stay alive, ingesting all the elements known to man, food par excellence, good for the body, even plutonium. Swallow it all, head first."

"But I want a Big Mac!" she said.

"Okay, let's saddle up," Andrea said.

"Stay!" J.G. said. "I was just about to explain to you the relationship between your book's ending and Miss Rember's being born again."

"I think what she really needs right now is a hamburger."

"If you wish," picking up his bucket and walking behind the altar. "You'll find the answer in terminal five on the information pod."

"What a strange man," Ybette said. "Do you think he washes all the feet that come in here?"

"No. That's not *the* Jean Genet. It was *a* Jean Genet, known only by a few people, mostly French philosophers."

That he was so familiar with the name suggested to him that the image of the man was a mental transformation of some sort, like a holographic idea. Maybe the edge of life was no thicker than a piece of paper and death resided on its verso. Hold it up to the light and you can see through it, not the mirror image of the letters and words, but the undersides of them. That was Genet's literature—not the noumena, which can never be seen or known, but the *inner face of the phenomena*. Not the reflection of the noumena on the back of the phenomena, but the expressions on the *back face* of the phenomena.

"What are you talking about?" asked Ybette. "What's noumena?"

"Did I say that?" Andrea said. "How did you know? My words didn't have quotation marks around them."

"Must be ESP."

"Well, then, that's it. Quotation marks give us perception. They give an idea its flying orders."

"Oh, I see. And tells the puzzle pieces where to go."

"Except one that I'm still puzzled about. Your last note. The period with quotation marks around it. What did you say it was? An embryo?"

"A fertilized egg, life size."

Before leaving, Andrea wrote the following in the chapel's book of intentions: **". "**

Then, looking back one last time, he saw the microcephalic head of a dirty white pit bull staring at him from behind the altar, growling terribly. It lunged at him, but an invisible chain around its neck yanked it back.

" . "

"I'm beginning to see," says Marge. "Do you think the hijacker is for real or just words inside quotation marks?"

"I doubt it," John says. "He's unusually silent though."

"I don't think many people are reading the book. What if he tests us at the end?"

"We might be in serious trouble if we flunk."

25/Sentence

A blast of wind swept down from the winged roof with such force, it felt like the building was flying away. Andrea struggled around to the front, holding Ybette close against his body and pulling his carryon up over a barricade and onto the sidewalk. But the entrance was still and silent—a nocturnal snapshot held steady by the bird's pointed beak and a door half open. He entered carefully.

The terminal by night varied so much from day that the intended buoyancy of the design was lost. Both day and night—the one by its blue skies, the other by its glassy blackness—the concrete body remained the same, but at night the exposure to the universe gave the impression that one was being spied on from above.

Running up the steps to the central information pod, he read his message, made signally visible by a split-second delay in flight numbers, gates, times, and destinations. *TWA congratulates Flight Attendants of the Year: Sandy Lee, Monique Bascle, and Wee Khim.* On the right side appeared the notice: *TWA congratulates pilot of the year Ten Williams, as humble as the gold cross around his neck.*

Predictably, a pilot came out of the tubular passageway that led to the gates, walked gracefully down the red-carpeted landing, and said, "I only wear that cross with my Sansabelt pants and guinea shirt." He was shaking a handful of nuts in his right hand.

Andrea looked at the mustachioed pilot curiously and read the nametag on his chest. "Are you, ah, him?" pointing at the pod.

"Pilot of the year?" the pilot asked.

"Yeah," Andrea said.

"Didn't you feel that landing? Smooth as glass."

"No, we weren't on your flight. We came over from the IAB and were looking for a message that's supposed to be on the information board. Then you're Ten Williams?"

"Yes."

"And there are really ten of you?"

The pilot counted the nuts and said, "Exactly!"

"What's with the white bucks?" Ybette said, pointing and laughing at the pilot's shoes. Andrea placed her on the information desk to give her some advantage.

"A pimp once stepped on these shoes while I was walking the Champs-Élysées, just to get my attention to go inside and watch a strip show. The easy-lay sailor I was dating cold-cocked him on the chops. Knocked him flat.

Then we went inside."

"Step on his shoes!" Ybette said over the PA system.

"She's been weak all throughout this story," the pilot said, "lacking in dramatic value and a pronounced tendency to be prosaic and didactic in dialogue."

"Who asked you?" Ybette echoed.

"Go on," Andrea said. "I need a way out of here. An exclusive tip from a genius."

"Genius, you say? I'm flattered."

"Then you are the one we're looking for."

"If you're looking for philosophical impact here, the characters don't create any mystery that will bring it off. You must omit content for effect. You are too literal. If you're writing about suffering from a terrible itching sensation all over your body, don't say you went to the doctor and he diagnosed eczema. Names destroy the mystery of things. Think back to when you were a child and didn't know the names of things; how *infinite* life was. When mommy went out of the house, you were terrified because you thought she was never coming back home. The world was like a universe; now the whole thing fits in your house and has lost mystery."

"Do you want to take over here? Finish this thing off? You know, Jean Genet said that we would find an answer here. We just met him in the Lady of the Skies Chapel. Do you have a climax we could use?"

"Genet, indeed. I read *Our Lady of the Flowers*. Well, I'm afraid you might be in for the same fate. What story are you talking about?"

The fact that the pilot hadn't asked about Ybette's size made Andrea think he was an apparition or a character in a dream. He pointed to her and said, "That should be evident. Didn't you even notice her?"

"Now you're going to make me as cross as two sticks! I don't know what you're getting at. If you keep up this dreadful banter, I'm going to have to...."

"Look, I know you make a living out of writing plays and have no use for anomalies like her that reach into science fiction. You think that people who look for the answers to life are arrogant because they always invent answers. Or their reason for having no answer is the only answer. But to say there are no answers because answers take the mystery out of life, is just rewarding your own destiny as a writer."

"Right," the pilot said with a chuckle. "I made a fortune on writing plays, and I couldn't have done so without showing mystery."

"The Catholic Church uses it as a crutch," Andrea said. "When boxed in a corner, it's a...hatchooo! Excuse me; I must be coming down with a cold."

"Roll up your sleeve," said the pilot.

"What for?" asked Andrea.

"Shot of some kind."

"What kind?"

"Ah, any kind. Don't they always give you some kind of a shot?"

"Yeah, beautiful! Thank you. Just what I needed to see the difference. Right out of your play. You kept the dialogue unidentified. The vial was filled with a mysterious substance kept in the refrigerator to stay cold and pure. Not good for the scientist or philosopher who needs to give it a name."

"You were saying about the Cath'lic Church?"

"Yes, I was always curious why you became a Catholic."

"Because the Mass is great theater," rasped the pilot. He put the nuts in his pocket, took out a cigarette and lit it. Taking a deep drag, he coughed and cleared his throat. "It has dynamic *and* organic qualities that you can't find anywhere else."

"I always thought it was about the priesthood. They can't get married. Their vow of celibacy. Did it attract you?"

The pilot looked up at the clock sheepishly. "I must be getting home. Donnie is expecting me."

"Their gene pool is lost," Andrea teased. "The priests, I mean. The men with the most fervent faith never get married to pass on their genes. That's why the church is doomed. There are fewer and fewer priests, because they are being genetically weaned out of society. Years ago, Catholics had large families and the parents expected one of them to be a priest. Now with just two kids, there's no way. That's why they ban birth control. To increase family size."

"Promise me you won't laugh, if I say that priests and nuns are undersexed, meaning just the opposite of what you say, resulting in a society that is oversexed, because the undersexed are being weaned out."

"Promise me you won't laugh," Andrea said, "if I say that homosexuals are being weaned out of society, because they are abnormally sexed and are not passing on their genes."

"Obscurantisme terroriste!" wailed the pilot. He turned and ran back toward the passageway and yelled again, "Obscurantisme terroriste!"

Andrea rushed behind the desk, picked up the microphone and said, "Attention! Attention in terminal five. There is a terrorist loose in the terminal; he is running for the departure gates. He's wearing a TWA captain's uniform and white bucks. He thinks he's Ten Williams, but he's only one short William. You can't miss him. He's wanted for writing plays in an obscure style and then criticizing people for their inability to understand.

Don't listen to anything he has to say since he's a homosexual who eats the sacred host and is guilty of the greatest sacrilege against the Holy Magisterium. You could read his plays all day and still not know one ounce of truth about life. Apprehend him and bring him here to the information pod in the main lobby."

The messages on the pod disappeared, and the departure schedules reappeared. Within minutes, a crowd came out of the passageway and approached the desk. In its midst was Tennessee Williams, unable to escape and forced to stand before the sentence.

"Step forward," Andrea said.

"What for?" Williams said.

"Trial of some kind."

"What kind?"

"Ah, any kind. Don't they always have a trial of some kind in a story?" jibed Andrea.

"This is bogus!" cried Williams.

"To deny that this trial is legitimate would be like saying that all your plays are illegitimate. You—Thomas Lanier Williams—are found guilty of impersonating ten men at once and ignoring the philosophical argument of the one and the many. Sentence?"

"Asphyxiation!" the crowd answered.

"That is not a sentence," Andrea corrected.

"Asphyxiate him!" the crowd shouted.

"That's better," Andrea said. "You are guilty of dancing to the beat of bongos and performing unnatural sexual acts with drunken sailors, thus corrupting the philosophical principle of causality and the natural generation of human beings. Sentence?"

"Asphyxiate him!"

"Guilty of writing this," pointing to the information pod on which appeared his sentence: *I've got a heart that's as big as the head of a baby.* "And using flamboyant figures of speech and mawkish symbols *ad nauseam*, erroneously participating in ideas separate from the body, showing only shadows, reflections, and mirages, and never abstracting ideas united to the body in order to reveal real objects, real light, and real being. Sentence?"

"Asphyxiate him!"

"Renouncing your baptism into the Catholic faith because you couldn't stand being upstaged by the greatest story ever told—the Holy Sacrifice of the Mass. Sentence?"

"Asphyxiate him!"

"For writing the movie *Baby Doll,* which was condemned by the Legion of

Decency for portraying a whore in a crib at Christmastime. What say ye men?"

"Asphyxiate him!"

"Other charges against this quotation mark abuser in violation of pure reason exist, but are not necessary to magnify the sentence. Will the Prince of Rokovoko please step forward?"

Marked by a plethora of scars and tattoos that resembled the impregnable skin of an alligator, a black man carrying a barbed harpoon came forward.

"You might wonder," explained Andrea, "as did Ishmael, whether this man has a soul, looking more like an animal than human being, or why he steps in the company of so many great philosophers like yourselves, but I tell you as did his author, this man is the equal to any philosopher, even though he cannot read and is said to be a savage, pagan, and even cannibal. Why? I ask you to look at this seaman and tell me that he is not as comfortable in his own skin as Socrates. I know you don't like the references to his Socratic spirit in Chapter Ten, but I have good reason to pick Queequeg as executioner of this sentence. Are any of you philosophers seamen that have been sodomized by Ten Williams? And as irrefutable proof that Ten Williams tried to pimp poor Queequeg off on his fellow pederast Donnie, look at this letter—his own words," pointing to the information pod once again. *I am reading Moby Dick. Have you ever? It is lovely writing, and the tattooed cannibal in it would please you, as he apparently did the hero if I understand him correctly. Ten*

Queequeg looked up at the pod and smiled at the incomprehensible words, then walked around Williams once to size up the rotund body. Placing the harpoon on the floor, he bent over as if bowing, prompting Williams to bow in return, which gave Queequeg leverage to pull Williams' arm over his shoulder and, with one smooth draping motion, lifted the body into the air. Holding the arms tight, he began an *airplane spin*, swirling about with such velocity, Williams felt like throwing up.

"That will teach him," said the young Marx, "amusing the rich with the heartaches of the destitute."

"Looks like he's going to blow," Andrea warned. "Who's got the Corpus Capum?"

A man with a long, bushy mustache came running out of the passageway yelling, "Ich habe. Ich habe es." The philosophers made way for him to approach, and he came forward holding high over his head a pill bottle cap.

"Friedrich you-flunked-me-because-I-couldn't-spell-your-ficken-name Nietzsche will do the honors."

"Aber ich kann nicht...how you say? Drive it home? Williams ist ein Dichter."

"Ja, ich verstehe," Andrea said. "Das Blut zwischen Dichtern ist sehr dick. Okay, die naechste! Herr Kant, konnen sie verleicht?" Kant nodded in agreement. "Jawohl! Herr Kant can. Nietzsche, give Kant the cap."

Williams was so distressed by the centrifugal force, his face turned beet red, his eyes bulged out of their sockets, und so weider und sofort.

"Queequeg, stop spinning!" Andrea shouted. "Stop! Stand him up. Get him ready. Herr Kant, if you please."

Out of fear of exploding into a critique of pure reason, Williams opened his mouth and allowed Kant to push the bottle cap deep into his throat.

"Halt!" shouted a mustached man wearing a swastika armband. "You are condemning an innocent man. All of you have devoted your lives to thinking, but you are not thinking here. Ten Williams, author of *Ten Blocks on the Camino Real*, is a great poet and has committed no crime other than a leap of faith, one block to the next."

Shouts of protest and jeers came from the crowd. "Wait!" Andrea pleaded. "He's got a right to talk. Settle down!"

Pointing at the information pod, Heidegger continued. "You see there, his words from *Camino Real*, not a blockbuster like *Streetcar Named Desire*, but an honest and innocent portrayal of man's confrontation with death, hardly an exploitation of dramatic art for profit. True, it doesn't solve the riddle of the universe, but it is a deep journey into the sources of being. Who among you would dare execute Dante for the *Divine Comedy*? Also a journey. It is a trip, a journey similar to those we are now on, but one that doesn't carry around excess baggage, a trek to the unknown without the aid of a compass or sextant, a trek none of you would dare undertake. Such was the journey of the Pequod; Queequeg himself would surely confirm. You philosophers have failed to understand the origin of thought, preferring the historical route that conceals the origin, our true source. I tried just like you. *Sein und Zeit* is studied by all philosophy students, but it stands as a failure, because in order for the man of common sense to understand it, he needs to study twenty-five centuries of logical arguments that have confounded the original quest for truth. But once he has mastered your *Metaphysics*, Aristotle, your *Meditations*, Descartes, and your *Ideas*, Husserl, he will find that his mind has been adulterated by unoriginal thinking. He will have learned just enough to cloud his thinking for the rest of his life. He will be a man of science, attaching labels to things and ideas, but unlike the scientist, will not know truth."

Applause comes from many of the philosophers. "And in conclusion, I turn to his very words. *Nothing untrue comes off the tongue quickly. It is planned speeches that contain lies, not what you blurt out so spontaneously in one instant.*"

"Wordiness and tiresome!" said Edmund Husserl, stepping forward. "This is true of all his works. Truth comes off the tongue quickly, is better, wouldn't you say? *Nothing* is problematic, as proven by modern quantum physics. Let me offer a conclusion to the dilemma we face here tonight. We have witnessed all the arts of argumentative dialectics—weak efforts and compromises, oppositions between idealism and empiricism, relativism and absolutism, subjectivism and objectivism, and positivism and metaphysics, giving us only half-truths and abstract one-sidedness that can only be resolved by my phenomenology that will someday torpedo the natural attitude!"

This sentence, declared to be Williams' sentence, was made whole by only one word—the predicate, the essence of speech, the *I am who am* to the *E=mc²* of the intellect. The predicate, and the predicate only, was the essence of man's genius, and here employed by one of the greatest minds that ever lived, came down to being just one word. *Torpedo!* It was a feeble attempt to avoid causal relations between abstract ideas, to avoid comparing things existing in space and time thus falling into the trap of never knowing whether they exist inside the mind or in the world. It was the mind crediting itself for discrediting itself, believing in itself for disbelieving in itself. It was a torpedo turning around in the water, not to *torpedo* the submarine from which it was launched, but to be the torpedo of itself.

Andrea looked at Husserl's face as the perfect image of a philosopher. Round glasses, graying beard, pensive eyes. He smiled, holding back laughter as best he could, but eventually burst out in one huge explosion over the PA system—"Torpedoes los!"

"Das ist *mein* Metapher," yelled Heidegger, "which is feminine for metaphor, derived from the Latin topere, meaning to stun, as in the eclectic torpedo ray that can really hit you."

"Ah, shut up, you, you rectorial blowhard for Hitler youth!"

Heidegger picked up the harpoon and gave it to Queequeg. "Topere!" he shouted.

Over the PA-system arose a terrifying scream that made Augustine grab Andrea by the arm, Aristotle duck behind Socrates, and Thomas Aquinas pray, "Mea culpa, mea culpa, mea maxima culpa," striking his breast three times.

Ybette screamed again and shouted, "Get off me, you filthy pig!"

Andrea pushed through the crowd and managed to seize Queequeg by the shoulder just as he was about to take a bite out of Ybette's belly. Holding her in his hands like a big turkey leg, Queequeg grinned, showing in his eyes the cannibalism to which he was addicted. Andrea swung his tightly closed fist, striking the savage on the chin, pushing the lower lip up into the bare incisor, causing blood to stream over his chin. The blow, though strong, put Andrea more off balance than his opponent. While grabbing onto a nearby arm for support, he felt something heavy slip secretly into his pocket. Immediately, the savage put Ybette back down on the counter and, without saying a word or holding the slightest feelings of anger or revenge, pushed Andrea away and picked up his harpoon.

Almost falling from the push, and, somewhat humiliated by it, Andrea pulled out the pistol, causing the crowd to disperse and open a space for them to battle. He glared at the savage, holding him at bay with the pistol, his face turning as cold and shiny as the stainless steel in his hand.

Unlike the savage, who would kill with the same dispassion that he would on a whaling boat, Andrea wished someone would jump between them and forge a truce. As the seconds passed, his look became more troubled, and he was like a man forced to stand before a firing squad and wait for a commutation of sentence that was never requested. His isolation transformed the space between them into a pain that he couldn't bear. The bullet's name chambered in his gun was *isolation*.

Rapidly, three cap-gun-size shots rang out. Stung in the back of the head, Queequeg reached behind and felt the warm, sticky wetness of blood on his skin. Ignoring the pain, he raised his harpoon, reared back, and took aim, but hesitated at the sight of Andrea cocking his pistol.

The gunsight at the tip of the barrel rose to a spot right between the harpooner's eyes, but didn't hold steady there. It kept rising, and, at the instant it cleared the top of his head—fired—sending a bullet directly into the face of the information pod.

Unlike what he would do to a whale, Queequeg speared Andrea's heart *tenderly*, pulling back and securing the barbs without the least effort. Suddenly, the tattoos throughout Queequeg's body became alive, swarming around his skin as spermatozoa looking for something to fertilize. They weren't illustrations of snakes or hearts, or words of any known language, but more like hieroglyphics, though inexplicable and beyond interpretation of any cipher. To borrow Ahab's hermeneutic, they were a "devilish tantalization of the gods!"

It was the one and only answer to the riddle of the universe, the knowledge of Being that existed without contrasts, not a god opposed to a devil, or good versus evil, but a being existing only for itself.

Rising to a fever pitch, the enigmatic idols interlinked and stretched out into a long chain, a gigantic double helix that wrapped around the shaft of the harpoon. Now spinning wildly, the genome of the species *truth* screwed itself into the body of the condemned.

Now filled by an endless strand of organic philosophical information, Andrea fell to the floor.

"Period!" Augustine said. "He has become an end for which there are no words."

"I get it," Marge says. "I get it."

"You get what?" John asks.

"Why this doesn't have a theme or plot."

"Okay, tell me why it doesn't have a theme or plot."

"The book succumbs to the same fate as his philosophy. It rejects literature for being *derivative*. It's the word I was looking for, but it didn't come to me till just now. Derivative . This book is doomed to remain at its initial stage, because it refuses to move on without first discovering the source of existence, which it can never do."

John tries to put on a face like Marlon Brando and says, "Instead I'm a bum, which is what I am."

"You don't get it, John. You're a derivative."

26/Nymphet

Early next morning, Ybette jumped out of bed and hurried to the bathroom. Five minutes later, she climbed back into bed and said, "I cannot tell you how good that felt. It must have been a week since my last."

"Did you flush the toilet?" he asked.

"No. I almost dislocated my arm trying. Could you please?"

He went to the toilet and started to laugh. "A three-pound woman does not a baby poop make."

"What was that?" she asked.

"Nothing," he said. "I'm going downstairs to buy a paper."

Ten minutes later, he returned. "Did you know that one Sunday *Times* has more information in it than a Renaissance man was exposed to in a whole year?"

"French crullers!" she said. "You darling," jumping off the bed, climbing up the chair and onto the table. "Cream and sugar, please, Andrea."

The news of the previous day, especially the local news, filtered through his eyes quickly, as was his special skill to process titles and relate them to the unanswered questions in his mind. But there was nothing inside to relate to them.

What am I looking for? A name in the obituaries? But I don't know anybody here.

"What are you looking for, Andrea? You skimmed over every page and haven't read a thing."

"All finished," he said, carefully folding the paper and throwing it on the floor. "I have a photographic memory."

"Can you remember what happened last night?"

The image of the info pod from the TWA terminal came back to him. He braced himself at this brief glimpse into the past, perplexed by the blank stare of the eye, such as affects parents when, after receiving a spirited letter from their son, an officer comes to their door and says he recently died in combat. Preparing himself to hear differently, he said, "Yeah, I had a weird dream about being killed in the T-way terminal."

"Andrea, that wasn't a dream."

"No? Not a dream? If it wasn't a dream, how come I'm still here?"

Ybette dunked a piece of donut into her coffee and said, "Because, my dear, it was a miracle."

"A miracle? How do you know that?"

"Because I was there and saw it."

"Nonsense. You were in the dream all right, but that's all it was."

Satisfying her hunger before proving her point, she finally said, "Okay, I'll prove it to you. Ask me a question about the dream."

Andrea thought a moment and said, "What was the message on the information pod in the terminal?"

"I've got a heart that's as big as a baby."

"Well, that's close enough. It's as big as the *head* of a baby."

"Ask me another question," she said.

"Okay. Who was the pilot?"

"The pilot was Tennessee Williams, and he was wearing...white bucks!"

Surrendering silently, Andrea found himself in a haunted house, a house he had entered without crossing a threshold, constantly looking for himself, yet never totally appearing, a house whose rooms were all locked and occupied by strangers—the real persons behind his cover stories.

He stood up and threw himself dejectedly onto the bed, landing on something under the covers that jabbed him in the back. Groaning, he rolled over and uncovered a pen, and further down, his journal! Opening it to the last few pages, he read about his encounters the night before at the airport. "A miracle?" he said. "Here's your miracle."

She said something, but it was out of earshot. "Your bullets travel farther than your voice," he said. She repeated herself, and he still didn't hear. Frustrated, she broke off a piece of donut and threw it at him. It landed short, so she kept breaking off pieces and throwing until one finally hit him. Then she started laughing.

"The maid's going to get pissed," he said.

She hopped onto the chair, down to the floor, and climbed up onto the bed. Now close to his face, she was able to see sugar crystals on his lips and chin. "I said," she yelled, "It was a miracle!"

"Anyone ever tell you that you have a heart-shape face?"

"It's a miracle!"

"No. It was a cover story, an exaggerated fantasy. And you wanna know why? You want proof?" He opened the journal and pointed out the scene where "Andrea tried to shoot the Indian with his thirty-eight. I don't own a pistol. I haven't shot a pistol in ten years!"

Just then, the radio alarm came on with Boz Scaggs singing, *Look What You've Done to Me*. Ybette smiled and started swaying slowly with the melody, mouthing the lyrics until she came to the last line, which she sang aloud, pointing directly at him, "Oh, love, you wouldn't lie to me, leading me to feel this way...."

"No, I would never...," conceding with a smile.

Their flight appeared on time, but when they went to check in, the ticket agent said that the plane was fully booked and that they would have to reschedule. The only consolation was an offer to upgrade to first class. They took the offer.

"Now, where are we going to sleep tonight?" Andrea said. "I can't afford another night in that airport hotel."

Without thinking of consequences, Ybette said, "Let's call Carol. She should be home."

"Carol? Where? I thought she quit and went back to Boston."

"True. And got married and divorced like everyone else. But she came back and started flying again. Andrea, she married an ambassador and had a baby. Let's give her a call just to save face with her."

After an awkward conversation on the telephone in which Ybette had to scream her lungs out to be heard, they took a taxi out to Carol's house in Bay Shore. A maid answered the door.

It was to be expected that a woman as well built as Carol would eventually wind up in a home to match. Carol knew that her figure was her main asset, and, from her appearance that night, she had kept herself in marketable shape.

"Where's Ybette?" Carol asked, looking past Andrea at the hallway.

"I'm right here," Ybette said, emerging from Andrea's jacket. "A might weak from lack of food." Carol took one look at the little white Disco Wanda and passed out cold. "Must be postpartum blues," Ybette said. "Andrea, help her!"

Andrea put Carol's legs up on the couch and took off her slippers. "Where's her husband?" he asked.

"Must be abroad," Ybette said.

"She certainly is," massaging Carol's feet.

"There, that proves it. You always had a crush on her."

"Crush what? I was just wondering why she wasn't overseas with him. Are they having problems?"

"Don't you wish? She happens to be here because she delivered the baby here. The ambassador wanted the baby born here just in case someday he might want to be president."

"Who, the ambassador?"

"No, you silly. The son!"

"Run for president? Don't you think they're being a little too optimistic? What are the odds of someone becoming president?"

"Much higher than your son."

"I don't have a son," he said.

"Well, that settles it. Let's go to bed."

"Where?"

"Do you think that an ambassador who has designs on his son becoming president wouldn't have a guestroom in the house? Upstairs, you silly...."

"Stop with that silly stuff. I'm sick of it."

Early in the morning, when it was still dark, the distressful sound of a baby crying awakened Andrea. Going downstairs to check on Carol, he found her in a rocking chair breastfeeding the baby.

"I brought him downstairs, but I guess that didn't help any," Carol said.

"I'm sorry. Where's ...?"

"Still upstairs sleeping. She's going to be very hungry when she wakes up." Staring at the baby, he thought that it was born with a silver spoon in its mouth and fed by the most beautiful breasts in the world. "Maybe he *will* become president someday."

"Oh, you heard."

"I'd like to be twelve inches high again."

"You could never," she said curiously, coaxing him to tell the story about Ybette. By the time he was done, the baby had fallen back to sleep.

"He makes me feel so happy for you, Carol, and so sad for Ybette."

"I should put Thomas back to bed. I'll be right back."

After five minutes upstairs, she returned to the living room, sat beside him on the couch, and asked him to explain what he meant by being sad for Ybette.

"It's just that you both started out together, like twins almost. You've made amends for that first mistake, but Ybette seems to be still so plagued by hers."

"What are you going to do?" she asked.

"I don't know. We're on the run. Keep running, I guess."

"Why is she like that, so small? What happened? Is she still the same?"

The question disarmed him. He didn't respond; his lips trembled, and she thought he was going to cry. He looked away to compose himself, and then said, "When we first met, we both knew at once that—I can't describe it without using a cliché—like it was something out of the movies, like seeing a Christmas tree loaded with presents, all just for you."

Carol wiped a tear from her eye, got up, and poured him a glass of cognac. "It goes down smooth," she said, "but watch out for the landing."

"Looks more like perfume," he said, provoked by the shape of the bottle.

"It might be more expensive," she said.

"Your husband must impress, I guess," he said, taking a sniff. "Wow! One sniff of this stuff will last me all night."

"Go ahead, Andrea. Take a sip."

Andrea's attraction to Carol was predestined. He wanted their relationship to have a special meaning, so he kept dropping back, trying to find a receiver downfield in the open. The idea of distilling his struggle in one story seemed impossible, if not absurd. Nonetheless, he prayed that she would return to the seat beside him, and when she did, he reared back and let go a Hail Mary pass.

"Carol, I feel something between us. Don't get jumpy; it's only a spiritual thing. But it's powerful, nonetheless." He took a sip of the cognac and smiled. "Roses? Violets? Incredible. Thank you. I'm overwhelmed." He laughed at himself and said, "I lost my train of thought."

"Something spiritual," she said.

"Yes, indeed. Like this cognac. It's a physical thing but so close to the spiritual. You know, Saint Bonaventure believed the soul was...," pausing a moment and asking, "You are Catholic, aren't you?"

"Yes."

"So you can relate to what I'm saying."

"Maybe."

"Anyway, he thought the soul actually had a *material* essence. He couldn't conceive of pure spirit as having individuality, and this is something, I'm hesitant to say, I see in you. It's as though your soul has a material essence. It's not a thing or part of you, like your legs or arms, not *what* you are, but *who* you are, your singularity, your being the person no one else can be." He took another sip. She leaned back, very receptive to what he was saying. "It's not that your hair is a special color, or that your skin is the softest I've ever touched. Nor is it because you sit here in a specific space and time. You're different because you are unique, not unique because you are different."

An expression of disbelief came to her face, making him pause for a reaction. "Sounds crazy, I know," he said. "How can I talk like this? It must be the cognac. I hope you don't think it's too weird, but just consider how simple it really is. Without being individuals, our love and union wouldn't exist! This is how we can be in love without having each other. Submit to the attraction of our absolute centers, forgetting about what we are. I'm *not* looking at your red hair and pink skin. I'm trying to pull our centers together."

Carol didn't quite understand his thought, but she felt the attraction. She wanted to tell him to stop, but he kept talking. "You returned to work because you love to fly, the feel of your feet leaving the ground, the ascent into the skies. Our mastery of space in this century has been a great thing. It carries our voices, radio waves, microwaves, even our bodies. It has turned us into masters of the heavens. Flying was supposed to give us total freedom and understanding, but we have been there and found it empty. That's what I'm afraid of; what Ybette saw." He paused again, afraid to continue. She held his hand as tears again came to his eyes. Half crying, he said, "Our journey is not over. We are still reaching, still not believing in ourselves. We are heading for outer space. Let's head for an inner space together and conquer that black ocean that Ybette saw. Wherever we are, we can do it."

They held each other tightly and silently until daylight came through the patio window revealing a clear blue horizon crowned by a gray overcast sky. "The ocean is still blue," she said.

"Would you like me to stay longer?" he said.

"Wonderful," she said. "You can meet Thomas. He's home next week."

"I don't know. It's going to look funny having a strange man living in the house."

"I'll tell him you're my cousin."

"And let's keep Ybette a secret," he said cautiously. "He's bound by oath, you know."

Even realizing that it might not be possible, she said, "Okay. Let's keep her a secret just between you and me."

"And promise me not to tell her about this."

"Cross my heart," she promised.

"This will give us more reason to explore our, ah...."

"Celibate energies," she said, making him laugh.

Later that day, he wrote in his journal: *The sublimity of our togetherness put us on the threshold of another universe, beyond the rainbow of merging colors into a light so white, we were nearly blinded.*

"Andrea, you look good in that suit," Carol said, showing him into the great room.

"It feels tailor-made," he said, feeling up to the challenge of entertaining a sheikh with small talk as the ambassador was held back at the UN.

"Thomas is really going to appreciate this."

A bodyguard in a black suit stood quietly in a corner, while the sheikh, dressed in white robe and turban, sat in a large leather chair. Andrea was prepared to greet the sheikh with *salaam alaykum*, but didn't when he realized Carol was not welcome in the room. He poured himself a glass of cognac as Carol left the room to help the maid in the kitchen.

"I've flown through your country," Andrea began. "The terminal at Abu Dhabi is terrific. It gave me one impression. Gold! Gold everywhere."

"What's your name?" the sheikh asked.

"Andrea High. That's spelled *H, i, g, h*. And yours?"

"Sheikh Avveroes."

Andrea smiled wryly. It was a name he knew well, but in a context wholly other than a sheikhdom.

"You think my name amusing?" Avveroes asked.

Taking a sip, Andrea said, "Would you like a drink? It's excellent spirits."

"Muslims don't drink alcohol," Avveroes said. "It's forbidden by the Holy Koran."

"Not spirits in the philosophical sense, hey?" Andrea said. The sheikh looked coldly at him. "I shouldn't think so, since the Avveroes that I know was a...what?"

"What are you getting at?"

"You don't know? Well, maybe not, but it's interesting that you should have a family name and not know that it once belonged to one of the greatest Arabian philosophers."

Avveroes got up, went out into the hallway with his bodyguard for a few minutes, and then came back and sat down. The bodyguard stood in the same corner and began jerking hairs out of his nostrils and flicking them on the floor.

"You were saying," Avverroes said.

"I was saying that Avveroes was a famous medieval philosopher. I should say infamous for what he thought about the human soul."

"Yes, infamous" the sheikh said. "Go on."

"He tried to reconcile philosophy with religion, just like the Christian philosophers did. That's what I meant by spiritual. Two understandings of spiritual: religious for the people and philosophical for the ones who know."

Andrea realized that he was getting in over his head, but he had something else in mind other than hermeneutics. "It all relates to my work," he said. "My experiments with the soul."

"What do you do?"

"I'm a geneticist."

"And you study the soul?"

"In a philosophical way. I'm trying to integrate philosophy with science. Averroes interests me because he believed like Aristotle that the soul gave the body life, and without the body, it could not exist. Body and soul were dependent upon each other for life. This meant that the soul could not live on its own separate from the body and, at death, was somehow subsumed into a universal soul. One soul. But this was contrary to Islamic belief in eternal life of the soul for each person. It was similar to the Hindu idea of universal consciousness. The cosmic consciousness that's hip these days."

Andrea let the idea sit for a moment, thinking that the sheikh might come up with the argument that if the soul is subsumed into the cosmic consciousness at death, where is the final reckoning, the justice for good and bad deeds during life?

The sheikh answered, "This is a philosophical question."

"True, but I seek a scientific answer. Quantum mechanics."

"Scientific...."

"Hey, don't look at me like that. I'm not trying to snowball you. Quantum mechanics is a theory of wave function collapse. It all has to do with measurement of electrons, which can exist as waves or particles. In some experiments, our consciousness of the results determines whether it can be measured as a particle. Measured in the sense of where it exists at any point in time. Consciousness, in other words, is the determining factor in our reality of space and time. It determines objectivity in the world. If this is so for one particular electron, what about the entire universe of electrons? There must be one cosmic consciousness keeping all the electrons in a state of objectivity rather than random probabilities. Otherwise, our Newtonian physics would not be possible; we wouldn't be able to measure the weight or movement of objects."

"You say all this comes from Avveroes?"

"Well, not exactly, but it does have implications on ethics. Saint Bonaventure and Saint Thomas had a lot to say about Avveroes, and their arguments against him are pretty standard and can apply to Hinduism and the cosmic consciousness movement, as advocated by egotists like Timothy Leary. There's no justice in their equations. Criminals meet the same end as saints after death. There's no God to pronounce the final sentence, so what good is there in being good?"

"You are a very convincing philosopher."

"Saint Thomas, Saint Bonaventure, and Saint Augustine all believed in the individuality of the human soul, though in different ways. But they all agreed that it had to be connected to a human body. And they thought a *fully formed* human body was the only thing dignified enough to receive a human soul from God. God would never infuse a human soul inside a pollywog. That was abhorrent. The human body had to have all its functions ready to receive the human soul. This was standard Christian belief up until the nineteenth century. Though they didn't talk about the morality of abortion, they would not have thought it to be murder in the sense that the human fetus did not possess a soul."

The sheikh appeared interested, though Andrea wasn't sure he had understood the logical argument. He went on anyway. "This is a dark secret in the Catholic Church, something they don't advertise, for they can't decanonize a saint."

The sheikh looked pensively at the glass of cognac, prompting Andrea to ask, "Are you sure you don't want a drink?"

"I'm fine. Go on."

"The main reason why the Catholic Church changed its dogma was to control the masses. There's nothing more frightening to a priest than to have no one attend Mass. That's why they call it the Mass. You see, it fits that birth control and abortion are grave mortal sins. The soul and body are united at the moment of conception. However, according to the saints, it is not necessary that the body receive the soul at conception, since the body too can exist without the soul, and vice versa. The embryo might have an animal soul, as Aristotle said, but not an immortal soul. A human soul. As the embryo grows, so does its appetite for being enlightened by the soul. In the human species, so great is the development of the brain, that there is a time in human fetal development that the brain cannot go on without the soul. There is a spiritual conception separate from the physical. I'm trying to discover when this takes place."

Avveroes leaned forward and said, "And you proved this in experiment?"

"I'm working on it.

"What have you worked on so far to prove this?"

"Well, it's not actually proof. But I've gotten some results that might interest you. It's kind of a, well, what should I say, an offshoot? Like striking oil where you least expect it. Maybe I should show you. Would you like to see?"

"Yes. You have here?"

Andrea took the sheikh upstairs to the playroom and opened the door slowly, allowing him to peek inside at baby Thomas in his crib and Ybette on the rocking horse eating a candy bar. "My first experiment," Andrea said. "Isn't she a beauty?"

Baby Thomas pointed at Ybette, and then he grinned to show off his baby teeth.

Averroes pointed at a video camera attached to the wall. Andrea explained, "No, she's not a hologram. She's as real as you and me. A great baby sitter, don't you think? She eats a lot of ice cream, peanut butter, and tiramisu, things like that, but she can't get fat. Always skinny."

"Is she a clone?" the sheikh asked.

"A clone? Not actually, but along the same line."

"You can duplicate this process?"

"She's one of a kind. Let's discuss downstairs. But first, you must agree not to reveal this to anyone, especially the media or the government."

While returning to the great room, Andrea was tempted by the notion that he could actually offer Ybette to the sheikh for a small fortune. He could propose that she be purchased as a nymphet, kind of a concept model ready to go into full production.

When the sheikh stopped at the fireplace and stared at the portrait of the ambassador hanging over the mantel, Andrea assumed that he was hedging, diverting attention away from the issue at hand. "Beautiful portrait," Andrea said. "It's by Jonathan Howard and cost seventy-five thousand. Very affordable, don't you think?"

"We don't admire such things in our country," the sheikh said. "It's against our religion Islam to create graven images of ourselves."

Although an acceptable explanation, the remark sounded hollow, as though he had read it from a script. Andrea said, "I'm sorry for suggesting it. I didn't know." Then he used the faux pas as an excuse to avoid the sheikh the rest of the evening.

Later that night, after searching the bedroom for bugs, Andrea lay beside Ybette and whispered softly but worriedly to her, "Sheikh Averroes is an FBI agent. I could smell him."

"How could you tell?" she asked.

"He didn't know that Averroes was an Arabian philosopher. Or maybe he knew and didn't want to say, because what little he knew about Avveroes was no match for me. I got an A in medieval philosophy."

"Look at you, brilliant Andrea."

"And the things he said were too convincing. I mean a real sheikh wouldn't have tried to explain himself."

"What did he say?"

"That Muslims don't drink alcohol nor have portraits painted of themselves, because it's against their religion."

"So, what's strange about that?"

"Islam is a closed religion. Muslims don't try to convert people. And they don't make a point about justifying their behavior to anyone, especially to Christians."

"Carol ratted on us," she said.

"What else? She's married to an ambassador that wants his son to be president."

"I think we better start packing," Ybette said.

27/SwissMiniGun

The thought that he had tried to sell Ybette to an undercover FBI agent weighed heavily on his conscience. In addition, over the course of his conversations with Carol, he had become convinced that Ybette was a curse on his life. Indeed, she had conceived his child surreptitiously and had aborted it without his knowledge, but his philosophizing about the independent life of the soul had actually ameliorated his need for revenge.

The Pan Am terminal felt like an oasis to the long-lost sky marshal, and he moved with the determination that every step he took was going undetected. He knew the day would come when the police would be able to read his intentions as he passed through the front entrance, using a scanner of some kind that read brain waves.

He took the risk of carrying the SMG in the carryon, and, being so small, it went undetected by the magnetometer. When he boarded the plane and sat in the comfortable first-class seat, he gave in to Ybette's demand to have it back, and he sneaked it to her fully loaded under his jacket. "Be careful!" he whispered. She massaged him to keep the peace. It was indeed consoling that Pan Am had followed through with its offer to upgrade his seat to first class.

A man in his forties with the unruffled manners of a diplomat settled into the aisle seat next to Andrea. Andrea avoided him and looked out the window.

After takeoff, the man picked up his briefcase and went to the lavatory. When he returned smelling of Brut, Andrea had a hunch that it might be a sky marshal. This was possible, since the FAA had a token force still flying international flights. When the man ordered a Bloody Mary, Andrea recognized the voice and said, "Mick Jagger. Are you Mick Jagger, my old roommate?"

Now looking at each other face-to-face, they smiled together. "High!" John said. "Andrea High, I remember. How long's it been?"

"Ten years about," Andrea said.

"It shows in those grays, man," John teased.

Andrea came back with, "And in your waistline, man. Looks like airline food agrees with you."

"So what's you been doing all these years?"

Andrea had in mind posing as an ambassador but, realizing that he might be asked to prove it with a passport, said, "I'm on the personal staff of a sheik in Dubai. Sheikh Avveroes."

John blinked as if trying to clear the haze from his eyes. "How'd you wheedle into that deal?"

"Do you remember Carol, my ex-roommate from Eastern? Well, she married an ambassador, and I happened to be staying at their home for a few days and met this Bedouin sheikh. He said that I was the only westerner he ever met that knew the Arabian philosopher Averroes. And they used to tell me in college that studying philosophy was a waste of time. Man! Well, he offered me a job on his personal staff, and now I travel around the world buying things for him. You should see the Ferrari we had delivered last week. He had it customized and cost a mil and a half. When I got behind the wheel, it was as if I had passed heaven and earth all at once. He was so happy with it, he gave me his old Testarozza. He didn't like it because it reminded him of 'the *redhead* Carol.' He had the hots for her something fierce."

"Wow, out of sight, man."

The flight attendant brought the Bloody Mary, and John took a quick drink, placing the glass back down on his tray. Andrea picked up the glass, took a sip, and smiled. "Bloody Mary my ass!" he said. "Ten years of phony drinks."

John smiled, as though it were a seal that would keep his identity undisclosed—the cover story that Andrea didn't care to know. The stash of hashish wasn't there anymore to mystify his identity. John's identity was not the real secret between them, but *his* cover story.

"Ever get tired of this airline food? Must get to you."

"Say, whatever happened to that skinny blond flight attendant you were dating? Did you two ever get hitched? What's her name?"

"Youbet," Andrea quipped. "No, we never got married," Ybette's punched him in the side and he flinched.

"Are you okay?" John asked.

"Yeah, it's nothing. Just an old war wound."

"Well, anyway, about Youbet. Yeah. What a chick." John leaned closer to Andrea and said, "One night on a deadhead to San Juan, she called me into the blue room and started to give me...." John stopped, distracted by the moving bulge under Andrea's pants. "Is that what I think it is? What d'ya got under there?"

"Hatchooo!" Ybette sneezed.

"It must be catching a cold," Andrea said.

John laughed, but when he saw a small arm reach out from under Andrea's jacket, and then a small body snake down his leg, he leaned back in his seat dumbfounded and frightened that he might have been drugged.

Ybette climbed onto the tray, stood up, and looked directly at John.

"What are you?" John said. Then to Andrea, "What is this?"

"That's what I want to know," Ybette said, aiming her gun at him. "You...you...no account, lying son of a...lying ...lying...bully bastard!"

John reached out spontaneously, grabbing her by the waist and pushing her up against the seatback. She opened fire with a volley of three shots that went wide of John's face and hit the seat. The impact of the bullets into the leather was so slight, he didn't notice. "Wow! She's even got a little cap gun. What are you two, Bonnie and Clyde?"

Ybette struggled but couldn't get her hand free and aim at his eyes. Still holding her at arm's length, John got closer and taunted, "You missed me. Ha! Ha! You missed me."

Desperately, Ybette fired a hip shot that went straight into John's open mouth, through his tongue and into the back of his throat. The red-hot bullet gagged him.

Unable to catch his breath, John released his grip on her and unfastened his seatbelt. Taking proper aim, she fired again, this time hitting just under his eye, making him recoil in pain. Blindly, he reached for his pistol while she kicked the glass, splashing the Bloody Mary into his face and chest.

The confrontation now totally out of control, Andrea grabbed John's pistol and twisted it out of his hand. John started swinging (his blackjack having been banned from the sky marshal's arsenal), testing Andrea's nerve to go deadly. Catching a punch on the lip, Andrea had no choice but to whip John in the head, causing him to fall out of his seat and start crawling down the aisle.

"Holy shit!" Andrea said. "Now you did it. You little bungling fool. Do you realize what you did? Now you're the silly fool, not me."

Ybette jumped onto John's seat, sat down, and reloaded her gun. "Did you see that?" she said. "Do you know what I just did to that pig?" She moved over and looked down the aisle at John still crawling, obviously trying to reach his partner in the tail of the plane. Looking across the aisle at a passenger staring at her in disbelief, she yelled, "What are you looking at!" pointing the gun arrogantly. The man cringed and held up his hands. "You better, you wimp," she yelled. "You're all wimps."

Andrea was tempted to stick the gun butt into her back and blow her away. He would become a hero. *Andrea High, an ex-sky marshal taken hostage today by a human-clone terrorist, thwarted a hijacking and saved the lives of three hundred passengers!* It was the break he had dreamed about for so long; it hurt just to think about it. He cocked the trigger, pointed the muzzle of the stainless-steel chief's special at her, and....

Before squeezing the trigger, he looked across the aisle at a man watching him, his eyes glaring with envy, his head jabbing forward like a knife attacking and stabbing. He's a Spaniard, Andrea thought, and this is just another bullfight. The hell this is!

Andrea uncocked the pistol, reached under the seat, and picked up John's briefcase. It was locked, but before prying it open, he tried one combination—007—and voila, it opened. Inside were John's passports, flight schedules, and boarding pass on which were written the two numbers: 8G, 62H. "Stay here," he said. "I'm going to check the back."

As he walked down the opposite aisle to the rear of the plane, he couldn't tell what the flight attendants were doing to help John, who was still struggling for life on the floor. Concealing the pistol in his pocket, he knew that the sky marshal in economy class was still seated and not inclined to help his partners and blow cover no matter how critical the situation became.

Andrea stopped just behind seat 62H. He sized up the man sitting there with hands folded over his belt buckle, obviously concealing a weapon clipped to his belt. A sharpshooter with a detective special, no doubt. Only the sharpshooters were kept on the force; all the marksmen were let go long time ago.

The sky marshal sensed someone's eyes on him. He turned his head and glanced upward at Andrea's face, squinting as if straining to recognize it. Andrea pulled out the pistol, pointed it at the clean-shaven face, and said, "Recognize this?"

"What?" the sky marshal said.

"Don't move! Put your hands out front! On top of the seat! You're under arrest."

"For what?" holding his hands up in the air.

"On the seat!" Andrea yelled. "Put 'em on top of the seat!"

"Okay, don't get nervous. There must be some kind of mistake here."

"What kind of mistake?"

"I don't know," the sky marshal said, not wanting to give out any clue to his identity to the people nearby.

"Where are your cuffs?"

"In my pocket."

"Okay, take 'em out slowly and put 'em on. Slowly!" Andrea cocked the trigger to show gravitas.

"Sure, man. Don't shoot," he said nervously. "You got it. Whatever you say."

After the sky marshal put on the handcuffs, Andrea said, "I'm going to take your gun, so don't get jumpy. This might be a mistake on my part, but...." He reached slowly under the belt and took out the pistol. A woman sitting next to him gasped for air. "And what else? Packing another piece? You guys always pack two pieces." Andrea frisked the man's pockets and came up with only a badge. "Aha. A skyjacker posing as an undercover sky marshal. Look at this, folks," holding up the air marshal badge. "A skyjacker posing as a sky marshal. But don't worry. We have everything under control. This guy's going nowhere."

Andrea walked away but stopped and looked back to make sure. The sky marshal was trying to get something that was taped to the inside of his belt. "Oh, yes," Andrea said. "I'm glad you reminded me. It's been a long time. I almost forgot. Your cuff key! Hand it over!" He took the key and went back up the aisle.

The curtains hiding the first-class section were now drawn, and Andrea walked through cautiously. At once he noticed that Ybette was missing and that the seat where the third sky marshal was supposed to be sitting—8F— was empty. Instinctively, he went for the spiral staircase and walked upstairs, now at a disadvantage.

No sign of Ybette! The lounge was empty, but the presence of death was there, lurking in the pressurized space, bouncing back and forth off the walls, unable to escape. He waited, turning strained ears toward the lavatory, listening for a sound other than the whir and vibrations of the fuselage, or the ringing in his ears.

"Help, help," Ybette squealed with a weak, small voice that went no further than the lavatory door that caged her. Sky marshal Konig, excited about having her alone in private—whatever she was—said, "What are you? An alien?" He pulled at her Barbie stewardess outfit, trying to see underneath. "A habeas corpus? Yes, I think I see a little habeas corpus there." He pulled off his necktie and tried to tie her up, but she scratched, punched, and kicked to get free. "Come here you little corpus delicti. You're my ticket. They'll never believe this. I'll bring back the *Twilight Zone* at thirty-five thousand feet."

Ybette bit his finger and screamed at the top of her lungs. The screams carried into the lounge, alerting Andrea.

"Come here you little bitch!" Konig said, grabbing her by the ankles and dangling her over the stainless-steel toilet. "If you don't stop it, I'll flush you down and write in my report that you were a stowaway that tried to hijack the plane with a SwissMiniGun. The press will play it like you were an alien from outer space carrying a ray gun."

Konig started laughing and couldn't control himself. He held Ybette up to get a closer look at her body. "Look at those little titties," he said. "It would be a shame. They look good enough to eat, like pink jellybeans!"

"Okay," Ybette said. "I give up. Whatever you say."

Andrea put his ear up against the door and tried to open it. It was locked.

Konig put down the seat cover and sat down on the toilet, getting ready to have his way with the little perp. "Okay, now. Let's get down to real business. Want to join the Mile-High Club?"

Again Ybette screamed. "No one will hear you," Konig said. "The captain has turned on the seatbelt sign, remember? And this old tub has no seats in the lounge. I command this plane."

"Rape! Rape!" she screamed.

Andrea heard clearly and cocked the pistol. Knowing that a kick would never open the door as it was hinged to open outward, he stepped back and fired a shot sideways at the latch, praying not to hit anyone inside. The bullet tore a hole in the door, exposing the latch and allowing him to open it quickly.

Konig, still sitting on the toilet, held Ybette in one hand and fumbled about to get his pistol with the other. Andrea reared back and, taking care not to hit Ybette, drove his boot directly into Konig's face. The connection was so forceful, Konig's head bounced off the back wall like a basketball off a backboard, and then he fell to the floor as conscious as wet meat.

"We're in a fix now," Andrea said, emptying Konig's pockets. "The captain probably alerted the crew and radioed ahead about this, ah.... This what? What is this? Are we skyjacking this plane?"

"Of course not, you...," Ybette said, putting on her Barbie uniform. "He almost raped me!"

"How'd it happen?"

"Where did you go? I got so worried. I was trying to hide under the seat when he caught me from behind. Somebody in the cabin crew squealed on me."

Wrestling Konig's arms behind his back, Andrea moved quickly to get the wrists cuffed before he regained consciousness. "What do we have here?" he asked.

Ybette looked around and said, "The upper deck of a seven-forty-seven." She ran across the floor, jumped onto the bench seat, and stretched out. "Do you know this might be the last upper-deck lounge? They're putting seats up here and turning it into world business class."

"Remember the first time we met?" he said, sitting next to her. "At the card table over there, where you snaked your foot up my leg."

"I did what? What for?"

"To excite me."

"Did I?" she said; then, feeling the plane change attitude, "He's turning. We're heading back to New York."

Konig started to stir and then sat up.

"Well, where do you want to go?" Andrea said. "Rome or Bangkok?"

"Rome!" she said. "Go tell the captain."

"Me?" he said. "It was your idea in the first place." Konig stirred on the floor and began to crawl toward the stairwell. "What are we going to do with him?"

"Let him go," she said.

"Stop fighting! Down your weapons! Go home!"

Startled, Ybette awoke and heard Andrea repeat, "Stop fighting! Down your weapons! Go home!" She punched him in the arm but didn't wake him. He kept repeating the commands.

"Andrea, wake up!" she yelled into his ear. "You're dreaming." He opened his bloodshot eyes swollen in their sockets. "You were asleep for the longest while."

He didn't respond, just stared at the raised coin patterns on the black, rubber carpet of the lounge. "How ugly," he said. "Even Pan Am has gone off the deep end." Then, realizing that he had pistols in his pockets, took them out and checked to see if they were loaded. This cleared his mind, and he said, "I used to be able to remember the whole dream, even back four or five layers to the beginning. Now it's only the last one."

"Nothing happened," she said. "I think we're still on course. No one came upstairs."

He stood up and looked out the windows at the clouds below, unable to tell whether they were flying over water or land. She said something that he couldn't hear, he being as tall to her as a three-story building. Looking up at him, she yelled again, "My neck is aching, Andrea. Get down here."

He sat beside her, looked closely at her face and said, "I just wanted to write a story that would make me famous. I wanted to turn all skyjackers into a book and then burn it."

"Hmm…. You certainly know how to dream," she said casually, more concerned about her hunger pangs than the meaning of his dream. "Do you think we could ask for some breakfast?"

He pressed the call button, to which the brave steward responded, coming up the stairs cautiously. They ordered two first-class dinners, which they ate without hesitation, knowing that the airlines didn't have a method for subduing skyjackers with drugged food or drinks.

After the meal, they relaxed on the floor for a full half hour without uttering a word, just drinking the wine and listening to the steady hum of the mighty jumbo jet.

"Ladies and gentlemen, this is your captain speaking. I have turned on the seatbelt sign, and everyone must remain seated, including the cabin crew. I have something important to tell you. Please don't be alarmed, but this plane is being hijacked. We are now flying to Tehran instead of Rome. I assure you that I will do everything in my power to ensure your safety, but we must listen to and obey the demands of the skyjackers. Please remain seated and do not do anything foolish. They have assured me that no one will be hurt if we obey their orders, so be calm and do exactly what they say. I repeat, stay calm and do as they say."

"What?" Andrea yelled. "Hijacked? Who's he kidding? How do I get on that thing?" pointing to the interphone on the wall.

"Call the steward," Ybette said.

"He's not getting away with this. I'm not falling into that trap."

Now patched into the PA system, Andrea said, "Ladies and gentlemen, this is Andrea High speaking. I am not, never have been, and never will be a skyjacker. The captain is making the whole thing up to make himself look like a hero. To prove to you that I'm not hijacking this plane, I have ordered the steward to open the bar to all passengers. Drinks are now on the house!"

"How generous, Andrea," Ybette said.

All the passengers were relieved, and some started clapping.

"Ladies and gentlemen, this is Father Boland speaking. Please don't applaud yet. The hijackers have made a demand and asked me to carry it out. I am an ordained priest and have been given orders to pray for their success and our forgiveness. I will now pray for us sinners. Everyone on this plane has fallen into sin of one kind or another, at one time or another. We cannot deny it. Everyone—Protestant, Jew, Buddhist, Muslim, Catholic. We must confess our sins to receive forgiveness. Therefore, everyone must come to me in person, one at a time, in the cockpit; otherwise, they will blow up this plane. I will call you by seat number, starting with seat one-A. Please come up the steps now. One-A, come! It's your turn to come to terms with the Lord before it's too late. Come!"

A tall woman of about thirty, handsomely dressed, came up the steps, gave Andrea an absentminded look, and walked toward the flight deck. She knocked once, waited a minute for the door to open, and then went inside without looking back. Andrea and Ybette glanced back and forth at each other and the door, not knowing what to make of the visit or what to do next. After ten minutes, the woman came out of the cockpit and walked down the stairs.

No sooner had the woman cleared the staircase than another woman came up and followed the same path into the cockpit. Andrea stood up, went over to the stairwell, and saw a line of women waiting at the foot of the steps. Just then, the door opened and the woman exited.

Ybette ran to the door before the next woman came up. Using the handle of the SMG, she knocked, and the door opened. She went inside. When the next woman came upstairs, Andrea signaled to her with his pistol to go back down. He waited at the door a minute until a voice came booming over the PA system. "INFERNO! INFERNO! INFERNO!" He stepped back and was about to shoot the door open when Ybette came walking out, head hung low.

"What was that all about?" he asked. She didn't answer. He looked down the stairs and noticed that all the women had gone back to their seats. "What did you say to him?"

"I asked him to tell my fortune. He got mad, and, you heard what he said." She slumped down on the floor and sighed, "Andrea, I'm not feeling well. Not well at all." An expression of pain came to her face, normally pink, now pale.

"You drank too much wine," he said.

"No, it's that man in there. He talked so strange…." The dryness in her mouth made it difficult for her to go on. Suddenly, she felt a numbness creeping down her arms and legs, signaling that the end was near. She was scared, very scared, and looked into his eyes for pity. She nudged his arm and tried to smile, and then she gave up her SwissMiniGun.

He put the gun in his pocket and said, "Maybe there's a doctor on board. Let's ask for help."

"No, Andrea! Don't go in there!"

He carried her to the cockpit door, but before knocking, put his ear against it. He heard two men arguing heatedly. He knocked hard and at once something smashed against the door, a book perhaps thrown at it. Within a minute, the flight deck was filled with the clamor of a drunken brawl—shouting, grunting, rumbling, banging—all terribly foreboding to Ybette. Nonetheless, Andrea kicked the door a few times and stepped back ready to fire at anyone or anything with death in its eyes.

"Let's not," she said. "Leave them be."

Instantly, the tumult stopped and the door opened slightly, tempting them to step inside. Letting her down to the floor, he kicked the door open wide and held the pistol out in a combat stance ready to fire. The cockpit was intact and the autopilot turned on, keeping the plane on a steady course. It was awaiting their arrival.

"What is that?" Andrea said. "The smell. Do you smell it?"

"Smells like cheap perfume," Ybette said.

"Roses in a garden," he said, filling his lungs deep with the fresh air. "It's not perfume. It's fresh air from outside."

Sitting in the pilot seat was an old man staring fixedly at the instrument panel. He wore a captain's uniform and stroked his gray beard as though it might help him understand the way the plane was flying. He said, "They said

I flew a mission to ward off an attack on San Giovanni during the war. Would you believe that?"

Andrea shook his head, not daring to entertain the apparition before him.

"That I should be such a war hero, flying in the air like some kind of a superman, was the start of all my troubles. The stigmata—the pain—I could bear, but the publicity of flying without wings was too much."

"Where's the pilot?" Andrea asked.

"I gave him a break. Poor man was getting too tired to keep his eyes open."

"And the priest? What's with the priest hearing confessions?" And then to Ybette, "Is this the guy you saw? The fortune teller?"

The old man responded, "The doors of their hearts were not open, because they feared grace would take away their external beauty."

"What?" Andrea said.

Ybette climbed up onto the flight engineer's seat and said, "Go ahead, Andrea. Try him on for size."

"Who were you fighting just now," Andrea asked, "before we came in? Was that you?"

"Actually, the nights when they used to beat me up are over. My guardian handles the roughhouse now, whenever I'm traveling on earth, thank God. Take over," pointing to the copilot's seat. Andrea sat down and adjusted the seatbelt.

"Well, little one," the old man said. "Are you ready? You don't have much time."

"I think you're right," she said. "I feel terrible. How much time do I have?"

"One minute. Maybe an hour."

Propelled by the fear of dying again, this time for good, she said, "Can you help me?"

"Yes," he said. "Your eyes are crystal clear, like the beads of a rosary. I can see through them, into your soul, and it longs to be saved from the black sea of darkness. You thought there was nothing else after death because that was your fate. You didn't see the light because you were never baptized!"

"What?" she said. "I was never baptized? Are you sure?"

"Positive," the old man said.

"Andrea, did you hear that?" she said. "I was never baptized. Why didn't you know? I'm so thrilled. I'm so…. Can you imagine never being baptized in the United States? I didn't even think of it. That was the reason why the boy.... I'm so lucky."

"But first," said the old man, "do you believe in Jesus Christ as your Lord and Savior?"

"Yes," breathing a big sigh of relief. "Andrea you almost sent me to hell."

"Limbo," Andrea said. "It would have been limbo."

"It doesn't exist," said the old man. "No limbo."

"Why don't you have faith?" she asked Andrea.

"Oh, he has faith," the old man said, "when he prays to God. He just has the bad habit of giving monks like me a hard time. Now, if you will come up here, young lady, I can administer baptism before heaven calls." Reaching into his flight bag, he pulled out a small bottle of French spring water and said to Andrea, "If you will be the godparent, we can proceed."

"Wait a minute," Andrea said. "Aren't you forgetting something? Doesn't she have to go to confession first? Come to terms with her past?" He was hoping to hear her sins and clear up the mystery that was plaguing him.

"No," asserted the monk. "She has accepted Christ in faith, and he has forgiven her sins. Now we will give her a sign, the absolute assurance of God's forgiveness. She is a newborn baby in Christ. This is the beginning of her eternal life."

The all-encompassing profundity of baptism hit him hard. If she was not a life history of sin, what was she? There being so many transgressions, she couldn't even count the number of pages it would take to describe them all. And to what end? To be washed clean as if they never existed? The end of her story must have more meaning than that, something to hang a hat on— a disclosure of condemning evidence, an act of final revenge, an apotheosis perhaps. Why was she given life in the first place, if it was to become null and void in the end? Where was the final accounting, the counting of talents as prescribed in the gospels?

The monk was so graceful in administering the rite, Andrea was overwhelmed with admiration. Every sign, every intonation, was not only sacred in itself, but seemed to crown the little princess for whom it was intended—a queen—and Andrea saw his own faith inherited rather than freely accepted, that he had been branded, stigmatized, caged, and imprisoned by it.

When done, the monk placed the newly christened Ybette on the pilot's seat to fly out the rest of her life as captain of her own destiny.

"Do you want your kiddy wings?" Andrea asked.

"Hush, Andrea High," she said. "Can't you see I'm flying?" Pointing out the window, she said, "Look at the beautiful clouds out there! They're no bigger than before, before I got small."

Andrea looked out at them and agreed.

" . "

"So, it does have a resolution," Marge says, "at the end of chapter twenty-eight, though not the one he wanted. It really is a mystery."

"You mean the bit about baptism?" John says. "A flawed resolution that puts him further in debt to the reader."

"So, you would have him take up with the likes of Bert Russell?"

"He missed the boat at the Passover Plot."

"I don't think so," says Marge. "He's charting new ground here. It's not about good versus evil, good guy versus bad guy. It reaches beyond the characters and any action they might devise. It's about the passing of poetry and philosophy, two very fragile endeavors in our century, don't you think? We have come down to this. Very sad."

"I'll grant you that," John says.

29/Being Taken

Not seeking as much to be flown as to fly, the old man's face floated peacefully in the sky in front of the plane. It changed to a fair-skinned baby, and then to a young man with a thick, dark beard, and then back to an old man's face. The changes started over again, displaying each year of the man's life, and, as the slideshow progressed, the faces melded together into an imperceptible blur. But the eyes, innocent and unchanging, were no longer hidden by a heavy brow, and he stared at them like a baby. "Adai nanda," he said softly.

"That's incredible!" Ybette said. "He's outside, can you believe?"

"Neat trick," Andrea said.

"Mother! Father! I'm home," a small voice said behind them.

"It's him!" Ybette said, turning around.

The boy ran up to Andrea, touched him on the shoulder and yelled, "You're it!" Then he ran out of the cockpit.

Andrea put on the copilot's headphones, pressed a button on the audio panel, and said, "Ladies and gentlemen, this is Andrea High speaking. Everyone must remain seated. There will be perfect silence on this plane. Anyone caught talking or laughing will be dealt with severely. The three air marshals are to leave their seats at once and move to the back of the plane. I have all their guns so they are now disarmed and helpless. Don't do anything that you'll regret, for you won't live to regret it. No, I'm not trying to sound like Yogi Berra. No one could. I just don't have any demands on you other than you do as I say, when I say it. I was once a sky marshal and scored sharpshooter with a thirty-eight pistol, so don't mess with me."

Andrea went to the cockpit door and opened it slowly. When the boy saw him, he ran down the steps. Thinking that it might be a feigned retreat, Andrea moved forward slowly and, when he saw the two air marshals waiting for him at the bottom of the steps, fired two shots into the stairwell. The sounds of the blasts echoed throughout the plane. He returned to the cockpit, locked the door quickly, and repeated his demands, adding, "Next time I'll shoot to kill."

Ybette had remained quietly seated throughout the ordeal, but when Andrea looked at her imploringly, she said, "No, Andrea. I can't anymore. You're on your own."

Emboldened by the rejection, he stepped out the door without even looking. Holding two pistols and carrying one in his pocket, he went down the stairs ready for battle, but was amazed to see everyone sitting quietly. Feeling like he had broken a long, deadly fever, he felt an inexplicable calmness flood his body, an ebbing of foamy intrigue, an exposure of real innocence. His aim was steady, and he could hit a bull's eye a mile away.

He walked smoothly and matter-of-factly through first class looking for the boy. The passengers saw him as nothing more than a skyjacker, and when he passed by, they held their breaths for fear the psychopathic killer would take a disliking to them. If they had read his thoughts at that time, however, they would have felt as calm as he.

Their vulnerability was so touching that he no longer carried his pistols ready to shoot, but now at his sides, as though the floor were his main threat. As he sauntered slowly down the aisle, passing row to row, everything seemed to point toward a different explanation for their presence. They sat in their seats just for his amusement. Then, over the PA system, a voice said, "I am Said, but you are not said."

Andrea was astounded by this logic. To think of himself as not existing just by saying it was absurd. Who could it be professing philosophy at a time such as this?

"You are maneuvering for a landing and cannot find an approach because you do not have a destination. And you do not have a destination because you do not have an approach." A roaring laughter filled the airplane, but subsided all of a sudden in order to hear the next line. "A real Mark once said, 'show me whar a man gets his polenta, and I'll tell you what his 'pinions is.' You have no source of polenta; ergo, you are being unsaid."

"Polenta?" Andrea said laughingly. "You mean corn pone. Show me where a man gets his corn pone, and I'll tell you what his 'pinions is."

"I said *polenta*, and I mean polenta. You must know that the Romans carried it everywhere they went and thus were of the opinion that everything—the entire world—belonged to them. Polenta power is what they preached, and it nourished itself to such a degree that those who worshipped bread—the Christians—were fed to the lions. Have you ever seen a pride of lions tear apart a woman and eat her alive? Her intestines are dragged the length of the Coliseum and she is consumed in toto. But with all the violence, the possession and consumption of the body, the nourishment of the lions and the sadistic pleasure of the Romans, something escaped total triumph. The thousands of eyes aiming only at the flesh and blood did not see the vision in her eyes. It resisted perception and became holy other than all the power and all the wealth of the world."

"I didn't see it," Andrea lamented.

"Of course you didn't see it. They didn't want you to see it. They didn't see it either, because they were pagans thirsty for Christian blood."

"They wanted power...."

"Yes, power over the authority that condemned promiscuity and sadism. The same power the devil offered to Jesus in the desert, the same power released in the world wars, the civil wars, genocides, and terrorism. The same power that rules the universe, tells planets, stars, and even galaxies how to move. Andrea, where is your power? In the eyes of the people you hold hostage or in your eyes that cannot find your son?"

Andrea raised his guns as if to shoot the loudspeakers. "I'm Andrea High!"

"You think the secret to the story—the perfect revelation of your cover story—is your son. There, look! There he is. Behind the galley. You're it, Andrea. Go tag him and release yourself from the name."

The boy walked down the aisle holding a book high in the air so all the people could see. "There it is, ladies and gentlemen," Said said, "everything that he aspired to since the beginning of the story. And nothing that he can possibly be."

When the boy came back down the opposite aisle, Andrea crossed through the galley, jumped out in front of him, snatched the book, and ran with it down the aisle into first class and up the steps to the lounge.

It didn't matter that he hadn't tagged the boy, for now he had the book—the Rosetta stone to his future. He placed it on the floor, opened it slowly, and found only blank pages. "Where's my story?" he yelled.

"Look closer!" Said said. "You'll find it."

Paging through the book, he asked, "It's not here!"

"You don't see it," Said said, "though you drew it, Andrew. It's unreasonable, nonphilosophical, because you drew it."

"An-drew?" Andrea asked.

"Yes, by Andrew. A *baby* in a manger. The greatest cover story ever told. The prereflective, prephilosophical story before you learned how to turn colors into ideas."

No longer holding himself hostage to the plane for the sake of a story, he sat perfectly still and serene, moving through the sky at 550 miles per hour. Nothing was easy about remaining perfectly still in a plane with six million parts; nothing was hard about it either. The faster it went, the slower he went, and the slower it went, the faster he went. Nothing was to be written down now; there was nothing to remember. There was no drinking or eating, no reading or talking, no aiming or measuring. There was no skyjacker or hostage, no bullet or gun, no target or shooter, only the perfect failure of words. This he realized. I'm the same dead or alive and different dead or alive. My body is a frail eggshell easily cracked by my fingers; my body is solid marble, thoughtless, fearless, and sinless. Here I sit, there I sit, everywhere I sit. Andrew D'Oria, one hundred fifty pounds of weapons grade ready to ignite.

As the auto pilot turned the plane to the left, beams of sunlight passed through the windows and illuminated the dust particles floating in the air. Without leaving the slightest visible trace, the photons of light vibrated the dust as loudly as wind rustling leaves. Raising a hand into the sunbeam, the shadows of his fingers moved across his chest, feeling delightfully gentle and leaving traces of hairs standing on end.

"Very good," Said said. "A very satisfactory result, but only a lukewarm enlightenment attained by the intellect, not the soul. You are not home to the eternal world of beauty and harmony yet. This you must create on your own. You *have* the idea, but you refuse to *be* the idea."

"I *have* the idea?" Andrea repeated as a question. "But I refuse to *be* the idea?"

The two sky marshals were now at the bottom of the stairs and heard him laughing. They walked halfway up to peek.

"Okay, then," Said said, "let's see how smart you are. What is larger than a jumbo jet and lighter than a feather?"

Andrea closed his eyes to see the answer to the riddle floating along the ground. "I see it," he said laughing loudly. "The shadow floating on the ground is caused by the airplane floating in the sky."

"You couldn't resist," Said said, "turning perfectly good poetry into philosophy. You'll never learn."

Peeking over the top step, Konig whispered to his partner, "Let's rush him!"

"Too risky," the partner said. "He's still armed."

A great elation filled Andrea's body, and slowly he began to rise off the floor, not letting go or submitting to an external force, but floating into the air as one floats in water by not struggling against it. Unlike the state of weightlessness where the body needs to push off on something to move, he propelled himself freely. He glided to the ceiling, gloating over his new power to transcend gravity, the original sin. With lighthearted playfulness, he flew to each corner of the lounge and then hovered over the stairwell waving at the astonished sky marshals below. Though he was within reach, they dared not grab him, fearing that any man with the power to fly, even a magician with a death-defying trick such as this, surely had deadly force up his sleeve. They backed down the steps and let him pass immediately through the stairwell and into the first class section, over which he glided, showing each passenger the invisible drawing of himself in the book. "Herr Four *D*...Madam Six *A*...Sir Six *B*." Even the sight of John, now recovering in his seat, didn't faze him as he said politely, "Signore Seven *B*, this is Andrew, see," and moved on again to the next person until he floated undisturbed out of first class.

All the passengers being seated, it was only natural that he should pass over them and put on a good show, the sullen veins on his skin swollen blue.

Predictably, he took extended looks at attractive women and glanced over the others, because he was for them a real man in the flesh, not the Vitruvian idol concentric with all male figures.

Arriving at the rear of the plane, he fishtailed around and started back up the opposite aisle, smiling at passengers that waved their hands as he passed, recognizing them by number as previously. They all thought a miracle was moving past them, and they wanted to reach up and touch it, but dared not. Nonetheless, they felt relieved that the skyjacker was not a terrorist bent on their destruction.

Once again, he retraced his path down the aisle, feeling that he had served his parade duty and was now ready to receive a medal. "Think lovely philosophical thoughts," he said to each row, "and they will lift you up in the air. Think lovely philosophical thoughts…."

About halfway down the aisle, his legs began to grow numb, and he began to sweat profusely, a yellowish sweat that smelled like….

"Petrol!" recoiled Mrs. *17D*. "Did you smell petrol just now as he passed?"

"Di miele," smiled Signora *18C*. "I hava strong taste honey my mouth."

"Yes it is," agreed *18D*. "It *is* honey. So sweet."

Soon, the good on the plane were feasting on honey.

"Give me a pencil!" Andrea said.

Quickly, pencils of all sorts were passed up to him, and he proceeded back into first class and up the stairwell. He sat in the middle of the lounge, opened the book, touched the drawing with a pencil, and said, "Beautiful little boy."

"You can't do that!" Said said.

The smile flew off Andrea's face like a leaf taken by the wind, then returned, landing in the same spot, upside down. The curls on his head unfolded into waves and became as straight and colorless as dead grass withering in the hot sun. His eyes shriveled into red grapes that sunk deep into his brain and disappeared. His feet pirouetted into a smudge.

On the flight deck, still entranced by the machinations of the autopilot, Ybette felt peaceful but uncomfortable as her uniform became too tight all of a sudden. Thinking that it was the food she had eaten, she paid no attention until more skin started to show. When her heart beat slower and heavier, she knew it was something inside, something growing all over. "What's the matter with me? What's happening?"

Like the creepy, tingling sensation of blood returning to an arm that has fallen asleep, it came rushing through her whole body—arms, legs, head, breast, abdomen—making her shriek in terror, "Get out! Get out of me!" She held out her hands, fingers tingling madly, and watched them begin to swell. The pretty little body that she had grown used to for so long was changing rapidly, and she was beside herself when the uniform began to burst at the seams, revealing her breasts in bulbous glory. After five minutes of gyrations, vibrations, and pulsations, the commotion was over and she had returned to her normal size of five-six, one hundred and ten pounds, wearing nothing but the doll outfit between her legs.

"Look at this," she said to her sensuous body veiled in skin as clean and soft as a baby's. She stroked her legs and, not finding a blemish or ugly hair anywhere, said, "Am I an angel?" She repeated the question and even felt behind her shoulders to see if she had wings.

Opening the closet door, she discovered herself in the full-length mirror. Not only was she the exact height of her former self, her body had attained the symmetry and balance she had always dreamed of having. Refusing to be deceived by the mirror, she felt herself all over, relishing the silky smooth skin, the fat-free definition of muscles and, of course, the two incredible breasts, not injected with lumpy silicone or artificially propped up, but naturally erect, an endowment of faith stacked on her chest the way Venus' pair must have been.

"How can I be so perfect?" she said.

Now catching up with her nakedness, a chill spread over her body, prompting her to grab a coat and put it on. She did so gracefully, without the least stress, feeling more feminine than any woman could feel. It was a special blessing that she had received and, even though unworthy, required an all-out commitment to holiness toward the one who had endowed her so.

But what good is there in having the most beautiful body in the world while being programmed to be a saint? "And this smile on my face—this upturned rose petal floating on my lips—where did it come from all of a sudden? Is there any man good enough for this?"

After taking one last incredible look at herself in the mirror, she opened the cockpit door and called out, "Andrea! Andrea, where are you?" Keeping the door ajar, she stepped out into the lounge to look down the stairs. Distressed by his absence and thinking that maybe he had been arrested— and she would be next—she scurried back inside the cockpit and locked the door.

"How'd you open that door?" asked the flight engineer.

Her bare feet on the black floor gave the three men simultaneously the idea that she was naked under the coat, uniting them for a moment in one implication. The captain suppressed the temptation and asked, "How did you get in here?"

She felt insulted yet relieved about being looked at as an intruder. "I was concerned," she said, "that you have so many male flight attendants. I counted five on this flight. Isn't that a little strange?"

"Don't you know what's happening, lady?" the captain asked. "You must return to your seat."

"Who are you?" the second officer said.

"My name is Ybette Rember, and I'm a flight attendant with Eastern Air Lines."

"Well then, Ms. Rember, Eastern Air Lines flight attendant, please return to your seat, and we'll have the flight supervisor bring you that answer."

"It's okay?" she asked. "You mean we're all clear?"

"All clear. There's nothing to worry about."

"Well, then, may I have that back?" she said, pointing to her uniform on the floor.

"So that belongs to you?" asked the captain. "We thought maybe the previous crew…. We had a real laugh over it."

She bent over to pick up the uniform but the first officer got to it first and held it out to her. Taking it back, she said, "Thank you," without smiling or even sneaking a glance at the pilot's ring finger, a pilot that was remarkably good looking, and a pilot that she would have surely made a pass at, even if married.

Though endowed with the most irresistible face and figure, she folded up the uniform, put it in her pocket and walked out of the cockpit. When she closed the door, she inspected the uniform and found the SMG still there. The notion that the skyjacking had been reconciled in another dimension flashed through her mind, while she felt relieved to be in possession once again of the thing that had given her the courage to be so small.

She moved through the plane as if through a thick fog at night, collar up and hands in her pockets. Taking a count of the male flight attendants along the way, she came up with a total of five and no sign of Andrea.

She sat in a vacant first-class seat, thinking of his lips that always looked sanguine and ready to be kissed, and his smiles that framed white, even teeth, good enough for any scene in Hollywood or even heaven.

"May I have hot tea with cream?" she asked a flight attendant.

"Sure ma'am," he said with a flashy smile. "Tea with cream coming right up."

You too were like that, a smile with a name on it—Ybette Rember—flight attendant, glorified waitress, ready, willing, and able to please the next available man, the man of status for whatever success in life, it didn't matter, always enough money to pay first class wherever he went, whomever he met. Every day at work there was always one man sitting there waiting, and you abhorred working in coach.

The tea had a cup of cream *and* a lemon wedge on the side. "How long have you been flying, Mister ah...?" she asked, pointing to his chest. "Where's your nametag?"

"This is my first flight ma'am," he said.

"I asked for tea with cream, not lemon."

"Well, I thought you might change your mind."

"Are you wearing lipstick?"

"No, ma'am."

She floated the mini-cup of cream in the hot water for a minute, then, pulling back the cover, drank it straight.

The court's ruling was in your favor, Ms. Rember," the attorney said. "It's a rather long statute; would you like me to read the whole thing?"

Ybette cleared her throat and said, "Yes, go ahead."

"A person who is absent for a continuous period of three years, during which, after a diligent search, he or she has not been seen or heard of or from and, where absence is not satisfactorily explained, shall be presumed, in any action or proceeding involving any property of such person, contractual or property rights contingent upon his or her death or the administration of his or her estate, to have died three years after the date such unexplained absence commenced."

"Could there be a longer sentence?" she said.

"I guess not," he said. "But it does apply in this case. The court did not originally issue a death certificate because there was no satisfactory evidence Andrea High, your benefactor, had actually died on that plane three years ago. There were many eyewitnesses that testified he had performed some kind of trick of levitation, and the court concluded that his disappearance might have been a feat of magic. It even mentioned the D.B. Cooper case of nineteen seventy-one. Do you remember the skyjacker that jumped from a plane in a parachute? He was never found. But there was absolutely no evidence that High did the same or even had a parachute. The only evidence the FBI found on the plane were two bullets fired during the skyjacking, and this—an old M-sixteen bullet found on the lounge floor. Well, you already know this, being on the plane yourself. You must have already gone through the mill on this."

"A hundred times," she said. "What can I tell you?"

"Understandable. With three sky marshals aboard and a stowaway midget as his accomplice, I can't imagine anyone other than a magician pulling off something like that."

Ybette kept silent, though she had cooperated with the FBI during the investigation, telling them that she had no recollection of Andrea ever taking up magic or the occult.

The attorney gave her a copy of Andrea's last will and read it aloud. Then he read Andrea's separation agreement, adding, "Not what I would call mutually exclusive documents, which is to your advantage, Ms. Rember."

"Thank you, sir," she said.

"And there was no evidence of suicide, which frees up a sizeable sum of insurance money. There's his basic federal employees life insurance, two private policies—one dating back to nineteen-forty-eight—and, of course, his retirement account refund, totaling well over a half million dollars, say nothing of the house in Maryland, and his condo and boat in Palm Beach."

Ybette smiled and asked, "All in my name?"

"His former wife must have really done him bad."

"Yes, she did," she said. Then, pointing to the bullet, "May I have that as a souvenir?"

"Yes, by all means, Ms. Rember. It's included."

Of all the possessions willed to Ybette, the one that intrigued her most was Andrea's journal. She read it repeatedly, each time getting more attached to it, and each time getting more detached from how to end it. She was so possessed with the task of finishing the book that she enrolled in a creative writing course at a local community college.

The instructor was an elderly professor with a British accent that made him sound erudite and very convincing. As was the rule for most British poets, he had a special interest in using language to reveal man to himself rather than to explain man to himself, "as say in philosophy or science," even going so far as to say that the great literature of the past was so powerful, "it superseded history. So, be forceful, expressive, and persuasive!"

And such was her assignment, to record one day in someone's life, right down to the most accidental occurrences, as though the person were an accumulation of words in a sentence. Without deliberation, she chose to write the story of Andrea, hoping it would become the same with him, pulling out of his being a new being, as an X-ray pulls out of the body an inner picture of the person.

She spent a week at his home gathering details about his life, looking for the key that would open the door to his revival. But that last day, that specific encounter on the airplane when he had vanished, was impossible to identify and describe. What was there in his life that could be rewritten without upsetting the continuity in it? Would the substitution of one event in space and time for another event in space and time upset the unity that bound the multiplicity of events into a meaningful whole? It was a task as difficult as taking out one pearl in a necklace of pearls without cutting the string that bound them together.

What could possibly be the answer? Never before was she so possessed by an intellectual challenge, and she feared that maybe the truth resided only in the language, a language that had no basis in reality. To dispel this pessimism, she turned to Andrea's library of ancient, medieval, and modern philosophy. Overwhelmed by the enormity of the task, she read only the flyleaves on which he had recorded interpretations of the texts. But nothing captivated her more than the journals of notes taken during his research into the mystery of her transformation. The words made real for her strange ideas that were as formless as delicate angels dancing in air. Though the words themselves were concrete, their special combinations evoked a presence on a higher plane, making her feel ecstatic yet forsaken at the same time. So high flying, so transcendent from the physical world, they couldn't have possibly brought his book to bear. They were creatures from the microcosmic world of which he wrote, foundations for the macroscopic world in which he lived, but having no identifiable causal relations with it.

The words were a spiritual link to her rebirth back to normalcy. She loved him all the more dearly for it and worried that her very existence depended upon them. The journal was the confession of a man who had attempted to understand his love for one woman and had failed. The same doubts about her pregnancies and death now weighed heavily in her hands, and they became her doubts as well. But how could she not know about herself other than what she read in the journal? Life didn't take its marching orders from a book, and neither was it congruent with it. The meaning of her life had a structure entirely independent from semantics and the *Jack-and-Jill-ran-up-the-hill* paradigm. This much she understood from his hand.

Nonetheless, she went ahead with the writing project, using as her primer, *Our Baby; The First Year*, kept by Andrea's mother and containing facts about his birth, the time and place of arrival, weight, length, circumference of head, color of eyes, complexion, and even a lock of auburn hair taken at his first haircut. *Andrew was a breast-fed baby. I weaned him when he was 10 months. It was not easy for he was very attached to the breast. He never had a formula. When he had been weaned, he did not gain weight so good. He began to get sick with colds. He had bronchitis at one year old and chicken pox at 18 months.* Especially intriguing was the remark written on the page that recorded growth milestones: His Favorite Word: *Always.*

Always? Always what? How strange.

No matter how carefully she wrote, the story still contained enough evidence to arrest him if ever he returned. She was being watched, because an unsolved skyjacking was still on the books. She couldn't resolve Andrea's dilemma without turning the story over to uncontrollable forces.

Now that the author was gone, there was nothing she could write to bring him back. There had to be another way. In reading his journal, she thought that maybe there was a way of writing the story without leaving evidence, *like a thief smudging his fingerprints at the scene of a crime—not* wiping them out, but leaving irreparable traces that allow him to pass totally undetected.

The first philosophical epigrams were logical and easily understood, pointing to where he was headed in his thinking.

"Nothing can ever become more or less in size, so long as it remains equal to itself." Plato

I did not increase or diminish in size, but in her sight, I grew all at once into a giant. I was, it seems, afterwards, what I was not before, and I did not become so in reality. It was impossible for me to become larger without becoming, and without gaining any size I could not have become larger.

This contradiction puts into question the key tenet of philosophy, namely, that what was not previously, could not afterwards be without becoming and having become. Our whole idea of "Being" is based on this simple premise.

But when she came upon his final entry, her insight took a fatal turn.

My boy was a period pinned to a page by a double set of wings that couldn't fly. Just like this: " . " Though microscopic, he had all the information needed to become a man. Augustine, Bonaventure, and Acquinas didn't understand the totality of the human genome when they said a fetus was merely a primordial animal incapable of supporting a human soul. Where the human genome-heart is present, so too is a human soul. And since conception is the first instance of human genome creation,...

All day long, the passage lingered in her mind, squiggly lines on a sheet of paper abiding fully to the laws of grammar, incapable of being changed in the slightest—a dot between two quotation marks. Yet, she hoped that it would change—a period into a picture that would be easily understood. But it hadn't changed, and her understanding was no better. The thought that she would never finish his final sentence made her cry. It was not a castle in a fairy tale that appeared real, but a fortress made impenetrable by a forsaken mind.

31/Deadheading

Ybette Rember lived the next twenty years in anticipation of the day when another miracle would happen, returning Andrea to her once again. Though the airlines had changed, the job was the same, and, now being a supervisor at the age of fifty-nine, she had only one thing to look forward to—retirement.

Her favorite pastime was to describe passengers in her journal, to *show, not tell*. It was the formula to success—*show, not tell*—a formula that Andrea refused to take, so addicted to the breast of life was he.

Animals of the same species look all the same, but humans look different, regardless of the clothes they wear. Take their clothes off, and they look even more different. And no two parts of their bodies are more different than head and foot. No other part is furthest from the self than the foot. I can practically read their minds by watching their heads and feet— this woman upset that her Italian leather sandals are slipping on the marble floor and slowing her down; this man concerned that he'll blow the contract because of a head-splitting migraine.

Podiatrists and psychiatrists are all medical doctors, but do they really have to be? The smartest graduates from medical school become shrinks, and the dumbest ones foot doctors.

There I go again. Telling, not showing. How will I ever...? I'm simply too opinionated to be an effective writer, to make this thing come alive!

Ybette had always stressed security in her job, even before the 9/11 attacks, but now that everyone was on the security bandwagon, and threat protection measures had improved significantly, she began sounding more like a passenger's rights advocate in her briefings to cabin crews.

"We must empathize with passenger concerns," she said, "especially now that we are in level yellow—elevated risk of terrorist attacks. We should hope that TSA has done its job of screening passengers. And as for air marshals—there won't be any on board this flight. So, let's keep our eyes open. And do remember that the three-ounce rule does not apply to life-support liquids that have already been cleared by TSA, and that includes formula and breast milk. We don't want any more incidents like we had in the past."

"Thank you, Ms. Rember," said the senior flight attendant. "We should all hope to look as good as you when we reach forty years old."

The cabin crew applauded and cheered.

"I promised myself one thing," Ybette said, "when I reached a six-figure income, I would retire. So, let me say that this will be my last check-ride on this airline." Again the cabin crew applauded. "And it has been a wonderful twenty-eight year ride. Enjoy! And be proud of your work."

As she buckled-up in her jumpseat, a new flight attendant sitting next to her said, "Ms. Rember, they mentioned your name at the flight attendant academy."

"I hope for something good," Ybette said.

"They said that when you flew for Eastern Air Lines, you helped stop a skyjacking."

"What else did they say?"

"That the skyjacker was never caught?" The upward inflection on the word *caught* turned the statement into an overly gracious question.

"Well," Ybette said, "it was a Pan Am flight, not Eastern. But that's immaterial now, isn't it? Both went out of business."

"I'm sorry, ma'am."

"Oh, don't be. Look, I have something to show you. It's true that the sky marshals didn't catch the skyjacker. But look at this." Ybette pulled on a golden necklace that was hidden under her red scarf; on it dangled a gangrenous pendant.

The young flight attendant looked at it with a serious eye and said, "Looks like it's been buried a thousand years. What is it?"

Ybette let the bullet drop down between her breasts. "A relic," she said. "It's the thing that keeps me looking twenty years younger."

"I can't imagine," thinking about the number of miles her mentor must have flown and the people she must have met over the years.

After takeoff, while the crew was preparing for beverage service, the senior flight attendant came out of the cockpit, went immediately to the interphone, and announced, "Ladies and gentlemen, the captain has turned on the seatbelt sign. Please return to your seats. I repeat, all passengers must return to their seats." Then confronting Ybette with a terrified look on her face, she whispered, "Threat level *red*! We're now in threat level *red*. Two planes have been blown up in mid-air."

In another supervisor's ears, the fiery warning would have emitted a shocking response, or at least some clarification, but Ybette asked in a calm voice, "Is there a threat on this plane?"

"What do you mean?" the senior asked.

"Is there a threat directly on our flight?"

"I don't think so."

"Call your crew into the galley and instruct them to search their sections thoroughly, including the lavatories. And tell them to report back on anyone fitting the *profile*."

In the case of a suicidal terrorist bent on bombing the plane rather than taking it hostage, there was no time to waste. As Ybette walked down the aisle, an elderly woman seized her arm and, trembling with emotion, said, "A dark-skin man got out of his seat and walked toward the back. We know what's going on. We've heard the news reports of bombings."

"What seat was he in?" Ybette asked.

"That one," the woman said, pointing to a seat on which stood an empty water bottle.

Ybette picked up the bottle and squeezed the soft plastic until it crackled. For several seconds she had the feeling of being a nurse again, which had never once occurred to her after leaving that job over thirty years ago. There was something bizarre about the bottle, like an X-ray that reveals the inner fluids of the body without showing its surface. Yet it was empty.

The contents were immaterial to the mystery. The bottle didn't have to go crashing to the floor to expose a deadly substance inside. The thing that really mattered was the form, without which the thing would not exist. It was an argument she had read in one of Andrea's notes about how the first molecule of DNA must have been endowed with some mysterious power to form a protective pellicle around itself to create the first living cell. That was the true mystery of life, not the DNA!

"Did he carry anything with him?" she asked the woman.

"No," said the woman. "But he couldn't stay still in his seat. Like he had the runs or something and needed to go in a hurry. He kept looking back down the aisle, then got up, and ran back."

As Ybette walked down the aisle, the bullet between her breasts started to get hot, and she had to pull it out and let it hang outside her shirt. Andrea's hysterical laughter came to her at that moment—his amusement with her distress overhearing the neighbors argue about the morality of sodomy. Ah, that's the one, she thought.

Liquid bombs other than nitroglycerin were not said to be highly explosive, but inside the pressurized cabin of a jumbo jet, they could cause devastating results. But how could a terrorist smuggle one on board, if not in his carryon bag?

The most predictable thing about a terrorist attack was that it was unpredictable. It hit without warning at the most unexpected moment. All the sky marshals, police officers, and special agents in the world would give anything to stop one cold. All it took was one bullet, and Ybette believed she was carrying that bullet around her neck.

She had walked this aisle at least one hundred thousand times, but would this time be her last? She hesitated before reaching the end, holding the hot bullet in her hand. Was Andrea with her or not? The vibrations of the plane and rush of the air outside were more evident now, and she felt as if she were floating quickly downstream toward a towering waterfall.

When she reached the tail, there was no sign of him, but one lavatory was occupied. She took a deep breath and knocked on the door. When no one answered, she knocked again, much louder. She knew he was inside and, by now, probably trying to cover up whatever it was he was doing. Instead of opening the door right away, she backed off and waited.

Should I call for help, get a couple of strong men to take him? He's been in there too long. Maybe he's ready to explode this very second, blowing a hole through the fuselage and sending the plane into a furious tailspin.

Fear stronger than she had ever known, made her shudder. For an instant, she was once again tumbling helplessly through the black void. But this time, an idea that had once been her own undoing, rescued her from eternal darkness. She was the only one now that could save the plane, and the moment was now!

She waited another minute to give the impression that she had retreated. Then she stuck the tip of a pen in the small hole of the *occupied* sign, pushed the latch to *unoccupied*, and opened the door. The door began to close, but she stuck her foot out to keep it open. Using both hands, she forced the door open, revealing the dark-skin man squatting on the toilet with a green plastic bottle sticking out of his rectum. He held out a trembling hand as if to signal *stop!* Ybette reared back and was about to kick him hard between the legs when she realized that the bottle might be filled with explosive.

On the sink was a tube of petroleum jelly and inside the sink were a pair of dentures connected by red, green, and black wires.

"Walk!" shouted the toothless terrorist.

In an instant of underserved sympathy, she gave way to the face of a young, innocent boy with disarming black eyes. Then a voice told her, "Don't give in! He's one hundred percent evil."

"No!" she shouted, grabbed the dentures out of the sink, and ran for help.

Ybette had stopped the bombing cold and had saved the lives of three hundred passengers and crew. Picking out two of the hardest bodies on the cabin crew—Flint and Keyla—it was now time to finish the job. Her heart was racing so fast that she could hardly tell them. "The teeth are capped with explosives," she said, "to detonate a liquid bomb. I caught him in the lavatory trying to put it together." She knew it was very risky doing it alone, "but I didn't have time to get help. Get the handcuffs. We have to get him before he does anymore harm."

There was no doubt in her mind that the man in the lavatory was a suicidal bomber, but when she returned to the tail, there was no sign of him, only the large green bottle caught in the trapdoor of the toilet, now empty. The flight attendants searched the whole plane, but the so-called bomber had disappeared.

The certainty that Ybette had shown was suddenly tempered by the notion that she had been fooled by an embarrassing stunt. Yet, the evidence was significant enough, and the culprit was hiding somewhere on the plane.

The two stalwart flight attendants were not so convinced by the veteran's story.

"Isn't this where you make an *executive decision*," Flint said, "and order me down to the lower galley and search for him."

"Nice try," Ybette said. "You've been watching too many reruns. I'm quite familiar with the new seven-eighty-seven configurations."

"Well, what about me?" Keyla asked. "Am I supposed to crawl above the ceiling and get hung by cables?"

"Then go falling through," Flint said, "scaring hell out of everybody. You know, dangling there."

Upon hearing this, Ybette lifted her shoulders to relieve tension in her spine, threw out her chest, and said, "It comes under the distinct heading of *other duties as assigned*." She looked them in the eyes momentarily, then turned toward the curtain of the galley and opened it swiftly.

All at once, the ceiling lights in the aft section of the plane went out. Oxygen masks deployed, making some passengers scream for help. Though fanatical in his drive to commit suicide, the bomber was now just as fanatical in his drive to stay alive.

The bullet in Ybette's hand started to grow hot again, and she had to let it go. But instead of dropping down, it started to float in midair, pulling the chain taut.

The astonished attendants watched as it led her out of the galley and started aiming at passengers in their seats, one at a time. Ybette followed the bullet down the aisle, using it as a divining rod searching for gold. When they reached the rear galley, the bullet pointed upward at the ceiling.

"It's pointing at something," Keyla said.

"Get a flashlight," Ybette said.

"They're inside, hanging under the steps," Flint said.

"Did anyone check the rest area?" Ybette asked. "Are there any crew inside?"

"We always keep the door locked," Keyla said.

"Well, if he's nowhere else to be found, then…."

Flint passed the handcuffs to Keyla. She glared at him and passed them back. They did this back-and-forth routine several times until Ybette said, "Stop it!" Then, going up to the door, "The key, if you please."

Flint unlocked the door slowly and stepped aside to let Ybette enter. "If only we had such luxuries when I was your age," she said, and then went inside.

She retrieved the flashlight and ascended the steps to the secluded and private place, a refuge where the crew could go and get a few winks to recuperate from jet lag, or even a good night's sleep. But now it had become a magician's cabinet into which a body had stepped and, with a brilliant flash of light and a cloud of smoke, disappeared into thin air.

The small cabin was dark and lit by only an emergency exit light over the entrance. The blue curtains were drawn around each of the bunks, three on either side of her. Sensing that someone was there, she said, "Hello!"

"It's only me," a man said.

Until that moment, she had been disconnected from Andrea and was merely a fifty-nine year old flight attendant. The attempts to resurrect him in words had been all in vain, but the traces of those things that were just as much a part of him as the bullet were there surrounding her. He covered her body with indelible fingerprints that couldn't be read, fingerprints that he had smeared on purpose before leaving the scene of the crime.

"Who are you?" she asked.

"Jack," he said.

"What are you doing here? Aren't you supposed to be on duty? Don't you know what's happening?"

"I'm deadheading," he said.

"Has anyone else come up here?" she asked, afraid of opening the curtain. She remained standing on the stairs, holding the handrail tightly.

"Yes, as a matter of fact," he said, "there was someone, but only a figment of your imagination."

"My imagination? Who are you?"

"You made the whole thing up. You're only a character in a book looking for a way to book me back into it. Well, here's your chance. Go ahead."

Downstairs, Flint heard the conversation and was just about to go inside when the senior flight attendant approached and said, "Captain Ferrel has decided to return to New York. He's not taking any chances. He'll make the announcement in a few minutes. Three more planes have been blown up."

"My God," Keyla said.

"Where's Ms. Rember?"

"Inside looking for the missing passenger," Flint said.

"Well, don't just stand there. Go up and help her!"

As Flint went inside, a flicker of light came from above. He unhooked the remaining flashlight, turned it on, and began ascending the steps. "Ms. Rember!" he called. "Are you okay?" There was no answer. The metal steps were narrow and steep; he slipped and had to hold onto the railing to keep his balance. When he reached the top, he pointed the light beam at the bunks but saw no one, just four flat mattresses framed by drawn curtains and supplied with neatly-placed seat belts, pillows, and blankets.

"Ms. Rember?" he called again, sensing she was there but somehow invisible. Her flashlight lay in a corner, faintly lit.

He crawled into the space and inspected each bunk, patting down the pillows and mattresses, hoping to find a clue to her disappearance. Not finding anything, he turned back and headed for the stairs but stopped to look at himself in the vanity mirror on the wall. Reflected in it was a figure lying on the bunk behind him. He turned around to look, but it wasn't there. At first glance, the figure in the mirror looked like two people making out, but there were only two arms and two legs to one body half-dressed as a man and half-dressed as a woman. The man kissed the woman so hurriedly that she could hardly breathe, and she had to break away from time to time to catch her breath. The man's hand reached around her body caressing the flesh and trying to find a way into it, and her hand did the same with her right side—his body. Then, the mattress on which they lay suddenly slipped away from the cabin and fell out of the plane. Floating downward, the two-as-one lover disappeared into the clouds.

Amazed by the apparition, Flint reached out to touch it but felt only flat, impenetrable glass. Startled, he stepped back and fell onto the bunk. Instantly, something stabbed him in the backside. It was Ybette's pendant. Upset, he threw it at the mirror, and it flew into the sky.

32/Hylomorphic Soul

The bullet hit the tray with a clang, bounced once, and rolled to a stop, leaving a thin trail of blood along the white enamel surface. Embedded and hidden in the patient's brain for forty years, it had become a substance other than itself, a force greater than four grams. To the physicians, it was purely a quantitative, material presence that had ruined the patient's life. It had turned him into a social misfit that needed to carry a gun for courage, and now it was just a harmless piece of corroded metal.

Every time Andrea visited Elizabeth Smith, he felt an immediate sense of relief that she wasn't like the others. Working in a profession dominated by men, and, having an appreciation for traditional values, she didn't accuse him of shooting a paramedic in the eye, running away from the scene of a suicide, beating up a homeless man in a grocery store parking lot, shoplifting in the Miami airport, and writing a trip report claiming to have hijacked a plane to Rome, followed by an intel report detailing his coronation in heaven as the patron saint of flight attendants. He could believe all the things recorded in his journal. It didn't matter to her. What mattered was his heart, which she loved in a motherly sort of way.

"You didn't forget our appointment," she said. "I'm proud of you, Andrea."

"Does that mean my lobotomy is working?" he said, sitting next to her on the couch.

She laughed and said, "I see you still have a sense of humor. How are you otherwise? Any pain?"

"Only when I laugh."

"Headaches? Dizziness?"

"Haven't had a headache in three weeks."

"The ringing in your ears?"

"Almost gone."

"I think Doctor Locke did an excellent job," she said. Then, noticing that he was staring at the little black box on top of her desk, "Are there any other things happening with you?"

"Yeah. I've been kind of tired lately. Taking too many naps during the day."

"Do you sleep well at night?"

"Seven hours straight. No problems."

"Any memory loss the next day?"

Andrea looked at her disappointedly, prompting her to say, "Oh, of course not. You were on time this morning, weren't you? That's terrific."

"I should have had this operation years ago," he said. "It would have saved me a lot of trouble. The thing made me a writer. I'm really an artist, but.... Now, I don't have any more time. I'm old enough to be your father."

"Many great artists did their best work in their sixties, and even seventies and eighties. You have a lot to look forward to."

"If I commit myself, can I make it? Will you help me?"

Dr. Smith was overwhelmed by his trust in her. "I'd be happy to, Andrea," she said. And now, thinking that it was time, she went and got the box off the desk. Sitting closer to him, she said, "I'd like to make a trade with you." She opened the box, took out the bullet, and offered it to him in the palm of her hand. "This for Ybette."

"So that's the culprit," he said, picking it up.

"So many years of pain," she said.

"I'll say. So, what do you want me to do with it? Wear it around my neck?"

"It is rather corroded," she said. "With a little polish, it will look as good as new."

"Just what I was thinking, doctor. I like the patina better. I'll take it," putting it into his shirt pocket.

"So, it's a deal?"

"Oh, yeah. Now I get it. It's my turn," he said, leaning back on the couch and expanding his belt as if measuring to see how much weight he had lost.

This was the moment of truth for the therapist. She could have taken the judicious approach—crossed examined him with visual gadgetry, discredited his nocturnal ephemera, or softened up his emotions with strategic chemicals—creating in him a mental milieu that was individually impotent but socially desirable. But she didn't. He was a person, and she believed that by disclosing his true identity, he would become whole again, revealing to her the same person that he was to himself, now and in the past. And the best way to achieve that was by disclosing herself.

He reached into his pants and pulled out his twelve-inch character actor dressed in a flight attendant uniform. "I know what you're thinking," he said, "so don't get uptight."

"And so, you get the better part of the bargain?"

"Well, that depends on what you do with it."

"I'll put it on my bookshelf. How's that?"

"Great idea!" he said. "Put it in the fiction section. I could never write anyway. Especially after...."

"So, you do remember."

"Yes. The suicide? Yes. Like it happened yesterday."

"So, the bullet was obstructing your vision."

"Blinded me. Yes. Like philosophy."

"So now, you might be able to decipher this note that was found by her bed. It had the police baffled. Not a suicide note. Just a period inside quotation marks."

"No, doctor, it *was* a suicide note."

"I don't understand."

"Well, as you know, we were all once that small."

"And couldn't talk."

"She was trying to give me back what she took from me but couldn't."

Later that morning, while driving home, Andrea noticed an estate-sale sign in his neighborhood and stopped to take a look. Though several cars were parked in front of the house, he felt at an advantage, this being two days prior to the weekend.

It felt more like a funeral home than a place where people lived, and the fact that almost everything had a price tag on it made it feel doubly depressing.

"What a wonderful pool, and what a view of the golf course," a woman remarked.

"They're not selling the home," the sales woman replied. "They plan to rent it out."

Who were *they*, the survivors of the deceased? Sons and daughters? Husband or wife? And why were they selling almost everything in the house? When he saw that all the artwork was for sale, he suspected that it was the husband, but when he saw that all the tools in the garage were not for sale, he suspected the wife. The things for sale in the library, however, made it clear that it was the wife—an easy chair, a collection of coffee mugs representing every state of the union, and even two framed certificates for player of the year at the Zephyrhills Country Club.

Andrea selected Elmo Zumwalt's *My Father, My Son* off a bookshelf—a good buy at five dollars, being signed by the admiral. Standing next to it was the largest book in the library—the 1971 *Lucky Bag*—a college yearbook as big as they come. He placed it on the desk to have a look inside. Suddenly, a picture of Ybette Rember shot out at him. It was unmistakable. Eastern Air Lines uniform and all, standing in the aisle of a plane filled with United States Naval Academy football players. There was a look of astonishment on her face, as though she had just walked into a surprise party. He flipped through the pages coming before and after the picture, looking for more of her, but there were none. How could she have been buried between hundreds of pages like that, as nameless as the person that took her picture?

Returning to his empty home, it felt like a theater that had just let out, and he was denied the pleasure of witnessing the end of the movie. It was a paradox of time that closely resembled the span of one's life, starting out slowly with a full reel of film, and then speeding up the closer it came to the end, even though the second-by-second, frame-by-frame action was constant throughout. It was an amusing analogy, the way one's view determines one's behavior.

With the passing of time, he became more yielding about Ybette's death. He had even forgotten where she was buried, though he knew it was in Kentucky somewhere, probably where she was born. Then one morning, *On This Day* column in the newspaper revealed that the first shot fired by an American soldier in combat was on April 19, 1776. Though the name of the soldier that fired the shot was not known, the name of the town in which he fired the shot was. Lexington! One name, two possibilities—Massachusetts or Kentucky. "And there she must be resting. I have to find her."

The house was old, narrow, and recently painted a light value of sap green. Set back ten feet deeper than the other houses on the street, it lacked the distinctive Victorian façade of its neighbors. The sidewalk leading to the front steps came up short and had been extended by a five-foot path of paver bricks. At once Andrea realized that the front porches of the house—upper and lower—had been removed, leaving the door on the second story exposed, flat and useless against the front, like an empty picture frame hanging on a wall.

He walked up the concrete steps and rang the doorbell. Peg Rember answered and invited him inside. He hesitated a minute as a small Chihuahua barked frantically at his feet. Worried that it was about to have a heart attack, she picked it up and said, "Sugar Baby's always in a fit when someone calls."

"I'm sorry," he said.

She was spry for a woman in her eighties, walking on bare feet that looked too hearty for shoes or slippers. Obviously raised on a farm, they were weathered to the bone, but still strong.

"Please have a seat," she said, pointing to the couch. She sat in a chair opposite him. "You've come a long way from Washington."

"Not exactly. I live in Maryland."

Her eyes were clear and lively, and her voice became more animated as she talked about her life. "They took my car away from me. Said I was too old to have a license. They want you incapacitated so they can stick needles in you and use you for experiments to improve the medicines for the next generation. I'll die soon enough so that your generation will live to be over a hundred. Your generation, the baby boomers."

He took it as an insult. "*Baby boomers?* That's not fair," he said. "As if we never grew up and will live forever."

She hooked her straight hair behind her ears. He thought that Ybette would have eventually done the same once it had begun to thin out.

"I told her to find a fine, young doctor, settle down, and raise a family. But no, she had to go off to Miami and become a glorified waitress. Wasted her life and her education. I warned her."

He didn't know how to approach her with the big question, like she was a time bomb that he had to disarm. He was sure that she knew. "I wouldn't say that about flight attendants," he said. "They have an important job. Security and safety of passengers."

"Ybette had innate breeding, is all. Innate breeding."

Andrea knew the phrase had been copped from some forties movie, probably a Bette Davis line. It was another example of "the error of isolation," and what he called the *terror of language*.

"Well, what do you do for a living?" she asked.

"I'm a magician," he said.

"Magician? Can you make me disappear?"

He pulled out a deck of cards and said, "I can do card tricks. Want to see?"

"Card tricks?" she said. "Everybody does card tricks. They drive you nuts."

He put the deck back in his pocket.

"Would you like a glass of iced tea?" she asked.

"Yes, thank you."

She put down Sugar Baby and went into the kitchen. Andrea got up and admired the family photos on the fireplace mantel, especially one of Ybette riding a horse. Suddenly, a loud noise of a door slamming shook the side of the house, and the pitiful sounds of a man crying came from the hallway leading into the kitchen. "Take off your clothes!" Peg shouted. "And get ready to take a bath."

Returning to the living room, she handed him the glass, and he took a sip. It was perfectly brewed with just the right measure of sugar and lemon, and a sprig of fresh mint.

"Sorry about the row," she said. "He gets a little cranky after program."

"Do you know how she died?" he asked.

"Ybette? Well, I know only as much as the authorities told me. I have the death certificate around here someplace."

"Have you ever seen the police report?"

"No. They said I could get one in Miami. But I'm not going down there just for that. I know what happened."

"Is she buried here?"

"I had her cremated," she said.

"Oh, I see."

"Just as well. She would have never had children to bury her anyway."

The horror of her death suddenly came back, racking his spirit with terrible images from the past. When they subsided, he came to himself as if out of a dream. "I didn't know," he said.

"You would have, sooner or later. You see she had premature menopause caused by my taking thalidomide. Was for my nerves, but look at Radar. Came out a jumble of nerves. She could have been worse."

"Premature menopause?"

"When she reached her twenties." Peg looked up at the ceiling as if to pray. "It's just as well."

Just as he said "I'm sorry," the same cries came from the hallway, this time making Andrea think of a man having his tongue pulled out. Then Radar wheeled around the corner, totally nude except for a towel held loosely against his genitals. His microcephalic head was bent to one side, his eyes looked in different directions, and his feet were so flat that arches had formed on the opposite sides of the insteps. He was silent and unable to keep still.

Mrs. Rember frowned as she stood up slowly. "Have you a look at Ybette's room," she said, "it's first one on the left. I had the walls recently painted; everything else is just the way she left it."

The invitation warmed Andrea's heart, and he said, "Yes, I will."

In the bedroom, he found Ybette's life much like she had abandoned it before becoming a stewardess. There was nothing there that he could appreciate, for nothing seemed to belong to the material present. It left his senses reduced to their lowest levels. He touched the quilt on the bed but couldn't feel it. He sniffed the clothes hanging in the closet but couldn't smell them. He looked at the graduation photo on the desk, but didn't recognize her. The years that she was alive were before him.

Opening the desk drawer, he was delighted to see a set of drawing pencils, all unused and very sharp. He opened the window blinds and let the daylight fill the room.

In his college years, he had forsaken art to study philosophy, yet he considered himself very gifted, able to draw elegant renderings quickly, whereas others labored painstakingly over the rules of proportion, perspective, and form. Everyone thought him gifted, an artist in whom the external object found a home, whereas in them it took up immediate opposition, like an enemy at war with their souls. Their art was modern; Andrea's art was inspired. He was in love with his work, and it didn't matter what anyone else thought or said about it. It didn't conflict, incite, or shock. It was simply beautiful.

Displaced for forty years by a foreign object, stripped of all his talent and gifts, he had been a living, breathing, walking work of art. The fact that no one had noticed, made it the greatest breakthrough since pop art and, in fact, its exact opposite, reversing everything modernity stood for. It was one step beyond the ready-mades. It was the almost-made in flesh and blood, the art idea incarnate, the perfect sacrifice that atoned for all the failures of the past that never got into galleries or museums, the lost, burned, trashed, and buried canvases painted by the millions that no one ever wanted. Was he about to resurrect his own talent and redeem them?

Ybette was not *in* the room but inside him, and he had to externalize her presence in lines. On the wall! Without shifting his eyes from the internal image, he drew blindly, his hand feeling every curve and angle of her body, and the pencil being guided along the ivory surface by the form of her spirit—a true hylomorphic soul! Edgeless, borderless, and multidimensional, the lines swept around the soul, not trying to wrap it around a skeleton, but giving it an external presence in which her energies could flow, an infinity of possible paths that she could take to reach him.

The result was extraordinary. He didn't realize it at first, but he had created something alive. The work didn't hit him as lines drawn on a wall— the things that he could see. What hit him was a feeling, a feeling he couldn't describe in words, the act of appearing rather than the thing appearing. It was an image that was not only appearing to him, but giving itself to him. Yet, it was a giving of a special kind, not as something to be used for a purpose or a cause, but to be taken into sight, arriving and departing, advancing and withdrawing, rising and passing away. It was Ybette on the make, turning the line without her being the line.

He was overjoyed that she had found him and had given him this perfect image. And he felt indebted to thank her. But he couldn't find the words. The gift could never be repaid.

He put the pencils back in the desk and sat on the bed. "Thank you," he said earnestly. "Thank you!" Two little words for so much to say. "How can I repay you for this?" The words lingered in the air, waiting for a reply. Hardly had they come out of his mouth when he lost sight of the drawing for just an instant, and not without a tremble. Quickly, he pressed his fingers against his lips as the drawing lost some of its definition momentarily.

"Are you tired, son?" Peg asked, walking into the room. "Would you like to take a nap?"

Startled, he stood up and said, "No. I was just recollecting."

"Do you like the color?" she asked, turning around to look at the walls.

That she had not taken his drawing as an obscene piece of graffiti was a surprise. "Do you like it?" he asked.

"It makes the room brighter, don't you think?"

"No, I mean the drawing. How do you like the drawing?"

"What drawing?" she asked.

"That one, there," he said, pointing at the wall.

"Where?" She moved closer to the wall, thinking that maybe her eyesight was failing.

Andrea stood beside her and gazed at the beautiful figure, baffled by its disappearance in her eyes. "Don't you see anything?" he asked.

"My eyesight is as good as yours," she said.

"Are you sure?"

"Is this some sort of magic trick you're playing?" she said. "Look, I can see that gold cross hanging around your neck perfectly."

"This is not a cross," he said. "It's my...!"

Peg examined the wall one more time closely and shook her head in disbelief. "No, son. No need to fret over something a body can't see."

The absence baffled him all night.

Waking up in Ybette's bed the next morning, he had an inspiration. Peg couldn't see the portrait because it was detached completely from everything around it. It didn't belong to anything but itself. It was withdrawn from whatever it was she knew about Ybette—her expression, color of hair, every detail that would divert her attention from the person, the selfhood present there. It was the glory of Ybette that her very own mother didn't recognize. But how could she not?

At breakfast, he complimented Peg on her "big, fluffy waffles."

"It's all in the machine," she said.

"Where'd you get it?" he asked.

"You can't find 'em in the store. But you can have this one. I'll clean it up and put it in the box, and you can carry it on the plane. I'll buy another one."

"How much does one cost?"

She showed him a catalog, and he immediately pulled out his wallet. Reading a price of $9.95, he gave her a twenty. "Do you have change?" he asked.

She rushed out of the room puffing like she was blowing out candles on the way, then returned shortly afterward with her purse. She counted her bills hesitantly, not sure if she was the one that should make change.

"Is there something wrong?" he asked. She waved her little finger at the catalog, and he took another look at the price, this time using his reading glasses. "Oh, I see. It's fifty-nine ninety-five. I'm sorry. I read the five as a dollar sign." Having committed himself to the purchase, he gave her two more twenties, leaving him with only one twenty left. And, there was no time to stop on the way to the airport to get more cash.

No sooner had he started his car than a young woman knocked on the window and signaled him to roll it down. He did so. She said, "I know you must think this is crazy, and that I'm not telling the truth, but I need your help. We just used up all our money on gas to fill up the tank, and we don't have anything left for food. It's getting late, I know, and it's going to take us five hours to reach Richmond. Look, I'll show you anything you want to see. Here's my sister's driver's license."

"Where's your car?" he asked.

"It's over there, behind that row of cars. It's the small, red one. My sister and her baby are inside."

He turned around but couldn't see it through the rear window. "How old is the baby?"

"One year old," she said.

"Where are you going to eat?"

"We'll find a fast-food place. The baby likes French fries."

Andrea shifted to park and turned off the engine. He pulled out his wallet and gave her the twenty, making sure to open it wide so that she could see there was nothing left. "You've got everything I have," he said.

"Nice car," she said.

"Thanks, but it gets lousy mileage."

"Thank you. God will bless you for this," she said, holding out her hand. He reached for it, but, noticing that it was her left, he used his left also, awkwardly shaking hands. "A good thing is going to happen to you," she said. "A very good thing."

"I hope so," he said.

After she walked away, he realized that she had not used her right hand, only her left hand, to signal him to roll down the window, to pull out the driver's license, and to shake hands. She kept it concealed in her coat pocket all the time.

"What was she holding in there? A gun? A knife? Damn, I could have been robbed!"

Quickly, he backed out of the parking place and drove around to find the red car, and there it was, just as she had described, with two women inside with a small baby.

"So, what was she holding in her pocket? Mace? That was it. Must have been a can of pepper spray. How else could she be so sure about me?"

During the trip home, he was constantly on the lookout for that good thing that was supposed to happen to him. He wanted it to happen. Just happen. He would take whatever it was, without question, as long as it was a good thing.

He knew that the further he got from the scene of the good deed, the less likely his chances were of being gifted.

Being Given, he thought, was just a book. A new way of paraphrasing phenomenology. It speculates that death too is a gift. How bizarre. My death—the possibility of impossibility—denies me an infinity of possibilities all at once in its oneness. Nothing else is possible when I die. Only death. As though it could never happen, but does. It's the ultimate possibility of impossibility. As long as the good thing is possible, I will not die! Is that the good thing?

He had always thought that the *Second Coming* would happen before he died. He could never die beforehand. He laughed aloud, then looked out the window at the clouds.

The last leg of the trip was a short fifty feet up his driveway. He reached for the garage door opener and, before he had a chance to press the button, the door opened. He was stunned, as if someone inside had beaten him to the trigger. At a complete loss, he closed the door, backed out of the driveway, and approached again, making sure to replay his exact movements. Nothing happened. The door stood unmoved, as it was supposed to until he pressed the button, heard the solid click, and watched the thing open. He waited a moment, finger just one inch away from the button, taunting the door to open. Then he touched it softly, massaged it, pressed it halfway, but no response.

Matt Bando was dumbfounded to see Andrea enter the room. His black and blue arm crossed over the bed, dragging IV tubes to reach out and shake hands. He smiled through a thick, gray beard.

"This place is like a SCIF," Andrea said. "I had to be escorted to your room." The ICU monitors connected to Bando's body kept steady and silent watch over his vital signs. "Picture window too. You're on the best side of the building. You can watch planes take off and land at the airport."

Bando moved slowly to butter a biscuit on the tray before him, and then used a spoon to eat his scrambled eggs. He looked at the TV on the wall broadcasting congressional confirmation hearings, and said, "I'd be embarrassed to date her."

Andrea glanced at the TV, then down at a blue polo shirt on the floor. He walked over and picked it up. It was soaked with sweat. He opened the small closet under the TV, but there was nothing inside and no hangers. "Where's your stuff?" he said.

"I don't know," Bando said.

Andrea looked around for a place to hang the shirt and found Bando's pants in a corner, also wet with sweat. He hung them both on a valet stool next to the sink where he sat down on a padded seat. "Where's your bathroom?" he asked.

"You're sitting on it."

Andrea lifted up the seat and exposed the toilet. Outside the door a shapely nurse was sitting at a computer looking over patient records. "Close at hand," he said.

"It's here," Bando whispered. Andrea moved closer and asked him to repeat. "It's here," Bando said again.

"What's here?" Andrea asked.

"I can feel it. You have to help me."

"Help you what?"

"I haven't gone in three days. Help me up."

"Don't you have an orderly for this? I mean you must be paying a small fortune."

"Come on, help me," lifting himself up from the bed. Andrea helped him get up without detaching the tubes and cords of the monitoring devices. Then Bando sat on the toilet and released his load. "Flush it!" he said.

Instantly, Andrea knew that Bando had intentions on the nurse and didn't want to spoil it by passing a *honeymoon's-over* shit.

Back in bed and now finishing his breakfast, Bando said, "Did you hear

Congress passed a law increasing the age limit for air marshals? It's now sixty. "

"Really?"

"TSA was attracting too much bad blood, so they changed the job to fifty percent investigation, fifty flying. No more airport security. They boosted the age to attract retired agents back in, and their salaries aren't offset by retirement annuities. They're now grade twelve. If I hadn't taken a buyout, I'd go for it."

"Yeah, your buyout. That's incredible. I can't believe they gave you *five hundred thousand*."

"Better than taken a bullet for this President. I figured my time was due, so I cut out."

"So, they're still hiring air marshals."

"Still got your clearance? And your ten-point preference?"

"Yeah."

"There you go. Only problem is they don't fly first class anymore."

"Oh, man, that ruins it. What's the sense of flying if you can't go first class? Flying economy class to Bangkok and back?"

"But it's still a free ticket."

The seat was more comfortable than the usual for economy class, but no consolation for not being able to fly first class. Nonetheless, he wasn't about to let the regulation bother him. This was his reprieve, and he now took pleasure in the mundane aspects of the job, which were many. The routine gave him a happy sense of security, something he hadn't felt thirty years ago.

Fully healed now and far enough away from the specter of war to think of his gun as a burden rather than a life-saving companion, he was now a public servant, not a knight on a white horse ready to save the world from evil heretics. And his faithful travel companion was no longer a journal filled with clonal machinations, but a simple stainless-steel bracelet engraved DANIEL C LEWIN MA USA, AA FLIGHT 11, 11 SEP 01 VOT. This was now his *verifiability criterion*, and nothing else. No longer a sky marshal wearing out his welcome with warrantless search and seizure authority, he was now a federal air marshal, a criminal investigator entrusted with top-secret information. But, therein dwelled the temptation.

When the plane reached cruising altitude, he opened his laptop, turned it on, and smiled at the logo on the front page. The woman sitting next to him stared at the big red letters on the screen: TOP SECRET//TALENT KEYHOLE//ORCON, NOFORN//MR. He typed in his ID and password, made a few clicks, and started a flow of images that flashed by without logical sequence or arrangement. Pictures, statistical data, and documents appeared, one at a time. And, like pornography imprinting itself on the mind until inanimate objects become sexual organs, the multifarious phenomena gradually became Flight 11 out of Boston heading for Los Angeles. A 787-200 with 81 passengers and 11 crew members aboard.

The details conjured to recreate that fateful morning were not to be organized, arranged, or classified in any way, not because they were too numerous, but because the description of even a chosen few would have been a submission to poetics, which had no place in truth. Linguistic cadence that attempted to keep rhyme with the beating of one's heart in order to mime entry into the past was an awfully deceptive thing. Superlatives had no rights in his mind.

He watched the clock ticking intently, waiting for the time to change—the second the present would cease and the past begin. He wanted to record the change precisely, thinking that if he didn't, he would miss it. And, when he blinked, three to four tenths of a second, 7:34:00 A.M. appeared on the screen.

The bracelet was gone, a sign of absolute verifiability.

There was a taste of ashes in the memory of 9/11. He repeated the numbers over and over again, a date that could never be shaken from the terror and horror.

He knew the sequence of events precisely, watching the minutes go by, until at 7:40, the plane backed away from the gate. Then, nineteen minutes later, it took off.

Sitting in 34B, he had a clear view of the left aisle—fifteen rows of economy, five of business, and two of first class—all the way up to the cockpit door. He assumed his partner in 11B, last aisle seat in business class, was still there, doing his job, blending in and looking inconspicuous.

He kept an eye on the clock. Five minutes after takeoff, the plane was still climbing. At 8:10, it reached cruising altitude—29,000 feet. The fasten seatbelt signs went off, and the flight attendants began to prepare for service. He couldn't believe that it was about to happen and caressed his gun to calm his racing heart. He looked into the aisle to spot any signs that it was beginning. The reports all said that it started fifteen minutes into the flight. But what was *it*? No one knew exactly. There was nothing left of *it*. Total annihilation. Not even a gold filling.

8:15, and he was getting anxious though of steady heart. He thought of the Miracle on the Hudson and how the passengers had diverted disaster by praying. Was this possible? He typed in the words "Help me Lord," and out came a psalm.

Help, LORD, for no one loyal remains; the faithful have vanished from the human race. Those who tell lies to one another speak with deceiving lips and a double heart. May the LORD cut off all deceiving lips, and every boastful tongue…. "I will now arise," says the Lord. "I will grant safety to whoever longs for it."

Daniel prayed this in the den of vicious lions and was *delivered* unharmed. But that was just fiction, a myth written by someone else. Daniel really was a magician that drugged the king and the lions as well. Now, he sat in their midst once again, in business seat 9B, follower of a different Lord, ex-officer in the elite Sayeret Matkal, and content delivery network entrepreneur. Content deliverer of a mirrored Zionist conspiracy to be closer to the end user, the jerk that believes everything he sees on the screen because it comes in just a split second.

The shadow of a man carrying a dagger passed up the aisle, freezing everyone. It edged slowly, waiting for someone to move. A woman ducked behind a seatback. The man stopped, turned, and stabbed her back. When he removed the dagger, blood flowed.

A woman cried. Two flight attendants came out of the galley to look. He stabbed the first repeatedly in the face and chest. She fell to the floor.

A charge ran through Danny Lewin. He unbuckled his seatbelt and rushed into the aisle. Landing a solid kick into the man's back, he followed with a crushing hit to the head. Two men sitting in the first row stood up and came at him, carrying daggers. Two more in business class came at him, also carrying daggers.

Matt Bando drew his weapon, released the safety, and stood up to get a clean shot at the hijackers. He watched helplessly as Lewin's arms were torn to shreds by the stabbing daggers. He couldn't shoot. But when the hijacker slashed Lewin's throat and threw him into an empty seat, Bando grasped the handle of the gun with his left palm, eyes pointing at the closest target, sinking into it. Hands trembling, he managed to keep the gun level and steady. He pulled the trigger. The gun fired, and fired, and fired, shocking hearts and bursting eardrums. And, to the amazement of the brave that were watching, from a span of six seats, Bando had missed his man.

The man ran down the aisle and stuck a dagger into Bando's chest, between the ribs, drilling into the lung, springing pink blood. Another dagger followed with a strike on the opposite side of the chest, causing Bando to drop to the floor.

The awful failure stunned Andrea. His partner had missed at close range. The bullets were real, not blanks. Bando was a sharpshooter with hundreds of hours of target practice that had honed his skill with a pistol to a fine edge. He couldn't have missed. This is not real. He must have been shooting blanks, or else the attacker was superhuman.

Andrea dared not move or show a sign of his identity. Though seriously outnumbered, he had the firepower. But would his fate be the same?

Knowing that another air marshal was aboard, the terrorists didn't enter the economy section. Suddenly, the business and first class passengers came down the aisles choking, looking at passenger after passenger, even at Andrea, for help, but no one came forward.

Three terrorists moved toward the cockpit while two stood watch in first class.

Andrea stood up and moved toward first class, determined to take back the plane. He drew his pistol and pointed it straight at them and was ready to fire, but the stainless-steel bracelet took its place.

The hijacking was a *mental* construct without a particle of metal in it, a metaphysical assumption the likes of matter and form not having any substance of their own until they came together as one. Reason said it should be so, because there was no other way substance could be absolutely verified. Reason was a given, a gift that should not be denied, despite the anomalies seen in the world.

The stainless-steel bracelet, whose absence said the hijacking was happening, now said by its presence that it was a construct, a having, not a being. It was a tremendous breakthrough to have this verifiable constant in his life, something that told him what was real and what was not real.

It was the retirement of his superiors—those that knew about his post-traumatic stress disorder and that year of recuperation and rehabilitation—that put him in good standing for the job in Bangkok. And, when the old hag retired, he got the assignment.

The customs inspection of his household goods was conducted in his house before the shippers packed, and it was a cinch for him to add his stash after the inspector left and when the packers were not looking. Old, but still fifty thousand dollars in cash!

It was mid-January and the sun was hot, but the breeze made being outside very pleasant. He couldn't remember feeling so happy, walking freely down the street like he had just been cured of a deadly disease.

His entire manhood had been confined to a sentence, from the day of his birth when his mother discovered a linear mark running from navel to genitals—a sign that required circumcision, tightly-pinned diapers, and a boyhood of undersize Jockeys—to the first year of his puberty when he pointed to a pain in his groin, prompting his father to take him to Dr. Gallzi, who examined him utterly with fat fingers and said, "He must wear a jockstrap!"

Now, briefless, he was freer than he ever felt in his life. Andrea unbound.

Waiting on a corner, he wasted no time catching a taxi and arriving for his reservation on time. It wasn't a restaurant, but a private apartment in Ploenchit. He had waited a week for them to procure the delicacy and paid the agreed upon price—three hundred U.S. dollars in cash.

The setting wasn't elegant, though the table was set with sterile white linen and china. A large glass kitchen door isolated the heat and steam, but it didn't close out the tintinnabulation of metal woks and the scent of sautéed ginger and garlic that prefigured the treasure being prepared. It was a square chamber that provided an aphrodisiac of scintillating magnitude, not just a booster of penal hydraulics. Whereas the popper of pills would say, "I'm hard again but don't feel it," the eater of *RMB* said, "I feel like eighteen all over again."

"You want drink?" Daksin asked.

"Yes," Andrea said. "Oolong tea, please."

"You eat with chopstick?"

"Yes, I do."

When the glass door slid open, the solemn meal was brought before him. The sight of it made him still and silent. Daksin thought he was saying grace silently before eating.

Andrea put on his glasses and leaned forward to get a closer look. He didn't wonder what it might be. He knew exactly what it was, but couldn't believe it was floating in a bowl of brownish broth garnished with medicinal herbs.

Sensing Andrea's reluctance to indulge, Daksin said, "I'm sorry if too small. We can get better one if you want."

It smelled unbelievably sweet and was unmistakably female.

"*RMB* from China," Daksin said. "You must eat all. Leave nothing."

"What does RMB mean?" Andrea asked. "The letters, what do the letters stand for?"

"Renmimbi," Daksin said. "It Chinese word for money."

"Chop chop," Andrea added as he picked up a piece that was floating beside the body.

Daksin smiled and said, "Ah, cord very good, very sweet."

Andrea bit off a piece from the end and began chewing. "Very tasty," he said. "Do you have chili?"

"You want chilies?" Daksin said. Andrea nodded yes, and Daksin retreated to the kitchen.

Though the body was still steaming, Andrea rescued it from the bowl, wrapped it in a linen napkin, hid it under his shirt, and rushed out of the apartment. He ran down the street and turned a corner to get out of sight. Then he hailed a taxi.

When he reached his apartment, he didn't know what to do. Sitting down on the sofa, he unfolded the napkin, trying hard not to visualize the body as food. But there was nothing else his mind could think of—the idea of pulling apart the leg and eating it like a chicken wing. It was a craving that originated at the pit of his stomach, a true hunger that had to be satisfied. It was then that he remembered the stripe connecting his genitals with his navel. It had the presence and rigidity of a tree trunk, the carrier of chi—the life-giving force that was his doom.

He brought the body to the kitchen, wrapped it in aluminum foil, and put it in the refrigerator. Then, he began planning for a burial, maybe even a cremation at a church.

Text message to Mel Gatongay: *I'm from the FBI. Fine Body Investigators. Pls come to my boudoir tonight. Andrea.*

Reply message: *Hi, Grand! I'm MFI. SU8. Melissa.*

"Enter the most beautiful ladyboy in all of Bangkok," Andrea said, showing Mel into his apartment.

"Sorry I'm late," Mel said, entering.

"You said eight, so I planned on nine."

"You're so considerate, Grand. Will you put me in your will too?"

"I have no children," Andrea said. "Might as well."

"But I have one for you, Grand," Mel said, handing him a brown paper bag.

Andrea opened it and exclaimed, "Durian!"

"Durian High," Mel said laughingly.

A cry of hunger came from Andrea's stomach as he brought the medieval fruit to the kitchen and cut the apparently impregnable ball of spines along the stripe that ran from the stem to the bottom. They divided the sections equally and watched each other eat like cannibals the richest and most pungent flesh imaginable.

When finished, Mel pointed to Andrea's bracelet and said, "Your boyfriend in the States?"

"Oh, no," Andrea said. "I don't have a boyfriend, or a girlfriend for that matter. It's a memorial bracelet. Daniel Lewin was a victim of nine-eleven. He was on the first plane that went into the Twin Towers."

"Oh, I see. Very tragic," Mel said.

"He sat between two terrorists, and some say he tried to stop them, but there was another one sitting behind him that slashed his throat with a box cutter. He was an Israeli commando, but against stiff odds."

"Grand, are you a spy?"

Andrea smiled and said, "If I told you, I'd have to...."

"You'd have to what, Grand?" Mel asked, eager to hear his fate.

"I'd have to ravish you," Andrea said.

But that wasn't the thing that excited him. Mel's mere presence close to him, his youth and vigor, his lithe body, his energy and strength, made him feel more alive and, somehow, very innocent. All he really wanted was Mel's strong hands to massage his aching body, to pull the triggers embedded deep in his muscles and tissues, and release the blocks to his wellbeing. It's what made him abstain from disgrace, he thinking the man was in fact himself. I am he, and he is me; therefore, neither one of us is guilty!

Andrea felt proud. The restraint and innocence was like nothing Mel had ever experienced, and he decided to stay, thinking that it could actually be love.

Hunger pangs woke Andrea early next morning, and he was surprised to see Mel sleeping beside him. He got up, went to the kitchen, and noticed a ball of foil on the countertop. Quickly he opened the refrigerator and couldn't find it anywhere. He unwrapped the foil and was shocked to see bones with not a stitch of meat on them. "Mel!" he cried, "What did you do?" He ran into the bedroom and continued to rant until his lover woke up.

"Grand, why so early?" Mel said groggily, rolling around the bed.

Andrea held out the ball of foil and said, "You stupid, stupid, dump, son-of-a-bitch. Do you know what you ate?"

"I had sore throad. Durian gave me sore throad and I had to eat something."

"When did you get up?"

Mel wrapped a pillow around his ears.

"Answer me! When did you get up?"

"I can't remember."

"Didn't you look at what you were eating?"

"Yes. Leftover."

"Leftover? Don't you know what you ate?"

"Goat? Taste like goat?" Mel said skeptically.

"GOAT?"

Mel smiled with a gorgeous look on his face. It was prettier than Andrea had ever seen, a glow that seemed heavenly.

"Where did you get that makeup?" Andrea asked.

"Makeup? I don't have makeup. I never sleep with makeup."

"Take a look if you don't believe me."

Mel got up and looked at himself in the mirror. He blinked a few times, and then cleared his eyes with water. He felt his chin and said, "Grand, I can't believe. I don't have beard. What happened to my face?" He turned to Andrea to show off.

"How can you not have a beard?" Andrea asked, taking a closer look.

"What did you do to me, Grand?"

"Nothing."

"It must be something you did last night. Look at me. Can you believe the way I look?"

"No. I mean, yes, I have to, shouldn't I?"

"Wait till everyone sees me. I can't wait to show them."

Andrea went to Daksin's place every Friday at twilight, bringing with him ten one-hundred dollar bills, but never daring to enter. Mel's transformation was surely due to the RMB he had eaten. There was no other possible cause. The thought that one could do the same for him was tempting.

It was a temptation based on the rationale that the unborn innocent was abandoned anyway, that it would only perfect another person's libido. But then, paying a thousand dollars for it would only support the smugglers he so detested.

Then, one evening, Daksin saw him lingering outside and asked what he wanted. His tone was congenial and not reproachful of the first incident, so Andrea said, "RMB."

Daksin said "Come back next Friday. Will have for you."

When Andrea first looked at the little body in the bowl, his face turned sadly happy, devilishly good. He tore into it as both cannibal and lover. His mouth was brutal and soft, teeth chewing flesh that lips had tenderly kissed. It made him feel whole inside not to think about it, debating with himself over the otherness of the body, whether it belonged to him as purchased object, a name for a recipe, a baby, a boy, a man, whether a part of a whole, or a whole torn apart, whether sacred or profane, an object of adoration or one of evil. It was an indulgence lodged in flesh that guaranteed an ultimate pleasure. Nothing was being eaten but an oracle. It sought complicity and forgiveness, yet didn't say a word in defense of itself.

Tearing open the skull, his fingers picked out the vital tissues wherein no ideas ever had the chance to form. It was pure potency! In the end, he would have no other food.

RMB was deadlier and more costly than any drug, and Andrea became superior in subservience than even the most dedicated addict. He had distilled all his basic instincts and senses into one, siding with everything weak and base, with all failures, making an idol of whatever contradicts, corrupting his reason with the supreme insignificance of his most sinful, pitiful, and corrupt life.

All of his powers—cognition, reason, and judgment—were absorbed into one primal sense. He became indifferent toward others. He no longer found it necessary to be worthy. He lacked faith in them, charity in them, and especially hope in them. He was partaking in a special advent; he was about to be born a philosopher of the irrational. He was learning anew without moral and aesthetic evaluations, without logic, inspiration, or enlightenment, which all brought him untruths. Truth was no longer found in "I think…," grounded in an I, an ego, which could never be now present but was always lost in the past somewhere. He looked back at the world that he had tried to distill into words in so many ways, a world that now condemned him to a prison cell of nothingness, and, with a defiant thrust of will, he said, "Damn it!" He was no longer an eater of words but and eater of the nameless.

Eventually, he lost count of his visits but, one day, Daksin asked him excitedly, "We have source for number one! You like?"

"Absolutely!" Andrea said. "How much?"

"Thousand U.S. dollar."

Something he could afford for sure, but if it became a habit like his current fare, it would deplete his bank in less than a year. Nevertheless, he said, "Stiff price, but one taste can't hurt."

"Never the less," he kept reminding himself during the week, "never the less," even abstaining from meat as best he could in preparation for the feast. Finally, Daksin gave him a call, and he was at the restaurant in no time.

When served, he didn't know if the fetal being before him was a stillbirth or a live birth, a miscarriage or an abortion. Those were all words that didn't matter to him. All he was sure of was that it was a boy, a male, a sacred gender in that part of the world.

He ate slowly at first, looking for any difference in flavor. There was none. But it hit him all at once that this wasn't the possession or imprisonment of an innocent being, but an assimilation of everything evil in its being into him, and the removal of everything good. He was absolving this being of its original sin!

And that was his last philosophical thought. It was his last thought of any kind. He didn't talk to anyone unless spoken to, and he would reply with total thought reduction in one of three words—yes, no, maybe.

The days immediately following the meal, he ate nothing in its wake, fasting on fresh coconut water, not wanting anything else, seeking only the greatest nourishment from one source, the quenching of dialectics and revolution of the blood. The less his life passed into the thing, the more life there was in his body, the decreasing matter of the thing eaten, the fuller the life absorbed into his body. Feeling the power mount to its highest pitch on the third day, the ringing in his ears, alive since the war, suddenly disappeared, as though someone had pressed a mute button in his brain and, voila, gone. It was an elation of profound proportions, second only, he imagined, to skydiving or riding a rollercoaster. It was the demise of every schoolboy's favorite poem. Alas, the poetic earworm, the emaciated trace of Poe's masterpiece, had died. How terrific he felt.

On a Thursday afternoon, while going out of the office for lunch, he watched his supervisor approach and stop for a moment to inspect himself in the mirrored side of the front door. It was as though he were using Andrea's image to straighten his tie, comb his hair, and wipe loose hairs from his face. When satisfied, he looked into the iris scanner and the door opened, revealing Andrea staring at him. It was an embarrassing moment, and Andrea should have said, "Excuse me, sir," but he didn't even step aside to let the man enter. He just stood there blocking the entrance until the door slid closed. When the door opened again, the supervisor was standing to one side. "After you, Andrea," he said. Andrea smiled and walked out of the building and through the garden and into the street. He walked slowly to save his energy, but suddenly the ringing in his ears returned. And then, it turned into a voice with a message that he didn't understand, in a language that he didn't recognize. He knew by the crying, though, that it was a plea for help, a haunting presence inside him.

He couldn't stop it or talk back to it. The crying kept pace with his walking, getting louder as he went faster. It choked him, and he could hardly breathe. "Stop it!" he shouted. "I can't stand it." He became lightheaded, stumbled, and fell down. Then the voice began to laugh, for it had won a round. Trembling, he lay on the sidewalk, facing the brink of disaster and understood who was speaking to him. It was an indulgence in reason that he could ill afford, for now he became an outlaw on the run from justice.

A man, who had been watching him from across the street, walked over and helped him stand up. He waved for a taxi and, when it came around, put him in the back seat, and sat in the front seat next to the driver. They drove around for ten minutes and then stopped in an alley between two apartment buildings. "Okay, now tour over," the man said. "You owe me twenty dollar."

"What tour?" Andrea said.

The man turned around and knelt on the seat to face Andrea and said, "You want trouble? I give you trouble. Twenty dollar."

"I don't have any money on me," Andrea said.

The man leaned over the seat and gave Andrea a strong punch in the middle of the chest, knocking the wind out of him. "Business is business," he said. "Give me money."

A garage door opened, and a tall woman walked out to the taxi. She said a few words in Thai to the spurious guide, gave him and the driver a few bills each, opened the door of the back seat, and escorted Andrea into her house. "Welcome, Mister High," she said. "My name is Doctor Ketjap Manis. I hear that you are a connoisseur of RMB."

"Doctor who?" Andrea said faintly.

"Ketjap Manis."

"Surely you jest," Andrea said.

"Well, you might say that I'm a doctor with a client who is very serious about your work."

"Which work is that?"

"Please come this way. You'll understand inside this room." Doctor Manis opened the door, stepped aside to let Andrea enter first, and then slammed the door shut, leaving him trapped. Andrea tried to open the door but it was locked.

It was a blue room with nothing in it except a red plastic pail and a bottle of drinking water in the corner. Knowing that he was now a prisoner, he went into a hapless panic, much like a squirrel scurrying about trying frantically to find a way out of a cage. His whole life boiled down to this one place—a blue boxroom—that might just as well have been his coffin. Panic! Panic! Panic! And the only cure for it was a gun in his hand.

The minutes went by like soldiers patrolling through the jungle in the night. He was desperate but knew that the only way out was to keep his head. He sat down and began thinking that he had to somehow outwit his captor, and foremost in this plan was not to reveal what was on his mind.

Then, mockingly, the urge came to defecate the remains of his last meal. He knew that someone was watching, but couldn't tell from what vantage. Using the bucket, he squatted, and it came out in a long string, folding upon itself as it descended.

"I'm a pooet!" he crooned. But no sooner had he claimed this title, than the echo of it came back to his head. It repeated, "I'm a pooet! I'm a pooet!" trying to disown the mistake, the changing of his excretion into a person, which had propelled him toward this end. Weakened by the act, he returned to the corner, sat down, and closed his eyes. A moment later, Doctor Manis came into the room carrying a gun and said, "Very good, Mister High. You have done your duty, which will make my client very happy. Would you like some breakfast?"

"Yeah, eggs Benedict," Andrea said sarcastically.

Doctor Manis picked up the bucket, said, "Very well done," and left the room. Andrea wanted to check the door but was too weak even to stand.

Half an hour later, a servant came into the room with a tray on which was breakfast, as he had ordered. The man didn't speak and left it in the middle of the room.

The initial effect of the food was revitalizing, and he found himself thinking logically again.

Windowless, the blue boxroom presented no means for escape. The agency had trained him for this, but he was in no shape, physically or mentally, to put up any resistance.

After a short while, the servant returned and retrieved the tray. "Good fare," Andrea said. "Are you the cook?" The servant bowed and left the room. Now he was sure they were watching him every minute.

Something grew in his throat, feeling like a small piece of food that had lodged there. He coughed but couldn't get it out. It was a sore throat coming on and maybe a cold. He took a drink of water but couldn't swallow. The water ran out of his mouth and onto his chest. The symptoms of the flu—fever, chills, cold sweat, headache, muscle aches—hit him all at once. He felt dizzy, swaying halfway out of consciousness. He could see but only through a heavy haze. He heard voices outside the door, followed by the door creaking open and steps approaching. He couldn't see it but guessed there was a gun aiming at him. "Doctor, is that you?" he said.

"Yes, Andrea, it is Ketjap Manis."

"You poisoned me!" Andrea said.

"Just a taste of your own medicine," she said. "One hundred thousandth of a gram to be exact. Not enough to kill you, but untraceable even in its most potent amount. All made from fermented beans, corn, and a little human excrement. If I really wanted to kill you, I would have merely doubled the dose and your death would have been very swift from total respiratory failure. Fortunately for you, this is not what we have in mind. We gave you this wakeup call, so to speak, because we have distaste for torture, which would necessitate the incorporation of some nasty devices. But, as you know, such things only happen in the movies and cheap novels for dramatic impact."

Doctor Manis paced the floor a few times, then said, "Your passion for RMB is decidedly bound up with your sexual glands, which are *inter unrinas et faeces*, as your beloved Saint Augustine had long ago observed, which explains your desire for ladyboys and barren women. In Freudian terms, you are stuck in the anal zone where the erotic urge is also bound, and its product acquires the significance of being your own child, which you use as filthy lucre to finance your lovemaking. Your quest for eating RMB is nothing more than sublimation, an abandonment of your anal eroticism. Unfortunately for you, you came across the offspring of a man of significant means, just like yourself. It is now up to you to make reparation for your childish tastes. Fifty thousand U.S. dollars is what you must pay."

Andrea debated with himself whether it was possible to resist. He knew that Mel would never follow-up on his absence, and that the ICA was impotent in a crisis. And hostage training had taught him that the effects of torture ran up and down a bell curve, the peripheral nerves being the first to be assaulted, gradually leading up to the spinal cord, then the brain, which eventually snaps, creating a tailspin into unconsciousness. The less damage to the body the better the technique, so as to give the victim a sense of endless repetition, a true taste of torturous hell. And, given Doctor Manis' anal fixation, there's no telling what was up her sleeve.

It was some relief to know that they were after money rather than intelligence. Nonetheless, he said, "Looks like I need to play a little catch-up, if you pardon the expression. I know your client is from China, so I'd like to make him a counter offer, something that might be worth more than money to him, since he's a man of means, as you say. I work for a government agency, which is actually a cover for a top secret operation to gather intelligence from belligerent nations, especially intelligence regarding the development of atomic weapons. I would be willing to provide him with this intelligence in exchange for the amount he wants."

"Excellent proposition, Mister High," Doctor Manis said "I'll see what can be made of this."

An hour passed before Doctor Manis returned to the boxroom. "No," she said. "My client prefers the money."

Andrea wanted desperately to see sunlight again, which was surely flourishing outside, along with birds and busy people. His intentions were not treason, for he would never give them real information anyway. He needed to find a way to save his bankroll as well as his neck. There was no use in further bargaining, for he knew that the Chinese never changed their minds on anything.

"There is someone who might be interested in your offer," Doctor Manis continued. "But for now, your desecration of my client's fruit demands reparation of fifty thousand dollars."

There was no need to defend his case, to say that Daksin was to blame as well. But an American was more of a menace, the easier target. "Okay," he said. "You'll find forty-five thousand in cash in my apartment inside the mattress of my bed. And don't cut it open. Use the zipper!"

"Very dramatic, Mister High. We'll be right back to let you free." Doctor Manis looked at Andrea's soiled underwear and said sarcastically on leaving the room, "By the way, you wouldn't have a key on you by any chance." The muscles in Andrea's jaws rippled as he clenched his teeth in anger.

He had no way of telling time and, since the boxroom was an interior room, no sensual contact with the outer world. He slept curled up on the cold marble floor for several hours, losing track of the shift from day to night and night to day, not knowing whether he was awake or dreaming of being awake, both being unreal.

On what he thought was the dawn of the second day, he crawled to the door, turned the knob, and opened it! Darkness prevailed on him, and the sweltering sounds of a jungle in the middle of the night. He closed his eyes, held them tight for a few moments, then looked, but the dark jungle was still there. He waited for sunrise to prove to himself that it wasn't a dream, for inaction and tigers didn't go together. Besides, the bracelet on his wrist told him it was all real.

They had disposed of him on the outskirts of the city, and he didn't know which way to go.

Choosing the direction of the sunrise, he came upon a river and saw a beautiful woman emerging from the jungle on the other side. She waved at him and called, "Justin, lonely man in the stillness of the morning, come to me. I miss you. Come, come! I miss you."

At once he recognized that it was Ybette.

"Now I'm in love with you," she said. "Hear me, Justin? I said that I love you, AND—I'm *in* love with you. All at once. Can you believe me? Please believe me, dear. Now I will love you. I will love you. Come, come! I have built a nest here. See, my nest is here, my nest is here. Please come."

Andrea threw off his clothes and jumped into the river. Just as he reached the shore of the other side, she suddenly flew away in the form of nighthawk, laughing mockingly at him. Then, a lonely cry echoed through the jungle, "Keeeeeer! Keeeeeer! Keeeeeer!"

Quickly, he jumped into the water and headed back to retrieve his clothes. Halfway across, the black water began to liquefy his body, ultimately leaving only his head with which to float and breathe.

By ten o'clock, the sun had raised the tide high enough to lift him over rocks and fallen trees, where, without the slightest exertion and upturned face, he floated downstream on a constantly rising current, weaving through nature's silence."

"So, what do I do now?" Andrea said.

"Just wait till they come," Andrea said.

Mel Gatongay didn't go to the police on account of Andrea's disappearance until one day he heard his brother Toon share stories he had heard from fellow taxi drivers, especially one about an American being escorted by a bully who wanted to get paid twenty dollars for giving him a ten minute tour of the city. The BPB followed up on the lead, interviewing the taxi driver and getting the address where Andrea High was dropped off.

"Come, let us go," the police lieutenant said eagerly to Mel, and together they drove to the address. The garage door was closed but not locked, so they opened it and went inside. The dankness of the empty interior made the lieutenant sniffle, and a fright ran through Mel's body. He pointed to a black door, making Mel's face turn pale and his legs tremble. Then he opened it.

There, on the floor in the center of a blue room, lay a body covered completely in a light-blue surgical sheet.

"Do you think?" the lieutenant said, stepping forward.

Mel sensed it might be but was speechless.

The lieutenant reached down and slowly lifted the sheet, revealing a headless, naked body—emasculated, surgically transformed, and fitted with a device to keep the organ dilated. The revolting sight shocked him, but he kept calm and examined the body. When he came to a bracelet around the victim's wrist, he said, "This must be him. I'll bet they botched the operation, cut off his head, but forgot to remove the name tag."

Mel stepped back but fainted before he had the chance to run away.

"Ladies and gentlemen, this is your captain speaking. Please listen, since Mister High has some good news to tell you."

"Ladies and gentlemen, boys and girls, I hope you are having a comfortable flight and have enjoyed the entertainment provided. My little computer tells me that all of you have finished my novel, but I really don't believe that. I know some of you didn't and most of you didn't read every word. I understand, since this story will never be made into a movie, which you would prefer watching.

"Now, for the final exam. If anyone fails, I swear this plane will go down in flames! Zero tolerance level is where I'm at. Do I have your attention, everyone?"

"Yes!" the passengers say in unison.

"I can't hear you!"

"YES!" they shout.

"That's better. There's something really big about an airplane story that trumps everything out there. Our captain could have suffered indigestion while flying over Colorado, and it would have gotten breaking news. But now you're all breaking news. Isn't the media wonderful?

"YES!"

"Now I'm happy to inform you that you have accomplished your mission. I'm not going to test you to see if you've actually read my novel, since it doesn't matter anymore. As of this moment, over one hundred million people have downloaded the E-book, thinking they're reading a skyjacking in progress. And, they even think, get this, that by doing so, they will save your lives. Well, lucky for you, this is true.

"I must thank you for your cooperation. You have made me a millionaire and John Barefoot a pauper. Some of you book lovers may know John Barefoot and might be pleased to know that he's actually on this plane, flying first class, while the rest of you poor souls fly economy. Would he have shelled out to give you all first-class meals?"

"NO!" shout the economy passengers.

"Very good. You can't see him, but he's on tour touting his new book— I'm not going to give you the title, since it's a fraud that you don't ever want to read—trying to cash in on a story of an air marshal that knows nothing, giving you the impression that he's created something new and exciting only for the purpose of making money. The words are all cast in an artificial light, whereas this book, which has come into the consciousness of more people at one time than any other book in history, now basks in a natural light, the light of day, which I grant each and every one of you. Consider this day a holiday, a day that celebrates the death of a counterfeit, an eloquent composition of grammar and metaphor with no more meaning in it than a nursery rhyme, and a book that gives you life!

"My purpose is not to offer a new literature, to tear down the false hopes of eloquence or the opposition which breeds on it, trying to expose the moral and political agendas hidden in it by using innuendo, allusion, and understatement, but to make you see that this poetic freedom is nothing more than eloquence in turn, an attempt to throw in the towel on intentionality and the quest for meaning beyond rhetoric and poetry.

"Cool, hey? Okay, I'll admit that that wasn't off the top of my head. I read it, but that doesn't matter. It's the meaning that counts.

"Now for the coup de grâce. There's one last thing for you to do, and you'll have met all my demands. You must rate the book from one to five, five being a *must-read page turner*, as if you didn't already know. It seems to me you have no choice. Rate it five stars and you'll be telling the truth. Rate it lower and you'll be lying. So, be honest about it. There you go."

"Page turner my ass," John says. "Let me out of here."

"Aren't you going to rate the book?" Marge asks. "You'll get us into trouble."

"It's all a hoax, don't you see? A literary hoax."

Marge gives the book a five, and then suddenly, it disappears. "It's gone," she says. John, look, my e-book is gone. Do you suppose that all of them are...."

John rates the book one and his suddenly disappears. "Deleted and delighted," he says.

"Yours too?" Marge says.

"Okay, ladies and gentlemen," High announces. "Your time is up. If you haven't rated the book yet, it's too late now. *Bait and Switch* has done its job. The most wanted novel that no one ever wanted has become the most wanted novel that no one will ever have."

A sultry flight attendant stops at the last seat in the outermost row, bends down, and whispers something in a passenger's ear. He unbuckles his seatbelt and follows her up the aisle. When they reach the flight deck, the door opens, and he enters alone.

"Welcome, Father Berthelot," Jack High says. "I watch your show on TV every Sunday night. I admire your candor."

"Where are you from, Jack?" Father Berthelot asks, his long, white beard whisking his words like a broom.

"Western New York," Jack says. "But let's talk in private. This way up to my headquarters," directing him up the stairs and into the pilot's sleeping quarters. They sit on opposite bunks facing each other. Father Berthelot says, "How did you know I was on this flight?"

"I didn't. I guess I was lucky. But there's always a man of the cloth on an airplane, don't you think?"

"The young lady mentioned reconciliation. Is that correct?"

"Yes, I'd like to. You see, I took a chance and there you were. What luck. Priests these days are so wimpy. Well, they've always been when it comes to confession. They can't handle it. Like it makes them feel powerless. But you're a psychologist, which should give you a better handle on it. And not afraid to wear rags in public."

Father Berthelot looked at his tattered, ash-colored robe and smiled. "So, tell me, Jack," he said, "what are your sins?"

"Well, father, you've read my book. It's all there, basically."

"You mean it's an autobiography?"

"Yes," Jack says. "A true confession."

"But I don't see a wound on your forehead."

"Very observant, father. You actually read my book."

"So, which parts are true and which are not?"

"All the immoral acts with women. True."

"You sound boastful."

"For those? Hardly the kind of sex a man would boast about."

"So, you plead poetic immunity. This is not a true confession."

Jack thinks for a moment, then says, "Yes, I agree. There's a lot more that's not in the book. Yes, I have broken every commandment."

"Even the fifth, thou shalt not kill?"

"Well, if you consider killing in war a sin, but I know the church doesn't. So, maybe not."

"And the suicide of your heroine? Was that true?"

"No. I made it up."

Father Berthelot considers the explicit desire to kill skyjackers expressed in the book, but lets it slide. Then, hinting at his favorite advocacy, he said, "Anything else in the book?"

"You mean the book itself, is it evil? I purposely didn't use the Lord's name in vain anywhere, and no profanity."

"It's blasphemous!" Father Berthelot says harshly. "Blasphemous!"

Dejected, Jack looks aside a moment and thinks. "You just like to hear yourself say that, don't you?"

"Blasphemous!"

"But I shut it down. It doesn't exist anymore."

"Precisely. Doesn't exist anymore. Is there anything else that doesn't exist anymore?"

An epiphany hits Jack with a wallop. "That part was true," he says. "I really did drive Carol to the abortion clinic." Tears come to his eyes and he begins to sob. He is overcome with grief and covers his face with his hands. He cannot control himself. He cannot talk. The ringing in his ears disappears, and he wipes the tears from his eyes. It's a catharsis, a realization that he had failed to save a life. He looks away and cries uncontrollably.

"Are you all right?" Father Berthelot asks.

"I don't remember ever confessing it," Jack says.

"Your reaction tells me you never did."

Jack sits silently for a long time while the priest prays. Then he grabs the handle of the smart gun, pulls it out of its holster, and cradles it in his hands. Finally, making up his mind, he hands it over, and says, "Here father, take it. I give up. I'm through."

Father Berthelot looks at Jack's empty hand, thinking that maybe his patient has gone off mad, and says, "Take what?"

"My gun, father. It's invisible, but you must promise me not to give it to the captain or any of the crew on this plane. Wait till the FBI come aboard and arrest me. Then give it to them."

"Okay, Jack," reaching out, and to his amazement, takes hold of the gun. "Shocking!" he says. "You are for real, Jack. How do I hold it?"

"Don't worry, father. It's set on safe. Just don't drop it. Hold it tight. It won't go off by itself. Now, can you give me absolution?"

"Yes, Jack."

Before returning to his seat, Father Berthelot visits the first-class lavatory just to see how different it is from the economy. He feels proud of his accomplishment disarming a skyjacker, so proud that he gets excited about the possibility of media attention, even rehearsing his statement in front of the mirror.

"Good," John Barefoot says, watching Father Berthelot exit the lavatory and return to the economy section. "Well deserved."

"I wonder what that was all about," Marge says.

John's perturbation propels him to get up and go gruffly to the same lavatory. When he lifts up the toilet seat, something falls to the floor, something he doesn't see, something he can't see, yet it's there, a thing between his feet. He reaches down and, like a blind man feeling frantically, picks it up. In utter amazement, he says, "The gun! It's High's gun!"

He inspects it carefully, running his fingers around the edges to measure its size and shape. "Amazing," he says.

Carrying the gun like his hero Kelso would, John returns to his seat, throwing scornful glances at his fellow first-class passengers. "Johnny's got his gun," he says to Marge, sitting down. "Now we'll see who's going to break the bestseller records."

"What are you talking about," she says. He shows her the gun. "It can't be," she says.

"I found it in the john. Invisible, but it's real. Feel it."

Marge reaches out and touches it softly. "How in the world...?"

"It was on the toilet seat," he says. "Now we can end this charade once for all."

"What do you plan to do?"

"Pardon the cliché, but I'm going to give him a taste of his own medicine."

The window on the electronic multiverse opens, and John types words into a portal. Data disappears in a wink, jumps to a deeper level, ubiquitous yet so promising, drawing him into infinite smut and hearsay that pornographers, bloggers, buyers, and sellers try in vain to control. Scanning over the initial results, he settles on the encyclopedic offerings, which he refines by typing in more words and receives an instant two-part table of facts and figures. "The pain ray is an RJ-seven," he says. "So says the Federation of American Scientists. Although I think this is only speculation, since they don't have a picture or data to really verify it. *Top secret, hand-held weapon that has a frequency exactly tuned to stimulate the endings of human pain nerves...is said to cause unbearable pain in every external nerve ending of the body...with intensity matching that of fire all over the body...but does not damage the skin.*"

"Wow! Does it tell you how it works?"

"No. But I found something even more interesting on our hijacker. It seems Jack High is an impostor. A pseudonym. He is in fact a dog chasing its own tail—Andrew D'Oria—the name Andrea High had before he changed it—an *ethical information specialist* working for the International Communications Agency. It was abolished in nineteen-eighty-two, but I imagine still exists as a covert, top-secret intelligence agency, just like in the story, which would be a criminal offense to disclose. The FAS doesn't have any information on it though, but my guess is that it's a cover to transport intelligence from embassies back to the U.S. in innocuous forms such as books! Books carrying top-secret intelligence in code. Or, even, dare I say, material, like wipes from suspected WMD sites? Can you imagine? I'm guessing he's hijacking this plane, because this is the only way he can get his story told without being arrested by the FBI."

"That's in his book, John."

"And look at this. You know the alumni research spam they always send you? Well they're not so bad after all. I searched for Andrew D'Oria and found him as a graduate of Timon High School in Buffalo, New York in nineteen-sixty-three."

"Not a very revealing lead," Marge says. "So, what did he do, pee in his locker?"

"According to one of his classmates, D'Oria lied in the class yearbook. It states that he was a member of the drama club, but a former classmate who calls himself Pirate King—must have been in the *Pirates of Penzance*—posted a comment refuting this. He was never a member of any clubs in high school. I'll bet our Jack High doesn't even know he's been called to task on this. Look, here's his picture. He has only one activity listed in his bio. Drama Club."

"And he changed his name to hide his criminal record? John, I think this is amusing but hardly character-breaking news."

"It might seem innocuous, but it's the kind of bait we need. The play's the thing...."

"Wherein we'll catch the conscience of the king."

After sending an accusatory e-mail to High, Barefoot examines the smart gun once again, wondering how it works. "The captain claimed that it melted the locks on the cockpit door. It feels like a real gun."

"Does it have a trigger?"

"Yes, right here."

"Please point it in the right direction, John!"

Father Berthelot appears in the aisle, looks around for the gun he's lost, checks the lavatory for a moment, and then goes to the flight deck door and knocks.

"Let me out," John says. "Hurry!"

John steps out into the aisle and waits for his nemesis, but, just as he begins to have second thoughts about being able to use the gun, Jack High comes out of the flight deck and begins to talk with Father Berthelot. The priest shakes his head, mumbles a bit, and returns to his seat with an angry look on his face.

Jack High stands against the door looking no less in charge of the situation without his weapon. Yet, the vulnerability of his body standing alone makes him seem like an entirely different man. Could it be a captain instead of a hijacker?

"LIAR!" Barefoot yells.

The word hits High in the heart.

"You were a liar then, and you're a liar now. You're not an air marshal. Sky marshals flew for only three years and were grounded for over twenty-five years, which would have made you too old to be rehired after nine-eleven. You're a skyjacker, and you're finished. The story comes abruptly to an end. And here's the *deus ex machina* to prove it." Barefoot draws the gun in an arcing motion until it comes level with High's chest. "How do you want yourself? Slightly warm or burnt toast?"

The look of fear on High's face makes Barefoot feel elated. He has conquered the beast singlehandedly. A hero who reclaims the plane and, not only that, the reputation of his bestselling hero Kelso!

Suddenly, High's scared look disappears and a smile comes to his face.

"What are you laughing at?" Barefoot says.

"Are you telling me not to laugh?" High says. "Are you telling *me* not to laugh? I wouldn't, if I were you. And that gun," walking forward and holding out his hand, "hand it over!"

In a rush of panic, Barefoot pulls the trigger and the gun begins to hum, but High doesn't flinch and keeps coming. Thinking he's misfired, Barefoot steps back, takes careful aim, and pulls the trigger again.

Jack High lets out a wail and begins to shake violently. He falls to his knees and John Barefoot releases the trigger, thinking he's electrocuted his antagonist. "You got me, marshal!" High says and falls over. He shakes one more time, and then becomes lifeless.

Barefoot goes up to the body and taps it with his toe, which makes High giggle and then laugh. High laughs so hard, he has to hold his aching side.

Barefoot fires again, but nothing happens.

High gets back on his feet and comes forward, causing Barefoot to retreat, his face turning white with fright. Expecting Barefoot to use the gun as a club, High rushes him, head down. Barefoot clubs the back of his head with the gun. High takes the blow and comes up swinging, catching Barefoot a few times on the head. Now standing toe-to-toe, the two men slug each other wildly. Then, losing energy, Barefoot backs off and falls into an empty seat, but now has the advantage of using his feet for defense. He kicks High solidly in the chest, causing the skyjacker to lose his breath. A passenger jumps up and grabs High from behind, then another man, bigger than everyone, comes in to help. As cheers come from the other passengers, Barefoot gets out of the seat and begins a flurry of punches to High's face, ripping open gashes on the chin, cheekbones, and brows. Wicked rights and lefts still keep connecting on High's bloody face, for he couldn't move either arm to protect himself.

Barefoot stops for a moment to catch his breath. Then, like a boxer who has his opponent on the ropes, he measures the distance with an outstretched left arm, and powers a right fist into High's nose, breaking it with the sound of an egg cracking. Unconscious, High's head drops in defeat.

A flight attendant comes forward holding a pair of plastic handcuffs and says, "Better put these on him."

The word spreads throughout the plane that the skyjacker has been subdued. All the passengers are now applauding.

"Ladies and gentlemen, this is the captain speaking. We have won the battle and the hijacker is now in custody. We have been through a terrible ordeal, and I apologize for any damage that has been done. However, it's now over and we should be thankful no one was seriously hurt. I and the flight crew thank you for being cooperative, and we especially want to thank the three passengers who subdued the hijacker. I now ask those three men, especially John Barefoot, to let their presence be known. Ladies and gentlemen, let's give a big hand to our heroes."

The three heroes parade through the plane, Barefoot holding up the smart gun as unseen evidence of his victory. After taking more praise than they could stand, they return to their first-class section.

"I thought you'd never stop," Marge says. "A man your age winning a fistfight. My gosh."

"Well, High's not in his prime either, though if it weren't for the help, he would have taken me. I never hit a man in the face before. And I was never hit in the face before. How do I look?"

"Red and swelled up."

"I'll never be able to type with these knuckles. Look at them. Man, he's got a hard head."

"You were so steamed up, John. Good going."

"This gun was no help. It didn't even fire. I think it's a dud. Maybe a model of some kind."

"How could he get his hands on it anyway? Who would be carrying such a weapon; top secret and all? Maybe if he were a CIA agent or something."

"He's just a loser," John says. "A sky marshal that lost his job and went bad. Maybe he fabricated it. Looks authentic doesn't it? Well, it's like science fiction in a way. You have to suspend common sense to build a story. Anything goes. Maybe we're just imagining it's real."

"Didn't he claim to be a philosopher?" Marge asks. "Look, here he comes now. They're taking him away. Cleaned him up a bit too."

"Good. He doesn't belong in first class."

As Jack High walks by, escorted by two male flight attendants, he says slowly and distinctly, "Three! ... Two! ... One!"

"What's that?" Marge says.

"He's marking time," John says.

"No. There's that look on his face. He knows something; I can feel it."

"About what?"

"I don't know. Maybe it's the gun. What did he say it was?"

"A pain ray."

"Intentionality. That's what it is. It's in his book, isn't it? A philosophical term having to do with thoughts that you don't use. I think he said it was pure consciousness."

"The only way we think is on purpose, as in premeditated murder. Any other way is sheer obscurity. The whole discipline of philosophy is nonsense, and philosophers write in an obscure style in order to criticize others for not understanding them."

Marge gets up in her seat to see where they've taken High. "I don't know, John," she says.

"How can you honestly think that thoughts could be non-intentionally intentional, non-deliberate. It's absurd. Don't you see? They search for a source of existence called Being, which is nothing but an artificial construction, a bombastic abstraction."

"His gun didn't go off because it was aiming at *him*," Marge says. "The gun is programmed not to shoot a friend, John. Haven't you heard of smart guns? It's how he got on the plane in the first place. The brain scanners read him as a friend too!"

John looks closely at it, still amazed that it is invisible. He puts it to his ear. "I can't hear a thing. Can you?"

Marge listens and hears something that raises her eyebrows. "I hear a slight ticking sound, John." She places the gun softly on John's lap and gets out of her seat.

"It's just the battery," John says.

"I don't think so," she says and walks away.

In the wing of the plane, Jack High stares somberly at the blue monitor, which once displayed his *Bait and Switch*.

"What is that?" the flight attendant sitting next to him says, referring to the intricate face of a gold tiger strapped around his wrist. "A wristwatch?"

"It's my cover story," High says.

"Where'd you get it?"

"In Bangkok."

The flight attendant looks closely at the face and asks, "Does it open up?"

"Yeah, sure. Ever been to Bangkok?"

"No."

"You can have one specially made there. Look, to see the time, just push the tiger's right eye." High tries to do so, but is hampered by the handcuffs. "I can't quite get it. You mind?"

The flight attendant approaches with her index finger, stops, and says, "Right eye as in right side of the face?"

"Yeah, go ahead. Open it."

She presses the right eye but the cover doesn't open. "It must be broken," she says.

"No, it just takes a few seconds to relay the message."

"Relay what message?"

"The message to my gun," High says.

"Then that gun is for real?"

"Just wait till it blows his socks off."

The smart gun in Barefoot's hands lights up like a restaurant pager. When it begins to vibrate violently, he says, "Am I dying, or is this my birthday?"

www.ingramcontent.com/pod-product-compliance
Lightning Source LLC
Chambersburg PA
CBHW020735250626
47155CB00003B/763